NO HUMANS INVOLVED

Cathleen + Kevin

Happy reading!

Also by Kelley Armstrong

BITTEN

STOLEN

DIME STORE MAGIC

INDUSTRIAL MAGIC

HAUNTED

BROKEN

NO HUMANS INVOLVED

KELLEY ARMSTRONG

RANDOM HOUSE CANADA

 Published in 2007 by Random House Canada, a division of Random House of Canada Limited and in the United States by Bantam Spectra, an imprint of Bantam Dell, a division of Random House, Inc. Distributed in Canada by Random House of Canada Limited.

www.randomhouse.ca

Library and Archives Canada Cataloguing in Publication

Armstrong, Kelley
No humans involved / Kelley Armstrong.

ISBN 978-0-307-35576-8

I. Title.

PS8551.R7637N62 2007   C813'.6   C2006-905699-4

Book design by Lynn Newmark

Printed in the United States of America

10 9 8 7 6 5 4 3 2 1

To my grandmother Florence Taylor-MacGowan,
who taught me that you don't need to be tough to be strong

ACKNOWLEDGMENTS

Many thanks to the usual suspects: my agent, Helen Heller, and my editors, Anne Groell of Bantam Spectra, Anne Collins of Random House Canada and Antonia Hodgson of Warner Orbit. Your help is, as always, much appreciated.

Thanks too to my readers this time around: Danielle and Alison.

And a special thanks to my copyeditor, Faren Bachelis, who has been with me for a few books and never properly thanked. Someday, thanks to her gentle corrections, I may overcome my fondness for gender-indeterminate antecedents and learn the rules of collective noun-verb agreement. Until then, a big thank-you to her for fixing my mistakes!

NO HUMANS INVOLVED

I

Brendan struggled to stay awake. A tough battle—far tougher than it should have been under the circumstances.

They'd approached him behind a bank, its parking lot empty as evening turned to night. He'd been cutting through to the shelter, hoping it would still have meals. Hot meals would be too much to hope for at that hour, but he'd settle for free.

The bank had erected a fence between itself and the shelter to stem the flow of kids taking the shortcut from the bus stop. Brendan had been halfway up when the woman had hailed him. Fearing trouble, he'd only climbed faster, until she'd laid a hand on his calf and he'd turned to see not cops, but a middle-aged couple—well-dressed professional types.

They'd told him some story about losing their son to the streets and devoting their lives to helping other kids. Bullshit, of course. In real life, everyone wanted something. Despite their sincere smiles and concerned eyes, he'd decided that what they wanted was sex. And, as long as they were willing to pay for it, that was okay with him.

It wouldn't be the first trick he'd turned. He'd briefly teamed up with a kid from the shelter, until Ricky had found a better-looking partner. Brendan should have taken this as a sign. If he wasn't good-looking enough to be a whore in L.A. he sure as hell wasn't going to make it as a movie star. But it was too late to go home now. Too late to admit he didn't have what it took. Too hard to face everyone who'd told him so.

He did have talent. Won the top role in every school play. Got a job at the summer theater three years running. Did two TV commercials for local businesses. So, at sixteen, tired of his parents telling him to go to college first, he'd taken his savings and come to L.A.

Now the money was gone and he'd found no decent way to earn more, and if this couple wanted what he figured they wanted, that was fine by him. They had kind faces. Maybe in Hollywood that didn't count for shit, but where he'd come from it meant something.

They'd driven him to their home in Brentwood. He'd recognized the neighborhood from a "Star Tours" bus trip he'd taken when he first arrived. He'd sat in the back of their SUV, peering out the tinted windows into the night, watching the fabled neighborhood pass. They'd pulled into the garage of a modest-looking house, then led him inside. They'd offered food, but he'd claimed he wasn't hungry, despite his rumbling stomach. He might be naive, but he knew better than to accept food or drink.

When they'd taken him downstairs, through a TV room into a guest bedroom, he'd been certain this was where the situation would change. But they'd only turned on the lights, pointed out the adjoining washroom and said they'd see him in the morning. They hadn't even closed the door, but left it ajar, so he wouldn't feel locked in.

Now, as he fought the urge to sleep, footsteps sounded on the stairs. The woman's voice, sharp with an accent. Then the man's. Then another man's. And another . . .

Oh, shit.

Heart hammering, he tried to rouse himself. Why was he so tired? Goddamn it, he had to make a break for it, before he found himself in the middle of a gang bang or—

Outside, in the TV room, the woman offered refreshments. Two of the men asked for wine, the third accepted water. Then their voices settled into one place, as if they were sitting.

Wine and conversation as a prelude to sex games with a teenage boy?

Brendan strained to make out their words. They were talking about books. "Texts" as they called them, tossing around words like "belief" and "ritual," debating the different translated meanings of Hebrew and Latin versions.

Latin. That's what the woman had been speaking earlier. As he'd been getting into their car, she had been saying something to the man in another language, and with her accent, Brendan had figured she was reverting to her mother tongue to relay a private message. The language, though, had sounded familiar. Now he knew why. As a Christmas and Easter Catholic, he'd heard enough Latin.

Now these people were discussing religious texts, and that couldn't be a coincidence. The couple had said they wanted to help, as penance for their mistakes with their son. Good Samaritans.

"—too old," one man was saying, his voice rising enough for Brendan to hear him easily. "All of our success has been with kids much younger, and I don't understand why we need to change that now."

"We aren't changing," another man said. "We're expanding and experimenting. There's a limited supply of younger children out there and it's difficult getting access to them. If we can adjust the procedure to work successfully with teens, we open the door to limitless possibilities."

"Don's right." The woman again. "One or two a year isn't enough, not for the scale we . . ."

Her voice dropped soothingly until, once again, Brendan could only catch the odd word.

He couldn't blame them for setting their sights on children. By his age, most street kids had no interest in "rescue." They were too immersed in the life to accept help. But he would. Drugs weren't a problem—he'd never been able to afford them. They could spout all the Bible verses they wanted and he'd smile and agree if it meant getting on a bus home. He could tell his parents he hadn't *failed;* he'd just had a religious experience and had changed his mind.

He closed his eyes and pictured himself walking up his drive, imagined his mother's face, his little sister's squeals, his father's expression—stern but relieved.

The conversation outside his door seemed to have turned to a heated debate on the nature of suffering. *Yeah,* he thought with a chuckle, *definitely Catholic.* From what he could make out, it sounded a hell of a lot like a conversation between two Goths he'd overheard last week.

Morbid. The word popped into his head and he turned it over in his mind. A cool word. Described Goths and some religious types alike—that fixation with death and suffering.

In the room beyond, a male voice had picked up volume again.

"—Romans used crucifixion not only because it was publicly humiliating, but for the degree of suffering inflicted. With the weight of the body pulling down, breathing becomes difficult, and the condemned could hang for days, slowly suffocating."

"True, but according to accounts of the witch trials, burning was the worst way to die. If you keep the person from dying from smoke inhalation, they can live a surprisingly long time, and suffer unimaginable pain."

Brendan shivered. Okay, that went beyond morbid. Maybe these weren't mainstream religious do-gooders, but some kind of fanatical sect. Like the Scientologists or something. Most religious people he knew were good folks, but there were wackos. As much as he wanted to go home, he wouldn't put up with any kind of sick shit. He should get up, go in there, maybe tell them he'd changed his mind. But he was so tired.

The voices had stopped. Good. He'd rest for a few more minutes, then sneak out—

The door opened. In walked the man and woman, followed by three others: a younger woman, a balding man and a white-haired one.

"Hello, Brendan," said the woman.

Brendan struggled to his feet. "I want to leave."

The woman nodded. Then she stepped forward, lifted her hand to her mouth and blew. A cloud of white dust flew into Brendan's face. He tried to cough, but only wheezed. She started speaking in Latin again and his knees gave way. Two of the men rushed to grab him, each taking an arm, their grips gentle as they helped him to his feet.

The men lifted his arms around their shoulders. His eyelids flagged and closed. His feet dragged across the floor as they took him into a second, smaller room. The men exchanged words, then lowered him to the floor. A cold, hard floor.

He opened his eyes. There, from high above, a dog stared down at him. A terrier, like his sister's dog. But there was something wrong . . .

Legs. It didn't have any legs. Just a torso and a head perched on the edge of an overhang, watching him.

Hallucinating.

Drugged?

He should care—knew he should care—but he couldn't work up

the energy. He squeezed his eyes shut and huddled there, too weak to even think. He heard them talking and he could tell they were speaking English, but deciphering the meaning of the words required too much energy, so he just listened to the sound and let it lull him.

Liquid splashed onto his back, seeping through his shirt. Cold and wet and stinking of something he should recognize. Then, as he was about to drift off, his wandering brain identified the smell.

Gasoline.

He snapped awake, panicked, telling his arms and legs to move, his mouth to scream, but nothing obeyed. He cracked open his eyes just enough to see the people filing from the room. The woman stopped in front of him and bent. Her smiling lips parted, saying something reassuring. Then she struck the match.

JAIME VEGAS, CENTER STAGE

ONE DRAWBACK TO BEING ONSTAGE for most of your life is that eventually you forget how to act when you're off it. Not that it matters. In such a life, you're never really offstage. Even walking from your bedroom to the kitchen you can't lower your guard . . . at least not if you're on the set of one of the most anticipated TV specials of the season—one costarring you.

I'd started my career at the age of three, forced onto the toddler beauty pageant catwalks by a mother who'd already decided I needed to earn my keep. I should have grown up dreaming of the day I'd be off that stage. But when I stepped into the limelight, every eye was on me and I shone. It became my refuge and now, forty years later, while there were days when I really didn't feel like strapping on four-inch heels and smiling until my jaw hurt, my heart still beat a little faster as I walked down that hall.

The buzz of a saw drowned out the clicking of my heels on the hardwood. I caught a whiff of sawdust and oil, and shuddered to imagine what alterations the crew was making to the house. From what I'd heard, the homeowners weren't likely to complain—they desperately needed the money. The "official" rumor was a failed film project, but the one I'd heard involved an unplanned baby project with the nanny. Tabloid stories to be suppressed, a young woman to be paid off, a wife to placate—it could all get very expensive.

As I passed a young man measuring the hall, I nodded and his jaw dropped.

"M—Ms. Vegas? Jaime Vegas?"

I swung around and fixed him with a megawatt smile that I didn't need to fake. Shallow of me, I know, but there's no ego boost like the slack-jawed gape of a man half your age.

"Geez, it *is* you." He hurried over to shake my hand. "Could I—? I know it's unprofessional to ask, but is there any chance of getting an autograph?"

"Of course. I'm heading to a meeting right now, but you can grab an autograph from me anytime. Just bring me something to sign. Or if you prefer a photo . . ."

"A photo would be great."

My smile brightened. "A photo it is, then. I have some in my room."

"Thanks. Grandpa will love it. He's such a fan of yours. He has a thing for redheads, but you're his favorite. All his buddies in the nursing home think you're hot."

Just what I needed on the first day of a big job—the reminder that in Hollywood time, I was already a decade past my best-before date.

I kept smiling, though. Another minute of conversation, and the promise of a handful of signed photos for Gramps and the boys, and I was off again.

As I neared the dining room, I heard a crisp British voice snap, "Because it's ridiculous, that's why. Mr. Grady is a professional. He will not be subjected to mockery."

Before I pushed open the door, I pictured the speaker: a stylish woman, roughly my age, dressed in a suit and oozing efficiency. I walked in, and there she was—short blond hair, thin lips, small and wiry, as if extra flesh would be a sign of softness she could ill afford. Icy green eyes glared from behind her tiny glasses. Personal assistant model A: the bulldog, designed to raise hell on her client's behalf, leaving him free to play the gracious, good-natured star.

Facing her was a younger woman, maybe thirty, dumpy, with a shoulder-length bob and worried eyes. Director model C: the overwhelmed first-timer.

The dining room, like most of the house, had been "redecorated" to accommodate the shoot. The homeowners had cleared out anything they didn't want damaged, so the dining set was gone, replaced by a cheaper one. As for the dead guy hanging from the chandelier, I suspected he came with the house, and was probably tough to remove without an exorcism or two.

The hanging man was maybe fifty, average size but with heavy jowls, as if he'd lost a lot of weight fast. He swayed from an old crystal chandelier, superimposed over the modern one. His face was mottled and swollen, eyes thankfully closed.

I eyed him from the doorway so I wouldn't be tempted to stare once I was in the room. After thirty years of seeing ghosts, you learn all the tricks.

This one, though, wasn't a ghost, but a residual. What tragedy had brought him to an end so emotionally powerful that the image was seared forever in this room? I doused my curiosity. It would do me no good. When you see scenes like this every day, you can't afford to stop and wonder. You just can't.

Both women turned as I entered. The assistant's gaze slid over me, lips tightening as if someone had shoved a lemon wedge in her mouth. I flashed a smile and her lips pursed more. If you can't still turn the heads of twenty-year-old boys, winning the catty disapproval of women your own age is a good consolation prize.

I stopped a hairbreadth from the hanged man and tried not to recoil as his swaying body circled my way.

"I hope I'm not interrupting," I said to the woman with the worried eyes. "I was sent to speak to the director, Becky Cheung. Would that be you?"

She smiled and extended a hand. "It is. And you must be Jaime Vegas. This is Claudia Wilson, Bradford Grady's assistant."

I shook Cheung's hand. "Should I step outside and let you two finish?"

"No, no." Desperation touched Becky's voice. "This concerns you too. We're discussing a promo shot. Mr. Simon has decided he wants the three stars to say a line."

Claudia shot a hard look at Becky. "A specific line. Tell her what it is."

"Um . . . 'I see dead people.' "

The hanged man's stockinged foot swung past my arm as I managed a laugh. "I think I've heard that one before."

Becky's gaze went to mine, searching for some sign that I was offended. "We—Mr. Simon—thought it would be fun."

"It sounds like a cute gimmick."

"Mr. Grady does not do gimmicks," Claudia said, then strode from the room.

"Thanks," Becky whispered. "This isn't as easy as I thought. Everyone's taking it very . . ."

"Seriously? We're trying to raise the ghost of Marilyn Monroe. If that doesn't scream cheap thrills, what does? I'm in it for the fun." I grinned. "And the chance to spend a week in a neighborhood like this."

"Not everyone is so thrilled with that part. I think we're going to lose Starr Phillips."

"I heard she wasn't happy about the living arrangements."

"I know it's unusual, but the studio is all over us to cut the budget. Mr. Simon thought this would be the most efficient way to handle the preshow tapings. Put the three of you up in a rented house in Brentwood, a block from the Monroe home, where we can do all the preshow work and media in one swoop." A crew member motioned from the doorway. "Whoops. Gotta run. Here's your schedule for the afternoon, just media interviews and—"

My cell phone rang. I could tell who it was by the ring tone, and I'm sure I broke into a grin more becoming to a four-year-old than a woman of forty-four. I motioned to Becky that I'd just be a second, then told the caller I'd phone right back. When I hung up, Becky gave me a ten-second rundown on my afternoon obligations, and passed me the schedule. Then I was sprinting for the door as fast as my platform sandals could take me. Four-inch heels aren't made for anything speedier than a runway stroll, but I pushed them to a quick march, inspiring a look of alarm from two passing workmen.

I told myself Jeremy had a plane to catch, but even if he hadn't, I'd still have hurried.

I know I should have more self-respect. More dignity. The way I see it, though, it's karmic payback. I've always been the one leading the chase—inspiring the bad love poetry, setting the hoops ever higher—then waltzing away when I grew bored. Now I guess some cosmic force had decided it was time for me to make a fool of myself.

I'd taken a big chance asking Jeremy to join me for the week.

We were—despite my hopes—just friends. Then, a few weeks ago, we'd been talking about the show and, having had a few drinks, the segue came easily. To my shock, he'd said yes. Now he was flying three thousand miles just to see me. That had to mean something.

The patio opened to a terraced yard stuffed with perennial borders, gazebos, ornamental trees and statuary. As I trotted along the flagstone path, winding around one fountain, one pond and two oversized statues, I wondered whether a trail of bread crumbs would have been wise.

Finally, far enough from the house to mentally step offstage, I found a wooden bench. Jeremy answered after the first ring.

"Did I catch you at a bad time?" he asked.

"No, I was just getting my schedule for the day. Mainly interviews plus some meet-and-greets, culminating, of course, in the welcome bash tonight—which, lucky man, you'll be just in time for. I hope you're ready to play party escort."

I stopped for breath. Silence filled the pause, and I winced and mentally smacked myself. Jeremy at a Hollywood party? He'd rather face off against a pack of ravenous wolves.

"I'm just kidding," I said. "You'll be jet-lagged, and I'm sure you don't have a tux—"

"I do. And it's packed. The party isn't a problem, Jaime..."

When he let the line trail off, my heart started thumping.

"The babies are sick. It's just a cold, but it's their first—"

A scream drowned him out—less like the wail of a sick baby than the roar of a wounded lion. I recognized Katherine, one of his foster son Clayton's fourteen-month-old twins.

"Jesus, poor Kate," I said. "She sounds miserable."

Jeremy chuckled. "She's not that ill, actually. It's Logan who's bearing the brunt of it. Of course, he's not complaining, but he's quite willing to let her express outrage on his behalf."

"How's Clay taking it? Or dare I ask."

"Let's just say he's not making it any easier. We don't usually contract colds, so he's worried. I'm sure it's no cause for alarm but..."

He let the sentence trail off. I understood his concern. A werewolf's increased immunity meant sickness was rare, so even a cold would be worrying. If the situation worsened, Clay and Elena couldn't just bundle the little ones off to the emergency ward, or the doctors might discover they carried something far more alarming than a cold virus. Jeremy wasn't a doctor, but he was the Pack's medical expert and they'd need him there. Even more important, he'd want to be there.

"Stay," I said. "We can do this another time."

"No, I am coming, Jaime. I'll be there soon as I can, hopefully tomorrow."

My heart gave a little flip. "Good. Then look after those babies, tell everyone I said hi and I'll get an update in the morning."

When I signed off, I closed my eyes, listened to the birds chirp and rustle in the hedges and let the wisps of disappointment float away. To my surprise, they *were* only wisps. If Jeremy had made any other choice, he wouldn't be the man I'd raced at breakneck speed to talk to. Family—and family responsibilities—came first, and that was fine by me, even when I knew his priorities wouldn't change, whatever form our relationship might take.

The birds had gone silent, their song replaced by the soft whisper of the wind and the tinkle of distant chimes. I looked around as I rose.

"Hello?" I said.

Someone touched my arm. I wheeled, but no one was there. I rubbed the spot. Probably a butterfly brushing past. It wouldn't be a ghost—with them I only got sight and sound, no touch.

I checked the schedule Becky had given me. Three interviews plus—

Fingers clasped my free hand. Resisting the urge to yank away, I looked down. Nothing. Yet I could feel the unmistakable sensation of a hand holding mine.

My gut went cold. This was how it had started with Nan. A lifetime of seeing what shouldn't be there and eventually she started imagining what she knew *couldn't* be there. That's what happens to necromancers, and that's what I am, same as my Nan.

Like most supernatural powers, necromancy runs in the blood. It often skips a generation or two, but in our family no one is spared. We see and hear the dead, and they are relentless in their quest to be heard. I may have learned a way to profit from my powers, but if I could be free of the ghosts, I'd give it up in a heartbeat and muddle through like every other con artist in the business. Better that than this long, cursed road that ends in madness.

The fingers slid from my hand. I squeezed my eyes shut.

Once before I'd had a ghost who'd been able to touch me. Didn't hold my hand, though. She'd sunk her fangs into my neck and nearly killed me, all because she couldn't make contact the normal way. Typical vampire—thinks the world exists to serve them.

But the chance that I'd encounter another dead vamp was remote. Extremely rare to begin with, they're so uncommon in the afterlife that I'd found only unconfirmed ancient tales of necromancers contacting one. If a vampire is already dead when it walks this world, where does one go when it passes into the next?

Somehow Natasha had clawed her way back and made contact with me, *physical* contact, as this ghost had now done. I rubbed the spot on my neck and cast a nervous glance around.

I let my mind shift to the semitrance state that would let me see ghosts too weak or inexperienced to pass over. Around me, everything seemed to go still, the wind chimes faint and distant, the gardens blurring.

"Hello?" I said. "Is anyone here?"

I kept turning and calling out, but no one answered. A sharp shake of my head and I was back to Earth.

"Ms. Vegas?"

I spun as a security guard peeked around a hedge.

"Didn't mean to startle you. Were you calling for someone?"

"Actually, yes," I said with a rueful smile. "I'm hopelessly lost."

He laughed. "This place is a maze, isn't it? Come on, then, and I'll walk you back."

THE ANGEL OF THE SOUTH

DURING A BREAK BETWEEN INTERVIEWS, I decided to send the babies a get-well gift. As for *what* to send . . . well, that was a problem. I get a kick out of the twins—I even babysat them during one council meeting—but they were the only little ones I'd had extended contact with since I'd been a child myself.

My first thought was a balloon bouquet . . . until the FTD florist in Syracuse told me they didn't recommend balloons for kids—choking hazard, apparently. So I went with stuffed animals. Rabbits. Perfect.

I spent the rest of the afternoon following my schedule and using the spare time to poke around the house and meet the crew. To my disappointment, I didn't bump into Bradford Grady.

Grady was a bona fide star with a wildly popular show exploring haunted European locales. That was where the money was: television. Right now, I had a prime monthly spot on *The Keni Bales Show* and I was a regular guest on *Knight at Night*. But my own show? *That* was the dream. Always had been . . . even though I personally preferred a stage to a soundstage. With Keni's show skyrocketing in the ratings, now the second-hottest daytime talk show in America, I had two offers—one from a major network, the other an up-and-coming netlet. Whether those offers turned into an actual time slot depended largely on how I performed on this show. Spending a week learning from a master wouldn't hurt.

AT NINE, I was in front of the full-length mirror in my bedroom, getting ready for the welcome party and making sure my new dress fit as it should, not wrinkling or sagging unbecomingly as I moved. And, let's be honest, making sure *I* didn't wrinkle or sag in it. It was a daring choice for a woman my age—a Valentino silk peekaboo dress. It wasn't from this year's collection, but I'm not above shopping the sales rack.

The dress had come in deep golden yellow or black. I'd picked the yellow. Silk straps left my shoulders bare. The ruffled hem brushed my knees. Slits in the deep-cut shirred bodice showed off generous swatches of skin. Not something you'd wear if your triceps sagged or your thighs were dimpled with cellulite.

I was proud of my body. I worked damn hard for it. *Paid* for it, some said, the whispers growing louder with each passing year. But I hadn't had any work done and I didn't plan to, yet sometimes I suspected my resolve wouldn't outlast the first significant wrinkle or sag. Getting my own TV show wouldn't make it any easier to resist.

A rap at the door. "Ms. Vegas?"

I shook off thoughts of television and plastic surgery and gave my reflection one last mirror check. Then I was ready for my close-up.

THE WELCOME party for *Death of Innocence* was being held in the basement. An odd location, especially for a warm, dry fall night, but I'd heard the neighbors hadn't been thrilled with having a TV show moving in next door. Getting the permit couldn't have been easy. Palms probably had to be greased, favors pulled in and concessions made, including no outdoor parties.

As we reached the bottom of the stairs, I pulled back to let my escort—one of the security team—lead the way, and give me time to see what I was walking into.

The basement was one huge room and held only a collection of high, small tables for setting down drinks. A waiter who barely looked old enough to serve was making the rounds with champagne, flashing a camera-ready smile, unaware that no one here was in a position to give him his big Hollywood break.

The producer, Todd Simon, wasn't coming. He was on location in Amsterdam after filming *Red Light District*—a controversial but much anticipated new reality show—and was supposed to have returned by now, but had been delayed. Can't say I was thrilled about that. When I'd first signed on to the show, the producer had been a real sweetheart who was also a fan, and had seemed committed to approaching the special with just the right balance of showmanship and solemnity. Then, less than a month ago, I got a fax from the studio. The producer and his entire team had been replaced by Todd Simon, a guy best known for beer commercials.

I'd done my best to meet with Simon and his team, but it never happened. When I'd lived in L.A. I'd have tracked them down myself. Not so easy now that my condo was in Chicago and I'd spent the last two months on my live-show circuit. I hated going in blind, but my future in television was riding on this show. I'd make it work.

There were fewer than a dozen people in the room. There, chatting up the model who'd be playing Marilyn in the dramatized death scene, was Bradford Grady. Not much older than me, if the tabloids were right, yet his dark hair was streaked with silver, giving him the air of a distinguished gentleman. The old Hollywood double standard.

The waiter hurried over to offer me a glass.

"Thank you—" I checked his name tag. "Jordan."

I smiled and he blinked, bedazzled. My smile grew. When I looked up, Grady was heading my way, his gaze sliding over me as he walked.

"Ms. Vegas," he said. "This is such a pleasure."

He took my hand and kissed it. No one snickered. Amazing what the British can get away with.

"Jaime, please, and the pleasure's mine. At the risk of gushing, I'm *such* a fan. I bought your first season on DVD just last week, when it finally came stateside."

Actually, I'd ordered all three seasons from the U.K. when I realized I'd be working with him. Can't pull a convincing fan-girl if you haven't studied the material.

Claudia appeared from nowhere. "Mr. Grady, Dr. Robson wanted to speak to—"

He cut her off with a "go away" flutter of his fingers. Claudia glared at me.

"She's right," I said. "You have people to meet and I don't want to monopolize you. What do you say we do the rounds together, save everyone from having to introduce themselves twice?"

He gave me his arm and let Claudia escort us over to Dr. Robson, a parapsychologist the show had hired as an expert. As I asked about Dr. Robson's studies in electronic voice phenomena—more homework—Grady's hand slid to my lower back then began inching down. When Bruce Wang, a specialist in ghost photography, approached, I used the excuse to slide from Grady's grasp and shake Wang's hand. It's a balancing act—being flirtatious enough to flatter without arousing expectations.

As we chatted, talk turned to speculation over Starr Phillips's mystery replacement. Robson had heard a rumor that it was Buck Locke. I prayed he was wrong. Last time I'd met the abrasive TV spiritualist, he'd offered to teach me the secret of tantric magic—sex magic—to enhance my link with the afterlife, and I'd made the unfortunate mistake of laughing. Worse yet, I'd done so as he'd stood in my hotel room doorway, wearing only a robe, which he'd let hang open to display the full "extent" of his offer.

We were still naming names when a murmur rippled through the room. I followed it to the door. In walked two men in shades, like FBI agents from a B movie. Between them stood a tiny, ephemerally beautiful girl in a silver dress. She had long blond hair, perfect porcelain skin and blue saucer eyes—far bluer than anything nature could produce.

Her gaze went straight to me, and she clapped her hands together, giving a kittenish mew of delight. She floated over, chiffon scarf streaming behind.

"Jaime Vegas. Oh, my sweet Lord, it *is* you!" She took both my hands and clasped them as she gazed up in limpid adoration. "You're my idol. I've been following your career since I was—" a girlish laugh, "—knee-high to a grasshopper, as my daddy would say."

A cameraman and a journalist appeared behind her, recording every frame and word. I tilted my head to my best angle and swept my hair back so it wouldn't block my profile. The lens inched my way.

"That's so sweet of you," I said. "And you must be . . . ?"

"Angelique . . . but my friends call me Angel. The Angel of the South."

"Oh, of course. Let me guess, you're the third spiritualist."

"I am. Can you believe that?" An earsplitting squeal of a giggle. "My big chance to work with Jaime Vegas. I was so afraid you'd retire before I got the chance."

I gave a throaty laugh. "Don't worry, I'm not retiring for a while."

Around us, the party had stopped, everyone watching the drama unfold.

"So, do you have any theories on Marilyn's death?" I asked.

"Oh, it was *such* a tragedy," she said. "Someone so young and beautiful, called to heaven too soon. My daddy—he's a minister, you know—always says—"

"I meant theories on *how* she died."

A wave of titters.

"Oh, yes, of course. Well, er, that's what we're here to learn, isn't it? To free her from the limbo of a tragic passing, to discover who wronged so innocent a soul."

"So you think she was murdered? Are you leaning toward the Kennedys or the Mafia?"

"Oh, my Lord, that is such a beautiful dress. So daring. My daddy would die if I wore something like that. You're so brave!" She waved to the cameraman. "Doug, you have to get a shot of the two of us, for my press release."

I pictured that shot and realized how I'd look towering over the fresh-faced, virginal blond.

"Unless you don't want to . . ." she said, her eyes wide with innocence.

"And miss the chance to get my picture taken with a rising star? Never. Doug, hon, can you make sure I get a copy of it?"

"Absolutely. Is there a mailing address?"

"Just bring it up to my room. Top of the stairs."

He grinned. "Be happy to, ma'am."

I flirted with Doug as he set up the shot, then struck a pose that would give Angelique's daddy a rise in spite of himself.

ANGELIQUE WAS going to be a problem. Her sly jabs I could handle—you don't spend a lifetime acting without learning how to deal with two-faced starlets. But television is so much more youth-oriented than the stage. Put me on camera next to a slip of a girl barely out of high school and the network execs who were considering my show might start thinking they were making overtures to the wrong spiritualist. I could sex it up—I could out-vamp her any day—but it might not be enough. I'd have to play this one carefully, prove I wasn't just the "sexy redhead" but the better performer. And, as it turned out, I was going to get my chance a lot sooner than I expected.

Becky had barely finished introducing Angelique to everyone when some wit came up with the idea of a "test" séance. As long as you had three spiritualists in a room, why not put them to work providing the entertainment?

"That's a wonderful idea," Becky said. "We should tape it too. For the DVD extras."

"There's going to be a DVD?" Angelique said.

Becky grinned. "There's always a DVD. What about Tansy Lane?"

"Who?" someone asked.

"Starlet," another responded. "From the seventies. Murdered right next door, I think. The crime was never solved."

I struggled to recall the case. I wasn't big on Hollywood legends, but because Tansy had been a former child star, her case had struck a chord. After outgrowing her starring role on a top-rated sitcom about a fairy changeling, she'd faded away, only to reappear again at twenty with a headline-making comeback. She'd not only beat the odds, but KO'd them, winning an Emmy. And that's when both her career and her life ended. Shot to death at a postawards party in Brentwood.

Murmurs of excitement ran through the crowd. Grady glanced at Claudia. I kept my mouth shut, my expression intrigued but not committed, waiting to see how Grady would play it.

"How mysterious were these circumstances?" he finally asked.

"I've heard there was satanism involved," the guard piped in. "That's why no one saw anything. They were conducting a secret Hollywood black-magic rite."

Grady's face lit up. Satanic rites were his specialty. He found evidence of them everywhere. He and Claudia exchanged a look.

She cleared her throat. "As per Mr. Grady's contract, he is supposed to receive a minimum of six hours' notice before any attempted spirit communications. He's willing to forgo that tonight. However, I insist that he still be allowed as much time as possible to complete his mental preparations, so he must be granted the final position."

Taking the final spot meant he'd have our work to build on, plus the chance to leave the most lasting impression.

Becky glanced at me, but I didn't have any such stipulations in my contract. I could hit the ground running anytime, anywhere, so I saved my contract demands for important things like billing position and wardrobe allowance.

"It's all yours, Bradford." I smiled, then slipped in, "I'll take the final spot next time."

"Excellent," Becky said. "It's settled, then. Angelique will go first, Jaime second—"

"Oh, no," Angelique breathed, her face filling with genuine horror. "I couldn't go before Ms. Vegas. She's the star; I should follow her."

I shook my head. "It's your first big séance and I insist you take the premier position."

She opened her mouth, but there was little she could say to that. I accepted Grady's proffered arm and we headed upstairs.

WHEN I realized they planned to hold this séance in the garden, I thought of the presence I'd felt there earlier and a chill ran through me. As bizarre as it might seem, I avoid mixing necromancy and spiritualism whenever possible. I use my powers to give me an edge, but under controlled circumstances. When I'm booking a show in a new city, I always visit the venues myself first, to make sure there aren't any resident ghosts. Nothing buggers up a fake séance more than having a real ghost screaming in your ear.

So I stepped into that garden, steeled against the first sign that my reluctant spirit had returned. But, to my relief, the presence of others seemed to scare it off. Or, if I was really lucky, it had given up and moved on.

We stole into the garden like schoolkids cutting out on a class trip, snickering and whispering, hoping the neighbors didn't overhear.

It was midnight. The witching hour, which I'm sure the writers would make a big deal of when they wrote the introduction to this segment. The full moon and the wind rustling through the bushes didn't hurt.

"Too bad we can't do it next door," someone said. "Right at the site of the murder. That's where she was found, wasn't it?"

"Near the pool house." Becky turned to the cameraman. "Can we get it in the backdrop?"

"Perhaps we could get some dirt from the site," Grady said.

Becky looked at the security crew. "Any volunteers?"

"I will," I said.

All heads turned my way.

"Oh, come on," I said. "What will film better? A security guard jumping that fence? Or me?" I turned to Angelique. "Unless you want to."

She backed away as if I'd suggested she desecrate a grave. "Oh, no. I couldn't. My dress—"

"Then it'll have to be me." I pulled off my sling-backs and handed them to the nearest guard. "Now, which of you boys is going to boost me over that fence?"

SO I snuck into the neighbor's yard and swiped dirt from behind their pool house. By the time I got back, my feet were filthy, my hair had twigs caught in it and I was sure there was a dirt smear or two on my face. But I got my round of cheers—and my laughs—and some footage of a cute young guard washing my feet in the fountain.

"Okay," I said, putting my heels back on as I leaned against the obliging guard. "Time for the séance. Angelique? You're up."

TANSY LANE

THE MEDIUM HAS TWO PRIMARY TOOLS at her disposal, and neither has anything to do with summoning spirits. The tools are knowledge and statistical probability. Or, as they're often called, warm reading and cold reading.

Cold reading uses statistical probability to make random guesses about a person or an audience. For example, if I say I see the spirit of a man, someone you've lost, it's a given that you've lost a male friend or relative in your lifetime. If I say his name started with J—first name, but maybe a middle or nickname—there's a good chance you can find a dead male relative with that common initial. Then I'll throw out "details" supplied by your dead relative, talking fast, shaping my responses by reading your reaction, and soon you'll be convinced I am indeed speaking to your dearly departed second cousin Joey . . . who, by the way, misses you, but is happy and in a good place.

Then there's warm reading, which uses prior knowledge. Maybe you chatted to one of my staff on the way into the show—they're so helpful and friendly. Maybe they overheard you telling your companion about the person you wanted me to contact. Or maybe you wrote it on that questionnaire you sent in, the one that was supposed to be anonymous. However it happened, I know that you, in seat D45, are praying that your second cousin Joey comes by with a message. Well, he has, and he misses you, but he's happy and in a good place.

When summoning a specific spirit, though, like Tansy Lane, you can't use statistical probability, so the tool Angelique needed was knowledge—memories of what she'd heard about the case. Which posed a problem, considering she'd been born after Tansy died. If she'd gotten the spot after me, she could have built on my "revelations." Without that, she was in trouble.

"Tansy? Is that you?" Angelique squinted as if straining to see in the dark. "She's having difficulty passing over. That's common with traumatized ghosts."

After two minutes of this, Becky told the cameraman to stop filming. I took a seat on a stone bench and waited my turn. At this rate, it wouldn't be long.

"I think I see her," Angelique was saying. "Her hair . . . it's light. No, maybe dark . . ."

A whisper rushed past my ear and I spun, nearly falling off the bench. I fought the urge to look around and kept my gaze straight ahead. The whisper seemed to circle me, a *pss-pss-pss* that made the hairs on my neck rise.

Fingers brushed my arm. I narrowed my eyes, withdrawing into that most primitive response—mentally stopping up my ears, squeezing my eyes shut and repeating, "I can't hear you. I can't hear you." As silly and immature as it felt, there was nothing else I could do with people all around me. Just ignore it and hope it went away.

Someone slapped me. A smack across my cheek so hard I reeled, gasping. Fury followed surprise as I pictured my mother's face above mine, heard her voice: "Don't look at me that way, Jaime. I was only getting your attention"—even as her slap still burned.

My hand went to my cheek.

As I looked up, I saw all eyes on me and realized I'd gasped aloud. Even Angelique had stopped and was glaring daggers at me.

"Sorry. I thought I . . ." I shook my head. "Never mind. Sorry."

"Oh, my God, your cheek!" Becky said. "There's a mark. Brian, get the camera over here."

Damn it. There was nothing more unprofessional than derailing a colleague's séance. Angelique's glares turned lethal. Worse yet was Grady's frown, one that said he hadn't expected such dirty tricks from me, and would need to be wary from now on.

"It's not—" I rubbed my cheek. "Something stung me. I'm so sorry. Please, Angelique, continue, with my apologies."

"Actually, I was just going to ask Angel to take a rest," Becky said. "But maybe you can give her a hand instead. Help her pull Tansy out of limbo."

"I'm not sure I should interfere..."

Angelique wheeled, frustration blazing in her eyes. Her first big shot and she was blowing it. Damned if she was going down alone.

"Oh, Jaime," she said, gripping my hands. "I would be honored if you'd help. Unless you think you can't. I'd heard you've been having some trouble lately..."

I laughed. "I'd love to know who told you that. Let's see what I can do."

After a few minutes of intense concentration, I wiped sweat from my forehead. Unlike Angelique, I'd been at this long enough to make it look like I was working hard. When I "finished," my hands were trembling, and the cameramen zoomed in on them and my glistening brow. Even Grady looked impressed—though maybe that's because his gaze was glued to my heaving bosom.

"Oh, I think—" I said finally. "Yes, here she... Can you hear me, Tansy?" I paused. "Good. I was just checking. We had some trouble making contact there."

Another pause. Then a grave nod. "I completely understand."

Around me, all had gone silent. Even the most jaded leaned forward, hoping. That's the appeal of ghosts. Hope. That prayer for proof that we exist—in some conscious form—after death. With ghosts, even the staunchest paranormal skeptics wouldn't mind being proven wrong.

I played into that with the conviction only a necromancer can have—the knowledge that the spirit of Tansy Lane really *was* out there somewhere. Just not here. Not now. A minor hurdle easily overcome with decent acting skills.

"I have someone here who'd like to speak to you, Tansy." I moved aside.

Angelique glanced around, then took a slow step back. "You brought her through. You should talk to her first."

Becky motioned the cameraman forward. "No, Jaime's right. She helped. It's your turn."

After a few protests, Angelique gave in and started fumbling almost immediately, now unable to hide behind the pretense that Tansy was out of reach.

I took my spot on the bench and braced myself against the ghost. It was the only thing I could do, short of claiming illness and forfeiting my segment. Even if this was only going on the DVD, it would be seen by people who mattered, and knowing something about Tansy's background gave me the edge I'd need to outperform an amateur and an Englishman who, I hoped, knew little of the case. So I was staying put.

The spirit left me alone for a few blessed minutes, then started up again. No slaps this time, just the whispers and gentle strokes on my hand that seemed oddly apologetic.

I'd have to deal with this. Not now, but tonight, when everyone had retired. Get out my kit and do a full-scale summoning. As much as I longed to ignore it, I couldn't risk this ghost interfering with the shoot.

When a young woman slid up beside me, close enough to get on camera should it pivot my way, I gave a distracted smile and stepped aside to give her room. I'm used to that—people sidling into camera range.

The girl edged toward me again. "You wanted to talk to me?"

I motioned that I couldn't speak right now. Bad enough I'd already interrupted Angelique. I couldn't be seen chatting with guests during her segment.

"Who is she talking to?" the young woman asked.

I leaned over. "She's contacted the ghost of—"

I stopped as a nearby guard turned to stare at me. I recognized that look all too well. It starts with a frown of confusion, followed by a sweeping glance around me, then the cautious look one bestows on people who carry on conversations with thin air.

By now you'd think I'd be able to recognize a ghost. But here was a seemingly corporeal young woman in a party gown appropriate for tonight's event. The only sign that she was a ghost was that no one else was paying attention to her, despite the fact that she was young and beautiful.

"Who—?" I stopped as her first words came back. "Tansy?"

She grinned. "Who else? You're lucky I got your message. You must have done something wrong, because it didn't come straight through to me. Someone watching the show came to tell me. Too cool. I've never been summoned by a . . . What do they call you guys again?"

"Necromancer," I said, trying to speak without moving my lips.

"Freaky." She waved at Angelique. "Speaking of freaky, what's up with that chick?"

"Wait!" Angelique said. "Tansy's trying to tell me some—"

Tansy let out a peal of laughter. "She thinks she's talking to me? But she's not one of you. She doesn't have that weird glow."

"She thinks she does."

"Really?" A mischievous grin. "Maybe it's just running low tonight. Let's find out."

Tansy skipped over and planted herself in front of Angelique, then started making faces and gesturing wildly.

"Tansy?" Angelique was saying. "Is there something you want to tell me?"

"Besides 'stop raiding your granny's closet'?" Tansy said. "Where'd you get that dress? Little Shop o' Virgins?"

I snorted a laugh, and tried covering it with a coughing fit. Angelique turned on me, her teeth bared like an enraged lapdog.

"Sorry. I—" I put my hand over my mouth as if stifling another cough. "I'll get some water. Please, go on."

"No, since you're so eager to perform, *Miss* Vegas, let's see you give it a try."

Becky nodded, her eyes pleading with me to take over. I stepped up.

"Now, this will be cool," Tansy said. "Show her how it's really done."

"Tansy?" I peered into the darkness. "Are you still here?"

"Oh, come on. Don't play that. This is the closest I've come to a camera in thirty years!"

"What's wrong?" Angelique sneered. "Let me guess. She's *fading*. I *overworked* her."

"Could be. But I can probably . . ." I peered into the dark garden. "I can just make her out. She's tiny. Maybe your size. Pale skin but long black hair and almost . . . copper eyes."

"That's what got me the part in *Lily White*," Tansy said. "They thought I looked exotic, like a fairy changeling should. Mom always said it was because my dad was Italian, but really, he was black. I mean, African American. He died in Vietnam, and her parents made her spread that story about him being Italian."

It must have been obvious I was listening to something, because Becky prodded me to relay the message. After some encouragement from Tansy, I did.

The crowd pressed closer, giving me its full attention. I could say it was the love of gossip, but I've always thought that puts too harsh a spin on it. People like stories, and what is gossip if not stories?

"African American?" Angelique said. "You can't prove it."

"Check my birth certificate," Tansy said.

I relayed the message. Becky motioned for her assistant to write it down, though he was already scribbling furiously.

So we continued. A natural comedic performer, Tansy regaled the crowd with quips and anecdotes until there wasn't a distracted face in the crowd.

"This is a waste of time," Angelique finally cut in. "Ask her what we really want to know. What we called her here for. How did she die?"

"I'm sure that's no big secret. Tell her to ask me something good." Tansy grinned. "Like what color underwear I was wearing."

"This is ridiculous," Angelique snapped when I didn't relay her question. "Doesn't she want closure? The guilty party brought to justice?"

Tansy frowned. "Guilty party?"

The last minutes of a ghost's violent end are wiped clean once she passes over. Tansy might not even know she'd been murdered—and enlightening her now was a cruelty I'd never inflict. Instead, I reached out, as if pulling her back.

"Tansy! Wait! She didn't mean—" When Tansy cocked a brow, I mouthed "Gotta go," then called, "Tansy! Please. We won't bring that up again. Come back."

"Fine," she sighed. "I'll leave. But can I talk to you later?"

I hesitated. When a ghost says, "I'd like to talk to you," what she means is, "I want you to do something for me." But Tansy *had* helped me. Though I probably couldn't return the favor, at least I could hear her out. So I nodded, and she disappeared.

"I DON'T know how I'll top that," Grady laughed as I walked off camera.

"I'm afraid you won't get the chance tonight," Becky said.

Grady's hearty smile stiffened.

"We've racked up overtime for the crew already, and that's definitely not something I care to tell Mr. Simon on the first day." She motioned Angelique forward. "Next time, hon, if you're struggling, don't push it. Let the others take their turn. It's only fair."

Angelique's cheeks reddened. I fussed with my evening bag, as if I hadn't overheard. However gentle Becky's reprimand, it should have been made in private. Performers have to stomach public criticism with every review or snarky blog, and no one likes taking any more than necessary.

Had Becky been more seasoned, she'd also have known there was no reason to rob Grady of his segment. He was savvy enough to know his performance would pale after mine and had she suggested it was getting late, he'd have offered to step aside.

Instead, Angelique was humiliated, Grady was insulted, Claudia was outraged on his behalf, and all three stormed off as Becky gushed over my "amazing" performance. I'd alienated both my costars, discovered the garden was haunted by a malicious spirit and falsely raised the hopes of a murdered ghost. All in my first day on the show I hoped would take my career to the next level. Off to a rousing start.

ONCE I was in my room, my resolve to sneak out and conduct a full summoning wavered. I told myself I couldn't face disappointing Tansy, should she be out there waiting. What if she *did* know she'd been murdered and wanted me to find her killer? My gut twisted at the thought.

Turning down ghosts who wanted messages delivered was hard enough. As much as I wanted to say, "Hey, do I look like a courier service?" I could be, to a ghost, a once-in-an-afterlife opportunity to get that message delivered, and even if it was something as mundane as, "Tell my wife I love her," it meant the world to them, and it hurt to refuse.

Sometimes, if it was easy enough, I'd do it. But finding or punishing a killer? Not possible. Saying no to message delivery was nothing compared to telling a murdered girl that even if she handed me a name and address, there was no way I could bring her killer to justice.

Still, I'd have to deal with Tansy sooner or later, and deep down, I knew that what was really keeping me out of that garden tonight was fear. Not of the spirit who'd slapped me, but the possibility that *no* spirit had slapped me. That I was finally losing it.

Madness is the legacy of this "gift"—one that gives me more nightmares with each passing year. Jeremy was helping me to deal with this. He has some experience with psychic phenomena himself, and there's no one better for laying out logical arguments. Not every necromancer goes mad, he pointed out. I'd never denied or overused my power, as was often the cause of the madness. I was otherwise healthy and I had a good support network.

But every time I'm convinced I'm overreacting, that I'm going to *drive* myself crazy by worrying about going crazy, I see my strong, stubborn grandmother who died strapped to a bed, being fed like an infant, ranting about ghosts even I couldn't see. Then after helping Jeremy in Toronto last fall, I had another image to add—that of a necromancer driven so insane she could barely pass for human.

As hard as I clung to Jeremy's reasonable words, I felt my confidence slipping... and imagined my sanity slipping with it. So, while part of me said, "You're not going crazy, so make contact with this ghost and prove it," another, quieter but more persuasive part said, "Isn't it better just to tell yourself you *could* make contact, if you tried hard enough?"

No. I wouldn't give in to the fear.

I took my necromancy bag from its hiding place and snuck downstairs.

SICK PUPPIES

I FOUND A GOOD PLACE in the garden—on the other side of a wooden bridge where I'd hear the footsteps of any night walkers coming my way. No one should be surprised to see a spiritualist conducting a ritual, even at 2 a.m., but people like their summonings neat and tidy, with flowery words, herbs and incense. A true necromancer crosses the boundary between this world and the next, and for that, I need the remnants of death.

There's no preset list of items every necromancer uses. It's like a recipe for stew—we take a few common ingredients, test out the variations our families pass along, then add and subtract through trial and error until we have what seems to work best for us.

First, I removed an old piece of grave cloth—a relic handed down from Nan, who claimed it came from a Roman emperor. Walk into a necromancy shop and *everything* comes from a Roman emperor or Egyptian queen or African prince. It doesn't matter. The power the individual held in life has no bearing on an object's power. It just makes a better story.

Next, vervain, an herb burned to help contact traumatized spirits. Then dogwood bark and dried maté to ward off unwanted spirits and prevent summoning demonic entities. Considering how this spirit was acting, I added an extra helping of the banishing mixture.

I took out a tied bunch of hair. Different hairs, from different people at different stages of life, from infant to elderly, some for each sex. These came from the living. The advantage to hair is that because it's dead cells, I don't need to harvest it from the deceased.

Finally came the true remnants of the grave. A finger joint. A toe. An ear. Bits of bone. Teeth. The bone and teeth were ancient relics, also from my grandmother, also purported to have some wild and glorious history. With the flesh artifacts, I wasn't so lucky. To be potent they had to be fresh. Fresh, thankfully, is a relative term when you're talking about decomposing corpses. But after a year, they had to be burned and the ashes added to a jar. Then they had to be replaced.

I laid them on the grave cloth as prescribed, then put the jar of ashes in the middle.

If Bradford Grady came strolling back here and found me arranging bits of flesh and bone in a symbolic pattern, he'd fall on his knees, thinking he'd finally found concrete evidence of the satanic. Dark magic does exist, but not in the form he imagines. Satanic cults and devil worship belong in the realm of the mentally ill, the attention-deprived and the foolishly desperate. The power of magic lies in the blood. Without that blood, they can't use the power, no matter how many cats they sacrifice.

Now it was time to start the summoning. First I'd test to make sure this wasn't another vampire. I took a container from my bag and removed two locks of hair. I kept them separate to guard against loss. Vampires are the rarest of the races and I only know two.

Like Jeremy and me, Cassandra and Aaron served as delegates on the interracial council, a body of volunteers from each supernatural race who work together on problems that affect us all. When I'd asked Cassandra for a lock of her hair, she'd looked at me as if I were asking her to lop off a body part. Aaron had handed his over willingly, and would always provide more, but I liked having samples from both genders, so I was taking good care of Cass's.

I arranged the hairs. Almost the moment I finished preparing, fingers glided along my arm, as if the spirit had been waiting patiently the whole time.

"Can you hear me?"

The whispering began, distant and off to my left. Something brushed my arm. A finger poked my cheek. At the same time, a third hand lifted a lock of my hair, and the hairs on my neck rose as I realized this meant there was more than one spirit.

I conducted the vampire test. Hands kept touching me, voices whispering, but nothing changed.

"Can you hear me?" I said. "Can you give me some sign that you understand?"

The touches stayed gentle, like the voices, as if whoever was on the other side knew I was working hard to make contact. I repeated the ritual using the regular hair and entreated the spirits to speak or otherwise make themselves known. They just continued the whispering and touching. I redid the ritual. Twice. No change.

I dumped my purse, laying out a pen and paper and scattering some other items. I even smoothed a patch of dirt for finger-writing. The vampire ghost, Natasha, had been able to move objects, and had conveyed "charades"-type messages. Maybe that would work.

The touching and whispering had stopped as soon as I'd emptied my purse, as if the spirits were puzzling over the meaning of this new activity.

"Is there some way you can communicate? Write something on the paper or in the dirt?"

I demonstrated by writing my name on the paper, then in the dirt. The whispering and prodding stopped, but as soon as I ceased writing, it resumed.

"Move something. Anything. Just show me you can."

Again, they stopped, this time for almost a minute, but nothing in the pile moved. I shifted the items, encouraging and demonstrating. They'd pay attention, then go back to touching me.

Time to call in the big guns.

From my purse, I took out a plain silver ring. It belonged to my spirit contact, Eve Levine. To summon her, I needed an object that had been significant to her in life. The ring had been a gift from her daughter's father, Kristof, and Eve and I had had to work with her teenage daughter, Savannah, to track down and get access to a safety deposit box.

Until three years ago, I'd known Eve only by reputation. A bad reputation, as the kind of witch you didn't want to cross. By the time I met her daughter, Eve was dead, which should normally make a relationship impossible, but in my case is no impediment. When Eve had needed a necro, she came to the one who knew Savannah, and to our mutual shock, we became friends. Now when I needed ghostly help, I called on her.

But this time she didn't answer. No surprise. For months each year, Eve was gone and couldn't explain where, one of the many mysteries of the afterlife that ghosts were forbidden to discuss with the living. In an emergency, I could use the ring to summon Kristof, and he'd get a message to her, but this wasn't urgent, and I wasn't keen to summon Kristof Nast otherwise.

TROUBLED BY my failure in the garden, I didn't get much sleep. When I finally gave up and got out of bed the next morning, I had a text message from Elena: *J didn't want to wake you. Said you had a party last night. Call when you can.*

"Hey," Elena said when I called. "Jeremy's upstairs putting the kids down for a nap."

"I hear you have a couple of sick puppies."

She laughed. "That we do. Oh, and your delivery came this morning. Their first bunnies! Kate's already trying to chew an ear off. Clay's so proud."

"No bunny chewing for Logan?"

"Too crude. He's been examining his carefully. Clay says he's trying to find its weak spots."

A door banged open and Clay's voice rumbled something I couldn't make out.

"Jeremy's on his way down," Elena said. "And in a few hours, he'll be on his way there. The kids are doing much better. Just a cold, like I kept telling everyone."

Clay's voice sounded in the background, more a growl than a rumble.

"Oh, they'll be fine," Elena said.

"Logan's coughing again." Clay's voice came clear.

"It's not fatal." An exasperated sigh as she came back to me. "Pain in the—"

She gave a squeal that made me jump. The phone clattered to the floor. Elena shrieked a reminder that she was on the phone—or supposed to be. The phone clattered again, as if being recovered.

“Tell her I’m sorry,” Elena called from the distance. “And Clay apologizes for being rude.”

“I do?”

“Profusely.”

“Take it outside,” Jeremy said. “The babies are trying to sleep, and you could both use the fresh air.”

“Sorry,” Jeremy said as their voices faded. “They’ve been cooped up inside, worrying about the babies, and they’re going a little stir crazy. Elena told you they’re doing better?”

“She did. But Clay still seems worried. Maybe you should—”

“He’ll be fine, and I’ll be on my way soon. So how was the party?”

I tried to emphasize the humor of the situation, but when I finished he asked whether there was more.

“You sound tired,” he said. “Which I could chalk up to the late night, but . . .”

“Sounds more like a *sleepless* night, huh?”

I told him everything.

“If you can’t contact Eve, try Paige and Lucas,” he said. “Elena talked to Paige last night, and they’re both home. I could—”

“You concentrate on getting here. I’ll make the calls.”

He promised to phone back when he had an ETA, and we signed off.

REPRIEVE FOR EVE

I SPENT TOO MUCH TIME fussing with my wardrobe that morning. I was supposed to be wearing a burnt orange crepe tank top with a chocolate brown pencil skirt and a matching fitted jacket—the kind of thing you'd see in an old noir film. Sexy and sophisticated with a fun, retro twist. The look suited me, which is always a relief. There's nothing worse than finding a fabulous new style in the fashion mags and rushing out to track it down, only to realize it made you look like a frumpy middle-aged suburbanite or, worse yet, a frumpy middle-aged suburbanite who still thinks she's a smoking twenty-year-old.

But should I wear it today, when I might not see Jeremy until evening? Or save it for then? Not so much a burning dilemma as a way to postpone facing my colleagues until I was certain I was awake and focused on the task of winning them over. Finally, after taking it all off and trying on a couple of alternatives, I put on the original outfit and went downstairs.

AS I approached the dining room, the silence made me check my PDA to make sure I hadn't screwed up my schedule. Another three steps and I caught the murmur of low voices. Angelique sat alone on one side of the table, Grady and Claudia on the other, whispering together and ignoring Angelique.

The dead man now hung through a plate of melon slices. I tried to ignore him.

"Good morning," I said as I slid into a seat.

Grady hesitated only a moment before good manners won out and he poured me a coffee. I thanked him with a dazzling smile, then reached for a piece of cantaloupe. As the dead man's fingers brushed the fruit, I decided I was more in the mood for muffins.

Angelique's eyes went round. "You still eat carbs? Oh, my lord, you're so brave."

"Not really," I said with a laugh. "I'll pay for it when I can't do up my skirt later."

I took a big bite and chewed with relish. Angelique tried not to drool.

"I'm a sucker for comfort food," I said. "And after last night, I need it. I'm used to getting a lot more advance warning than that. My nerves are still recovering."

Grady thawed enough to speak. "It was rather more sudden than I like."

"I hope to God there won't be any more. No one mentioned warm-up séances to me."

"Nor to me." Claudia cut a muffin in half and took one piece. "I'm going to have a talk with Becky."

"Good. I'm not used to working that way. I felt awful about interrupting Angelique." I turned to her. "I'm very sorry. My nerves were just frazzled."

She studied my face, as if looking for a catch, then slowly nodded. "I might have been a little jumpy myself. I'm not used to being on camera."

"You specialize in live shows too, don't you? TV is a whole different medium, and I don't do a lot of it yet." I grinned over at Grady. "But we have a pro on the set. Maybe if we're nice, he'll pass some tips our way."

"Oh, good, everyone's here," Becky said as she swung through the door. "Did you all get breakfast? I'm so sorry I'm late."

She collapsed into the chair beside mine. I filled her coffee cup.

"Thank you. You have no idea how much I need this. I've been up half the night. First, calling Mr. Simon, who insisted on hearing the results of the Tansy Lane séance. Then he had me get the researchers to work confirming Jaime's facts."

"And how does it look?" Grady asked.

Becky slid a worried glance my way. "Well, I hate to be the bearer of ill news but—"

She reached over to a telephone on the side table. The top line was flashing. A press of the buttons and . . .

"They're all here, Mr. Simon."

Shit. Becky had no problem chewing out Angelique last night, but apparently I deserved different treatment—a direct reprimand from the producer himself. I braced myself.

"Only got a minute, folks." Simon spoke so fast I had to concentrate to keep up. "First, let me say how absolutely devastated I was that I couldn't be there last night. I was dying to meet you all. Heh, heh, that's probably not the best phrase to use with you folks, is it? Jaime. Jaime, hon?"

"Uh, here, Mr. Simon."

"Todd. Call me Todd. I hear you struck a home run last night. Hit the ball out of the park."

Becky grinned at me.

Simon continued. "Every question right, our researchers tell me. That is fucking amazing, pardon my French, folks."

As Grady's and Angelique's faces hardened, I chastised myself. I had to be careful when I really did contact ghosts as part of a show—getting enough answers correct to maintain credibility, but not so many that colleagues would accuse me of rigging things.

Simon continued, "So I just wanted to call and say 'atta girl.' You're the real deal, Jaime Vegas. Soon the whole world will know it, and believe me, no one is more thrilled about that than I am. You ever been in *Vanity Fair,* Jaime?"

"Um, no."

"Well, I'm lining something up for you right now. Know some people. Making some calls. My gift to you."

"Uh, thank you."

"Angel? Brad?"

"Yes, Todd?" Grady said.

"That's Mr. Simon to you, sir." Simon gave a laugh that could be interpreted as "I'm kidding," but suggested he wasn't. "Angel, sweetie, I gave you this big chance to get your pretty little ass out of the cornfields, and you aren't showing me the love."

"I—" she began.

"Brad, you're going to get your chance soon, and I expect results. That salary of yours is killing the budget. Don't make me regret it. *Comprendes,* amigo?"

"We understand," Claudia said.

"Good, good. Just so we're all on the same page, folks. Now, gotta run, gotta run, but I will be watching. Do me proud."

The line went dead. It took sixty seconds for Angelique, Grady and Claudia to remember previous engagements and clear the room. So much for smoothing things over.

I HAD a magazine interview at nine sharp—barely enough time to brush my teeth after breakfast. The interview part went smoothly. Then they wanted to take pictures . . . in the garden. Of course they'd want the garden—the house was half furnished and partially under construction.

All I could think about was photos of me, wide-eyed and jumpy as those damnable spirits tormented me. I panicked. I started babbling excuses about bad lighting and allergies. The harried photographer, who probably had a full schedule ahead of him, decided he didn't need to start his day this way and suggested the article could run without my photo. That wouldn't be good. Hit a certain age, and if your picture is missing in an article, people start to suspect there's a reason, especially when your costars' photos are there.

So I gave in . . . and it was every bit as hellish as I'd imagined. The spirits poked. They prodded. They whispered in my ear. And I had to ignore them and look like I was having the time of my life, which only made them poke and prod all the harder. By the time the session was over, my nerves were shot.

This had to end. I needed to figure out what these ghosts were and banish them before they ruined the shoot.

———

I LEFT the house by the front door and walked to clear my head. Normally, after a block in heels, my feet would have been screaming for me to stop, but if they were, I was too preoccupied to hear them.

Why couldn't I communicate with these ghosts? Spooks do play pranks on necromancers, but if that was the case, the dogwood bark and dried maté should have warded them off.

Souls can also get trapped in dimensional portals, but I'd encountered those and knew that wasn't the explanation here. Nor were they demons or demidemons or demideities. Again, been there, done that. Robert Vasic, the council research expert, always tells me I should keep a journal of my experiences for his records, to help other necromancers with odd cases, since I seem to have encountered them all. I think he's kidding, but I'm never sure. Just as I'm not sure whether my breadth of experience has more to do with untapped power or a talent for stumbling into trouble.

My gut told me these were normal ghosts in an abnormal situation. But how did they get there—in a place where they could touch me, but couldn't materialize or communicate?

One answer: black magic.

When it came to black magic, I had an excellent source of information. A former leading teacher of the art—and one who did not fulfill that "those who can't, teach" cliché. My absent spirit guide, Eve Levine.

Also known as "dark" or "chaotic" magic, black magic isn't necessarily evil. It's a blanket term for all magic with a potentially negative outcome. Like a spell to kill someone. You could use it for evil, but you're more likely to use it in self-defense. But the only type of magic likely to affect ghosts was the darkest of the dark arts: ritual sacrifice.

Human sacrifice is rare. Some dark-arts practitioners never conduct such rituals. Had Eve? It's not something you ask a friend about, but I'd guess that she had, though only when she'd needed to kill an enemy and decided his death might as well serve another purpose. That was Eve—never cruel, but coldly practical in a way I couldn't fathom, just as I couldn't fathom living a life where you *had* enemies you needed to kill.

When I reached the Brentwood Market, I headed around back, out of sight of passing traffic, took out Eve's ring and tried contacting her again, putting all my concentration into it, hoping that somehow, wherever she was, I could break through. After a couple of minutes, the air shimmered—the first sign of a ghost coming through.

"Oh, thank God! Eve, I need you—"

A man materialized. A big man—tall and solidly built, in his late forties with thinning blond hair and bright blue eyes.

"Kristof," I said. "I didn't call you. I called—"

"Eve, I know." He cast a look around the lot, nose wrinkling slightly, then brushed off the front of his suit jacket, as if it might have been soiled in the transition. "You've been trying to get through to her for a while, and obviously something's wrong, so I thought I should find out what you want." He checked his watch.

"If I'm keeping you, Kristof—"

"I'm in court, but I requested a ten-minute recess."

An afterlife with lawyers, three-piece suits and wristwatches. If I ever needed proof that Kristof Nast had ended up in a hell dimension, this was it.

"Is there some way you can get Eve for me?"

"I can try. She isn't supposed to be disturbed, but if it's urgent, I can petition for a special allowance. I presume it's urgent?"

Something in his gaze begged me to say it was, but with Kristof, it was wise to be wary. "Well, I'm not sure it's *urgent*—"

"If you say it's urgent, that's all I need."

Ah. So I wasn't the only one Eve was out of contact with. That's why he was here. Certainly not to help me. My only contact with Kristof in life—not in person, but through his employees, naturally—had not been one to encourage friendship. Eve was the only thing we had in common.

"If you did get access and it wasn't for something important, would Eve be pissed off?"

"Hardly. She'd welcome the break." His eyes glittered. "I'd even go so far as to say she'd be grateful."

"So, wherever she is, she isn't there by choice?"

His smile faded. "You know I'm not allowed to discuss that. But if you need her, which you obviously do, I can petition—"

"And if it's not urgent, would Eve get in trouble?"

That stopped him. "There's no way for her to know what you might consider urgent . . ." Another pause, then a sigh. "*Is* it urgent?"

It was. To me. But I suspected "saving Jaime Vegas from pestering spooks" wasn't a problem you should petition deities to fix, so I said, "Not really."

He swore under his breath. Then asked, reluctantly, "Is there anything I can do?"

He hated offering. But she'd *want* him to offer, and that's what counted.

I could ask him about ritual sacrifice. But sorcerers like Kristof Nast don't conduct dark-magic rites—they hire people to do them. So I thanked him for his time, then watched him go.

TIME TO reach out to others. Jeremy had suggested Paige and Lucas, and that was the logical next step. Paige was the witch member of the interracial council. At twenty-seven, she was the youngest delegate, as well as the most energetic. Just watching her work was tiring.

For Paige, helping supernaturals was a life mission. Together with her husband, Lucas, she ran a legal-firm-cum-detective-agency devoted to protecting supernaturals from the Cabals—the corporate Mafia of our world. The fact that Lucas's father was CEO of the most powerful of those Cabals made their lives all the more complicated.

They would help, of course . . . as soon as they could. The spirits weren't going anywhere, and I wasn't in mortal danger. Whomever they were helping right now probably *was* in mortal danger. So they couldn't be expected to drop everything for me, but I knew they wouldn't turn me down if I showed up on their doorstep and only asked for an hour or two of their time. I could run the problem past them, get their input and ask them to point me to their library or computer files, so I could do the research myself.

According to my schedule, I only had one work obligation today. I was supposed to sit in on some discussions with the parapsychologists—playing "interviewer" as they explained their methods—but Angelique could take my place. In fact, if I suggested it, the offer might go a long way toward easing the animosity between us.

Now for an excuse . . . I decided to use my mother, claiming she was ill and needed me. Most people would feel guilty using a parent like that, but the way I see it, it's a fair exchange. She used me for years. Still does. Her spot in the retirement village costs more than my condo in Chicago, and she isn't the one paying for it.

Last time I heard from my mother had been when she'd decided she wanted to upgrade her monthly spa package. When I argued, she'd used her usual threat: to tell the tabloids about my abortion at sixteen, conveniently leaving out the fact that she'd arranged it and I'd thought I was going to the doctor for a prenatal checkup. I'd paid for the upgrade, as I always did, not so much because her threat worried me but because it was easier to throw money at her than to deal with her. A coward's ploy, maybe, but with some wounds, slapping on a bandage and pretending it isn't there is easier than dealing with the pain.

ZOMBIE SLAVES

IT WAS DURING TAKEOFF that I began to repent my haste. Was flying to Portland really necessary? When I'd called Jeremy and told him, I'd heard the hesitation in his voice, though he'd taken the change in stride and switched his plane ticket to Portland, where he'd meet me for dinner and help me slog through Paige's files.

Exactly how much faster would this route be, when I wouldn't get back on the set before tomorrow? How annoyed would Grady and Angelique be when they realized I'd swanned off—even if it was on a family emergency?

Yet as foolish as I felt, I knew why I'd done it. To prove to myself that I could handle this.

I'd gotten my job as necromancer delegate because, frankly, no one else wanted it. I had zero experience at resolving supernatural problems and, as I quickly realized, no one cared. They expected me to do what the last guy did—answer necromancy questions when called, but otherwise sit back and let the others work.

I wanted to be a full-fledged delegate, doing everything the others did, including the investigative work. So far, they'd included me, but with lots of supervision and safety nets, until I felt like the overeager rookie everyone fears will just mess things up.

Last year, I'd done something just like this—flown to help Jeremy and Elena when a phone call would have sufficed. And even then I'd had to fight for every step I took off the sidelines.

But this was *my* case. And I couldn't bear to call up Paige or Robert and push the research—and maybe the entire investigation—onto their laps. It probably would have made more sense to swallow my pride and call, but now it was too late, and part of me was glad of that.

I STOOD on the sidewalk and tried not to shiver. I'd been so wrapped up in getting here that I was still dressed for Southern California. So I'd go to Paige and Lucas looking like a ditz who couldn't even remember to wear a warm coat to Portland in November. It would be nice to make a different impression now and then, just for variety's sake.

I looked up at the building. Double-checked the office address Paige had given me when I'd called from the airport. I wondered whether I'd misheard. The taxi idled behind me, the driver apparently as uncertain as I was.

The building seemed to have been a warehouse or other industrial sort, deep in a neighborhood of industrial sorts. It had no nameplate or other sign, but when your clientele is supernaturals, you don't advertise with flashing billboards.

I waved the driver on. Then I decided to check the street name before knocking on the door. As I approached the corner, a young woman in jeans and a shearling coat hurried across the empty road.

"Excuse me!" I called.

She didn't slow. In this neighborhood, that was probably wise. I trotted another few steps.

"Excuse me! Is this North Breton Road?"

She turned and lifted her sunglasses, features drawn in confusion. I'd seen that "you talkin' to me?" look often enough and my gut sank as my gaze dipped to take a closer look at her outfit—bell-bottom jeans, tie-dyed shirt, fringed purse...

"Uh, sorry," I said. "I thought you were... Sorry."

I turned and marched back toward the building, my heels clacking along the empty road.

"In a hurry, necromancer?" she called from behind me.

I cursed under my breath, plastered on a vacant grin and turned to see the young woman bearing down on me.

"No, of course not," I said. "I was looking for directions and—"

"You didn't think I could provide them? Being dead and all?"

"I didn't want to presume. So is this North Breton Road?"

She kept walking until she was well into my personal space, something ghosts can do much better than people. Her hands passed through my shoulders as she gestured.

"You aren't worried about asking something I can't answer. You're running as fast as you can before I ask *you* something."

"I wasn't—"

"Cut the crap. I've met your kind before. Two years after I die, I'm lucky enough to bump into a necromancer at a KISS concert, and I beg the guy to pass along a message to my kid sister. Just a phone call, no big deal. He gives me this lecture on the *proper* way to approach a necromancer."

"Some necros can get a little touchy, especially at social events—"

"Ten years later, I see another, I try again and she walks away. Doesn't even have the courtesy to answer me."

"Well, I can't promise anything, but if you'd like me to get in touch with your sister—"

"She's fifty years old! Do you think she wants to hear from me now?"

"I'm sorry you had a bad experience—"

"Fuck you." She wheeled and stalked away.

As I walked back toward the building, I concentrated on the questions I'd ask Paige and Lucas, and tried to forget the young woman. Another day, another ghost. One of hundreds. Hundreds of hopeful, disappointed—

I cut off the thought and picked my way past a ripped-open garbage bag to the front doors. They were full-length dark glass—one-way glass, I presumed, so they could see out and I couldn't peek in.

I pulled on the handle. Locked. To my left was a small speaker marked "Deliveries and Visitors." I buzzed.

"Hey, Jaime!" It was Savannah, Eve and Kristof's seventeen-year-old daughter. Not a ghost, thankfully, but very much alive and the ward of Paige and Lucas.

Savannah's voice was so clear, I looked around to see where she was. When she laughed, I spotted a tiny camera lens.

"High-tech, huh?" she said. "We get all the bells and whistles. Very cool . . . and complicated as hell. I need a damned instruction book for this— Oh, there it is." The door buzzed. "Come on in. We're on the second floor. You'll need to take the stairs. The elevator's card-activated."

In the background, Paige yelled for Savannah—something about boxes—and a male voice cursed. Obviously not Lucas—if he used profanity, I'd never heard it.

As I entered, it was like stepping into an upscale corporate office under construction, the gleaming floors dusty with footprints, the richly painted walls awaiting artwork, cardboard boxes stacked by the gleaming elevator doors. I should have remembered that this was originally supposed to be a Cortez Cabal satellite office. I'd been in one once, and it had been just like this—a grungy exterior hiding plush offices.

As for how Benicio Cortez's anti-Cabal youngest son ended up with an office that was built for a Cabal, I only knew that Lucas's father had been building it in Portland and somehow Lucas and Paige ended up buying the unfinished offices instead. That had been over a year ago, and they were just moving in now. A big leap for a young couple, but I guess it was better than having Daddy and his mob move into town.

The stairwell was as silent as the foyer, but the moment I opened the second-floor door, it was like someone had hit "play," the air filling with noise: the whine of a drill, a woman's laugh, the bang of a dropped box, a man's shout. Top-notch soundproofing between floors—another bonus from the Cabal construction crews.

The drilling came from one direction, the voices from the other.

"Don't touch the books. I have a system."

"What system?" Savannah answered. "Dump them all in a pile?"

It took me a moment to recognize the first speaker. Adam Vasic, one of my fellow council members, who was joining his friends in their new venture.

"Just leave the books." Paige's voice, a deep contralto. "Adam, keep bringing up those boxes. Savannah, make sure all the books get into Adam's office, but don't unpack them. They'll need to be arranged in a recognizable system, so we can all find what we need when our librarian isn't here."

"Librarian?" Adam said. "The title is head of research."

"And security guard," Savannah added.

"*Head* of security."

"Right. In charge of all those other librarians and security guards we've hired."

"It's a growth position. Just like yours. Someday, I'm sure you'll be in charge of the entire secretarial pool."

"These boxes aren't moving on their own," Paige cut in as I approached the open door. "I need them all upstairs and sorted into the proper rooms. Then I need Adam assembling the bookcase while Savannah helps Lucas with that alarm system. And when that's done there's—"

"A shitload more," Savannah said. "You know what you really need? Zombie slaves."

"I've got you two. Close enough."

"You don't want zombies," I said as I walked in. "You'll spend a fortune on air fresheners."

Adam was digging through a box of reference texts. He didn't look much like a librarian . . . unless the library catered to surfers. A stereotypical California boy, well built and tanned with sun-bleached hair and a quick smile. He didn't look much like a kid with a demon for a dad either, but that was typical for half-demons. They appeared and acted human, inheriting from their father only a set of abilities, usually elemental or sensory. Adam's power was fire. When he lost his temper, his touch could give third-degree burns. Fortunately, it was hard to piss him off.

Paige was busy on the computer, fingers flying and eyes on the monitor even as she spoke. A voluptuous twenty-seven-year-old with long dark curls, she was dressed in jeans and a sweatshirt. Practical moving-day attire. It was rare to see Paige out of a skirt. A girly girl, as Savannah always teased.

Savannah didn't follow her guardian's tastes in clothes—or much else. One look at the seventeen-year-old—almost six feet tall and slender with long dark hair and perfect bone structure—and anyone who'd known Eve could tell who Savannah's mother was. Only her eyes, big and bright blue, came from Kristof.

Even in ripped jeans, old sneakers and a tight concert T-shirt, Savannah exuded elegance and grace . . . until she opened her mouth. Paige no longer commented on her ward's language. I guess parents need to pick their battles, and with Savannah, there were far more important ones. As the daughter of a sorcerer and a half-demon witch, she was a powder keg of supernatural power. At thirteen, panicked and trying to contact her dead mother, she'd leveled a house—an incident that I suspected was responsible for her father's death, though even Kristof pretended he'd died in an unrelated accident.

Savannah greeted me with an exuberant hug. Paige started to rise, but I waved her down and leaned in for a hug.

"I guess that lock on the front door still isn't working," Paige said. "I'll have to get Lucas to take another look at it. Poor guy. Really *not* his area of expertise."

"It's working," Savannah said. "I buzzed Jaime in."

"And didn't go down to escort her up?"

"How? You've got us working our asses off while you play on the computers."

"I'm getting the network up. If we don't have everything in place by tomorrow—"

"The earth will stop revolving around its axis. And we might lose our first paying client."

"Which is even more important." Paige looked up at me. "Sorry. Things are a little nuts. We've been slowly moving in, but now we've got a lead on a very big client . . . who expects to see a fully functioning professional office—tomorrow."

"Well, don't worry. I won't take up much of your time. I just want to run a scenario by you."

"Sure. We'll grab coffee and talk." A glance at the others. "Can I leave you two alone?"

"Please." Savannah turned to me. "Take her for as long as you want."

Paige pulled a face and ushered me out of the office. The drilling down the hall had stopped, replaced by Lucas's voice, quiet but insistent. We found him on his cell phone, examining a drill hole in the wall.

He peered at his drill work, his already serious face dropping into a frown. Paige caught his attention, and his eyes lit up.

"No, I don't believe you understand," he said into the phone. "We allowed for leeway on the understanding that if our needs changed and we needed the work completed promptly, it would be. If you cannot provide that . . ." He paused. "Good. Then I shall expect a crew at . . . ?"

He lifted two fingers to Paige, who nodded. He signed off, then hung up.

"We were coming to see whether you have time for a coffee break," she said. "But I'm guessing the answer is no."

"I'll take one anyway. I could use the air. Jaime, was your flight—"

His cell phone rang. A soft sigh and he checked the number. "Jack McNeil."

"The client," Paige explained to me. "Take it. We'll bring you back a coffee. Jaime can explain her situation then."

WE WALKED to a bakery a block up. Paige swore the neighborhood wasn't as bad as it looked. I put my trust in her hands . . . and her defensive spells. We were still catching up when we returned to the building, coffees in hand.

"Savannah's working for us this year while she decides what she wants to do about college."

"Is she still leaning toward graphic design?" I asked.

"She is, but she wants our advice and we're really torn. Part of me wants to tell her she's doing the right thing, preparing for a reliable career while she pursues her art in her spare time. The other part wants to say 'forget practicality' and tell her to enroll in a fine-arts program."

"Getting a job to fall back on isn't the worst idea. Jeremy worked as a translator for years before his paintings started to sell."

She led me onto the elevator. "I think that's who she's taking her cue from. But I worry that Lucas and I are both too inclined to push practicality and maybe *that's* what's driving her decision. Anyway, she has a year to think about it."

We met Adam and Savannah in the hall.

Savannah lifted her hands. "Before you crack the whip, we're heading out for more boxes."

"Take this one instead. Brownies, plus a Coke for Adam, and a mocha cappuccino for you."

"Thanks," Adam said.

"Don't thank her," Savannah said. "It's zombie slave fuel. Sugar and caffeine to keep us going."

"You got it. And sandwiches for later, so you don't need to take off for dinner. Jaime? The meeting room is the first door on the right. Go on in while I find Lucas."

BE PREPARED

"I ASSUMED IT WAS A NECROMANCY PROBLEM, but now I'm thinking dark magic," I said after I told them what was happening.

Lucas frowned. "Dark magic? As in ritual sacrifice?"

"Eve would be your best bet for anything dark," Paige said. "But I'm guessing if you're asking us, she's out of contact again. My experience with stuff like this is practically zero. I've witnessed ritual sacrifice." Her face went pale at the memory. "Not intentionally. Some kind of high-level protection ritual."

"That's the primary use," Lucas said. "A life given for a life protected. Ritual sacrifice is very rare. If I encounter it, it's peripheral to a case I'm investigating. When a Cabal passes a sentence of execution they may perform ritual sacrifice as the method of execution. Purely a matter of economics."

Paige nodded. "If they're already killing someone, might as well use it."

"But in all cases, the soul passes over," Lucas said. "It's even written into the Cabal legal code that if an executed victim is used for ritual sacrifice, an independent necromancer must be on hand to confirm that the soul has safely passed over."

"That's the Cabal version of the Geneva convention. They can only torture you until you're dead."

"Huh." I sipped my coffee, thinking. "What about Druidic sacrifice?"

"Rare these days," Paige said. "Even rarer than dark-magic sacrifice. Remember Esus? He didn't even try to ask for a human sacrifice. We gave him his pint of blood and he was happy. But even if a Druid was performing human sacrifice, it doesn't explain damaged souls. It's the act that matters. A show of respect for the Druidic deity."

I drank more coffee. Hoped the caffeine would help my brain work faster.

"What *you* have are damaged souls," Lucas said. "Somehow they've been fragmented or drained, and there's no magic we know of that works that way. That doesn't mean such a thing cannot exist—simply that it defies the basic principles of sacrifice. We'll look into it further after we get through tomorrow."

"That's fine. In the meantime maybe you can steer me in the right direction and I can run with it. Paige has the council records, right? I can search those, see whether I find anything similar."

"You could, but they're, uh, on a disk, which is . . . somewhere in this mess. I decided they'd be more secure here than at home. I'll find it for you after tomorrow, though."

"Oh. Well . . . is there someone I can speak to, then? A contact in dark magic?"

Lucas shook his head. "One needs to be careful with this sort of thing. Expressing excessive interest in dark magic can be extremely dangerous. You should leave this to us."

Even when I showed up on their doorstep, I couldn't get anywhere. Just give us the details, Jaime, and let us do the work. I argued for a while, but it was clear they weren't giving me anything that could get me into any trouble.

SAVANNAH CALLED me a cab, then stepped outside to wait with me. "So, you need to talk to someone about dark magic."

"Eavesdropping?"

"Beats working. I might be able to help."

"Oh? What would you—" I stopped. "Your mom, of course."

"Nah, Mom didn't teach me that sort of stuff. Nothing darker than a chaos spell—and even then, only to protect myself. She kept that part of her life separate."

"I should have guessed that."

"Doesn't mean she was ashamed of it. It's just not the kind of stuff she'd talk about around her kid. But I know someone who *will* talk about it." She took out a BlackBerry. "A dark witch my mom knew. She tracked me down last year, saying she wanted to talk, share some stories about Mom."

"That was nice of her."

Savannah gave me a look. "You think I bought that shit? She just wanted to make contact with Eve Levine's daughter before her competition did. That's one thing my mom *did* teach me. Someone like that always wants something."

"So you didn't meet with her."

She smiled. "Never said that. The corollary lesson from Mom? People like this might want something from me, but I can use that—turn it around and get something from them." She glanced over her shoulder, then lowered her voice. "We've been in e-mail contact, and met a couple of times. She's useful. Paige and Lucas can't get information from someone like this. But me? I just pull some 'confused teenager' bullshit and she's putty in my hands. She'd tell me anything in hopes of winning Eve Levine's daughter as an ally. An idiot, but a useful idiot."

The look in her eyes chilled me.

"So, yeah, I've used her," Savannah continued. "Just to get stuff for Paige and Lucas. Without them knowing, of course. If they found out I was even talking to someone like this, they'd shit bricks... then use them to wall me up in my room for life."

"In that case, I'd better not wave your name around to get access to this woman."

Savannah hesitated. "You're right. But you can use Mom's. Tell Molly you'll grant her an exclusive audience with Eve Levine and she'll give you anything you want."

I shook my head. "Not without asking your mom first, and she's out of contact right now."

"Huh." Savannah fingered her BlackBerry, toying with it as she thought. Then she smiled. "Molly's boyfriend died last winter. Half-demon. They'd lived together for years and when I saw her this summer, she was still really broken up. Let's say you offer to put her in touch with him..."

I hesitated.

"You can offer to *try*. She'll still have some of his belongings and can even take you to his grave, so that gives you, what, about a ninety percent chance of success?"

"Eighty... maybe."

"Good enough. Don't promise, but say if you can't, you'll arrange a backup session with some other dearly departed." She flipped her BlackBerry around, tapping on an address. "She's just across the border in Vancouver."

VANCOUVER, WASHINGTON, was a cab ride from Portland. I checked my watch. Jeremy would be here in about two hours. As much as I wanted to meet him at the airport, I wanted to impress him even more, which I could do if I'd found and scoped out Molly Crane's house before he arrived to help interview her.

I called Elena and asked whether Jeremy had her cell phone with him—the only one in the family.

"I tried giving it to him, but he wouldn't take it. You know how he is. God forbid I should drive home without an emergency line. I told him to buy a prepaid phone. He had no idea what I was talking about, but of course he wouldn't admit it. You'll have to help him. Might have to show him how to use it too."

I laughed, remembering the first time I'd met Jeremy. When Paige introduced us, I'd been hoping, really hoping, for that "Oh, my God, *the* Jaime Vegas?" reaction... and had gotten only a polite hello, prompting Savannah to inform him that I was on TV sometimes—which hadn't changed his expression one whit. Elena had teased Jeremy about his lack of technological savvy, kidding that he didn't know what a TV was. And, perhaps for the first time in my life, I'd realized I was glad. I could make my own impression.

When I told Elena that I'd hoped to get a message to him about meeting elsewhere, she said, "If you don't mind me relaying that message, I can give it to him. He'll find a pay phone as soon as he arrives, to check on the kids."

Of course he would. Perfect. I found a coffee shop near Molly's address as a meeting place, then called Elena back.

NOW, TO prepare for the interview. As hard as the other council members worked to keep the celebrity necro away from anything that might break her manicured nails—or leave her death on their conscience—I'd been taking notes, and I understood enough about interviewing a hostile witness to know one does not blindly walk up to a potential dark-magic contact and say, "Hi, my name's Jaime and I'd like to ask you a few questions about ritual sacrifice." Before it even reached the point of introductions, I should determine the best method of approach, map out escape routes. Be prepared.

Molly Crane lived at 52 Hawthorne Lane. Coming into the area by cab, I'd had a feeling this was going to be the second time today I was surprised by where I ended up.

I was savvy enough to know that even if Molly was a dark witch, I was unlikely to find myself in a dingy alley outside an unmarked black-market spell shop. Such a shop might exist, but only in the back rooms of an otherwise normal business. Yet, except for the plaza where I'd found the coffee house, the neighborhood was residential, with row after row of matching houses, all with minivans and basketball hoops, the lawns pristine, kids' toys on the drives. I had the driver drop me off at the coffee shop, then I walked down three streets: Hemlock, Cedar and Hawthorne. Suburbia: a place where they cut down trees and name streets in their memory.

The house at 52 Hawthorne was a tidy bungalow on a street of tidy bungalows. The small house wasn't anything fancy, but in the drive stood a gleaming Mercedes SUV, as if Molly couldn't resist indulging herself a little. The basketball hoop over the garage suggested kids, but there were no toys to be seen. Maybe they were too old for pedal cars. Maybe they preferred spell practice to hoop practice. Or maybe she had no kids, and the net just came with the house—a standard feature like a paved driveway.

I started with a very slow walk past. Noted that the backyard was enclosed by a privacy fence. Noted a calico cat, but no sign of a guard dog . . . though anything could be behind that fence. Noted a light shining from a window overlooking the drive, a window with kitchenlike curtains.

It seemed safe enough—I was just a nicely dressed forty-something walking down a suburban street. And yet, when the door to Molly's house opened and a woman's figure darkened the doorway, I realized I had a problem.

If I came back later with Jeremy, she'd recognize me and know I'd been checking out her house, which would start the interview off badly. Yet I wasn't ready to question her. So I made a split-second plan. I'd look her way and if she wasn't watching me I'd take a chance and keep walking.

I looked. Our eyes met.

As I headed up her sidewalk, I got my first good look at the woman. She was probably in her late thirties. Short blond hair worn in an easy-maintenance but stylish tousle. An elfin face with bright green eyes. Small and compact, she was dressed in a designer sweat suit, maybe heading to the gym, maybe just wanting to look as if she were.

"Molly Crane?"

A bright smile, the welcome mitigated by a wary look in her eyes. I searched those eyes for some sign of recognition. With an average American, my chances of being recognized are on a par with any C-list movie celebrity. To those who follow spiritualists or certain talk shows, my face is unmistakable.

In the supernatural community, though, my face recognition goes up . . . usually accompanied by either disapproval or contempt. Spellcasters like Molly Crane can use their talents to make a living, but God forbid I should do the same.

I saw that "I know her from somewhere" spark in Molly's eyes, and cursed. I would have been safer using a false name, but she'd realize who I was the moment I mentioned ghosts.

I climbed the steps and extended my hand. "Jaime Vegas."

Her eyes lit up in recognition. "My daughter and her friends tape you on *Keni Bales* every month. Please come in."

COMEDY OF ERRORS

THERE WAS NO WAY TO REFUSE without making Molly suspicious, so I stepped inside.

"Did I hear something about you serving on the council now?" Molly said as she led me into her living room. "I suppose that's what you're here about? Council business?"

Damn. Another detail I'd been hoping to keep to myself. If Molly didn't want to deal with Paige and Lucas, she might not be so keen to speak to another council member.

I took the chair nearest the hall doorway. "Not so much council business as delegate business. Helping a fellow necromancer with a minor problem—one too small to warrant the council's attention. More of a research issue, actually. A puzzle I'm trying to solve so we can document it."

"Oh?" Intrigued, but not suspicious. "So what brings you to me?"

Another smile, this one wry. "Well, I'd say you came recommended as the top witch of the dark arts and I couldn't even *imagine* asking anyone else, but blatant flattery doesn't work so well on people outside of Hollywood."

She laughed, relaxing now. "We have our egos, but they don't impede brain function."

"Truth is that, yes, you came highly recommended, but when I took a close look at the possibilities, you seemed the most—" a mock throat clearing, "—approachable."

She laughed hard at that. "Now, that I believe. Between the weirdos and the recluses, it can be hard finding a viable contact among our bunch."

"I was also told that there might be something I can offer you in return. Which is what I want to do. I'm not asking for favors."

"Oh? Now I *am* intrigued. Can I get you something to drink before you satisfy my curiosity? Coffee? Tea? Soda? Bottled water?"

I opted for the water. There are too many things a witch can do with a brewed beverage.

When she came back, I gave her a version of the story, with this fellow necromancer being bothered by spirits who couldn't make contact. So far, I said, my investigation suggested a magical explanation.

When I finished, Molly nodded, thoughtful, then said, "I'm sure you've been told that doesn't sound like the results of normal ritual sacrifice."

"I have."

"Perhaps I can help but—" She met my gaze, eyes deceptively mild. "You offered an exchange?"

"I've heard you lost someone this year," I said. "Your common-law partner, I believe. A half-demon."

She hesitated, gaze down, then nodded slowly. "Mike. Yes."

I switched to my "dealing with the grief-stricken" voice. "If you'd like to make contact with him, I could try. With articles belonging to him plus access to his grave site, there's a good chance I can do it. Not perfect. But maybe a . . . ninety percent chance."

Molly said nothing, just stared down into the glass cupped in her hands. Still grieving, as Savannah had said. Or maybe wondering if I was trying to con her.

I hurried on. "If I don't make contact, I'll owe you. I *will* contact someone for you. Guaranteed."

Still she stared into her glass, her thumbs now caressing the sides.

Unlike humans, supernaturals know there's an afterlife. There must be, or there couldn't be necromancers. Through us, they also know that most ghosts are happy enough. If you know this, then perhaps contacting a loved one isn't such a wise idea. What if he's stopped grieving for his lost life, and you only rip open those wounds? What if you rip the scabs off your own grief?

"If you'd rather not contact him, maybe there's something else—"

Her head snapped up. "Why wouldn't I want to contact him?"

"I just meant— I'm not trying to renege on the offer. I certainly will try, if that's what you want. But if *this* isn't what you want, then I'd completely understand—"

"Would you?"

Molly's voice had gone cold. She set her drink aside, deliberately. My gaze swung to the door. She followed it and gave a brittle smile.

"Thinking of leaving already, Jaime? And why might that be?"

I laughed. "Leaving? No. I was just wondering—"

I leapt from the chair. Her hand flew up, lips moving in a sorcerer's knockback spell. I tried to duck, as Lucas taught me, but wasn't fast enough. Instead of hitting me in the torso, it slammed into my shoulder, whipping me around. My feet flew out. I saw the edge of the coffee table sailing up to meet me. Tried to twist. Too late. Impact. Pain. Darkness.

I AWOKE to the blast of a car horn. Something held me down, tightening around my wrists and ankles when I moved. I opened my mouth to call out, but tasted plastic and glue.

Everything was as dark as when I'd fallen. Blindfolded? I moved my head, testing for that pulling sensation against my temples. Sadly, I know what a blindfold feels like. Know what being kidnapped feels like too. For a second, that's all I could think: *Goddamn it, not again.*

But when I moved, instead of a blindfold, I felt something scratchy against my bare hands and face. Like an old blanket. Bound, gagged and covered.

The floor vibrated beneath me. The steady hum of moving tires. I remembered the horn blast that woke me. I was in a vehicle. In the trunk— No, I wouldn't be able to see light in a trunk. I pictured the car in Molly's drive. An SUV.

She'd bound and gagged me, then managed to haul me into the garage, drove in, put me in the back and was now taking me . . .

Where?

Well, I was pretty sure it wasn't out for daiquiris.

I'd taken self-defense courses. They'd given me more confidence than skill, but one piece of advice I remembered was that if someone tries to get you into a vehicle, you do everything you can to fight it, because you can be damned sure that wherever he's taking you, it's someplace private, to do something you won't like.

I had to get out before Molly—or whoever was driving—got wherever we were going. But how? I was trapped. I had no spells. No demonic powers. No superhuman strength. I was just a necromancer. Defenseless.

Bullshit.

Ordinary women got out of situations like this all the time. Okay, maybe not this *exact* situation, but if you took the black witch out of the equation, it wasn't that much different than any kidnapping. I wasn't sure what the statistics were for escaping a kidnapper, but I told myself they were pretty good.

As I shifted, the blanket scratched my cheek and it made me think of why I was covered in one—because I wasn't in a trunk, meaning someone could look into Molly's SUV, see the rear seat folded down and a bound woman in the luggage compartment. Goal one, then? Remove the blanket.

I'd just moved when a voice stopped me.

"You got home from school okay? And your sister?"

Molly. In the driver's seat. On her cell phone. Talking to her children. I allowed myself a flutter of relief before I started wiggling again, squirming out from under the blanket.

"There's a box of Twinkies in the cupboard over the stove, but don't let Tish see where you found them. They're meant for school. Tell her it's a special treat and Mommy's sorry she wasn't home to see her after school."

A sliver of light appeared above my eyes. I kept wriggling until the edge of the blanket slid down past my nose, then took a deep breath of cool air. In front of me, Molly's head was hidden behind the headrest, only her arm visible as she held her cell phone.

"I might be late, but I'll pick up dinner and call you on the way to find out what you want."

The blanket slid down to my neck. There. Finally. Another deep inhale through my nose as I relaxed. Then I looked up . . . way up . . .

at the tinted window, and realized the chances of anyone peering in from a passing transport and seeing me here were next to none. I had to get closer to that window.

Using my feet, I pushed toward the side. Then I twisted around so I could use my bound hands to pull myself up—

Molly's gaze met mine in the rearview mirror.

"Hon? I have to go. I'll call you as soon as I can. Look after your sister, okay? Love you."

She disconnected, then, without a word to me, cast a spell. An energy bolt slammed into me, and I dropped into darkness again.

CAPTIVE AUDIENCE

I WOKE TO MOLLY SLAPPING MY FACE.

At first, I could only moan. Everything hurt, as if I'd been dragged over rocky ground. As I inhaled, that's what I smelled: damp earth. Trees too, that crisp odor of autumn. And another scent, fainter and not nearly so pleasant—rotting vegetation and brackish water.

Quiet. Very quiet. The sigh of rustling leaves yet to fall. The soft, almost tentative call of a bird. The creak of a broken branch in the wind.

Lying on the ground. Damp earth, the ripe smell of it surrounding me. Something digging into my spine—a rock or a twig.

Another smack, harder.

I opened my eyes to see trees, and more trees. No sign of the SUV. Or the road. Or people. Just Molly, crouched in front of me.

She grabbed my hair and wrenched my head to the side, calling my attention to the source of that rotting smell—a swamp visible through the trees. "Who sent you?"

The threat was clear: if I didn't talk, there was a convenient body-disposal site nearby. She ripped the duct tape off my mouth, taking a layer of skin with it. When I gasped and paused to catch my breath, she cuffed me again and I glared at her.

"I don't know what this is about, but—"

She slapped the tape back on, then laid her hands on my forearm and recited a spell. It was like I'd spilled boiling water on my arm—a moment of confusion followed by blinding pain. I screamed behind my gag, more outrage than fear.

When I turned a fresh glare on her, she only smiled. "Didn't like that much, did you? Maybe I should come up with an inducement better suited to the lovely Jaime Vegas."

She backed up on her haunches, looked around and found a twig. Another spell, then she lifted it and put her finger to the end, making it glow like a lit cigarette. She brought the burning end so close to my cheek I could feel the heat.

My heart hammered but I resisted the urge to shut my eyes.

"I'll bet you wouldn't find it so easy to make a living with scars on your pretty face."

She moved the twig even closer. An ember dropped onto my cheek and I jumped, then held firm. Molly wielded the twig like a pen, pretending to write.

"Perhaps a nice big W. Let the world know what the rest of us think of you—a whore who uses her gifts to make a quick buck."

The tip touched my skin. I gritted my teeth and steeled myself. I wouldn't think about what she could do—to me and my career.

"Or maybe that's still not incentive enough . . ." Molly said.

She lifted the stick until it was level with my right eye. I instinctively tried to close it, but found myself caught in a binding spell, my eyes glued open, that brand coming closer, the end glowing red hot.

My brain went wild with panic.

Molly laughed. "That's better. Now, let's get this over with or you're going to have a hell of a time fumbling your way from this forest blind." She said it as casually as if she were threatening to break my fingernails.

She stood, stretching her legs, and circled me. "The person who sent you here. It was Mike, wasn't it?"

For a second, my brain just whirred. Who was Mike? Then I remembered. Her dead common-law husband.

She made no move to remove my gag, just kept circling me, brandishing the burning twig. For one moment, I felt the almost irresistible urge to giggle, thinking *I've seen this scene*. Only this wasn't a B movie and, no matter how ridiculous it looked—this suburban mom playing evil interrogator—there was nothing funny about it. She could do exactly what she was threatening, and from the look in her eye, she would. She'd put out my eyes to get the information she wanted, kill me and dispose of my body in the swamp, then call her kids to remind them to finish their homework before she brought dinner.

"Mike contacted you," she continued, "then you decided to come to me with this silly story about needing help with trapped spirits in return for 'contacting' him. What I want to know is why. Did the council send you? Or are you acting on your own, hoping to collect a bribe for *not* going to the council?"

With a jolt, the pieces fit together in the only way that made sense. What could her dead lover tell me that the council would investigate? Or that I could blackmail her with to *avoid* an investigation? Proof that the grieving widow wasn't so heartbroken after all.

"Ready to talk?" Molly said, crouching in front of me.

I nodded. As she ripped off the gag, my brain raced. I could point out that murdered ghosts rarely remember the circumstances of their deaths, but that would only confirm I knew he'd been murdered.

"It's a council investigation," I said. "I was walking past your house scoping it out, waiting for my partner, when you opened the door and I had to approach alone."

From her expression, I knew this was what she'd feared. If it was blackmail, that was easy. Kill me and the situation was resolved. It wouldn't be so simple if others already knew.

She eased back on her haunches. "So Mike told you what happened, and you contacted your delegate partner..."

In other words: please tell me there's only one other person involved.

"I took the problem to the whole council at the last meeting. That's proper procedure and, being new, I always follow protocol. They assigned an investigative partner—the werewolf Pack Alpha—" I added for good measure, "—to accompany me."

Fear, maybe even panic, touched Molly's eyes. Good.

"I don't know what Mike told you," Molly said, "but that bastard earned it. After five years of living in my house, he decides he's tired of me. But he's *not* tired of my money. So he offered me a deal. Give him fifty grand and he'd leave quietly, without telling the council . . . a few things. I told him I didn't have that kind of money lying around, and you know what he told me to do? Empty the girls' college funds."

Flecks of saliva flew from her mouth as she snarled. "He spends five years in our house, winning my girls over, getting them to call him 'Dad,' and then, as his parting shot, he's going to steal their college tuition? Over my dead body." Her snarl twisted into an ugly smile. "Or over his, which was much more to my liking."

I was quiet for a moment, then said, "That's not the story he told, but yours sounds a lot more believable. If you can support that with evidence, we can explain it to the council. You were furious—rightfully so—and you wanted to teach him a lesson about messing with a master of the dark arts. But things went wrong."

Molly nodded. I blinked to hide my relief.

She stepped away, then took her cell phone from her jacket and called her daughter, telling her to pack overnight bags and take her sister to a family friend down the street. Molly would pick her up there.

"They aren't in any danger," I said. "My partner would never touch your girls, not even to find out where I am. It would be totally against council policy. Plus he has little ones of his own—"

"I'm not taking that chance."

"Okay. I understand. Then let me call—" I remembered Jeremy didn't have a cell. "Better yet, take me back and if he's there, we'll settle this right now—"

"I'm not taking you anywhere but there."

She pointed at the swamp. Panic welled up. Before I could protest, she slapped the tape back on.

Molly straightened, then flew backward, knocked off her feet. I looked around wildly, but saw only forest. I rocked, trying to get up without the use of my hands. I had to stand, escape before she—

A binding spell caught Molly in midrise. Then I heard a woman's voice, chanting another spell, somewhere behind me, growing louder as if approaching. A sizzling sound, like the air electrifying.

Then Molly toppled forward, binding spell broken. She scrambled to her feet, took one hard look at me, then ran.

The sounds of pursuit followed, the other witch still out of view in the thick woods. I struggled to my feet. A corner of the overused duct tape gag got caught on a branch, and I managed to rip it off. I opened my mouth to shout for help . . . then reconsidered. Another witch didn't necessarily mean a helpful one.

Heavy footsteps sounded, each punctuated by a mumbled "fuck." That gave my rescuer away even before her dark head bobbed into view.

Savannah jogged toward me, still cursing as she untied me.

"Hold the binding spell, cast the energy bolt," she muttered. "Easy, right? But no. I try it, I lose the binding spell and the energy bolt flops."

"We have to warn Jeremy," I whispered as I pulled my hands from the loosened rope. "She knows he's heading to her house and she'll—"

"I'm sure Jeremy could handle that bitch, but he won't need to. She isn't going anywhere."

As if on cue, a distant motor ground. Stopped. Tried again, making the same grinding sound.

Savannah grinned and tossed aside the rope from my hands. "Little trick I learned from Lucas. So, did you get what you wanted from her?"

"No, but I'm well beyond caring—"

"She owes you. Sit tight, then. One wicked witch coming up."

Savannah started to leave, then turned. "Maybe you should hide. In case she circles back."

Hide? Like hell.

I didn't argue, though. Just let her run after Molly, then yanked off my pumps and gathered up the pieces of rope Savannah had tossed aside. She'd never think to take them—she was too confident for that. A confidence that had gotten her into trouble before, and while I had no doubt she could handle Molly Crane, I wasn't taking any chance that I'd need to tell Paige and Lucas I'd gotten their ward killed rescuing me. As for telling Eve and Kristof their daughter died because of me? I shivered and picked up my pace.

Heading in the direction of the car, I stuck to the line of tall bushes. Today's fashion choices might not have been ideal "running through the forest" wear, but at least the colors were camouflage friendly.

A metallic bang reverberated through the forest. I envisioned Savannah thrown against a vehicle. Then I recognized the sound. The slam of a car hood.

Molly's voice drifted over. ". . . need a tow truck out at—"

A yelp. Now I *did* run, hiking up my skirt, twigs biting into my stockinged feet. Ahead, the woods opened into a sunlit clearing. I could make out the gray side of Molly's SUV, then Molly herself, scooping up her cell phone from the ground.

Another yelp, more anger than surprise now, as the cell phone flew from her grasp. She grabbed the door handle.

"That's not going to help." Savannah's voice rang out across the clearing.

I ducked behind a wide tree.

"Your car's not going anywhere," Savannah said. "And neither are you."

Molly was less than ten feet from me, but facing the other way, head ducked as if squinting into the late-day sun.

"Sav—Savannah?" A shock-stutter of surprise. "What are you—?"

"Did you forget Paige is on the interracial council?" Savannah stopped a few yards from Molly. "That means I have friends on the council. Friends like Jaime. Not a good idea to fuck with my friends, Molly."

Molly gave a short laugh. "Seems you inherited your mom's attitude. Maybe it'll fit in ten years, but right now, you're a little girl with a big opinion of herself."

Savannah's face darkened, her blue eyes blazing, fury palpable enough to make most people hesitate, but Molly only shook her head, as if this were just another rebellious teen, something she was used to handling.

Savannah's lips started to move in a spell. I tensed, ready to run and knock Molly over if she began a cast of her own, but she only sighed, the sound rippling through the clearing.

"For the sake of my friendship with Eve, Savannah, I'm willing to let this interference today pass, and I'll even discuss letting your 'friend' walk out of here alive, but if you cast that spell—"

"You'll what?"

"I don't think you want to test that," Molly said, voice dropping.

Savannah smiled. "Oh, I think I do."

She flung her hands up and shouted a spell so loudly I jumped, almost tumbling from my hiding place. The words boomed through the forest. Molly froze, caught off guard. Savannah's arms flew down. Molly slammed into the side of the SUV so hard she left a dent.

Savannah's hands sailed up again like a conductor hitting the crescendo. Another booming cast, her lips curled back, snarling the words to the sky. Then she convulsed, her arms flying out, her head jerking back. I ran for her. There was a tremendous bang, like a car backfiring. As I stumbled, the sky lit up.

Around us, the trees shook and moaned, dying leaves raining down. A strong wind rushed past me, and I could tell it wasn't a wind at all, but spirits. Not ghosts, but something more primitive, more elemental. Before I could get to Savannah, one knocked me off my feet.

Everything had gone still, and the sky above us was tinged with an eerie red, warning of the calm before the storm. Then the redness seemed to twist over our heads, gathering speed and size like a tornado. It turned blue. Then a greenish yellow. Then it shot down, hitting the earth next to Molly. She screamed and backpedaled. Another hit behind her.

I struggled to my feet. Savannah still stood there, rigid, on her tiptoes, eyes closed. Around us, a strange illuminated mist rose from the earth, then shot into the air. Elemental spirits. I could feel them. They shot up all around now, like geysers, ripping up chunks of earth, raining down dirt and rocks.

"Sav—" I began, but an earsplitting yowl cut me short.

I tried again, but the spirits kept screaming, flying around Molly. Then one shot right up under her, hitting her, and her mouth opened, eyes going wide as she gasped for air. Another veered her way, then another, their howls turning to shrieks as they found their target. Molly dropped to her knees, hands going to her throat, mouth working, trying to get air but only letting the spirits steal her breath. Her eyes bulged.

"Savannah!" I shouted to be heard over the din.

She turned on me, lips pulled back. "I told you to wait!"

I strode forward until I was close enough to see uncertainty flicker in her eyes.

"She's down," I said. "You got her. Now what are you trying to do? Kill her?"

Savannah hesitated.

"Maybe right now it doesn't seem like such a bad idea. She did kidnap me. She could pose a threat. But can you justify it to Paige?" I paused a beat. "Can you justify it to yourself?"

She flushed, raised her hands and cast again. For a second, nothing happened. She cast again, faster, eyes bright with worry, and I knew the first cast had failed. I held my breath as she finished the second. A seemingly endless pause as Molly clawed the air, face going blue. A second thunderous clap. A second red flare in the sky. And the spirits vanished.

Molly fell forward onto her hands and knees.

"They're just koyut," Savannah said as we ran to Molly. "They'd only have knocked her unconscious."

"Are you sure?"

She flushed and I knew she wasn't.

As Savannah cast a binding spell, I grabbed Molly's hands and tied them behind her back, and while it felt pretty good to be tying *her* up, it was more than revenge. Most of a witch's nasty spells are sorcerer ones, which require hand gestures. Bind their hands, and they're almost helpless. Not completely—they still have witch spells—but I'd rather get hit with a binding spell than an energy bolt any day.

"Good idea," Savannah said, her voice almost apologetic.

"Now we need to take her into the forest to question her, in case anyone drives up."

A smile. "Yes, ma'am."

She grabbed Molly's left arm. I took the right, and we hauled the witch into the woods.

HUMAN MAGIC

WE FORCED MOLLY TO KNEEL. She wasn't gagged or silenced by a spell, but she hadn't said a word. Hadn't tried to escape. Just watched us warily, tensed for a fight, but making no move to start one.

I waved Savannah back. She hesitated—maybe a reflection of her faith in my interrogation abilities, but more likely just an instinct to take charge—her parents' daughter to the core. After a moment, she backed off with a nod.

I stood over Molly. "You screwed up. You've been on the dark side so long, you think everybody is just as devious and dangerous as you. I was telling you the truth. All I wanted was information, and I was offering a fair deal in return. I had no idea what really happened to Mike until you got paranoid and started confessing."

"I never admitted—"

"True. We can go that route. I take you into custody. You plead your innocence before the council."

Molly's eyes narrowed.

"Or we can leave the council out of this. Killing Mike wasn't the solution I'd have come up with, but from what you've said, it wasn't completely unjustified. You had a good reason—"

"I did. That bastard tried to—"

Savannah cut her off. "Heard it already."

I glanced over at the young witch. She'd settled onto the grass, cross-legged, leaning back on her hands. A cocky pose—as if so unthreatened by Molly she might as well make herself comfortable. Molly's lips pressed into a thin line. I strolled behind Molly and motioned for Savannah to sit up. She did. Molly relaxed.

"The council doesn't know I'm here," I said. "The werewolf is only coming as unofficial backup. Friendship, not duty."

Molly's gaze slid to Savannah.

"I'm the unofficial unofficial backup," she said. "I sent Jaime to see you because I thought you'd help her. Then, after she left, I had second thoughts. So I followed."

"Do *they* know you're here?"

By the contemptuous twist Molly gave "they," she meant Paige and Lucas.

Savannah shook her head. "I said I was driving Jaime to the airport, hanging out until her plane left. By now they're probably figuring I skipped out on my chores, but nothing more than that."

"So, Molly, your secret is safe . . . if you want it to be," I said. "We can back up and start over. Pretend we're in your living room again. I just told you my problem and you want to help."

"In return for . . ."

Savannah barked a laugh. "You think you're in any position to bargain?"

"I'll offer the same deal," I said. "If you help me, I'll contact Mike."

Molly scowled.

"In that case, how about this deal: you answer my questions in return for me forgetting who killed him."

I TOLD her the story again.

"First piece of advice?" she said. "Go back and take a hard look at whoever is giving you this cock-and-bull."

"Cock-and-bull?"

"Someone's having you on. Feeding you bullshit."

"I've tried contacting these spirits myself and—"

A brittle smile my way. "Step one, then, would be to find a better necromancer. Either there are no spirits or they're in on the game. Whoever came up with this story doesn't know jack shit about magic. They trolled the Internet or maybe checked out a few reference books at the library. What they researched isn't our magic. It's human magic."

"Human magic?"

"In human folk magic, you kill someone to drain his energy, his power, and take it for yourself."

Savannah made a rude noise, summing up her opinion of humans.

"But human magic doesn't work," I said.

Molly pinned me with a withering look. "No kidding, which is why I said someone's pulling your leg."

I looked at Savannah.

"She's right about this not sounding like a sacrificial ritual. Same as Paige and Lucas said. But if you've tried contacting them yourself, then it's not a problem of power."

Molly rolled her eyes.

"Could the ghosts be playing a trick?" Savannah said. "That does happen, doesn't it?"

"A trained necromancer can tell if she's being played."

A sniff from Molly.

"You say it sounds like a human's version of magic," I said. "Could that be what it is? The results of humans sacrificing people in some kind of fake black-magic ritual?"

Molly and Savannah looked at each other. In that exchanged look, all grudges seemed forgotten—sister witches considering an academic question.

"What *does* happen when humans play at ritual sacrifice?" Savannah said, half asking, half musing. "They can't get any powers from it, but does anything happen to the soul of the person they kill?"

Molly said, "If it did, necromancers would have seen this kind of thing before."

"So maybe it doesn't happen every time. But under certain circumstances..."

"Who can tell with humans—the lengths they'll go to in pursuit of magical powers. Sacrificing babies? Children? Torture? We have nothing on them."

So said the woman who, less than an hour ago, had been ready to put out my eyes with a red-hot stick. But I knew even Savannah would agree it wasn't the same thing. I'd been a threat. I'd knowingly walked into the house of a dark witch, so one could argue that I'd taken my chances. It wasn't the same as killing a baby in hopes of receiving some magical boon.

Savannah and Molly discussed this further but came to no conclusions. Investigating human magic would be a wise next step, but not something either of them could help with.

When we finished, the sun was setting.

Savannah said to Molly, "Your kids are at a friend's place, right?"

She nodded.

"So they'll be fine if you're later than you expected. Here's what I'm going to do. First, I'm not untying your hands. That's your job. Second, I'm leaving you in a binding spell. When I'm far enough away, it'll snap and you can walk to the parking lot, find your phone, make that tow-truck call. But if you come after us—now or later—you're launching a council investigation into Mike's death."

AS WE drove to Molly's neighborhood to find Jeremy, Savannah explained how she'd followed me, but stayed back until it was obvious I needed help.

"What gave it away?" I said. "When she loaded me bound and gagged into the back of her truck? Or when she actually said 'I am now ready to kill you and throw your body in the swamp'?"

"Hey, for a while there, it looked like you were going to talk your way out of it. I didn't want to interfere."

In other words, she'd been giving me a chance to escape on my own.

"Don't feel bad," she continued. "It's not your fault you don't get the cool superpowers."

"Thanks."

She threw a grin my way.

I picked twigs from my hair, then checked my reflection in the visor mirror. "I do appreciate you coming after me, Savannah. When I tell the story to the council, I'll leave your name out of it."

She hesitated, then shook her head. "No. I'd better come clean now or it'll bite me in the ass later, and I'll get in more shit for making you cover for me. I'll take my licks. But if you could . . ." A glance my way. "You know, tone it down a bit? Maybe leave out the koyut spell?"

"So long as you tone down the 'I had to rescue Jaime again' part."

A grateful grin. "Agreed."

AS SAVANNAH circled Molly's block, I saw a flash of someone through the slats of Molly's fence.

"There's Jeremy," I said. "In her backyard."

"Where?" she squinted into the near dark. "Ah. There. Good eyes."

She didn't add a sly remark about my uncanny Jeremy radar. I flatter myself that Savannah doesn't know how I feel about him, but if she doesn't, she's the only one.

She pulled over as Jeremy leapt the fence, taking it as easily as a two-foot hurdle.

"I'd better let you out here and hightail it back home before Paige calls out the National Guard."

"Running off before I can tell him what happened?"

"Running as fast as I can, but tell him I said hi and I'll see him at Thanksgiving." She paused. "On second thought, don't mention that part or they're all liable to decide that keeping me from going to Stonehaven is a suitable punishment."

WHEN I crossed the road, Jeremy was gone. Standing in front of Molly's house, I had a strong sense of déjà vu . . . and an even stronger sense that standing here really wasn't a bright idea. I pictured Molly arriving home to find the necromancer who'd escaped her clutches hanging out on her front lawn.

I was looking for a safer place to stand when a voice behind me said, "Hello, Jaime."

I wheeled so fast I tripped over my own feet. Fingers clasped my forearm, steadying me. I looked up into a face with high cheekbones and slightly slanted black eyes. Dark hair fell over his forehead as he leaned forward. I resisted the urge to reach up and push it back . . . then lift onto my tiptoes, press my lips against his, my body against—

Damn it, was I ever going to see Jeremy and not start blushing like a schoolgirl? It was ridiculous. I'd had erotic fantasies about men right in front of their noses and never batted an eye. With Jeremy, even the thought had me in vapors.

"Jeremy," I managed.

"I'm sorry," he said, still holding my arm. "I didn't mean to startle you."

"We need to bell you, like a cat."

A twitch of his lips. Not much of a smile, but I knew it was one.

"So," I continued, "you *could* follow my trail from the coffee shop."

"Not easy in the daylight, when I can't crouch to sniff the sidewalk. Fortunately, your perfume is distinctive."

"It's worth the price, then."

He released my arm and gave me a once-over, and while I'd love to think he was checking out my hot new outfit, I knew the truth—he was trying to figure out what had happened. He plucked a leaf from my hair.

"I ran into some trouble," I said.

"So I see."

His voice and expression were impassive, but he was worried. With Jeremy, the emotional signs were never obvious.

His gaze flitted toward Molly's house.

"She's . . . tied up for a while. But you're right, talking here probably isn't a wise idea."

"I didn't say that."

"No, but you were thinking it. Come on, then. Let's get someplace safer and I'll explain."

As we walked down the street, I snuck another look at him. Just over six feet, he was lean and athletic, though that side of him rarely showed . . . unless he was leaping over six-foot fences. Not the kind of maneuver you'd expect from a fifty-eight-year-old, but it was easy to forget how old Jeremy was. Werewolves age slowly and—with silver just starting to thread through his dark hair, and shallow lines around his mouth—I'd peg him at my age, if that.

Paige swore Jeremy had Asian blood, presumably from his mother, but there was no use asking him; he knew nothing about the woman. She'd disappeared from his life shortly after his birth. That was the world of werewolves, where mothers and sisters played no role, wives were unheard of and even lovers came and went quickly. Elena was the exception—the only living female werewolf.

It was a world of men. The Pack and its bonds were everything, and everyone else was an outsider. And this was the man I'd fallen in love with—the leader of a world in which I would always be "the other." My heart, it seemed, could be as feckless as my brain.

"Here," he said, guiding me into a darkened playground.

His fingers rested on my arm as he steered me, and I found myself trying not to read too much into the casual contact that tingled up my arm. Yet it *did* mean something. Werewolves, while very physical with one another, don't extend that attitude toward others. Clay, the most wolflike of the Pack, avoids even handshakes. Elena's politer about it, but I figured out early on that she wasn't someone I should greet with a hug.

Jeremy doesn't avoid contact, but doesn't initiate it either. In the last year or so, though, that's changed.

I found myself evaluating his touch. Gripping me tighter than usual? Lingering longer? I searched for a sign that something had changed—that something was *about* to change, proof that he'd come here to take that next step. A lot to read into a touch, and, of course, I couldn't.

The park was barely half the size of the small surrounding lots, just enough room for the developers to plop down swings, a slide and a bench and say, "Look, we gave you a playground." It was dark now, the equipment deserted.

Jeremy motioned me to the bench. "I'd like to check that blow to your head."

"How—? Oh, you smell the blood."

I pointed to the spot. He brushed my hair aside, then examined it, his touch so light I barely felt it. Then he checked my pupils and asked whether I was feeling nauseous or experiencing any pain other than at the point of impact. I wasn't.

"I'll need to keep an eye on you, to ensure it isn't a concussion, but it seems fine. Now . . ." He sat beside me on the bench. "What happened?"

I told him.

AS WE waited for a taxi, I pulled the jacket tighter against the bitter wind. Jeremy's jacket. He'd offered, and I'd hated taking it, but as the sun dropped so had the temperature.

I looked up at him. "Ghosts do play pranks. I've had it happen. But these ones are breaching the physical barrier. That is different."

"I know. But about this human folk magic business, I'm not sure what to make of it. I don't know enough about magic to give an educated opinion."

"Well, I'm not the best-informed supernatural around, but even I know that human magic doesn't work. Robert would be our best source on that."

Jeremy stared down the street, his expression unreadable. "I don't suppose there's any need to follow up with Molly Crane, something we might discover by breaking into her house later or interrogating her further."

I shook my head.

"Did she give you any other contacts? Let a name slip? Another dark-magic practitioner or black-market contact we should investigate?"

"Nothing."

He looked almost disappointed. Then he said, with a soft sigh, "I suppose it's on to Robert, then. I'll call the airport and see when we can get a flight to San Francisco or San Jose."

"One there for you and one to L.A. for me, I'm afraid. I need to be back on the set first thing in the morning."

"Ah. Of course." His gaze dipped away and I was certain he *did* look disappointed. Then he cleared his throat. "I'll see Robert alone, then, and come to L.A. tomorrow. I'll help him with the preliminary research, to be polite, but I'll get away as soon as I can."

II

This was always the hardest part. Not only was it delicate work, but the smell was enough to unsettle even the strongest stomach. It didn't bother her as much as it did the others, and it wasn't so much the smell itself as the thought of what was burning.

They'd been careful not to use too much gasoline on the boy, but the flames had still licked the artifacts high above the concrete floor. An interesting experiment, but not one they were likely to repeat... not unless this material proved significantly better than the rest.

She adjusted her mask and checked the temperature on their tiny version of a cremation oven, designed to incinerate the organs, which was all they needed.

This oven burned at a lower temperature than ones used by funeral homes, so only the soft tissue turned to ash. Even then an auxiliary power supply was necessary. In Brentwood, a power spike would likely be attributed to marijuana growing and ignored—there were better uses for the police budget than stopping movie stars and pop singers growing a little weed—but it was always safest to provide no excuse for investigation.

After they'd taken the organs from the body, they'd needed to dispose of the remainder. Burning an entire corpse wasn't feasible. The boy's body—larger than that of their previous cases—would have been difficult to transport whole. So Don had recruited Murray's help, and they'd cut the body in two so they could carry it out in reinforced garbage bags.

It was then that Murray had snapped. Odd, she mused as she

unraveled the bolt of cheesecloth. After all they'd been through together, it had been helping Don bisect the corpse that had done it.

Tina had calmed him down. She was good at that, one advantage to having a psychologist in the group. To reap the magic, they had to do things that were bound to affect the weaker among them, but Tina could always get the shaky back on track . . . and assess how likely they were to stay there.

The door opened, and Don walked in, nose wrinkling. She pointed at the stack of surgical masks, but he waved them away.

"How's Murray?" she asked.

"Better. Embarrassed about the whole thing now. Work's been stressful this past week."

She nodded. "It happens."

The timer sounded and she opened the oven, stepping back as heat poured out.

"He should take a vacation," she said as she examined the tray of gray and white ash.

"I'll suggest—"

"No. *Insist.*"

Their eyes met. Don nodded.

"How was the new disposal site?" she asked.

"It's not as convenient as the garden, but it'll do."

She nodded. The terraced gardens had been convenient. Too convenient, and they'd used them more than they should have, with each disposal increasing the chance of being caught. Unacceptable.

She donned heavy gloves and shook the tray of ash, helping it cool faster.

"Looks like more this time," Don said, peering at it.

She smiled. "That's the advantage to using an older one."

PENALTY BOX

HAD MY TRIP TO PORTLAND and near-death experience put me any closer to banishing the spirits in the garden? I'd like to think so, but I was convinced I'd only made things worse. First, in the midst of problems on the set, I'd taken off, which wouldn't help. Second, Jeremy had finally joined me . . . only to leave again.

I needed to stop worrying about how to contact these ghosts and simply get rid of them.

My Nan raised me to regard ghosts the same way the average person sees door-to-door salespeople and telemarketers: an unavoidable nuisance of life, one that should be dealt with firmly and swiftly and, ultimately, ignored. As cruel as that sounds, it was rooted in self-preservation. Like salespeople, if you say yes to one, you'll suddenly be on the contact list for hundreds more. Rather than weed through the requests, taking only those you can manage, it's better to slam that door to all of them and walk away.

If I could speak to my Nan again, I'd ask her this: did it hurt you to say no and does it ever stop hurting? She always acted as if it didn't bother her, so I feel that it shouldn't bother me, and when it does, I feel weak. As much as I long for the day when it will stop hurting, part of me dreads it too, because I'm not sure I ever want to be that hard, that cold.

But now I needed to be cold. I had to banish these spirits. So when

I finally got back to the house, as the first light of dawn broke, I went to my room only long enough to retrieve my kit. Then I headed into the garden.

The moment I stepped out there something whizzed past me. Then the whispering started. Fingers brushed my hand. I kept walking until I reached the far rear corner, where I knelt in the shadows between the fence and a towering tiered garden bed, and tried to contact them one last time.

I performed each ritual methodically, completely focused on each step. As before, as long as I appeared to be trying to help them, they behaved, stroking my cheek or patting my hair as if telling me I was doing a good job. Though I still couldn't find any words in their whispers, I had a feeling that if I could, they'd be telling me to keep going, to keep trying.

I had to smile, reminded of when I'd first started doing this, under my Nan's guidance. I could see myself, kneeling in the basement of her old house, trying to summon a spirit. If I closed my eyes, I could feel her in those pats and caresses, hear her encouragement in those whispers.

When I tried to persuade the spirits—again—to find another way to communicate with me, they went silent at first, as if trying to do as I asked, but soon returned to the whispering, their caresses becoming pokes and prods. Like easily distracted children.

A chill raced through me.

When I did as they wanted, they caressed and patted me. Treating me as if I were a child? Or rewarding me in the only way they knew how.

I stood. A hand pulling at my top fell away, as did the one touching my hair. The whispering continued, but lower now. Fingers pulled at the edge of my skirt, like a child trying to get someone's attention. Pulling, poking, prodding . . . and when that failed, hitting and pinching.

Not possible. Necromancers rarely encountered child ghosts. There were stories of young-adult ghosts who'd made contact, and were later discovered to have died as children, then allowed to grow to physical maturity rather than spend their afterlife trapped in a child's body.

How would a child ghost remain a child? Only if it was caught between dimensions, unable to step into ours and get help, unable to pass over and grow up.

That's what I had—not adult ghosts, but children, trapped between the worlds. I couldn't just banish children. I had to help.

When these spirits first contacted me, I'd thought it was a random event. Happens all the time. I go someplace new and I attract some ghosts. But was that really all there was to it? Coincidence? I just happen to be billeted at a house with trapped child ghosts, a puzzle best solved by a necromancer with connections to the rest of the supernatural world?

Where others see coincidence, I see fate. And where I see fate, I see the hand of a higher power. I'm not sure if I see "God" as others would recognize him, but I see someone—a benevolent entity, maybe not as all-powerful as we'd like, but a concerned being with the ability to watch and the power to do something about it.

Maybe that higher power couldn't free these ghosts alone. Or maybe that's not her place—we must solve our problems ourselves and the best she could do was put someone here, in this house, who might be able to help. And maybe I've got too high of an opinion of myself if I think *I'd* be that person, but I still felt like I'd been given a mission, and damned if I wasn't going to do my best to fulfill it.

I PACED along the cobblestone path, Eve's ring clutched in my hand.

"Goddamn it," I muttered. "You said I could call you. Well, I'm calling and you'd damned well better not be ignoring me, you arrogant Cabal son—"

A sound behind me. I turned. Kristof stood there wearing . . . skates. And holding what I was pretty sure was a hockey stick.

" 'Son-of-a-bitch' is the phrase you wanted," he said. "I suppose it could have been simply 'Cabal son,' which, while accurate, isn't much of an insult." He leaned on the stick, musing. "Or perhaps . . ."

"I didn't mean—"

"Of course you did. I wasn't ignoring you, Jaime. If you've been calling me for a while, I'm afraid I didn't hear it. But now I'm here."

"If you're busy . . ."

"I was only in the penalty box. Again. Might as well serve my time here." A murmured incantation. The stick vanished and the skates changed to shoes. "What can I do for you?"

"I need Eve. And now it's urgent."

I told Kristof the story. He insisted on every detail, then tried to make contact with the spirits himself.

"There's something here," he said, frowning. "I can make out . . . flashes. And I heard the whispers, on both this side and the other."

"As if they're caught between the two."

"I don't like jumping to conclusions, but yes, I suppose so. And they *may* be children—your deduction is sound enough, but one has to be careful presenting a case to the Fates. Unlike human jurors, they aren't swayed by supposition, sympathy and theatrics. They deal in facts. The fact in this case is that these spirits exist, and they appear to be unable to cross either way. I'll ask them to send Eve back."

"Will it be enough?"

"It better be."

THE CATERER hadn't finished setting up for breakfast, so I went into the kitchen and helped myself to a coffee.

"Another early riser, I see," Becky said, walking in as I added cream.

I told her I'd been outside meditating. If I was going to be spending more time in the garden, it was good to establish an alibi up front, and this was one I always used in any situation where I might be seen sitting on the ground, talking to myself.

"Sounds like you found a little peace in this insanity. Now I really hope that I'm not about to undo that." She looked troubled. "It's about Grady. He's still upset about the other night. I don't think I handled that as well as I could have. Now he's demanding—through Claudia of course—that he get a private performance to compensate."

I could feel her gaze on me, studying my reaction.

"Sounds fair to me," I said.

"Thank God," she breathed. "You're such a trouper, Jaime. I swear I won't let him steamroll over you after this."

"He's not steam—"

"He may be a huge name overseas. But you're a huge name here. I won't let him forget that. There'll be no more costar bashing on this show."

"Costar bashing?"

"I won't stand for it. Now, about this private séance. Do you mind watching, just to show support?"

BEFORE WE headed into breakfast, Becky's assistant, Will, came to tell her he'd conveyed the same invitation to the private séance to Angelique, but she'd refused, claiming she had a manicure appointment. Becky fumed, and I offered to talk to Angelique, but she didn't want me getting involved.

Over breakfast, we discussed the séance.

"First, where to conduct it?" Becky said. "Mr. Simon has checked all records for this house, and the only reference to a death he could find was some has-been producer who hanged himself. For excitement, that rates about a two. Must-snore TV."

I glanced at the hanging residual and sent up a silent apology to his ghost, wherever it was.

Grady leaned forward, tapping his knife on the table. "Perhaps, but it's the ones whose deaths *weren't* reported that are the most entertaining."

"Accidental deaths, you mean?"

A smile creased his tanned face. "No, purposeful. Very purposeful. I have felt a dark presence in this house, a force of great evil, death so vile, so despicable that the heart freezes at the very thought—"

Claudia motioned for him to take it down a notch.

He cleared his throat, then sliced into his egg. "I have, you see, some experience with these things."

"And you sense . . . evil in this house?"

"Not surprisingly. It is in the seats of power that the demonic reigns. Those who crave the trappings of power—wealth, fame, beauty—are often driven into the service of Satan to achieve their goals." He turned to Claudia. "Have we ever visited a castle or an ancestral home where I *haven't* found evidence of satanic rites or devil worship?"

Claudia gave a soft sigh. "Never."

Grady smiled.

DOWSING ROD FOR EVIL

"I FELT A STRONG PRESENCE down here the other night," Grady said as he led us into the basement. "I know, Becky, that you were simply using the best available space for the party, but you should be careful about bringing spiritualists to subterranean realms. They're simply rife with evil spirits."

"Jaime?" Becky said. "Are you picking up anything?"

"I don't have Mr. Grady's nose for evil, I'm afraid."

"Of course she doesn't," he said. "What evil would dare show its hideousness in the face of such beauty?"

Claudia looked like she couldn't decide whether to gag or scratch my eyes out.

Grady took a compact from his pocket, did a makeup check and hair fluffing, then drew himself up straight.

"Camera, please." He lifted his hands, like a pianist preparing to play. "Robert, are you there?" Pause. "Yes. Yes, he is. Thank you, Bob."

Grady opened his eyes. "I have made contact with my spirit guide."

Huh. That was easy. *Eve? Are you taking notes?*

"For this session, I have selected Black Robert McGee as my guide," Grady continued. "He was a notorious pirate who terrorized the Caribbean. In the afterlife, he is trying to make amends, seeking redemption by helping my quest against the dark forces. Having lived on that dark side, he is the perfect guide for this segment of my journey."

A pirate spirit guide. Cool. Eve had been known to hang out with pirates, but I don't think that counted. She was, however, well acquainted with dark forces. As for seeking redemption, though . . . questionable. Very questionable.

Grady and "Bob" proceeded to wander the basement, Grady with his hands out, dowsing rods for evil.

"I see a dark room. Very dark. I—" His head jerked up, eyes closed, and he let out a whimper, then said in a high-pitched voice, "It's dark, Mommy, so dark . . ."

His head twitched and bobbed like a bird, then his eyes flew open. "Bob? Yes? Thank you, Bob."

He pivoted and stopped, facing a half-door that led into a crawl space under the stairs. He gave an exaggerated shudder, then looked into the camera.

"Bob tells me we will find the source of this great evil under those stairs. Inside there is a room. A room whose walls once ran red with blood. A family slaughtered. The satanic altar is beneath those steps."

"Amityville?" I mouthed to Grady.

"Yes!" Grady's face was feverish now as he spit the word. "Thank you, Bob. Bob has reminded me of another case similar to this. An American case in Maine, I believe."

"Long Island," I mouthed for him.

He nodded his thanks. "Long Island, thank you, Bob. The infamous Amityville horror. I have long believed that the rituals conducted within those walls were part of a wider ring of satanic activity."

"Faked!" I mouthed, gesturing to get his attention.

"Yes, Bob? Bob is trying to tell me about something but— Bob? Are you still there?"

Grady signaled for the camera to stop filming. "He's gone, I fear. This happens from time to time, particularly in places with such intense negative energy." He rolled his shoulders and rubbed his neck, then looked at me. "Jaime, I believe you were saying something?"

"Amityville was a hoax," I said.

I explained. The house had been the site of infamous killings—a young man who'd murdered his parents and four siblings. A year later, a family bought the house, claimed they saw blood dripping down the walls, demonic pigs, what-have-you, but stayed there—with their terrified kids—until they had enough details for a book. A best-selling book. And the guy who killed his family? His lawyer had been trying for a "devil made me do it" defense, and had been in contact with the haunted homeowners. The lawyer later claimed he and the couple had dreamed up the whole scheme over a bottle of wine. The family had since admitted, in court, that at least *some* of the things they claimed had never happened.

When I finished, Grady glanced at Claudia, who eyed me as if suspecting I was making it up.

"All true," Becky said. "A couple of years ago the Catholic Church revealed it had submitted a list of inaccuracies to the book publisher . . . which ignored them. Big hoax. Paid well, though," she added with admiration.

"I'm not surprised," Claudia muttered. "It's America. Land of 'anything for a buck.' "

Grady waved her to silence and went still, head cocked as if listening. "Bob has returned. We may begin again."

The camera started rolling.

"Thank you, Bob. Bob tells me the events of Amityville were, I fear, a false case predicated on greed and the lust for fame." A slow, sad shake of his head. "Unfortunately, such counterfeits do exist and we must be vigilant for them. However, as Bob also says, we must be careful not to let one falsehood blind us to the overwhelming truth of evil. It seems those responsible for Amityville used real events elsewhere as the basis for their fabrication, and here, in this house, we see one such example—"

His head jerked back, eyes closing. He started shaking so violently that Becky tensed as if fearing a convulsion, but Claudia waved her down.

Grady's arms shot around his body, hugging himself, his teeth chattering, and I realized that his "convulsions" were supposed to be shivering.

"Momma?" he said in that high-pitched voice. "It's cold, so cold and so dark. I'm s-s-scared." A whine, more like a car engine than a child. "The bad man is coming. The bad man is—"

Grady roared, his head whipping back, teeth bared. His eyes flew open, rolling. Anyone who'd watched enough of his shows would have seen this coming, but Becky jumped and dropped her clipboard. As she scrambled for it, Grady allowed himself a tiny smile of satisfaction that morphed into a snarl, his head jerking back and forth, hands clawing the air.

"He's fighting possession by an evil spirit," Claudia explained in a monotone.

"I see," Becky said. "Is there any chance this spirit will win?"

"About ninety-five percent."

Becky smiled.

Grady jolted up onto his tiptoes, then went still. A moment's pause before he collapsed against the wall, panting and trembling.

"Damn," Becky muttered.

"Wait," Claudia whispered.

"Outside," Grady said between gasps. "Bob has shown me a room, a small, dark room. We mistakenly believed it was this one, but now he has realized his error and says we must go outside, to a shed."

He motioned for the camera to stop filming.

As Grady marched for the stairs, Becky hurried up beside him.

"The shed idea is great," she said. "It avoids, you know, connotations of Amityville, but there's a small problem. There isn't one."

"One what?"

"Shed."

He threw a smug smile over his shoulder as he started up the steps. "My dear, I never said there *is* a shed. I said there *was* one. It has, of course, long since been torn down . . . to hide the evidence."

OUTSIDE WE went. On the way, Grady thanked me for the information about Amityville. While unwarranted, he appreciated the thought. It was a step back into his good graces.

He stopped beside a koi pond. As our shadows passed over the water, the fish zoomed from under the lilies, their mouths breaking the surface. Was someone feeding them in their owner's absence? Probably. They looked expensive.

"Here, Bob?"

Grady lifted a hand for silence, although no one had spoken. Then he checked to make sure the camera was rolling before continuing.

"The shed was here? You're quite certain?" He paused. "No, no, I understand."

Grady turned to the camera. "Bob says he can't be certain this is exactly the right spot. The sense of darkness in this entire yard is overwhelming. This, however, appears to be reasonably close to the original location."

And so, Grady picked up where he'd left off, channeling the "spirit" of the dead girl. I tried to relax, but startled at every noise and movement, waiting for the children to come and make their presence known.

"What the hell is that?"

I jumped and glanced over to see Kristof staring at Grady, who was waving his arms, rolling his eyes, shaking and moaning.

"I think he's possessed," I said.

"By what? Epilepsy?"

"He's a famous TV medium from the U.K.," I said, as if that explained everything.

Kristof sniffed. "Not so famous that he can afford a decent tailor, evidently. Or acting lessons."

"They aren't letting Eve come back, are they?"

"No." He spat the word. After a moment, he went on. "I have, in the past two years, on occasion, tried to find reasons for them to let Eve return, if only temporarily."

"And they think you're tricking them again."

A humorless laugh. "Not 'again.' I haven't tricked them yet, damnable spirits. Eve's tried too. No luck. You can't blame us, but they get . . ." A dismissive wave. "Offended, as if we're insulting them, when the fact is that *we* are the ones who should be offended. We play by their rules. We assist in their enterprises. We are—" a twist of his lips, "—their *humble* servants, and yet when we ask for the briefest respite from our bargain, you'd think we were the most unrepentant convicts asking for a day pass."

I had no idea what he was talking about, but knew he couldn't explain.

"So they said no."

"They'll 'look into it.' And, perhaps, should I prove to be telling the truth, they'll find someone to help you."

"But not Eve."

He looked away, but not before loneliness and disappointment pushed the bitterness from his eyes. "No. Not Eve."

He pushed to his feet. "This is ridiculous. They cannot expect us to wait on their forbearance and trust that they will find someone suitable. Eve isn't the only person who can help us. The Fates won't like my choice, but that is their problem."

It seems to me that forbearance and trust are things a higher power *can* reasonably expect from mere mortals. But men like Kristof Nast are not accustomed to being refused, and being dead didn't change that. If his insolent determination helped my case, I wouldn't argue.

"Who are you—?" I began.

A dismissive wave. "You'll see."

NATURE AND SCIENCE

I HAD ANOTHER INTERVIEW after the séance, then nothing. Jeremy would be here in a few hours. Robert hadn't found anything useful. Kristof hadn't returned. So I was stuck cooling my heels. I decided to call Paige, check what *she* knew about rituals involving children. This wasn't a call to make in a public place, so I headed outside.

As I sat down on the front porch, Will hailed me. I greeted the portly young man and he handed me an icy bottle of water.

"I saw you heading outside and thought you might need this. The sun's a killer today."

"That's so sweet. Thank you."

"Oh, and I also wanted to tell you how much I enjoyed your segment the other day, with Tansy Lane. Incredible. The whole crew's still talking about it. I think you've made some believers, Ms. Vegas."

I laughed. "Jaime, please. And I hope they're still believers when all this is done, because that definitely wasn't a typical summoning for me. I got lucky, which I can only hope is a good omen for the show."

My gaze strayed toward the cell phone in my hand—a subtle hint that there was something I'd come out here to do.

He stepped closer and lowered his voice. "I also wanted to commend you on how well you handled Angelique."

My mouth opened in protest, ready to say I hadn't "handled" her at all, but he continued before I could.

"I can't believe they brought her on the show after the things..." He coughed. "Well, you know what I mean. Anyway, as far as most of us are concerned, you're still at the top of your game, and we're looking forward to seeing you put her in her place."

I could tell by his expression that he was willing, even eager, to go on, but would it help me to know what she'd said? No. If I heard her insults or insinuations, I would indeed want to "put her in her place" and I couldn't afford to do that. Not on this shoot.

"I appreciate the support. Now, if you'll excuse me—"

"Absolutely. And thank you for helping with Mr. Grady this morning. Becky really appreciates it. She was really afraid this was going to be difficult, knowing you're lining up a show of your own, and Grady's hoping to relocate here."

"Relocate—?"

I snapped my mouth shut. This one was tougher to ignore. A lot tougher. But I promised myself I'd investigate later. Right now, I had to concentrate on the ghosts.

As he headed into the house, I stepped off the porch and caught a flash from the shrubs, like the sun reflecting off a mirror—or a camera lens. A slower, more careful look around, listening for the rustle of a quick retreat. Silence.

It could have been nothing. Or it could have been a crew member sneaking around with a camera, hoping for a shot he could sell to the tabloids. Photos of C-list celebs aren't worth much, but if you can get ones that are embarrassing enough, you can make a few bucks. One last survey, then I headed toward the road, making sure I wasn't slouching or squinting unbecomingly, just in case.

AFTER CALLING Paige, I went to the kitchen to grab a sandwich. I hadn't been in the mood for a communal lunch, and it was almost two now. Out of the corner of my eye, I saw Grady stride in. His gait was fluid, almost gliding.

"Hello," I said without turning.

"I need to speak to you."

My fingers tightened around my coffee cup, but I kept my tone even. "Good. I need to talk to you too."

"A private word, then. In the garden, please."

Hmm . . . That sounded suspicious, but there was nothing in his bearing or his manner to suggest he had seduction on his mind. Quite the opposite. Cool and professional.

"I'm right behind you," I said.

I followed him through the house to the back doors.

He still walked with that odd gait—graceful and relaxed yet purposeful. Some affectation he was practicing for an upcoming segment?

When we reached the garden, I tried to catch up, but he only moved faster. Afraid Claudia was peering from a window? Seeing me "following" him into the garden wouldn't make her any happier.

Finally he stopped, his back still to me. Then, as he turned, he inclined his head in an oddly formal nod, coupled with a tiny smile.

"Jaime O'Casey. A pleasure."

A dart of panic raced through me. No one in the business knew my real name. But if Grady thought this gave him some leverage over me, he was wrong. Vegas was just a stage name; I wasn't hiding anything.

I looked at him. His gray-blue eyes now shone a blue brighter than the sky. Impossibly and unnaturally bright. I backpedaled. He grabbed my arm. His fingers were so hot I could feel them through my sleeve.

That dart of panic found its target and exploded. I yanked back. His grip didn't tighten, but didn't give either. Firm as an iron shackle. This wasn't Grady but someone—something—using his body, and I had a good idea what that something was.

"Kristof Nast sent me."

Damn Kristof! This was why he hadn't told me who he was calling: I'd never have agreed.

"I'm sorry," I said. "There's been a misunderstanding. I don't talk to—"

"Strangers? A wise choice, but I'm hoping this time you'll make an exception."

Amusement sparkled in those beautiful eyes. Entrancing eyes.

"I've come to help you, Jaime."

"I've had my share of help from your kind."

He tipped his head, his gaze searching mine. "Ah, I see. A youthful indiscretion. The price seemed fair, didn't it? That's the way it is.

A demon's price always seems fair when you're blinded by the boon. Then you always end up paying more than you expect. But that's long past. You've received your boon. You've paid the price. An unpleasant learning experience, but it certainly could have been worse."

"Whatever *bargain* you're offering—"

"My dear child, I do not barter like a common merchant. Do you know who I am?"

I shook my head. He released my arm.

"I am Aratron."

Seeing my blank look, he gave a rich, warm laugh. "Does no one educate their children in demonology these days? For centuries, I had only to speak my name and even your kind would prostrate themselves before me, promise me their gold, their wives, their firstborn child in return for but a speck of my knowledge. Today? Bewilderment dulled by apathy. Not *nearly* as gratifying."

"Sorry."

He laughed again. "Eve knew who I was. Properly respectful even."

He walked to a bench and waved for me to sit beside him. When I resisted, his eyes sparkled. "I'm not going to gobble you up or incinerate you in a ball of white-hot flame. The last, while quite spectacular, doesn't promote good relations with mortals."

I perched at the far end of the bench.

"May I hope you at least know what a eudemon is?" he asked.

"Oh, yes," I said, a little too enthusiastically. "There are two kinds of demons. Cacodemons are the ones we can summon and make deals with. The chaos demons. The same kind that father half-demons like Eve. But eudemons..."

I drummed my fingers against my thigh, as if I were back in school again, proudly volunteering the answer only to get halfway through and realize that's all I had. "Can't say I know much about eudemons. Other than they aren't cacodemons. We can't usually summon them. They don't father children..."

"To most supernatural mortals, that's all that's important. It's almost impossible to summon us. We can't create you. We are, you might say, neutral. Indifferent even. To both your joys and your suffering. You do not interest us... except in the most academic way."

"And that's what you are. A eudemon."

"That's what Aratron is, a fact you can easily confirm with a call to Robert Vasic. And I claim to be Aratron. But whether I truly am is not so easily established. In fact, I daresay, it cannot be established all. You know, from my voice, from my touch, from my eyes, that I am no low-ranking demon. These things I cannot fake and even one unschooled in demonology knows the marks of a demon of power. But could I not be a cacodemon such as Baal or Balam or Lucifer? Were I one of them, would it not be wise to come in the guise of a eudemon like Aratron?"

"I guess so . . ."

"You look at me as if I'm mad. Why raise such possibilities? Because, child, if I do not, you will—now or after you've given the matter due consideration. I cannot prove that I am who I claim to be. You can call on Kristof, but you do not trust him. You trust Eve but she is, conveniently, unavailable. What you can do, though, is consider whether Kristof would do such a thing, not to you, but to *her*. Eve is very protective of her friends. Given their relationship, would he introduce one to a cacodemon?"

"No."

"Then, in the absence of absolute proof, that will have to do. Eve knows me. She has established a working relationship with me and I'm fond of her . . . as fond as I can be of a shade. I wouldn't want to damage my relationship with her by hurting you."

"Okay. So you're here to help me and you want . . . nothing for it?"

"Oh, of course I want something, but I cannot imagine you'll begrudge me what I wish."

"And that is . . ."

"Knowledge. I have little *except* that, but more of it than you could ever fathom. I collect knowledge and sometimes I share it. In exchange for new knowledge, of course. What you are investigating fits nothing you know, correct?"

I nodded.

"And nothing your scholars know, correct?"

Another nod.

"And, I must admit, nothing I know. Therefore it is new. That is what intrigues me and why I would guide your feet onto the right path."

"Which is . . . ?"

"You already know." He smiled. "I'm simply here to tell you that you're right."

I shifted on the bench. "I'm no good with puzzles."

"Then don't make this into one. Your scholars and your experts tell you this is not any known form of magic. They also tell you that it most closely resembles something else."

"Human magic. Which is impossible."

"Why impossible?"

Aratron leaned back, that tiny smile on his lips, not mocking but encouraging, like a patient teacher who wanted me to succeed at this lesson. I always preferred the sarcastic teachers, the bored teachers—the ones who expected little from me. Impossible to disappoint.

"This is not a graded assignment, Jaime."

I started, as if he'd read my mind.

And what made me think he hadn't?

"If you'd like me to give you the answers, I will," he said, the rich timbre of his voice muted, "but I think you'd prefer to work it out yourself. They aren't riddles or trick questions. You haven't *missed* any clue. You've simply overlooked a possibility that I don't blame you for overlooking. The possibility of the impossible."

"I don't understand."

"Why is human magic impossible?"

"Because it doesn't work."

"Ah."

I looked sharply at him. "Does it?"

"It's never been known to, aside from the occasional minor spell mastered by a nonspellcaster. But even then, the caster almost always had some diluted magical or demonic blood. And the spells were only the simplest. Certainly nothing that would drain or fragment a soul."

"Then it is impossible."

"Fifty years ago, man had never set foot on the moon. Does that mean such a thing was impossible?"

"Of course not. Science just hadn't evolved . . ."

I stopped.

"Evolution . . ." Aratron mused. "Funny thing."

He twisted and snapped a rose from the bush, severing the stem with his thumbnail. He caught his thumb on a thorn and a drop of blood slid down his wrist. He followed the path of the blood, then examined the bloodied thorn with the cool scrutiny of a scientist examining cause and effect.

He turned his hand over and touched his index finger to the puncture on his thumb. "Hurts, I suppose."

"You don't feel it?"

"I do, but it doesn't mean anything to me. Were you to have done that, you'd have learned to handle the rose more carefully."

He wrapped his hand around the rose and I shivered, imagining the thorns driving in. When he opened his fist, his palm was smeared with blood.

"To me?" He lifted his palm. "Merely interesting. Now, I am sure that the man who owns this body will not appreciate me having done that, but if what you call pain doesn't bother me, how am I to take pity on him? Yet, although I cannot feel the pain, I understand that it exists, and that explains to me the purpose of these thorns."

"To defend the flower. To increase its chances of survival."

"Evolution. As men might evolve so that they may turn into wolves, to better hunt, find food, defend themselves. An aberration, to be sure, but is that not the point of aberrations? The root of evolution? A man who is part wolf, with superior strength, superior sensory abilities. An advanced predator. It works and yet—" He lifted his bloodied finger. "There are drawbacks, flaws, imperfections in the design. A world of werewolves alone would destroy itself. As an aberration, though, it works . . . for now."

"That's what we are, then? Temporary aberrations? I've heard the theory. So it's true?"

"True?" He turned the flower over in his hands. "No, it remains a theory and ever shall be. That is the conflict of science and faith. I can say that supernaturals are random mutations that, from an evolutionary perspective, succeeded in some way. The facts support that. But if some higher power was to say, 'No, I did that—it was part of the plan,' how can I argue the point? What I can tell you is that these mutations come more often than you would imagine. Most last only a generation or two." A slight smile. "Evolution or a grand creator busily experimenting? It doesn't matter, does it?"

"I guess not."

"Some of these mutations persist for centuries only to die out when what makes them unique is no longer necessary . . . or no longer unique. Imagine if those scientists in there—" he waved toward the house, "—discover a way for any human to communicate with the dead. What would happen to your kind?"

"We'd . . . die out?"

"Nothing so drastic. You'd simply merge with the gene pool. Necromancers as a unique race would cease to exist. It's happened before. Dryads, elves, nymphs, all the woodland races—there was no place for them in the modern world. Their time had passed. It matters not. Others come."

"Genetic flukes evolving into races. But that must take generations."

"True, but sometimes it's more than a random genetic 'fluke' that causes change."

He lifted the rose to his nose, then offered it to me.

"Smell anything?" he asked.

I sniffed. "It's very faint."

"A mutation. Not by nature, but by man. Create a hardier rose, a more disease-resistant rose, a longer lasting rose. A decided improvement over wild roses and yet . . ." He sniffed and sighed. "There are drawbacks."

He looked at me. "You say man-made magic is impossible because it has never existed. But what if . . ." he dropped the rose onto my lap, ". . . something clicked? The collision of nature and science?"

LEARNING CURVE

TWO HOURS LATER, I was sitting across from Jeremy, in the corner of a half-empty restaurant. We were keeping our voices down as I told him about my visit from Aratron. I don't know why we bothered—anyone hearing us talking about the evolutionary theory of supernatural races and the potential emergence of a new power would only mistake us for screenwriters trying to cash in on a paranormal trend. As for my garden visit from a demon? It was Hollywood. Deals with the devil were a way of life.

We were in a tiny restaurant with better food than atmosphere. When my seafood linguine had arrived, I'd slipped some of it onto his plate. He didn't protest, just accepted it with a murmur of thanks, as he always did. A werewolf's high metabolism made dining out less than satisfying, and it wasn't like *I* needed the food. My stylist was already complaining about the three pounds I'd gained in the last year. I was trying to ignore him, but after a lifetime of panicking if the scale needle so much as quivered, it wasn't easy.

"So," I said as I picked at my plate, "the gist is that Aratron thinks someone—some group—has broken the barrier, by either in-depth scientific experimentation or plain old dumb luck."

"You mean they've hit on a form of human magic that works."

I nodded. He set down his wineglass and stared at the blank wall behind me, his dark eyes equally blank, shutters pulled as he thought.

After a few moments, he said, "I'm not the best person to investigate this. Man-killing werewolves I understand. Humans killing with magic? I barely know where to begin."

A chill settled in the pit of my stomach. "You'd rather not help, then."

"Of course I want to help." His knee brushed my leg. "What I'm saying is that I'm in over my head." A twist of a smile. "And it's not a place I'm accustomed to being. I'm the Alpha. I lead in full confidence." The smile sparked in his eyes. "Usually. But with this, I should do what any good leader does—take it to an expert. But to whom? It's a matter that might concern all the races. Where should that go?"

"To the interracial council. Which, unfortunately, is us."

"Sad, isn't it? There should be some . . ." He waved his hand.

"Body of elders? Wise old men and women who do nothing but send out troops of highly trained investigators to protect the interests of the supernatural world?"

"Instead they get us. Part-time volunteers, untrained, unbudgeted and usually flying by the seat of our pants."

"It's nice to know I'm not the only one on the council who doesn't always feel up to the job."

"Did you think the rest of us do? In werewolf matters, yes, I am an expert. In necromancy, you are an expert—"

"I wouldn't say—"

"You've never let us down. If you don't know the answers, you find them. That's all we ask. Paige? Magic is her specialty and, between her and Lucas, they do just fine—remarkably fine, given their youth. So if this is magic, does it go to them? They know little or nothing of human magic. So *who* is the expert?"

"I guess it's about to be us. Self-taught. With a huge learning curve looming in front of us."

AFTER DINNER we walked for a couple of city blocks, then Jeremy headed into a park. Trust a werewolf to find green space anywhere.

A park probably isn't the safest place to be after dark in L.A. but Jeremy didn't hesitate. For him, safety was rarely a concern. I envied him that—Elena too—able to go anywhere after dark, walk into deserted parking lots, cut through alleys, knowing that any rapist or mugger who thought that pretty blond looked like an easy mark was in for a shock . . . maybe his last.

We passed a couple of street thugs, not yet old enough to be out of high school, hidden in the shadows of a willow. Jeremy put his arm around my waist. I couldn't help noticing how he drew me a little closer, so his hip brushed mine, or how his hand gripped my waist, pulling me into his circle of protection.

He didn't speed up or slow down, but met the leader's gaze full on, dipped his chin and murmured a greeting. They let us pass.

We'd gone a few more yards when another figure appeared on the path. A man, shoulders hunched, dressed in black, face hidden in the shadow of his hood. I glanced at Jeremy, but his gaze was fixed on a point past the man, his face as relaxed as the arm around my waist. A single unarmed assailant doesn't pose much risk for a werewolf. But as confident as Jeremy is, he's never cocky, which meant he couldn't see him.

Sure enough, as we drew closer, the man lifted his head, his face pale under the dark hood, and stared at me, confused. He knew the glow he saw around me meant something, and was racking his brain to remember what it was.

Not slowing, I looked up at Jeremy. "Did I tell you I talked to Paige? About the children?"

"No, what did she say?"

The man stopped. "Hey, aren't you—?"

"She's going to look into it and ask around. We should run it by Robert too, see whether he knows anything."

The man had gone quiet, staring after me. I kept walking and talking. After a moment, he mumbled something under his breath and continued on his way, convinced that either he was mistaken, or I wasn't strong enough to hear or see him. I sighed—part relief, part regret, as always.

WE STOPPED on a slope down to a small, man-made lake. Downwind, as always, so Jeremy could smell anyone approaching from behind.

We sat on the grass. I hadn't done that in . . . well, probably not since I was old enough to worry about walking around with grass stains on my rear. Jeremy offered to put down his jacket for me, but I refused, insisting my pants were old and the night was cool. Neither was true, but I wanted to just kick off my shoes, settle in the grass beside him and, if I got dirty, laugh about it.

I started talking, as usual. It takes awhile to draw Jeremy out if the topic is anything *but* business. That used to discourage me, but Elena says he's like that with everyone—so good at getting people to talk about themselves that they rarely realize he never offers anything in return.

Even when he does share, none of his stories are about himself, but when he talks of his family or his Pack, he's always there, in the background. So I get my insights that way. Sometimes, in talking of Clay as a child or the twins, he'll make a brief segue into his own childhood, enough for me to know it hadn't been a pleasant one. That glimpse behind the shutters meant more to me than he could imagine.

I asked him about the twins' birthday and he told me about Elena's misadventures with the baking, how she'd tried to sneak the failed cake outside for the birds, but Clay, smelling food, had rescued it and shared it with the twins, reasoning that they needed to get accustomed to bad food in case Jeremy ever cooked them dinner. I watched him tell the story, his face animated, relating even the jibe at his cooking with a wry smile.

We sat there for over an hour, just talking. A cool wind blew off the water, bringing a fine mist as it slid over us and into the trees, rustling the leaves, then departed with a sigh. Beneath my fingers, the grass was growing damp. Jeremy's legs were outstretched, mine bent, our shoulders brushing when we moved.

"Thanks for tonight," I said. "For taking me out. You have no idea how nice it is to eat without a dead man hanging over the table."

His brows shot up and I explained. "But on the upside, I'm pretty much guaranteed to lose those few pounds my stylist keeps nagging about."

He shook his head. "I don't know how you do it, Jaime."

"Don't have much choice."

"Yes, you do. You could hide from it. Take your meals elsewhere and make some excuse to the others. But you never do. You'll sit there, smile and chat—with a ghost hanging a foot from your nose—and no one will ever be the wiser."

"It's a residual, not a ghost. And it's more like two feet."

He smiled and shifted, moving the arm stretched behind me to my back. His hand went to my waist, his face turning, lips a scant inch from mine, the look in his dark eyes sending a shiver through me.

I waited through five long heartbeats, but he didn't move, neither coming toward me nor pulling back. It was up to me.

The kiss started firm yet gentle, sweet yet strong, everything I'd expected from Jeremy. Then, as I pressed against him, an edge crept into it, an urgency and a passion that maybe . . . wasn't quite what I'd expected. Like being hit with a blast of hot air when I was anticipating a gentle breeze. I threw myself into it like someone who's been plucked from an icy river, lapping up the heat.

After several intense minutes, he pulled back.

"I'm sorry," he said. "That wasn't—"

"You don't need to apologize. I started it."

"Ah, yes, right."

He sat there for a moment, hair hanging forward, then gave it an impatient brush back. I resisted the urge to put my arms around his neck and bury myself in another kiss. His expression told me he wouldn't argue, but that this wasn't a step he was entirely ready to take.

I settled for resting my hand on his thigh. He laid his hand on mine, fingers sliding under my palm and squeezing.

"I love it when you're indecisive," I said.

A pause, as if he wasn't sure he'd heard right, then a laugh so abrupt it was almost a bark. "Oh?"

I eased closer, leg against his. His hand slid from my waist to my hip, bringing me closer still.

I said, "When I first met you in Miami, you were so sure of yourself, so . . . in charge. You spoke; everyone listened. Even Benicio Cortez. Hell, even *Cassandra* lets you tell her what to do."

"I'm not so sure about that."

"She just likes to pretend it's her idea. A vampire can't seem to be obeying a werewolf—it's just not done."

He laughed, rubbing my hip.

"It's a bit daunting, you know, being around someone that self-assured. So it's nice, now and then, to get a hint that the armor isn't as impenetrable as it looks."

"The armor is full of chinks, I'm afraid. The trick is to keep it polished to such a brilliant shine that everyone is blind to the holes."

"Is that it?"

He looked down at me, his crooked grin almost boyish. "Yes, that's it."

He stayed there, head angled, lips slightly parted. My heart started thumping. But he turned away.

"That's one problem of being Alpha. You have to act with complete confidence. It's the wolf in us. Uncertainty makes us nervous. Smacks of weakness. An Alpha must be resolute in all things. He should have no misgivings, no second thoughts, no doubts."

"But sometimes you do," I said softly.

He met my gaze. "Most times I do." He turned to look out at the lake. "I've always been happy being Alpha. It's a lot of responsibility, but I love that—not the power, but the ability to affect change. Sometimes though . . . lately . . ." He took his hand off mine and brushed back his hair. "Under certain circumstances, the restrictions can be . . . not what I'd choose, if I had the choice. Like coming here. For most people, a simple matter. Make travel arrangements and go."

"But you have responsibilities."

"Not just that. To come here alone, without backup, without a bodyguard . . ." He shook his head. "To explain to you how much work it took would make the whole thing sound ridiculous. But I am the Alpha. I cannot do as I like, go where I like. Even an outside werewolf who has no particular grudge against me would consider attacking me if I crossed his path. To kill the Pack Alpha would solidify his status in our world. For the rest of his life, every werewolf he met would clear out of his way. The Alpha before me—Antonio's father—was inarguably the best fighter of his time, but he never left Pack territory without a guard. To do otherwise is to threaten the stability of the Pack for something as petty as privacy."

My cheeks got hot. "I'm sorry. I never thought—"

He squeezed my leg. "No one expected you to. I didn't come to L.A. to be polite, Jaime. I came because I wanted to spend time with you. Alone."

His gaze met mine and held, making sure the words sunk in. "The area is as safe as we could make it. I even managed to convince them that I didn't need Antonio lurking in San Diego, awaiting an emergency call, though I suspect Karl isn't in Arizona this week by accident. Elena probably sent him there, hoping—being Karl—it wouldn't seem suspicious."

I nodded.

"I won't be Alpha forever," he said. "But I will be for longer than I planned."

"Because of the babies."

He nodded.

I said, "Elena needs to concentrate on them, on being a mom, not an Alpha."

"Which doesn't mean I can't continue to train her. Antonio and I will keep nudging her into leadership, getting her accustomed to the idea, but we can't push."

"And you shouldn't." I paused. "Does she know yet?"

He shook his head. "I don't plan to tell her for some time. If I did, she'd suspect I want out, and she'd do everything she could to help me achieve that. And, as you said, her priority should be her family, not her Pack. At least for a few more years."

I wanted to say, "That's okay. I'll wait," but I knew that wasn't what he was asking.

"That's best," I said. "It'll give Clay more time to recover too. How's his arm?"

"As good as it will get. He knows that. Whatever that zombie did to him, it's beyond what medicine can fix. The trick now is to learn to compensate. And to regain his confidence, get him back to a place where he feels he can defend his family, his Pack, his Alpha. If that Alpha is Elena, he's going to need to be in top fighting condition."

"Because other werewolves, outside the Pack, will see a female Alpha as a sign of weakness."

"Or, at least, of change and, as I said, we don't respond well to change. Elena's used to being in danger. It comes with being Clay's mate. His enemies might not dare take on Clay himself, but there are other ways to hurt him."

"Through Elena."

"Most werewolves will not believe that a woman, even a werewolf, poses a threat, and therefore Elena is seen as an easy target." He smiled at me. "Fortunately, she isn't." His smile faded. "But she's always been in danger, just by being his lover."

Another message for me.

"Having a female Alpha will be an adjustment for all. It took a long time for me to accept Elena as a werewolf. Logically, I was fine with it, but deep down?" He shook his head. "It wasn't easy. To Clay, having a mate was the most natural thing. The wolf in him is so strong it rules out everything else. But for me? Being raised as a werewolf means being raised to keep your distance from romantic entanglements. Pack werewolves weren't allowed to form long-term relationships, let alone marry. Open yourself up to someone and you might be tempted to tell her everything. Now that the werewolves are back in the supernatural fold, there are women who can safely know my secret. I still have trouble accepting that."

We sat there for a while, staring at the water.

I knew now that Jeremy hadn't come to L.A. to declare himself—or to let me down easy—but to give us both a chance to explore the possibilities and weigh them against the consequences. We could spend time together, away from being "werewolf Alpha and necromancer delegate." Time to decide whether it was better to stay friends or risk becoming lovers.

Becoming lovers *would* come with risks. He was letting me know what I'd be in for. A lover who couldn't fly to meet me for romantic getaways. A lover whose priority would always be his family and his Pack. A lover who would put my life in danger just by being with me, making me a target for anyone who wanted to get at the Alpha. Even if I was fine with all this, after a lifetime of one-night stands, avoiding emotional attachments, Jeremy might never be comfortable in a relationship.

My impulse was to say: "Put my life at risk for a difficult, long-distance relationship that might never work? It's *Jeremy*. Sign me up." But I had to approach this with my head, not my heart. It wasn't something I could just leap into.

"We should get you back to the house," Jeremy said finally. "I presume you have a segment to film tomorrow?"

"In the afternoon, plus an interview midmorning."

He helped me to my feet. "When things settle down with your

costars, I'd like to watch a segment or two. I'm looking forward to that."

"It's not nearly as much fun as you'd think. It's a lot of standing around doing nothing."

"I'm not here to be entertained, Jaime."

He put his hand on my back and led me from the park.

SPIRITUALIST BIG BROTHER

BACK AT THE HOUSE, I grabbed a cold drink from the kitchen before heading to bed. I was backing away from the fridge when something moved along the far wall. I turned and braced myself, waiting for a ghost to materialize. Another flicker—just a flashlight beam from a guard doing a walk-around outside. As I'd stared at the wall, though, something else caught my eye. Resting above the chair rail was a dark dot, smaller than a dime. I walked over. The dot became a hole, and recessed within the hole was the lens of a camera.

There could be a logical explanation for this. Maybe the family that lived here suspected the cook of spitting in their food. Or they had a dieter with a midnight fridge-raiding habit. But tiny wood shavings still clung to the hole, meaning it'd been drilled recently.

Time to take a tour of the house.

I FOUND four pinhole cameras in the shared rooms where we spiritualists were most likely to congregate. The crew-only areas were surveillance-free.

So we were being taped. By whom? My first thought was the crew. But if someone hoped for an ugly photo he could sell to a tabloid or a compromising video to post on the Internet, he'd be filming in the private areas.

I thought of Todd Simon. Beer-commercial director turned reality-show producer.

Becky said we were all in this house for budget reasons. Entirely plausible, and I was sure she believed that. But someone was hoping for *Big Brother*–style footage. Was it legal? That depended on our contracts.

I went upstairs, pulled out my contract and gave it a good read. I never sign without studying the contract and consulting with my lawyer. I don't care if it looks just like the boilerplate I've signed a hundred times—I don't take chances. But Hollywood contracts are notorious for their legalese and for their sheer size, and this one had covered every eventuality from *Death of Innocence: The Musical* to Jaime Vegas action figures.

I found the clause about agreeing to be filmed at the Brentwood house. Seemed obvious—I was going to the house to tape segments, so naturally I'd agreed to be filmed. When I reread that clause after finding the pinhole cameras, it took on a whole new meaning.

I'd run this past my lawyer, but even if I had grounds for raising a fuss, I'd be labeled difficult, and my hopes for my own show would fly out the window. Better to tuck the knowledge into my back pocket and use it to my advantage. If I knew I was being taped, I could put on a good performance. And I could make damned sure I didn't pick my nose, scratch my ass or badmouth anyone in the common rooms. As long as they weren't taping me in my bedroom . . .

I put down the contract and searched. No cameras. Whew.

AS I headed to breakfast the next morning, Becky called to me from the living room. When I caught up with her, she was already vanishing into the study that now served as a communal office.

"I wanted to thank you for helping us out with Grady yesterday," she said as she shut the door. "I really appreciate it, and I want you to be the first to hear Mr. Simon's amazing new idea for the show. I just know you're going to love this."

I braced myself. In Hollywood, the words "you're going to love this" are more plea than assurance.

"Rather than pepper our show with random séances, why not make it a theme?" She lifted her hands, punctuating her words with a jab as if pointing to them on a marquee. "One final curtain call for the tragic dead of Brentwood."

"You want us to contact more dead movie stars?" I said.

"Not just movie stars. *Brentwood* stars. Those killed under mysterious circumstances, like Tansy Lane. A theme, leading to the grand finale with Marilyn Monroe."

"It's an . . . interesting concept," I said carefully. "Certainly ambitious—"

"We don't expect you to do as well with every ghost as you did with Tansy. You can ask how they died, but we won't expect any real revelations. We'll intercut with some talking heads giving their theories, some old detectives reminiscing about the cases, and by the end of the segment, no one will even notice that we didn't actually find out anything new."

"It sounds . . . interesting."

Becky crumpled, bracing herself against the desk. "It's horrible. I'm so sorry. We're still having issues with Grady, and this is Mr. Simon's solution, knowing how much Grady loves working with mysterious deaths."

"I'm not comfortable with changing the format at this point. It's been changed once, when they set it in this house, and I was very understanding about that."

Terror filled Becky's eyes. Part of me wanted to stand my ground and tell her that if she wanted to make the show she envisioned, then she'd better grow a backbone and stand up to men like Bradford Grady. But another part of me remembered being young, ambitious and overwhelmed, and I wanted to be the one person not making this shoot a living hell for her.

"I'll consider a change of format, but on several conditions."

"Name them."

"I want a written guarantee of equal screen time in the final production and equal preshow promotion. Is the Tansy Lane segment in danger of being cut?"

"Definitely not. I'll get Mr. Simon to put that in writing. No matter how much weight Grady throws around, your success with Tansy stays."

Her cell phone rang. A few quick words, then she hung up. "I need to run. The next séance will be after lunch. We're keeping the locations and subjects a secret. Yes, I know—Grady is an expert and by tonight his team will be faxing him dossiers on every semifamous person who died in this neighborhood. But I have a plan."

She headed for the door, then stopped. "Oh, and before you leave, there's a release form on the desk. Just an addendum to your contract. It's in the blue folder. Take it with you to read over. No rush."

I OPENED the blue folder she'd left on the desk. Inside was a single printed sheet. On first glance, it looked more like a memo than a release form.

Subject: Gabrielle Langdon.

The name sounded familiar, but I had to read a few lines before I realized what I was looking at: a detailed summary of the life and death of arguably Brentwood's most famous murder victim.

I slapped the folder shut and scanned the desk, but there were no more blue folders. No folders of any color.

Becky said she had a plan, and now I knew what it was.

I HAD lunch and the early afternoon off, so Jeremy picked me up. He'd already checked in with Robert and a second potential source: Clay. Like Jeremy and Elena, Clay worked part-time and primarily from home—the advantage to having a healthy communal bank account and little desire for material goods. From Jeremy and Elena, I knew Clay was passionate about his work, but he rarely talked about it with anyone outside the Pack.

While Robert Vasic looked like the stereotypical professor, no one looked—or acted—less like one than Clay. Yet that's what he was: an anthropologist. His specialty was religions with animal deities. There's a name for it, which I can never remember, and it's not like he's about to discuss it with me anytime soon.

"Any luck?" I said, shutting the car door.

"Very little," he said as he pulled from the curb. "According to Clay, we're barking up the wrong tree. Of course, he said it in far more colorful language, but the point he made was that the link between pagan religions, like Wicca and Druidism, and sacrifice is significantly overemphasized in popular culture."

"You mean they aren't out there slaughtering babies every full moon? Bradford Grady would be mightily disappointed. And probably out of a job."

"Wiccans and satanists don't practice human sacrifice, whatever the tabloids might say. But even the more mysterious religions are far more benign than I assumed. Animal sacrifice, yes. But not human. Those that did practice it did so only in the very distant past and have since found substitutes more acceptable to contemporary mores. One sect Clay did mention was tantraism."

"That's related to Buddhism, isn't it?"

Jeremy shook his head. "This is different. It's a religion based in India that practices sacrifice. Usually animal sacrifice, but reports of human sacrifice do arise, sometimes child sacrifice. Then there are 'muti' murders, primarily in southern Africa. Not necessarily human sacrifice per se, but the killing of people, often children, for medicine."

"Does that kind of stuff make its way over here?"

"I don't know, but if I haven't heard of it, it's likely very rare."

"Good."

"They suggested we concentrate on the occult underworld in Los Angeles, which won't be easy." He turned a corner. "Speaking of tabloids, though, Elena suggested someone else who might be able to cut through the research for us. Hope Adams is here for six months, on a work exchange."

"Hope? Oh, right, the *True News* reporter."

I'd never met her. Her contact with the council was Elena, a fellow journalist. A half-demon with a sixth sense for chaos, Hope covered paranormal events for a supermarket tabloid. Through a werewolf in Jeremy's Pack—Karl Marsten—she'd hooked up with the council and alerted them to any potentially real supernatural activity that crossed her desk. Strictly a volunteer job, but to kids like Hope, money never seemed to matter. Working for a good cause was payment enough.

DEMONS AND DEBTS

WE PARKED IN A LOT so expensive that in Chicago, I'd have expected valet service and a car wash. It was still a few blocks to where Hope worked, so Jeremy offered to drop me off, but I refused.

As we walked down the street, the smell of falafels and fresh-cut fries reminded me I'd skipped breakfast. It was a business district, respectable enough, but with little else to recommend it. A hodgepodge of small office buildings and take-out restaurants, interspersed with nail parlors, boutiques and gourmet coffee bars, as if the neighborhood was taking one last stab at trendiness.

I updated him on the show situation: the hidden cameras, the newly scheduled séances and Becky's blue file folder.

"And when I made some calls about Grady, I found out that he is looking to move his show to America, but apparently only for one season, and his show wouldn't be anything like mine. Yet Becky's assistant seemed to think I should be concerned, and maybe I should. Hollywood executives are notorious for things like this: they'll see two spiritualism shows on the slate and won't notice any differences between them."

"Have you talked to Grady?"

"And say what, 'Get off my turf'?" I sighed. "I know, you mean just talk to him and get the details. I intended to, but now with him making more demands, I'm nervous. I'm already flustered enough over that memo leak about Gabrielle Langdon. I know Becky meant well, but if I win, I want to win without cheating."

I shook my head. "Listen to me. One minute I'm telling you I want to stop all this competition, the next I'm saying I want to win. I'm so tired of the backbiting, the posturing, the lying. Especially now. I have child ghosts trapped God knows where, and instead of helping them, I'm trying to thwart a twenty-eight-year-old beer-commercial producer who wants to turn this into *Spiritualist Big Brother*."

"You've been tired of show biz for a while."

"I know. I can't wait to get out. Not the stage shows, just . . ."

"The television work."

We turned a corner. "I know what you're thinking. I say I want out, but my sole reason for putting up with the crap on this set is so I can do *more* TV. But I only want a television slot for a few years. Once I've built up more name recognition, I can do live shows exclusively and be more available for the council. Last month, Paige invited me to join her on an investigation—after months of me practically begging—and I had to back out because it interfered with my talk show spots. If I could schedule a half-dozen sold-out live shows a year, I'd be set."

"Your shows almost sell to capacity now, don't they?"

"Yes, but—" Jeremy tugged me back as I'd nearly stepped off a curb on a Don't Walk signal. "I really need a TV show, just for a while, so I can say I had one. It's always been part of the plan."

"Your mother's plan."

He said it mildly, with no emphasis, not making a point, but I felt it all the same.

"No, her plan was for *her* to get me a TV show. Without her, I didn't stand a chance. Or so she thought."

Actually, she'd thought I'd never get anywhere without her. And in a way, she'd been right. At eighteen, I'd left home, still too young and inexperienced to make it on my own. I needed a mentor. And a world-renowned spiritualist had needed a student. But I'd only been doing spiritualism for a few years, and my rival for the position had been on the circuit since he was ten. So I made my deal with the devil.

It was my boyfriend's idea. He was a sorcerer I'd met through a friend of Nan's. He'd been older and smart enough to know that, as tempting as bargains with demons seemed, it was the kind of thing you really wanted someone else to test first... like a naive and ambitious young girlfriend.

The demon made me a deal: he'd get me the job, if I'd help him contact a soul in a hell dimension... and he'd even tell me how to do it. My only stipulation was that my rival wasn't killed. A week later, I'd been told my competition had left the business. I never found out why—never dared try. I had the job and he was still alive and that was all that mattered.

I contacted that ghost—the spirit of a serial killer. The demon questioned him about his crimes, getting graphic details that still haunt my nightmares. But what haunts me more is knowing that the demon couldn't have wanted those details for mere curiosity's sake. He must have had a supplicant that he wanted to reenact the crimes. Somewhere in the world, people had died horrific deaths, and it was my fault. That was the price I'd paid for fame.

After that, I climbed the ladder by myself—asking for no favors, indebted to no one, relying on no one. If my mother was surprised by how far I'd come, she never showed it. Almost the first thing she said to me every time we met was, "So, Jaime, have you gotten that TV show yet?" I didn't want it so I could say, "So there." I just wanted to prove to myself that I could do it.

"THAT'S THE building over there," Jeremy said. "I hope she hasn't left for lunch yet. Her voice mail said she's in the office, but when I tried leaving a message, it didn't seem to work." A faint smile. "Or, as is more likely, I was doing it wrong. Probably not much point in leaving a message, as I couldn't give a number for her to call back."

"That's right. We need to get you a cell phone. We'll do that this afternoon."

Jeremy led me around the corner and stopped in the alcove of a three-story building. He pulled on the door. A buzzer sounded and his gaze dropped to the Please Use Intercom sign. Below the intercom was a directory of offices. He scanned the list, frown growing.

"Perhaps 'just popping by the office' isn't going to be as easy as it seemed."

He pulled a notepad from his pocket and checked the address, then read the directory again. There was no listing for *True News* or anything resembling a newspaper.

"I'm not that surprised," I said. "Considering what they write, maintaining a low profile might be wise or they'd have a steady stream of UFO and Elvis reportings, and probably *not* from the sort of people you want walking into your office unannounced."

"True. So . . ."

"What's her number?"

"Ah. Right."

He gave it to me. I punched it into my cell, then handed the phone to him. He spoke for a minute, his voice too low to overhear.

"She'll be right down," he said as he handed the phone back.

We stepped out of the doorway. No more than a minute passed before the smoked-glass door flew open and a young woman stepped out. Dressed in sneakers, a T-shirt and blue jeans, Hope Adams looked like a Bollywood princess trying to pass through L.A. incognito. Fine-boned and tiny, with delicate features and golden brown eyes, she had the kind of face that would be as lovely at eighty as it was at twenty. Yet she wore that beauty awkwardly, like a farm girl handed a Vera Wang gown, not quite sure how to put it on or whether she even wanted to. Her long black curls had been yanked back in a careless ponytail. Ink smeared one cheek like war paint.

Her gaze lighted on Jeremy and she smiled, striding over to clasp his hand. Her handshake was firm and vigorous, and a little too much of both, like a junior employee called in for a meeting with the boss, pretty sure it wasn't bad news, but unable to shake that glimmer of fear.

"Mr. Danvers, good to see you again."

"Jeremy, please. And this is—"

"Jaime Vegas." She took my hand in a firm grip. "It's a pleasure. So you two wanted to talk to me about a council problem? My place is just down the block, if you'd like privacy."

I FOLLOWED Hope up the rear stairs to her walkup apartment. On the way we'd found a store with prepaid cell phones. I showed Jeremy what he was looking for, then he insisted on handling the purchase himself while I went on ahead, so we didn't take up too much of Hope's time.

She opened the door to a dark cave haunted by the ghosts of mildew and pungent food. Someone had tried to banish them with lemon-scented cleaner and fresh flowers, but the odors lingered. Hope strode in and started opening windows.

"Can't get rid of the smell," she said. "I swear it's embedded in the walls."

She flicked on lights, but they did little to brighten the place. Two of the three windows gave lovely views of a wall so close it defied building codes. I walked into the kitchen. Five steps later, I was in the living room.

"Tiny, huh? The place is a hole, but it fit my budget, it came furnished and it's close to work."

"It's nicer than my first few apartments."

"I had to fight with the landlord to let me paint it—doing the work myself and buying my own supplies." She ran her fingers over the wall. "Though, in the end, I probably didn't do him any favors. Apparently, you're supposed to wash the walls before you paint. I think that's why I can't get rid of the smell."

I looked over at an arrangement of fresh flowers on the coffee table. There was another, smaller one on the bookshelf. "The flowers brighten the place up."

"Courtesy of my mom's most recent visit. As are the curtains, throw rug, pillows . . . I probably have the only place in town where the accessories are worth more than the furniture. Every day I'd go to work, come back and find something new, then she'd explain how she chose the fabric or the color. Still trying to teach me how to accessorize. I keep telling her it's a lost cause—a gene I failed to inherit, among many." She grinned. "Moms, huh? They drive you nuts, but you know they're only doing it because they love you."

I nodded as if I knew what that felt like. She fluffed a pillow, a wistful look passing behind her eyes.

"You and your mother are close?" I said.

An almost embarrassed smile. "Yeah. I'm the baby. This is my first time living more than a few miles from home." She walked to the fridge. "Can I get you something cold? Or tea? Coffee?"

"Water would be fine."

She handed me a Perrier. "Also courtesy of Mom. When she saw my cheap bottled water, she had to take me aside for a little heart-to-heart on the state of my finances."

She got a Dr Pepper for herself. "Have a seat— Oh, I'd better clear my mail off the table."

She sorted as she cleared it, fixing bills to the fridge and tossing junk mail in the trash. An expensive vellum envelope formally addressed to "Miss Hope Adams" went into a basket with a small stack of others.

"Invitations?" I said as I pulled out a chair. "I wasn't that popular even after living in L.A. for a decade."

"My mom, again. When she was down, she had to make the society rounds. Not really her thing, but it's expected, if only to make connections for her charity and philanthropy work."

I nodded, as if I knew all about high society.

"So . . ." Hope waved at the basket. "Now they all know that Nita Adams's youngest daughter is in town, and they're inviting me to garden parties and luncheons, to check out my suitability."

"Suitability?"

She grinned. "As a wife, of course. Never been married. College graduate. Getting a little long in the tooth at twenty-eight, but if I'm half as pretty, witty, charming and well bred as my mother, then they'll overlook that and find me a match among their eligibles."

"That sounds very . . ."

"Arranged?" Her grin broadened. "Society here can be worse than in Bombay. In some families, background is still more important than making a love match. My father's family came over on the *Mayflower* and my mother has Indian royal blood in her veins, adding the dash of exoticism to a perfectly respectable American name. Of course, if they knew who my real father is, those invitations would dry up pretty quickly."

"You never know. You're a rare form of half-demon, which means your dad is probably pretty high up the ladder. Royal blood on both sides."

JEREMY ARRIVED and together we told her what we were investigating.

"So, this group, the ones you think have broken the magic barrier, presumably they'd be local, right?" she said. "Or at least have a local branch. That's why the ghosts would be here."

"Most likely," Jeremy said.

"Then I know the perfect people for you to talk to. Some paranormal scam-busters. They know every person and rumor connected to the supernatural. They hooked up with me shortly after I came to town and we've been trading tips ever since."

"Scam-busters?" I said.

"You know what paranormal investigators are?"

"The bane of supernaturals everywhere."

"Think of these guys as the opposite. Instead of trying to prove that the paranormal exists, they try to uncover the scams and the frauds."

"Like unmasking TV spiritualists?"

"Oh . . ." She paused. "I hadn't thought of that. But it shouldn't be a problem. I can't imagine these guys taking an interest in you. If you were bilking widows of their life savings for passing messages to their husbands, you'd be on their radar. But that's not what you do. If you're uncomfortable, though, Mr. Dan—Jeremy and I could meet with them . . ."

"No, I'll be fine. I might not be their favorite sort of person, but we'll come up with a good cover story."

HELPLESS

WE LEFT HOPE TO MAKE THE ARRANGEMENTS. In the meantime, Jeremy would make the telephone check-in rounds again, seeing whether Robert, Paige or Clay had anything new for us. As for me, as much as I hated being distracted from the investigation, I had a job to do. Time for the Gabrielle Langdon séance.

We wound up not at Langdon's house—where she'd been murdered—but at a place down the street, where she'd gone for a few community barbecues. As for why her ghost would linger there, the intro would give some heart-tugging speech about the good times she'd had in that place, and how those memories would attract her far more than the nightmares she experienced at her house. I'd bet my retirement savings, though, that this was at the end of a long list of potential sites, all of which had refused access.

Only after we arrived did Becky announce the subject of the séance. While we waited for Dr. Robson to set up his "electronic voice phenomena" equipment, Angelique sidled over to me.

"Isn't this exciting?" she said. "Lord knows, I was barely more than a tot when poor Gabrielle died, but I remember Daddy talking about it in church. He was certain the husband did it. A soccer player, wasn't he?"

"Baseball."

She nodded, processing.

"San Diego Padres," I added. "Star pitcher."

Her eyes narrowed as if suspecting me of feeding her false information. Then she lowered herself onto the bench beside a statue of a nymph that, apparently in keeping with Hollywood standards, had undergone a boob job. I glanced at the statue. Angelique followed my gaze, let out a squeak and vacated the bench, lest she be photographed under it. Not inconceivable—the cameraman was prowling the garden, getting his setup shots.

"Maybe you can give me some advice, Jaime. I know— Well, I get the impression you don't like me very much—"

"Then you're getting the wrong one, hon. I'm always thrilled to see a new star in the making. Plenty of room for all of us."

She lifted limpid eyes to mine. "Really? Lord, you don't know what that means to me. I've idolized you my whole life, waiting for this moment, hoping you'd still be around—"

"So you wanted to ask . . . ?"

A quick glance toward the others. "Your advice. I just don't think it's fair, picking séances with these people that I've barely even heard of. It's . . . what's the word? Ageist."

"Ageist?" I tried not to laugh. Tried even harder not to remind her she was supposed to be getting her stories from the dead, not from memories of past events. "I suppose it is."

"I think Becky has me scheduled to go first, and I was wondering whether there was any way you might . . ."

"Switch spots with you? Be happy to."

"Really? Oh, gosh, that's so sweet of you. So you'll go first and I'll take the last place, which is hard, but I think I can manage—"

Becky approached, shaking her head. "I'm sorry, Angelique, but the positions are set. Jaime goes last."

"I thought Mr. Grady had the last spot." Claudia hurried over. "What's this? Another change?"

I raised my hands. "I don't know what order we're supposed to go in, but I'll take whatever works for you two. First, second, last, your choice."

"No, Jaime, I'm afraid it isn't," Becky said. "You're scheduled last. I can't change that."

As she spoke, she shot nervous glances at me. Had I been the other two, I'd have interpreted those glances to mean Becky was indeed following orders: my orders. Protest, and I'd sound like a two-faced poseur. Take Becky aside and I'd confirm suspicions of collusion.

Damn it, I didn't need this. It was hard enough doing this silly séance, when all I could think about was those child ghosts. It took all I had not to say "screw it" and walk away from the whole thing. Screw the show. Screw my future in television. I had more important things to do—things I'd *rather* be doing.

I forced my attention back on task. As Claudia harassed Becky, and Angelique made pointed comments about special treatment, I noticed the cameraman, ten feet away, filming the spat.

"Becky," I murmured.

"I'm sorry, Claudia, but the positioning has been set—"

I coughed, and nudged Becky toward the cameraman.

She glanced his way, then continued. "If Mr. Grady has a problem with this shoot, then I'd suggest he go ahead and contact Mr. Simon because . . ."

I excused myself and walked away.

THE SÉANCE did not go well. Suspecting that my information was false, Angelique called Gabrielle's husband a soccer player, then started talking about bullet holes, when the woman had been stabbed. Seeing her failure on Becky's face, she tried to salvage the séance with boring personal details—Gabrielle remembered her mother brushing her hair, Gabrielle liked to walk in bare feet, Gabrielle liked puppies—the sorts of things impossible to confirm or deny.

On to Grady, who probably vaguely remembered the case, but not well enough to chance it, so he found a Spanish conquistador who'd stumbled on an evil pagan cult and claimed this ghost was so strong he blocked Gabrielle.

Then it was my turn. Becky could scarcely control her excitement. By placing me last, she'd given me the prime spot for using the details she'd provided.

I pulled my nonprescription glasses from my purse, and adjusted my hair from semipinned to a neater do—less sexy, more scholarly. Then I had them film me sitting under the double-D nymph, as I gravely explained the "challenges" of this séance.

The geographic connection was tenuous at best, which likely

explained why no one could contact Gabrielle. Even had we been on the very site of her murder, I doubted our results would have been much better, given the trauma of her passing. While we'd hoped to help lessen her burden by sharing her story with the world, we had to accept that she wasn't yet ready to do that for herself. Perhaps someday, the world would know the truth behind her tragic passing.

Cut.

"WHAT THE hell was that?" Becky said as I checked my cell phone for messages from Jeremy.

I closed the phone. "What's wrong?"

"You didn't contact Gabrielle Langdon, that's what's wrong."

I sighed. "It's the location. I could have worked it harder, but after Tansy Lane, I thought it best if I didn't try to show up the others." I returned my phone to my purse, took out a pen, then stopped, staring at it. "Oh, my god. I'm such a ditz. That release you wanted me to sign. I forgot all about it. I'm so sorry. After you left, I got a call and walked out without grabbing that folder. I'll do that as soon as I get back to the house."

"No," she said, words clipped. "That won't be necessary."

I asked if she minded if I walked back to the house while she finished up. She waved what I took for a "yes" and strode back to the set.

THE STREET was empty. The houses, pushed back from the road, peeked out from curtains of trees and evergreens. The rumble of the distant highway was only white noise. Even the lawn crew I passed worked in silence as they clipped bushes into submission. Across the road, a pool-cleaning truck idled in a drive, the fumes harsh against the smell of fresh-cut grass.

There was nothing to see, nothing to listen to, nothing to distract me from burrowing deep in my thoughts and staying there. I wanted to say "to hell with this shoot" and walk off before it got worse, but I'd earned my own TV show and I was damned well going to get it.

A throat cleared behind me. I glanced over my shoulder and caught a glimpse of a blond woman.

"Nice to see someone walking," she said as she fell into step beside me. "Around here, people drive to the corner store."

I nodded, torn between wanting to be polite and wanting to be left alone. We continued on, the woman staying beside me in silence.

"I hope I'm going the right way," I said finally.

"You are. Just another block and a half."

"Oh?" I glanced at her. "How—? Ah, there's not likely to be more than one TV special filming in Brentwood right now, is there? We're probably the subject of much discussion."

A small laugh. "Probably. But that's not why . . . I mean, that's not how I know . . ."

The sentence trailed off. I took a better look at her. Any other time, I'd have pegged her as a stereotypical Hollywood housewife, but considering where I'd just been and what I'd been doing, I recognized her.

I stopped walking. "Gabrielle, I didn't— Yes, they were calling you, but *I* didn't—"

"I know. Better keep walking. Bad enough you're talking to yourself. You don't want to be caught doing it in the middle of the road."

I resumed walking, my heart thumping. I pulled out my cell phone—an invention that made "talking to myself" much more socially acceptable. "I'm sorry. I'm so—"

"—sorry. But you shouldn't be. Like you said, you didn't call me. Some of us have been . . . catching your show, so to speak."

I glanced around, imagining ghosts, hidden on the other side of the veil, watching me, waiting for an excuse to make contact and ask for help I couldn't give.

"We don't get many of your kind around here, so it was big news. We're the ones who told Tansy you were calling her and, well, seeing you talking to her, being so nice, it gave us hope."

"Hope." The word echoed down the empty street, as hollow and empty as its promise. And it reminded me of an obligation I'd been trying to avoid—my promise to speak to Tansy. A double shot of guilt. I took a deep breath. "I don't blame you for wanting revenge against whoever killed you, but telling me who it was isn't going to help."

"Revenge?" She met my gaze. "I don't want revenge. I just want answers."

"Answers?"

"I don't *know* who killed me. I don't remember."

"That's normal—"

"Normal?" A bitter laugh. "I don't think 'normal' has anything to do with my case. Everyone knows how I died. Everyone has an opinion about who did it. Everyone thinks they know the truth. Everyone except me."

I didn't know what to say.

"All *I* know is who was accused. The man I married, the father of my children. A criminal court finds him innocent. A civil court finds him guilty. And I don't know. I *still* don't know." Her voice rose, then she steadied herself and rubbed her face on her sleeve. "How am I supposed to spend eternity not knowing?"

If I opened my mouth, I was going to throw up. It's happened before. Just last spring, I almost lost my dinner on the scuffed shoes of a very straightlaced old man who'd cried as he begged me to contact his dead granddaughter and find out who'd raped and murdered her.

That's the price I pay—for every hundred people I console with fake reassurances, there's one whose heart I break by saying no. I used to think the balance was in my favor, that I helped more than I harmed. But lately, I've come to question that.

"I—I don't know what to tell you," I said finally. "I can't solve your murder."

"I know, but isn't there someone you can ask? Some . . . higher power who can tell me the truth?"

"If there is, I have no way to make that contact. With the afterlife, I'm restricted to talking to ghosts like you."

She reached to take my arm, frustration and despair filling her eyes as her fingers passed through me. She met my gaze. "Then just tell me what you think. Did he kill me?"

As tempting as it was to tell Gabrielle what she wanted to hear, I didn't have that right.

"What if I tell you no, and you wait for him, only to learn I was wrong? What if I say yes, and you find out later I was wrong?"

"You're right. I'm sorry. I shouldn't have asked. Do you . . . do you want me to leave now?"

I shook my head. "Walk with me, if you don't mind. I could use the company."

AS WE neared the house, my gut started twisting again. How should I handle our parting? If I said nothing, I'd lead the other ghosts to believe that while I might not have been able to help Gabrielle, that didn't mean I wasn't willing to hear their stories. I'd spend the rest of this job with ghosts hovering about, waiting for the excuse to pop in, only to be disappointed.

But what was the alternative? Tell Gabrielle to bring them all by, like serfs granted an audience with the queen, telling me their stories, begging for help I couldn't give? I couldn't find a killer. I couldn't help a still-grieving spouse find love again. I couldn't take an inheritance away from an ungrateful child. I couldn't stop an unscrupulous partner from destroying the business they'd built together. Most times, I couldn't even deliver a simple message—at best I'd have a door slammed in my face, at worst I'd be reported for trying to scam the bereaved.

I couldn't handle listening to their pleas, knowing I'd disappoint them. Selfish, maybe, but every *no* hurt too much.

So what should I say? "Please tell all those other ghosts not to bother me"? How callous was that?

I tell myself that I *do* help—not ghosts, but the grief-stricken, with my show. But does it matter how many people I reassure if I raise the false hopes of one? By splashing myself on screen and stage, proclaiming my desire to help the grief-stricken make contact, aren't I lying to the spirits themselves? Misleading them into thinking that of all necromancers, *I'm* willing to help?

As we reached the drive, I turned to Gabrielle, to tell her . . . I didn't even know what. But when I looked, I saw only the empty sidewalk.

III

"Five years ago, in this very room, when we first decided to escalate our search for knowledge to the highest level, we made a pact."

She looked around the circle of faces, getting a nod from each member. There was no need to remind them what that pact had been. They were all educated and rational people. Indeed, that very rationality was what had led to the pact.

For over a decade they had searched for the secret that would unlock the arcane mysteries of the occult. It had to exist. Countless ancient texts detailing spells and rituals could not all be mere works of fancy. They were too pervasive, coming from every age, every civilization, every corner of the globe and yet, in many ways, so similar.

They'd come close several times. Even found success with minor magics. But what good was a spell that would levitate a pencil an inch? What they sought was true magic—the ability to fully control inanimate objects, the elements, human behavior, everything those old books promised.

For a long time there was one thing they'd refused to do. An ingredient they would not collect, one that many of the darkest, most obscure tomes called for. Even if that was the key, they'd find another way.

When they finally accepted that their progress had stalled—that they could go no further without help—they agreed to one human sacrifice, to reassure themselves that this wasn't the answer.

To be able to say "we did all we could do," they had to follow the practice most often prescribed. Not just human sacrifice, but the sacrifice of a child.

First, though, they'd needed to protect themselves against one another. They must all agree this was necessary. They must all participate. If it succeeded, they must agree that it would be repeated and that they would participate for as long as the group remained intact. Anyone who refused or changed his mind would forfeit his life.

Harsh, yes. But sound. Sharing responsibility meant sharing blame. That was the iron wall that would safeguard their secret.

And now they didn't need to know why they were being reminded. They had only to look around the circle and see who was missing.

Murray had not bounced back from his breakdown. For a while, he'd seemed fine. But he hadn't taken his share of the ash. A week later, he'd been late for a meeting. Missed a second. Withdrew from the group socially. Found excuses, made apologies. The vacation they'd insisted on had only made matters worse, as if it gave him time to dwell on his misgivings.

"Don has come to me with troubling news," she said.

Don nodded, face grave. "Murray has asked for a job transfer. Out of state."

A murmur of alarm.

"He didn't tell me directly," Don continued, "but when I stopped by his house to speak to him last week, I saw Realtor business cards on his table, and overheard him on a call to his firm's Rhode Island office."

"Should we . . . ?" Brian swallowed, as if his throat had gone too dry to continue. "Should we wait and see how it plays out, in case he changes his mind?"

She felt a twinge of annoyance, but reminded herself that this was the first time their pact had been tested. They were still civilized beings, capable of considering all options and allowing the possibility of mercy. So she nodded to Tina, ceding the floor to the psychologist.

Tina shook her head. "The only way to change his mind would be to remind him of the pact. To threaten him."

Brian shuffled, clearly uncomfortable with the option. As he should be—they weren't thugs.

"And even if we resort to threats, given Murray's personality, he will pretend to acquiesce, but inwardly become more resolved to leave the group. He will cover his tracks better, so we can't find him. If cornered he'll be more likely to betray us."

She let Tina's words settle over the room. Waited for everyone to absorb the idea. Give them the chance to question it. Then, when no one did, she said, slowly and carefully, "Are we agreed?"

They were.

MURRAY CAME to the next meeting, and they'd done what needed to be done. Now the others were gone and his corpse lay on the gurney. She and Don would dispose of it. There was no need to involve the entire group in that process—and safer if they didn't. Take part in the killing, yes. Know where to find the body? No.

Don was examining Murray's naked body as if it were nothing more than a medical school cadaver.

"He's a lot bigger than that teenager," he mused. "I'd suggest removing the limbs and head and disposing of them as we did the boy—in garbage bags."

She agreed.

He glanced from his tools to the small oven, then over at her.

"Waste not, want not," she said. "The others don't need to know. It will be an excellent way to conduct a blind test of the effectiveness of adult material."

He nodded and lifted his scalpel.

THE EHRICH WEISS SOCIETY

AT FIVE-THIRTY, I WAS BACK IN L.A. with Jeremy, walking to yet another office building, this one in a far better section of town. The directory was peopled with accounting firms, law offices and other professional sorts. The elevators coming down were jammed with fleeing workers, but going up we had one to ourselves. Hope pressed the button for the tenth-floor law office of Donovan, Murdoch and Rodriguez.

"Our contact is the head of the group," she said as the door closed. "May Donovan."

"A lawyer?" I said.

"These guys are professionals, in every sense of the word. We've got a couple of lawyers, a United Church minister, a psychiatrist, an *L.A. Times* journalist, a professor or two... All folks who take this kind of thing very seriously and can contribute to the cause in their own way. Like May. She does primarily commercial law, but she has a sideline helping clients fleeced by paranormal scams. Not a lot of money in it—mostly pro bono, I think—but she's very passionate about it. They all are."

The doors opened into a quiet lobby, the silence broken only by burbling water—a fountain set in the wall, water cascading over an artfully arranged rock pile. I could hear the faintest tinkle of Japanese music. The walls were done in muted shades of gray and yellow. The thick carpet absorbed all noise. Very Zen.

Though it was just past five, the office seemed empty except for a woman leaning over the receptionist counter, reaching down to peck at the keys and straining to see the distant monitor. She was tall and slender, maybe late forties, with short graying brown hair, a long patrician nose and stylish glasses. She glanced up.

"Caught me checking my stocks." Her voice was low and pleasant, with an accent I couldn't place. "Nasty habit. I know I should just wait out the bad days, but I can't help peeking." She put her hands on Hope's shoulders in a semiembrace. "Good to see you."

Hope performed the introductions.

May caught my hand in a warm, firm grasp. "Jaime Vegas. I read something about you being in town. A TV special, isn't it?"

"Yes. In Brentwood. Trying to raise the ghost of Marilyn Monroe." I rolled my eyes. "Cheesy as hell but entertaining . . . we hope."

"I'm sure it will be. I was at a show of yours in L.A. a few years back."

"Oh?" I managed a laugh. "Checking up on me?"

"No, actually I was taking my mother. My father had died a few months before and she was having a rough time of it. She'd never been a religious person, and I think that made it harder. She needed . . ." May pursed her lips, as if searching for the right word. "Reassurance. I knew from our dossier that your shows do that very well. Benign spiritualism. I was hoping that might help her, and it did."

"Oh."

"You look shocked." A mischievous glint lit her dark eyes as she laid a hand on my arm. "Rather like hearing about a temperance advocate visiting a saloon? Think of us more like MADD. We don't argue that people should turn away from the paranormal, only that it be used responsibly. For entertainment, yes. For setting a grieving mind at rest, yes. Where we become concerned is when it is misused."

She led us through the office, still talking.

"They say that if you scratch a cynic, you'll find a disappointed idealist underneath. That holds true for many of our members, myself included. Some of us have had bad experiences with paranormal scams. Others, like myself, are fascinated by the paranormal, and disappointed by our inability to find proof of its existence."

She opened a door and ushered us into a huge office. "As a child, I devoured stories of witches, vampires, werewolves, ghosts . . . I couldn't get enough. Then, in my teens, I began 'the quest' as so many do. Ghost hunting, paranormal groups, faith experimentation, I did it all. Nothing but disappointment. Or so I thought, until I realized I *had* gained something from it. Knowledge. Having been burned, I could see through the scams. Together with a few contacts I'd made along the way, I decided to put that experience to good use and the Ehrich Weiss Society was born." She glanced at us. "Do you know who Ehrich Weiss was?"

My mind went blank and I'm sure my face followed.

"Harry Houdini," Jeremy said.

May nodded. "Our choice of name reflects our philosophy. Harry Houdini was, in his time, both a debunker and a seeker. He uncovered many paranormal scams, and offered ten thousand dollars to any medium who could produce evidence of the afterlife under rigorous scientific conditions. Yet he gave his wife a prearranged message so that he could make contact from the afterlife. Exposing frauds while hoping for proof."

At the back of her office, she unlocked a door and pushed it open. "And here is the inner sanctum. It's a little unsettling the first time, so I'll leave the door open while I get coffee. Two other members of our group are joining us. They should be here soon."

"UNSETTLING" WAS one word for it, particularly after the Zen peacefulness of the rest of the suite. Like big-game hunters displaying mounted heads on the wall, this group displayed its trophies—paraphernalia from scams they'd busted. Beneath each was a newspaper clipping announcing the bust. I saw everything from tarot cards to a shrunken head, a wooden wand to an ornate sacrificial knife, an "ectoplasm" photo to a jar containing something I didn't want to speculate on.

"Are these real?" I asked.

"Depends on your definition of real." Hope glanced out the door, making sure May wasn't coming back. "Like that dried-up hand. The Hand of Glory. I've heard that some real witches and sorcerers use them, but that one's a fake. Fake in the sense that it's not really magical. Not fake in the sense that . . . well, it's a real hand."

I glanced at the shrunken head.

"Yep, that's real too," she said. "As for how I know that, let's just say I have it on impeccable authority."

"A vision?" Jeremy asked as he sat down.

She nodded. "Completely freaked me out the first time May brought me in here. I was sucked right into the Amazon and watched the former owner of the head lose it."

"That's your power, isn't it?" I said. "You see . . ."

"Death, destruction and all that fun stuff. Other half-demons get a special power without a demon's attraction to chaos. That attraction is *all* I get. Raw deal."

She said it lightly, but her expression wasn't nearly so flippant. I thought about that—walking into a place where someone died and not seeing a ghost, but flashing back to the death itself. Seeing it. Hearing it. Smelling it. Living it.

Maybe seeing ghosts wasn't so bad after all.

MAY INTRODUCED us to Rona Grant and Zack Flynn, and explained their backgrounds.

Rona Grant was a medical researcher, one of the founding members of the group. In the eighties, when she'd considered a career in psychiatry, her mentor had specialized in satanic-cult memory retrieval. In other words, he'd take patients with a specific set of presenting factors and "regress" them, where they'd discover they'd been child victims of satanic ritual abuse. What Rona saw in those sessions had made her uncomfortable enough to do some research of her own, and she'd become one of the leading proponents of the "false-memory syndrome" theory, which says that our memories, far from being representations of fact, are a mix of fact and fantasy. The work of Rona and others proved that most of the memories of these satanic-cult victims were, in fact, therapy-induced fantasies.

Zack Flynn was a newer member, not much older than Hope—the *L.A. Times* journalist she'd mentioned. His claim to fame had been a series of investigative reports, uncovering a pair of fortune tellers whose seemingly harmless business working the psychic-fair circuit had masked a multimillion-dollar identity theft ring. His area of expertise didn't seem likely to help us, but seeing him sneak sidelong glances at Hope, after May made sure they sat together, I could tell Hope's mother's society friends weren't the only ones playing matchmaker.

May had already explained our cover story to the others—which was that, having seen many cases of "paranormal abuse" myself, I was considering a documentary on the subject. While my area was spiritualism, my backers wanted to include more sensational topics, like ritual abuse, animal sacrifice—even, perhaps, human sacrifice. What I was looking for, then, was local groups who either laid claim to such things or were rumored to engage in the practices.

"An excellent subject," May said. "And welcome exposure for our cause. As titillating as such topics are, it is too easy to vilify innocent people. Wiccans, for example, are some of the most peaceable people I know, yet they're reviled as witches. And don't even get me started on the misunderstandings about the church of Satan. Even reasonable people who hold no prejudice against Wiccans and other pagans would hide their cats and babies if a satanist moved in next door."

Rona said, "Which is not to say that there aren't people out there practicing animal sacrifice and such. It does happen. As for who you could talk to . . ."

The three brainstormed a short list of contacts. Most were not practitioners, but experts or former practitioners with groups known or believed to practice the "darker arts." As shortcuts went, this one was more safe than short—circumventing the dangerous underbelly of the pseudoparanormal world. That underbelly was where we'd have to eventually go, but there was no way to tell these people that—not with the cover story we'd given.

We took the names, chatted for a bit, then thanked them. May gave us her phone numbers and offered to help in any way she could. As May and Rona led Jeremy and me out, I glanced back at Hope. She was laughing at something Zack said, and waved us on. In the lobby, May and Rona headed down to the underground lot while Jeremy and I went out the front door.

"Should we wait for Hope?" I said.

"We'll start walking. I expect she'll be along soon."

"Guess she's not seeing Karl Marsten anymore, huh?"

He glanced at me, brows knitting. "Oh, you mean..." He nodded. "As for Karl, I'm not certain she ever was involved with him. Whatever their relationship, they're still in contact. In staying behind to chat with that young man, I think she has something other than romance in mind. Did you notice when they were giving us the list? He clearly wanted to add something, but was uncertain."

"Missed that completely. I was busy jotting down names and groaning over the thought of doing all these interviews."

He chuckled. "I don't blame you."

"So you think the group's hiding something? Something they didn't want Zack telling us?"

Jeremy shook his head. "My guess is it's a wild—"

"Jaime?"

I turned to see Rona hurrying up behind us. Jeremy arched a brow my way, as if to say that Zack might not be the only one who hadn't spoken up inside.

"Sorry," Rona said as she caught up, her large form shaking as she wheezed from the exertion. "I wanted to give you my card. May can be difficult to contact at times—especially on court days."

She handed us each a business card.

"Please don't hesitate to contact me if you have questions or if you just want a sounding board. The paranormal can be a confusing area to navigate, and a guide is always useful."

"I'm sure that's true," Jeremy said. "Thank you."

When she left, Jeremy watched her go, then steered me into a coffee shop. "Let's take a seat in the window and watch for Hope."

HOPE PASSED the coffee shop window a few minutes later, as Jeremy was still waiting in line. I waved her in. Jeremy called her over to get her order, then joined us with take-out coffees. We headed outside.

"Did Flynn tell you whatever he was holding back in the meeting?" Jeremy asked.

"You picked that up too? You should be a reporter. Yes, Zack has a source he wanted to pass on, a shady one—and probably an unreliable one."

"Which is why he was reluctant to mention it in front of the others."

She nodded. "May is trying to give us respectable contacts. This guy is anything but. His name is Eric Botnick. Straddles the line between serious practitioner and wannabe. He runs an occult shop and heads a group that calls itself the Disciples of Asmodai. Not affiliated with any known faith practice. Into some . . . questionable stuff."

"How questionable?" I asked.

"Mainly sexual. Definitely not to be confused with Wiccan or tantric sex magic. This is hard-core S & M. Emphasis on submission and dominance. Group sex with bondage, flagellation and bloodletting. It's supposed to release magical energies."

"Uh-huh."

"Exactly. The whole thing sounds like an excuse to indulge in some hard-core fetishes. But Zack says Botnick is very serious about the magic angle, even if his group members may be there to scratch other itches."

"Any link to children?" I asked.

"As far as Zack knows, the Disciples are all consenting adults. While they haven't found any cause for concern, the group keeps a close eye on them. Zack says May has it in for Botnick."

"She thinks he's into something darker than consensual bondage?"

"Zack seems to think May just doesn't like *that* part, but May's never struck me as the closed-minded sort. Live and let live, I think she'd say . . . unless she suspected not all the women in the group were as consenting as Botnick claims. Then she'd be all over it."

"Ah."

"Now, with the cover story you gave, it's this Disciples of Asmodai group that Zack thinks might interest us. But what I think you'll find more interesting is something else about Botnick. One of Zack's informants in this underground told him that Botnick's been promising his group that something big is on the horizon. He's been hinting at a major breakthrough. Something about powerful magic. True magic."

I choked on my coffee. Jeremy patted my back.

"Sorry," Hope said. "I should have prefaced that by saying it sounds like a better lead than it probably is. According to Zack, Botnick has serious credibility issues. The guy's been promising his followers this 'true magic' for months. Zack thinks it's just a ploy to keep disgruntled Disciples from leaving the flock. He hasn't even mentioned it to May and the others—he had an embarrassing experience last year when he gave May a hot tip about Botnick that went nowhere and she was not pleased."

"Still sounds like something we need to check out."

DISCIPLES OF ASMODAI

HOPE FOUND WORK AND HOME ADDRESSES for Botnick. Jeremy, with his new prepaid cell, headed out on a tracking expedition. He invited me along, but I figured I'd only get in the way. Hunting was his area. I'd stay behind with Hope as she dug up details on the contact names the Ehrich Weiss Society had provided us.

We went to her office. No need to worry about being caught researching S & M cults on an office computer—in Hope's line of work, she'd get commended for putting in the extra effort.

No one else was working overtime. The office was barely larger than her apartment, and not nearly as clean. It stank of burned coffee, stale burritos and overflowing ashtrays that shot a middle finger to the state's workplace smoking ban.

There was one semiprivate room, presumably for the editor. In the main area, a central table was covered with papers, printers and fax machines. Four to six desks were crammed along the walls—it was tough to tell the exact number, the way papers spilled from one surface to the next, and cables snaked everywhere.

As we picked our way through the cable jungle, Hope explained that few of the staff worked from the office. Most spent their days on the streets, tracking down the latest celebrity infidelity or plastic surgery rumor.

We'd just settled in when Jeremy called to say he'd found Botnick closing down his shop. He'd follow him and see where he went.

When I hung up, Hope was tapping away at the keyboard. I glanced at a stack of papers. The top one looked like an edited printout of an article with her byline.

"Mind if I . . . ?" I waved at the article.

"Enjoy. Oh, and I think we need to bring that particular case to the attention of the council right away. Definitely threat potential."

"Demon transmitters in breast implants?"

"Hey, at least it's not alien transmitters. You have no idea how sick I am of aliens—sightings, implants, abductions . . . it never ends. But demons? That's a lot rarer. Obviously the whole 'impregnating human women and creating a master race to take over the world' thing isn't working out for them. If I'm the best they can do, the apocalypse is in serious trouble. As a backup plan, controlling large-breasted women isn't too shabby."

"Start with subliminal messages in *Hustler*. Work your way up to *Playboy* . . . I can see it."

"If anyone can bring down the politicians in this country, it's hot women with breast implants."

I laughed. "Any more tips for the council in here?" I asked, pointing to the stack.

"Nah. There's a piece on a body found with fang marks. Cassandra and Aaron suspect it's a vampire's annual kill. They're investigating, and will give the careless vamp a slap on the wrist, but they told me not to bother killing the story. Corpses with fang marks? Passé. And even if my editor had wanted me to investigate it for a full-blown article, I could convince him it wasn't worth the inches. That's mostly what I do—not so much suppressing real supernatural stories as downplaying them and, in most cases, like this one, even that isn't necessary."

"Must be an . . . interesting job."

She grinned. "Oh, come on. Say it. Cheesy is the word."

"You're talking to a woman who pretends to contact the dead and returns the same message every time. Cheesy is my life."

"Fun, isn't it?"

I smiled. "Yes. Yes, it is."

We talked about her job as she continued to search for information, multitasking like a pro. After a half hour, Jeremy called again to say he was outside Botnick's home. He'd keep watch for another hour or so, see whether this was just a pit stop or if the man was settling in for the night.

At nine-thirty, Jeremy checked in. Botnick—who lived alone—had eaten, and was now in front of the television. As it looked likely he was home for the duration, Jeremy decided it was a good opportunity to take a closer look at his store. He asked me to pass him to Hope.

At his request, she zoomed in on an aerial photograph of Botnick's shop, then relayed its layout and potential entry points.

"So you're doing a little B & E?" she said. "Too bad Karl's in Massachusetts."

She paused.

"Ah, Arizona this week, is it? Glad someone knows where that man is. If you need him, though, you tell him to haul his ass over here. Whatever job he's pulling, he doesn't need the money and this is more important." She tapped at her keyboard. "Speaking of help, could you use ours? We can be there in—"

She paused. "No, I understand, but I could help. Karl's taught me a few things about casing a place—strictly for information, of course—and I'm sure the extra eyes would come in handy."

Another pause. She nibbled her lip, eyes down as she listened.

"I know, but I'd love to help, risks or no risks. Hey, if things do go wrong, I'll even take the fall for you. I'm an ambitious tabloid reporter—no one's going to question why I'm breaking into a place like that. Plus, it's experience, right? If I'm helping the council, I need to build up my arsenal of skills, legal and otherwise."

There was a note of puppyish pleading in her voice. She reminded me of Paige—always in the thick of things, taking any risk to help others. Frustrated from hours of research, I found myself sharing her enthusiasm, even seconding it loud enough for Jeremy to overhear.

After a moment, she grinned at me, flashed a thumbs-up, then handed back my phone. "He wants us to meet him in the lot behind the shop in ninety minutes. That'll give him time to find a way in first."

She turned back to her computer, continuing down the list.

"So Karl Marsten is giving you break-and-enter tips?"

"Against his will. He doesn't like me doing stuff like that. But we have an agreement. He teaches me B & E and I cook for him. You know werewolves." She grinned. "Feed them well and feed them often, and you can win any argument."

I wished it were that easy with Jeremy. For him, food was just fuel. Which was okay with me, because cooking—like most domestic skills—wasn't one of my strong points.

"So I guess you and Karl are together?"

"Nah. Just friends." She printed off a page. "That's strange enough. I'm a half-demon with delusions of crime fighting. He's a werewolf jewel thief. Logically, we shouldn't be able to stand one another. But as a friendship, it works." She hit "print" again, then pushed back her chair. "Okay, let's see what we've got."

WE WERE eyeing the clock when Hope's cell phone rang. As she glanced at the display, she cursed under her breath, hesitated, then seemed to think better of it and answered. A string of "uh-huhs" followed, her shoulders slumping with each one.

After listening to the caller for at least thirty seconds, she said, "Could this wait until morning? I'm hot on a trail tonight—"

Pause.

"It's still in the early stages, but it's about ritual magic—"

Pause.

"I know we covered that new Voodoo club opening last month, but this is different—"

Pause. She closed her eyes, sighing softly.

"Yes, yes, I'm sure a 'Bigfoot in L.A.' story doesn't come along all that often but—"

Pause. A deeper sigh.

"Okay, I'm on it."

When she hung up, I said, "Bigfoot?"

"Apparently he's been spotted cutting through an alley near a nightclub."

I paused. "I hate to break it to you, but it's probably—"

"A guy promoting a new movie? Or 'Monster Pizza'? I know. So does my editor. It doesn't matter. The point is that multiple witnesses claimed to have seen Bigfoot. That's indisputable. So I go out, interview some stoned clubbers, collect grainy cell-phone pictures of the monster and write it up under the headline 'Bigfoot Spotted in L.A.?' "

"I see."

"It's the question mark that makes the difference. We're not saying he *was* in L.A., just that the claim was made."

"Uh-huh."

"Tabloid journalism: where the truth comes with many loopholes, and we know how to exploit every one of them."

She turned off her computer. "The club is on the way to Botnick's place. We can share a cab. I'm going to whip through this monster story, then fly back to help you guys."

I HAD the taxi driver drop me off a block from the shop, just in case Botnick reported the break-in later. As I scanned the road, lined with pawn shops and massage parlors, I realized I was being overcautious. Break-ins in this neighborhood wouldn't warrant more than a police drop-in. Even if someone did canvass the taxi companies' drop-offs, I looked suspicious only in that I didn't seem like someone seeking a late-night body rub. Giving them maybe.

My clicking heels echoed like a siren's call to would-be muggers. I walked slower, trying to muffle the sound. Rather than fret over being dropped off too close to the scene, I should have been considering the wisdom of wearing high heels to a break-and-enter.

Behind me, a car rounded the corner, engine revving. I walked faster. The entrance to the shop parking lot was less than a store length away. Better to get there before the oncoming car reached me or I might suffer the humiliation of being mistaken for a hooker within earshot of Jeremy. I did up a button and walked faster.

"Jaime?"

I jumped. Jeremy stepped from an alcove, hand going to my arm to steady me. I rapped him with my knuckles.

"We're belling you. I swear it."

He smiled, then scanned the street. "Is Hope coming?"

"Bigfoot took her away." I explained. "But she'll phone if she finishes in the next hour or so."

I let him guide me down the sidewalk. "Did you get inside already?"

He nodded. "Botnick seems the type who relies more on steel doors and bars than alarms. Probably wise in a neighborhood like this."

"But not so smart if your break-in artist has superhuman strength."

"Hmm. Still not easy, but I found a way."

He steered me into a gravel parking lot boxed in by buildings, each wall peppered with more No Parking signs than there were spots to park. It looked barely big enough to fit a couple of cars and a delivery truck—a small one.

The full moon shone from a multitude of rut puddles. A bright yellow orb with not so much as a wisp of cloud over it. I looked at Jeremy, but knew the full moon meant little to him. Real werewolves need to change form more than once a month, and they do so on demand, not with the phases of the moon. He'd said once that they often did take advantage of full moons for hunts, but only because it was easier to see.

I caught a movement in the shadows. Jeremy's head swung toward it, hand gripping my arm tighter, pulling me back as if shielding me. A cat slunk between trash bins. Seeing us, it froze. Its orange fur puffed up as it spit and hissed, a feline fireball, bright against the gloom. Jeremy made a noise deep in his throat. The cat tore off, its paws scrabbling against the gravel, a fiery streak racing for cover.

I twisted to say something, but Jeremy was scanning the lot, eyes narrowed, making sure that the cat was the only intruder. His hand still gripped my arm and he kept me so close I could feel the thump of his heart against my shoulder. His face was taut and wary, mouth a thin line, the pulse in his neck throbbing. When I shifted, he loosened his grip and rubbed my arm, as if reflexively reassuring me, his gaze and mind still busy checking for danger.

One last scan, then his hand slid to squeeze mine as he passed me a crooked smile, as if he didn't like being caught doing something that came naturally to a werewolf, but might look odd to me.

He led me to the farthest door. It was solid metal, and I could see no sign that it had been pried open, yet the plastic Deliveries plaque over the bell confirmed it was Atrum Arcana, Botnick's store.

"How did you get—"

He was already gliding alongside the building and came to a stop at a wooden box with a hinged lid. A garbage bin, judging by the stink and the oozing puddles beneath. He bent, getting a grip on the box, and heaved it away from the wall. Behind it was a window with a rack of bars propped beside it.

"I don't suppose those were already conveniently removed," I whispered.

He shook his head.

"Impressive."

A graceful shrug. "They weren't affixed very well. More for show, I'd wager. He probably thinks hiding the window is security enough. Not much of a challenge."

"You sound disappointed."

A soft laugh. He motioned me closer to the open window. As he handed me a flashlight, I noticed he was wearing gloves.

"Only brought one pair, I'm afraid," he whispered. "Not very well prepared."

"You bought gloves and a flashlight. I showed up in a skirt and heels. Who's not prepared?"

"Breaking and entering was hardly on our minds when I picked you up at the house."

"Maybe so, but next time, I'm packing a bag."

He helped me through. With the moonlight blocked by the trash bin, the room was pitch black. Even the flashlight only illuminated a basketball-size circle. I cast it around as he crawled in behind me.

It looked like a storage closet. In front of me, a shelf held mail-order supplies—stacks of folded boxes and bags of packing material. To my left, there was a narrow shelf tower with floor cleaner, bleach, rags, drain opener, rat poison and cat food. On first seeing the cat food, the optimist in me wanted to say, "See, the guy may run a hard-core sex cult, but he still feeds the neighborhood strays." Seeing the food next to the rat poison, though, I had to suspect it was more a lure than a handout. You can't run a decent black-magic cult without sacrificing a cat now and then.

Jeremy was leaning out the window, pulling the trash bin back into place. As I turned, I saw that the storage closet also doubled as the shop bathroom. No sign of a sink. Very sanitary.

There was a stack of reading material by the toilet. Magazines. The top one showed a woman bound and gagged, her eyes rolling in helpless terror. Judging by the size of her breasts, though, she wasn't *completely* helpless—swing one of those at the right angle and you could knock a guy out.

Jeremy stepped up beside me. His gaze followed the flashlight beam.

I whispered, "Something tells me the Disciples get more inspiration from those than from Asmodai."

He shook his head and looked away, distaste on every feature.

I reached for the door handle, then stopped and waved Jeremy forward. He opened it, then took off one glove and passed it to me. When I started to refuse, he pushed it into my hand.

"You can't search if you can't touch anything."

I pulled the glove on. "Is there anything else? Security cameras maybe?"

He shook his head. That made sense. A place like this, the clientele wouldn't want to be caught on camera.

We stepped inside.

HARD CORE

THE DOOR OPENED BEHIND A SALES COUNTER. My gaze went to the gray safe under it.

"Even *you* can't break that open," I whispered.

"I shouldn't need to. Imagine you're Botnick—"

"Rather not."

He smiled. "For the sake of argument only. If this store is robbed, where's the first place a serious thief will go, after the cash register?"

I pointed to the safe.

"So, while you may keep files, checks and valuable merchandise in there, it's not the place for anything not easily replaced, including items you can't report to an insurance company."

"Like a spellbook, a ritual journal or a list of contacts. Is that the kind of thing we're looking for?"

He nodded. "Documents, primarily. Books, journals, correspondence, contact lists, anything related to magic or his cult. I'm going to search his office. Could you take the shop floor?"

"Will do."

THE MAIN area displayed a mix of occult and S & M paraphernalia, everything from magic fetishes to toys for fetishists. Pretty mild stuff on both counts. A wall display of handcuffs, from metal to rubber to candy. A bookshelf of titles—*Occult Mysteries Revealed* and *Rituals for Beginners*—the type of texts you'd find in a regular bookstore. A rack of whips that looked more like props than torture devices. Candles, amulets, chalices, even a display of organic herbal teas made by a local Wiccan.

Keeping my flashlight down, so the light couldn't be seen through the smoked front window, I flipped through a few items. Under the displays, I found cupboards, but they were all unlocked and held only extra stock of items already out.

To the far left was a closed door marked Employees Only. Not a bathroom, which I'd already found. Not the office—Jeremy was in there. I walked over and tried the handle. Locked.

"Jeremy?" I whispered. "Got a locked door."

He stepped from the office, walked over and bent to check the lock.

"Looks like a good, sharp twist—" I began.

He held up a key ring.

"—or the key," I finished as he tried one.

"Makes our entry less obvious. I found them under the register. The office was locked, as well, so I think there should be one for—" The lock clicked. "There."

He opened the door. Pitch black. He peered around the corner, eyes narrowing as he strained to see, his night vision probably as good as my flashlight. I tapped his arm.

"I've got it," I said.

A small smile. "Sorry. Just curious."

He backed out and returned to the office.

I stepped through the doorway into a space no bigger than a closet and bare, with curtains on either side. I picked the one on my right and pulled it back. Inside was a larger storage area, maybe as big as the one we'd first entered. It was lined with shelves filled with boxes and jars.

I lifted the light to one large jar and jumped back. Inside, a fetus floated in preservative. I scanned the bottles. Mostly body parts. Organs, it looked like. I shone the flashlight into a box. It was filled with bags, each containing a dried piece of something . . . or someone.

All the bags and jars were labeled, but only with reference numbers. The code was probably in the office. I'd get Jeremy to look, but first I rifled through the bags, trying to ignore a pair of floating eyeballs that stared down at me.

Dried bits I can handle—been doing it all my life. It was hard to tell how many of these were human. Many were just indistinguishable, shriveled gray pieces. Some were clearly not human: a bat wing, a furry tail, a pointed ear. I pushed aside a bag of teeth—sharp, probably rodent. Underneath was something definitely human: a thumb. I lifted it. Even dried and shriveled, it was obviously adult.

I peered into the box. Under where the thumb had lain there was a tube of dried skin. Too big to be a finger. I lifted the bag into the light, took a better look and—yep, human. Male human. Definitely not something you'd find in *my* bag of body bits.

I looked at the rows of boxes and jars. Time to get Jeremy. As I backed up, my heel caught on something and I looked down. It was an odd place for an area rug. My heel had tugged it aside to reveal wood set into the concrete. I bent and peeled back the rug. Dust flew up. As I coughed, I thought of the dried bits and *hoped* this was dust.

Under the rug lay a trap door. Hinged. A recessed handle. No obvious lock. I grabbed the handle and gave an experimental tug. Nothing. I pulled hard. The door swung open. A ladder stretched into darkness. Even with the flashlight, all I could see was a narrow chute.

Definitely time to get Jeremy.

I closed the trap door.

As I pushed back the curtain, I remembered the room across the way. I should peek in there, so I could tell him I'd checked out everything. I opened the other curtain and . . . stared. A metal helmet stared back. Dull black metal with tiny nose holes, the eyes and mouth solid. There was a hinge on one side and a lock on the other. I thought of it closing over my head and instinctively gasped for air.

I pulled my gaze from the helmet and looked around. It was another storeroom, with shelves and hooks, stocked not with body parts but bondage gear. The room stunk with the ripe scent of leather and sweat and something acrid, vaguely familiar. Urine.

As I pulled back, my gaze went to a whip—one that bore no resemblance to the toys out front. Braided leather, with the braids undone at the end, each strand finished with a metal weight. The strands were stained dark. Blood.

I consider myself sexually experienced. Very sexually experienced, and for me, sex has always been about entertainment. But looking over those shelves, I felt like a convent girl.

"I think we can safely assume that we won't find any answers in there," Jeremy murmured at my shoulder.

I jumped, covered it with a small laugh. "Scary stuff, huh? Most of it, I can only guess what it's used for. And some of it, I don't even want to guess. That helmet alone is enough to give me nightmares." I let the curtain fall. "I was just coming to get you. I found a few things in there." I pointed at the other curtain.

"Good. I was hoping you were having more luck than me."

He pulled back the other curtain and surveyed the shelves, frowning.

"Parts, dried and pickled," I said. "And for me, way less disturbing than what's in that other room. This stuff—the dried bits at least—are right up my alley. I've identified some of them. Most seem to be animal." I lifted the bat wing. "A few hidden at the bottom are obviously human." I lifted a few more: the ear, the toe, the teeth and the "tube."

Jeremy frowned at the tube. "What is—? Ah, I see."

"Male."

"It would appear so."

"And almost certainly adult, despite the shrinkage." I waved at the jars. "I'm not so good with the pickled and the less whole pieces. You're better at anatomy, so I was hoping you could identify them."

He scanned the shelf. "Most are organs, primarily animal, though it's not always easy to tell."

I lifted my gaze to the floating fetus. "And that?"

"Pig."

"Whew."

He moved a couple of jars aside with his gloved hand, to get a look at the ones behind them.

"Before you get too involved in identification, there's something else I should show you."

I pointed the flashlight at the trap door.

"Now, that's promising." He opened it and peered down.

"See anything?"

"Not without going down." He turned around and started doing just that.

"Are you sure we should?"

He paused. "You're right. You'd better wait here."

That wasn't what I meant, but he'd already vanished into the darkness.

I knelt and leaned into the hole.

"Jeremy?" I passed down the flashlight.

"No," he said. "You keep—"

"Take it. All I'm doing is sitting here."

He came up a couple of stairs and took the flashlight, then disappeared, and the room went dark. Very dark. I lifted my hand and couldn't see it.

I tried not to think of those suspended eyeballs staring down at me.

A random thought flashed through my brain. Was there any chance I could reanimate those . . . bits? By accident? I tried not to think of it but, of course, thought of it all the more, images of B-grade horror movies flashing past, those bits and pieces taking on life—

Silly, of course. It's tough enough for a necromancer to bring a full body back to life. Not the sort of thing I could do accidentally—thank God. And if a zombie loses a body part—which they tend to do, with the rotting and all—the parts don't stay alive, creeping along of their own volition. But how much of a corpse had to be left in order to be raised? Would a head be enough? Were there any heads in those jars?

A light flickered in the hole. Jeremy coming back? The light bobbed away again. I stuck my head down as far as I could without toppling in headfirst, but the ladder stretched down a chute at least four feet long. I twisted around and put my foot on the first rung. Just a quick peek.

My toes slid off the rung and I had to catch the edge of the hatch to keep from falling.

Yet another reason why heels were a really bad idea. Maybe if I took them off . . . No, I'd probably miss the rungs in the dark and still fall down the ladder.

Someone laughed. I went still. A muffled male voice. Ghosts? A rattle, then the creak of an opening door, keys jangling against the steel.

"Think we're the first ones here."

"Looks like it." A woman. "Oh, here comes Eric."

Okay, not ghosts. Worse. I leaned into the hatch to call for Jeremy, then froze, picturing the open door just a few feet away. Feeling my way out, I went through the curtain, then slid behind the half-open door.

"Where's that light switch?" the woman asked.

"Beside the front door."

"Ah."

I eased the storeroom door shut with a quiet click.

"Let there be light. Hey, Eric..."

As the voices continued, I hurried back to the trap door, hands out again, feeling my way in the pitch blackness. As the curtain tickled my fingertips, I paused. Should I lock the door first? I hadn't felt a locking mechanism when I'd closed it. Did you need the key to relock it? Or, worse, did it engage automatically, and I'd just locked us in?

No time to check. I pushed past the curtain, then pulled up short as I envisioned myself falling through the hatch. I crouched and felt my way forward. A flicker of light from below answered my question. Before it disappeared, I found and gripped the opening, then I ducked my head into the hole.

"Jeremy?" I whispered.

My voice echoed in the chute. No answer came from below.

More laughter and more voices from the shop. Why were people coming here after midnight?

Uh, probably because the shop's owner is the head of a sex cult. They wouldn't hold their meetings Saturday afternoons at the library.

"Jeremy?"

My whisper bounced around again in the chute, swallowed by bad acoustics.

A voice sounded just outside the door—the door to the storeroom containing the magic and bondage gear needed for a proper sex cult meeting.

I found the ladder. Took two steps down. Paused. Maybe they'd go for drinks or something first. Loosen up the inhibitions. Always worked for me.

Keys rattled, then slid into the storage room keyhole. I grabbed the hatch lid with one hand and the rug with the other, and closed the door as I pulled the rug over it. It wouldn't be perfect, but it should pass a casual glance.

I hurried down the ladder, my toes somehow managing to keep their traction until I reached the bottom.

The roving light swung my way. I raised my finger to my lips and hurried forward, my heels clicking on the concrete. I stopped to yank them off. When I lifted my head, Jeremy was beside me.

"People," I whispered, pointing up.

A soft curse. He looked up, as if straining to hear, then shook his head. The floor must have been too thick.

"Hmmm, what have we here?" a voice whispered in the dark.

I jumped, but Jeremy seemed unperturbed. I took the flashlight from him and shone it around. A heavyset, middle-aged man with a receding chin walked through a stack of boxes, his gaze fixed on me.

"A redhead. Very nice."

"Who are you?" I whispered.

The man stopped, squinting, as if trying to figure out who I was talking to. Jeremy looked down at me and frowned.

"Ghost," I whispered.

"Gho—" the man began, then curled his lip. "Necromancer. Tried to trick me with that flashlight, hiding your glow. If you're here to report me—"

"Report you for what?"

He dropped his gaze. "Nothing."

"Ask him if there's another way out," Jeremy said.

"Way out?" the ghost said, hearing him. "Now, why would you want to leave?" He bared his teeth in a nasty smile. "I think you're really going to enjoy yourself."

I cast the light around. We stood in the middle of a large basementlike room with concrete floor and walls. To my left, some occult symbols had been painted on the floor . . . right beside a row of hooks embedded in the concrete. There were more hooks on the walls.

I turned to Jeremy. "I think we'd better find our own way out. Fast."

"Agreed, but . . ."

He looked around. I followed his gaze. A single room, with no adjoining doors or halls.

I turned to the ghost. "There's a way out, isn't there?"

He smiled.

"There is," I said to Jeremy. "Probably hidden behind these boxes and crates."

"You're not going to find it," the ghost said in a singsong voice. "It's very well hidden. And locked. Better just give up now."

Jeremy strode to the wall and waved me over. "You go that way. Stay along the wall. If you need any boxes moved, just whisper."

I nodded and we went in opposite directions.

Boxes and crates of various sizes were all around the perimeter, some stacked to the ceiling. I strapped my shoes together and draped them over my arm, then started moving along the wall, searching for any kind of door.

"Nice ass," the ghost said as he followed behind me. "Not too big, not too firm. You like to use it, don't you? Put that extra wiggle in your walk, teasing all the boys."

I reached the first stack of boxes. The gap behind it was big enough to slide through, so I did.

"You know what that says to me?" the ghost continued. "It says 'I'm just dying for you to throw me over a table, hike up my skirt and . . .' "

He kept talking. I stopped listening.

I reached a four-foot crate pushed against the wall. I grabbed the sides. It wouldn't budge.

"Jeremy?"

He was at my side before I could whisper again. One heft and the box was moved.

"Is that how you like them, hon?" the ghost said as we looked behind the box. "Strong men? Dominant men? Alpha males?"

I sputtered a laugh at the last. The ghost glared, this obviously not being the desired response. Jeremy glanced over and arched a brow.

"Just the ghost," I said as I moved along the wall.

"Is he bothering you?"

"Nah, just some old pervert waiting for the sex show."

The ghost's lips curled. "If I was alive, I'd teach you some manners. First I'd—"

"I'm sure there are lots of things you'd do to me if you were alive, but seeing as how you're not, I guess you're stuck with an eternity of watching and . . ." I made a jerk-off gesture.

Jeremy chuckled. The ghost started spitting threats and insults. I tuned him out and kept feeling along the wall.

"I've got it," I said as Jeremy pulled out a light stack of boxes for me. "You go on back."

Jeremy's head shot up, his gaze flying to the ladder. A laugh rang down it. He grabbed my arm and looked around.

"Now you're in for it, bitch," the ghost chortled. "A real prisoner. They'll like that."

I swung the flashlight beam around and stopped on a mountain of crates to our left.

HANGMAN

THE CRATES WERE STACKED three or four layers deep. Jeremy moved the front one just enough to squeeze through the gap, and waved for me to follow. He kept going, shifting stacks and sidestepping through. At the final row, he stopped and motioned for me to turn off the flashlight. I did just as he lifted a top box and stacked it on another.

Darkness fell. Feet clanked down the ladder. The swoosh of another moving box. A hand slid around my waist and guided me in farther.

The lights went on, and I saw that he'd cleared all but one box from a stack against the wall. A cubby seat. The crate was too small for us to sit side by side, so he gestured for me to turn and back onto his lap.

"You think that's going to save you?" the ghost sneered, his head sticking out from a crate. "They can still see you."

I was about to pull back farther, then took a better look. The path Jeremy had carved for us was zigzagged, meaning we couldn't see the main room from here . . . and no one in the main room could see us.

"Liar," I mouthed.

The ghost stalked off, probably hoping to alert the cult. Good luck with that.

The group filed in, chatting about their kids' baseball tournaments, layoffs at work, trouble with a broken dishwasher. I counted at least six distinct voices.

Scrapes and thuds followed, as if they were setting up something, probably an altar. They kept talking, the man with the appliance problem now soliciting advice on whether it was more cost-effective to hire a repairman or just replace the unit.

I wriggled back onto Jeremy's lap. He readjusted his hold on me, arms going around my stomach, as if reassuring me I was safe.

"They can't see us," he whispered.

His breath tickled the back of my ear and I shivered, thoughts of discovery vanishing as I became very aware of his body against my back. I shifted again, squirming in his lap, and felt him harden beneath me. I went still and concentrated on what was happening on the other side of the room instead. Wasn't easy, but after a moment, I made out the slap and hiss of matches being struck.

A faint smell of smoke, then the pungent scent of musky incense. The clink of thin metal. The glug of liquid. I pictured hammered chalices being filled with blood-red wine. In the background, one woman told the horror story of a recent appliance repair encounter—paying more to fix a ten-year-old stove than she'd have spent on a new one.

The low rumble of authority. Botnick. The voices faded, shuffles and clinks taking over as they arranged themselves, probably in some ritual circle.

Botnick intoned something in a foreign language—presumably an invocation to Asmodai. I'd spent enough time in spiritualism to know how these pseudorituals worked, and Botnick seemed to have it down.

When he finished, the Disciples took their turns pledging their body to Asmodai in English one by one. Eight people, including Botnick. Four men and four women.

I listened carefully to each voice, on the off chance I'd recognize one. Unlikely, but I listened anyway. From Jeremy's shallow breathing behind me, I suspected he was doing the same.

The ritual resumed with more foreign chanting from Botnick, his voice rising now to an impassioned boom. I longed to ask Jeremy what Botnick was saying—whether he could translate—but doubted it was more than gibberish.

Botnick's voice reached a fever pitch, then stopped, and all went silent.

"Now," he began. "We dedicate ourselves to the demon of lust, king of hell, prince of revenge, our Lord Asmodai."

Footsteps sounded, then a few foreign words, a sharp intake of breath, a choral chant, receding footsteps. The sequence repeated, then again, and I pictured each member walking to the middle of the circle for the dedication. Jeremy sniffed behind me and made a guttural noise, as if confirming a suspicion, and I knew what they were "dedicating." Blood. Dripped into a communal chalice, most likely.

The last member took her turn. Then a match was struck. More chanting. A faint, oddly metallic smell wafted over. Jeremy exhaled sharply, as if expelling the scent from his nose. The blood. It must have been dripped into a censer, not a chalice, and burned in dedication.

The chanting stopped.

"We receive the blessing of Asmodai," Botnick said. "And in return, we offer the mortification of our flesh, for his pleasure."

The glug-glug of wine being poured from a bottle. Then a scraping sound. Stirring—metal on metal. A gulp. The burned blood scraped and stirred into wine, then drunk. I shivered. Jeremy's arms tightened around me.

"Spirit of Asmodai!" Botnick cried. "I am yours to command."

Chanting from the group, rising in pitch. Then a snarl from Botnick.

"You," he said, his voice guttural, the word almost indistinguishable. "Prepare her."

The clink of chains, the click of locks, the slap of leather. Then it began.

The snap of the whip, the muffled cries of the gagged woman, smell of blood so strong even I could recognize it. And, worst of all, the shouts of the others, egging Botnick on, by turns ecstatic and enraged, lust perverted into bloodlust.

Hearing them earlier, chatting about broken appliances and children, I'd relaxed. Just repressed suburbanites playing S & M games. But now it was chillingly real. I could picture that woman, bloodied and writhing in pain—real pain, not the put-on horror of that woman on the magazine cover.

My stomach twisted, bile rising. I started to squirm, but Jeremy's hands went to my hips, holding me still. I flushed.

When I swallowed hard, Jeremy raised his hand to cover my left ear and leaned into my right, whispering, telling me to ignore it, to block it, but as hard as I tried, I couldn't. It was like upstairs, trying not to imagine accidentally reanimating those parts.

I thought of the ghost, tried concentrating on that pathetic spook getting his voyeuristic jollies, but then I heard his words again, about them finding me—a real prisoner—and my heart started hammering.

While that woman was genuinely in pain, presumably no one had coerced her into coming here. She'd submitted without protest. Maybe, in sexual dominance, that was the goal—willing submission. Or maybe it was just the closest facsimile they could get to what they really yearned for—an unwilling victim. If they found me here...

I tried not to think about it, but of course I did. I pictured that whip with the lead ends, that horrible mask, smelled the metal going around my head, felt the cold of it against my skin, the engulfing blackness, stealing my light, my breath, my screams...

"Shhh," Jeremy whispered, pulling me against him, his lips at my ear. "Block it out."

I tried. Really tried. Then I saw those jars, those bags, envisioned them not as magical aids stolen from graves and morgues—like my necromantic artifacts—but as body disposal, like hunters making use of every piece—

"They can't find you." Jeremy rubbed goose bumps from my arms. "I won't let them. You know that."

I nodded, but kept hearing fresh noises from beyond, grunts and whimpers, the sounds ping-ponging in my skull, refusing to leave, throwing up images...

I started to squirm again, then caught myself and stopped.

"Here," Jeremy whispered. He shifted me forward and took something from his jacket. His notepad, the pen stored in the coils. He flipped open the pad, past a few pages of notes to a clean sheet. He drew four lines—two horizontal and two vertical. Then he shifted me again, until I was leaning back against him, head in the dip of his shoulder as his chin rested on my shoulder, looking over it. He made an X in the center square and handed me the pen.

I stared at the paper, the layout he'd drawn so familiar I should recognize it, but my brain refused to work, still filled with unwanted sounds and unwelcome images. I blinked . . . and gave a silent laugh, seeing a tic-tac-toe board. I put on my O.

Every kid over the age of eight knows the trick to the game, but I was so preoccupied it took me a few rounds to remember how to win.

Once I remembered that, of course, the game lost its challenge. So he switched to hangman, starting with a four-letter animal. Got that one pretty quickly, and he doodled a wolf for me, then drew out a fresh game. On it went, with Jeremy challenging me with ever-tougher puzzles and making me smile with his doodles and intricate hanged-man sketches.

The sounds beyond seemed to fade into background noise, like an annoying neighbor playing his porn video with the volume jacked. My world narrowed to this little cubby, to the warmth of Jeremy's arms, stretched around me as he wrote, to the whispers that tickled my ear and vibrated down my back, to the scratch of his cheek against mine as he shifted, to the spicy smell of his breath—tacos or burritos grabbed on the run. I leaned against him, solved his puzzles and laughed at his drawings.

Who else would do this for me, play hangman while an S & M cult was in full swing only yards away? Who else would know it was exactly what I needed—a distraction so innocent, so innocuous, that it couldn't help but make what was happening out there seem equally harmless?

I didn't even notice that the ritual had ended, I was so engrossed in solving a hangman puzzle. The Disciples' conversation was sparse and subdued now, no one in the mood to discuss dishwashers. Chains rattled as they were unclipped. A hoarse voice asked for the wine. Chalices clinked as someone gathered them.

I went on to the next puzzle: a nine-letter American city. Minutes later, the basement light clicked off and the puzzle went dark.

The voices and footsteps receded as Jeremy put away his notepad. I slid from his lap, found the flashlight and turned it on, then picked up my shoes and slung them over my arm.

I whispered, "Do we wait for them to leave or try to find that alternate exit?"

"The latter is probably safer. Do you remember where you left off searching?"

I nodded, and slipped from the box maze. As I crossed the main area, I looked around it, ignoring the flecks of blood on the walls as I searched for the ghost. As unpleasant as he was, I might be able to blackmail him into telling us where to find that door, by threatening to "report" him. But there was no sign of the ghost. Typical. Always there when you don't need them, never when you do.

I found my place along the wall and resumed searching. I moved aside one box stack myself, then hit an immovable crate. Glancing toward Jeremy, I saw him crouched beside a dark square inset in the wall just on the other side of the ladder.

"Is that—?" I whispered, stopping as he heaved on the cover.

The crack of breaking metal. He pulled back the cover and stuck his head inside. I headed toward him.

As I neared the ladder, a foot appeared from the bottom of the chute. I stumbled back. Jeremy spun, seeing the foot appear and waving for me to take cover. I swung the flashlight along the nearest wall, stopping at the first stack tall enough to hide me. I turned off the light and raced forward, my hands out, measuring the distance and praying I was right.

My fingertips touched cardboard just as the main light came on. I swung behind the stack, my pulse racing, waiting for a shout.

When footsteps headed toward the other wall instead, along with a deep mutter of "where did I leave that?," I could breathe again. I hadn't been seen. Now I just had to relax while Botnick found whatever he'd left behind—

A shadow appeared across the floor, moving slowly, and I realized my mistake. I was hidden from the stairs, but not from the other half of the room. I glanced over my shoulder. Behind me was another box, on my other side. If I could wedge between the two, the shadows should hide me. I backed up into the gap. Too narrow. Using my hip and shoulder, I eased the one box over—

It scraped along the concrete, the soft whisper as loud as a shot. I froze. So did the shadow, now halfway into view.

"Hello?" Botnick called.

As he spoke, I eased back into the gap, wiggling and squeezing until I was—

Slap, slap, slap.

I looked down to see my dangling shoes swinging against the box.

ESCAPE HATCH

I GRABBED MY SWINGING SHOES with my free hand. A low chuckle sounded right in front of me, and I slowly lifted my head to see a bearded man standing less than ten feet away.

"Well, hello," Botnick said, his eyes locked on mine. "Come for the meeting? You're too late, but I'm sure I could arrange a private lesson."

He stepped forward. Eyes still on his, I resisted the urge to shrink back and flipped the shoes around so I gripped them just below the heel. Four-inch spikes. Maybe they were good for something after all.

Botnick kept strolling forward, in no rush, savoring the fear in my eyes. I let him have that, widening them and inching back, bringing my shoes up to my chest as if clutching them in fear, getting them higher, ready to—

A blur behind Botnick. The man flew from his feet as Jeremy swung him in a head lock. Botnick gasped for air, clawing at Jeremy's arm. Jeremy stood there, face impassive. When he tightened his grip, Botnick went wild, flailing and gasping. Jeremy relaxed his hold on Botnick's windpipe. Then he cupped his free hand under Botnick's jaw.

"Scream and I'll snap your neck. Understood?" Jeremy's tone was soft and even, like a patient teacher warning a difficult child.

When Botnick didn't respond, he tightened his grip on the man's jaw. Botnick's eyes flew open, wide with pain and something like excitement. He mouthed "Understood." Jeremy relaxed his hold.

"It's true, then," Botnick said hoarsely before Jeremy could speak. "About the magic."

My gaze met Jeremy's, but he looked as confused as I.

"Your strength," Botnick went on. "That's not . . . human. You're one of them. It's true about the magic. They've found the key." His eyes gleamed with a fervor bordering on the religious, and I knew that the excitement I'd seen hadn't been a reaction to the pain, but to the cause of it—a show of supernatural strength.

Botnick continued. "You—they—your group. They got my message, didn't they? That's why you're here. To see whether I'm worthy."

Even standing behind Botnick, Jeremy let his face betray nothing. But in the pause that followed, I knew what he was thinking—working through his options, deciding how best to handle this.

"How did you learn about us?" Jeremy asked after a moment.

"Pillow talk." A small laugh from Botnick. "It has been the undoing of many a man. In this case, it was a shared lover. A particularly attractive occult aficionado." His gaze traveled to me. "You know the type. Not terribly skilled, but eager to learn and pleasant to teach. One of your members let a few things slip, presumably to impress her, and she passed them on to me, for the same purpose."

"What did she tell you?"

"That you'd breached the wall. Discovered true magic."

Jeremy waited. After a moment, Botnick interpreted Jeremy's silence as meaning he wasn't satisfied and cleared his throat.

"Her exact words were that your group had found a way to harness the power of life." He smiled. "She had no idea what that meant. I think she expected me to tell her. I didn't, of course. I kept your secret."

Only telling a few of his closest contacts . . . like the one Zack Flynn knew. Jeremy didn't call him on it, though, just kept silent, as if still awaiting a full reply. Botnick shifted his weight, his eyes rolling back as he tried to gauge Jeremy's expression. Jeremy kept him facing forward. Botnick looked to me for help. I looked back, face as impassive as Jeremy's.

"I understood what she meant," Botnick said. "That you'd

harnessed the power of magic through the transference of the life force. Through sacrifice."

"Sacrifice?" Jeremy said. "She said that?"

"Well, not specifically, but I inferred it, given the wording."

"What do you know of us? Our group?"

Botnick straightened. "That you're serious practitioners. Not like most of them—wannabes and freaks looking for a place to belong, messing around with ritual magic and calling themselves witches and satanists as if it were no different than calling themselves Rotarians. Or indulging some socially unacceptable need—" he waved at the hook on the floor, "—and telling themselves it's an act of faith. You aren't like that. You are true seekers. Like me."

"And who told you this?"

Botnick shifted. "No one told me directly. But I've heard rumors for years now. About a group, very tight-knit and secretive, closed to newcomers. Dead serious, though. Scientific even, in their quest."

"These rumors. What else—?"

"Eric?" A woman's voice echoed down the chute.

Botnick opened his mouth, but Jeremy's forearm clamped on his throat. Botnick shook his head, whispering, "I'll get rid of her." Jeremy hesitated, then slackened his hold.

"Still looking," Botnick shouted. "I'll be up in a minute."

"Here, let me help—"

"No! I'm fine."

Jeremy motioned for me to circle around to the hidden exit. I did, steering clear of the chute. On the wall behind it was an opening, maybe thirty inches square. Jeremy had ripped the cover off by the hinges, the lock still intact. I shone the flashlight inside and saw a dark tunnel.

Behind me, Botnick was still trying to convince the woman he didn't need help, but the more he argued, the more suspicious he sounded. I'd just crawled into the passage when the entrance went dark and I glanced back to see Jeremy following me.

He pulled the cover on and the tunnel dimmed, lit only by my flashlight. As shoes clicked down the rungs, Jeremy crawled over to me, hand resting on my leg, and while I knew it was there to reassure me, I felt the heat of that touch burn through me, igniting thoughts very inappropriate under the circumstances.

"I said I was fine, didn't I?" Botnick snapped. "Now go back upstairs—"

"The office door was unlocked. Glen noticed when—"

"Yes, I was in there earlier. I probably left it unlocked."

The woman continued to argue, certain something was wrong and intent on figuring out what it was.

"Eric?" A man's voice now. "Did Dawn tell you about the office? You should have a look, see if anything has been—"

Footsteps on the concrete, coming our way. Jeremy waved for me to move fast.

"Eric? These boxes have been moved. The one in front of that old tunnel door . . ."

The voice faded as I moved away quickly, Jeremy at my rear. I crawled as fast as I could over the damp earth, the musty stink of it filling my nostrils, stones cutting into my palms and knees, skirt bunching up over my knees and slowing me down. I reached back with my flashlight hand, grabbed the skirt by the slit and ripped it, almost pitching face-first into a pit as my other hand came down on empty air.

I jerked back as Jeremy caught my legs.

"It drops off," I whispered.

"How far?"

I shone the flashlight down. As I did, a clanking sounded behind me and light filled the tunnel.

I leaned into the pit, holding the flashlight down as low as I could, afraid the sound of clicking it off would echo down the tunnel.

"Can you see anything?" Botnick's distant voice asked.

"No," the other man answered. "It's too dark. We need a light."

"Dawn? You'll find a flashlight in my office. Glen? Help me search the room, in case they're still here."

Shadows moved at the far end as they backed away from the opening. I peered into the pit.

"How deep?" Jeremy whispered.

It dropped down about four feet, then stretched into another tunnel. I twisted around and lowered myself. Water seeped through my nylons, my toes squelching in the mud below. It smelled foul but didn't stink like raw sewage.

Jeremy stepped down behind me, barely rippling the water. I

considered asking for verification that we were not, in fact, standing in sewage . . . and decided I was better off not knowing.

I shone the light down the tunnel, but darkness swallowed it after no more than a yard.

"Is it me or is this light getting dimmer?" I asked.

"Hard to say," he lied. "Give it a shake."

I did, and the light seemed to flare brighter. "Should we wait here, or continue on?"

Jeremy peered down the tunnel, then looked back down the one we'd come in. A clank. I recognized the sound of the trap door opening and ducked even as Jeremy pulled me down.

A beam danced over our heads. Mud oozed up to my ankles, swallowing my feet.

"See anything?" a woman whispered.

"No," Botnick replied.

"Where does the tunnel lead?"

"To the street, I was told. Guy who owned the shop before me ran some underground political paper. Always worrying about being raided."

"I'm going in," said the other man.

"Wait, you don't know what's . . ."

I didn't catch the rest. They'd pulled back, their voices now indistinct. Jeremy leaned down to my ear.

"We should move. Can you put on your shoes?"

"Not if I plan to walk in this. I'm fine."

I started into the tunnel. He caught my arm.

"You're in stockinged feet and can't see where you're stepping."

"I'm—"

"Here—"

"Don't offer me your shoes. Gallant, but it hardly solves the problem unless you're going to squeeze into my heels. I'll be careful."

"Feel before you step. I'll lead and take it slow."

We'd gone about twenty feet when the water level dropped to a trickle and the ground beneath it turned to concrete. I was about to whisper "Well, that's better," when my flashlight beam flickered and went out. That was fate for you. Gives and takes, keeping the balance.

Jeremy's fingers reached back and brushed my arm, warning me that he'd stopped before I smacked into him.

CHIVALRY

"WHAT'S WRONG?" I whispered as Jeremy stopped.

"I can't see. Give me a moment."

We waited, the distant drip of water the only sound. It smelled different here—stale with an almost musky odor. Cold too. I wrapped my arms around myself, trying not to let my teeth chatter, which would only have Jeremy offering me his jacket.

"Hmmm," he said after a moment. "There must be a distant source of light. I can make out shapes, but barely, and it doesn't seem to be getting any better."

"No light at all means even you can't see, right?"

"I'm afraid so. My night vision needs something to work with. I'll move slowly. Here, give me the flashlight and your shoes, and put your hands—"

He guided them to his hips. I moved closer . . . just for safety, of course.

We started forward again, creeping along in the dark. We made it about fifty feet, and around the bend, when I heard a sound that made the hair on my neck rise. The chattering of tiny, needle-sharp teeth.

"Please tell me that's mice," I said. "Or underground squirrels."

"Okay."

I poked his back. "Liar."

"Don't worry. They're a ways off yet."

"Do you remember the psycho rats in Toronto? Did Elena ever tell you we were cornered by them?"

"No, she left off that part. Left off a lot of parts, I'm sure."

"Well, I had to kill some. The rats. Squashed their poor little skulls with a two-by-four and I know payback's coming. Bad karma for the rodent slayer. They can probably sense—" I stopped. "Jeremy?"

"Hmmm?"

"Something brushed my foot. Something furry."

"Don't worry. It was dead."

"Dead?"

"I smelled it, but thought it best not to mention it and hope you passed by."

"Preferably without stepping on it?"

"I'll warn you next time. It can be hard to pinpoint the exact spot, though. The best I can do is say, 'By the way, there's a rotting corpse around here somewhere.' "

"On second thought, ignorance is bliss. So where—?" I stopped as an overpowering stench filled my nose. "Oh, God, I think I smell a ripe one."

"No, that's just the nest."

"N-nest?"

"It's down a side corridor, I think. We'll be past it in a moment. They shouldn't give us any trouble."

"Right. The predator thing. Like the cat. They smell you and run."

"Hmmm."

Not a terribly reassuring response. Elena had told me before that werewolves confuse other animals, that mix of wolf and human, and when confused and faced with a larger potential predator, they run. We'd had problems with the rats in Toronto only because they'd been infected and acting irrationally.

The chattering grew louder as the smell got worse. Mud oozed between my toes. And if it wasn't mud, I didn't want to know about it. I stepped on something that crackled under my toes, hard and thin like twigs . . . or bones.

"Almost past," Jeremy whispered. "When we reach the entrance to the nest, I'm going to stop and swing you by. All right?"

"Thanks."

A hiss in the darkness. I froze, my hands falling from Jeremy's hips as he kept moving. A loud chatter sounded right at my feet. I resisted the urge to kick and danced backward instead, wildly looking around, seeing only blackness.

"Jaime?"

Another hiss. I stumbled back. My foot slid in the muck and—

Jeremy's hands caught me around the waist and swooped me up. "Grab my neck and hold on."

As I slid my hands around his neck, my fingertips brushed through his hair, then down along the back of his neck. Just bad aim, of course. Couldn't expect me to see in the dark.

He took two steps, then stopped and cursed under his breath. More hissing. The scrabbling of tiny claws on concrete. The enraged shriek of a rat defending its nest, and I knew our path was blocked.

Jeremy made the low growling noise that had scared off the cat. A few rats' shrieks turned to panic, but more just kept chattering. Jeremy jerked back as he kicked a rat. I resisted the urge to bury my face in his chest like some nineteenth-century heroine.

"Hold on," he murmured. "This is going to take a stronger warning."

I tightened my grip. He twisted, as if leaning away from me, and let out a snarl that resounded through the tunnel. The rats squealed, claws scraping the concrete as they ran.

Jeremy took a few steps, getting us past the rats' nest, then lowered his lips to my ear. "My apologies. That wasn't very civilized."

I wasn't complaining. It'd worked on me too . . . though not in the same way. I readjusted my grip, pressing closer. His lips brushed my ear, sending a delicious chill down my neck.

"Sorry," he murmured, mouth still at my ear, breath hot on my neck. Then he straightened. "We should keep going."

I agreed wholeheartedly. Unfortunately, he meant walking. And just when I'd started thinking sex in a dank, rat-infested tunnel wouldn't be so bad after all. It would certainly be a first and, with me, that wasn't easy.

I rested in his arms, enjoying the heat of his body, the smell of him blocking the stench of the tunnel. After a few minutes, though, that twenty-first-century independent woman started nagging at me and, with a silent sigh, I said, "We're far enough away. You can put me down."

"I could. But the tunnel is wide enough here for me to carry you and, from the smell, people use this end, so I suspect there's a discarded needle or two on the ground. Not something you should step on in bare feet."

Couldn't argue with that. Another minute and we could see dim light. We soon reached the source—moonlight streaming through a partly boarded-up exit.

Jeremy put me down and I pulled on my shoes. Then we squeezed out through the door and found ourselves at the bottom of stairs leading from a parking lot to the basement door of some building.

We finally escaped the putrid, rat-infested tunnel, only to step out into a cold drizzling rain. Never fails. I catch a break and I pay for it. The story of my life.

So we ran, shivering and wet, from under one overhang to the next. Jeremy gave me his coat, and I didn't argue. We finally reached the street and darted under a store awning.

"Not the safe fact-finding mission you had in mind, was it?" Jeremy said. "Are you all right?"

"Sure. It was fun."

The corners of his mouth twitched. "Fun?"

"Well, fun is probably pushing it but, hey, this is the first adventure I've survived without being kidnapped, attacked, knocked unconscious or possessed by evil spirits. A ripped blouse? Ruined skirt? Bad hair? I'd call this progress."

He laughed. Then his eyes met mine, face turning serious. He moved closer, his hand going under my chin, warm fingers against my skin, tilting my face up, leaning down to me.

He wiped his thumb over my cheekbone, frowned and peered at it.

"You cut your cheek on something." He reached for the spot again, then pulled back. "I probably shouldn't touch it. My hands are filthy."

I met his gaze. "I don't mind."

He hung there, over me, one hand at my back, clutching my blouse, eyes darkening, body taut, as if fighting the urge to take me up on my invitation. If I made a move, his resolve would break. I could see that in his eyes. Just reach up, put my arms around his neck, press my body against his and I'd see that fire again, feel that passion. No tortured cab ride back to his hotel. That would take too long. Make my move and I'd be carried back in the shadows of that alcove and—

I swallowed hard and stepped back. Probably the hardest thing I've ever done, but follow through on that impulse and there'd be regret come morning. Take it slow. Make sure it's where I want to go—where he wants to go.

As I fussed with my shoe strap, Jeremy peered out into the dark, wet street, squaring his shoulders against the chill. "We need to get you someplace warm and dry—"

A taxi turned the corner.

A quarter-smile. "Now, there's the kind of magic I like."

He stepped out and waved it over, then turned to me. "I'm going back to the shop, to see whether I can pick up Botnick's trail. With any luck, he'll head somewhere interesting after his encounter."

"Are you sure? It might be—"

"Dangerous?" The corners of his mouth twitched. "Don't worry. I'll be careful."

The cab stopped. He opened the rear door halfway, then paused, looking back at me.

"You're welcome to come with me. I didn't mean—" He gestured at the cab. "I'm not trying to get rid of you. I just thought you'd probably had enough..."

"If you could use me, I'd go. But tracking is your field. I'd only get in the way."

I slid past him into the car.

He leaned in and swept a strand of wet hair back from my face. "You're never in the way, Jaime."

I turned my face toward his, lifting my chin...

"Call me when you get to the house," he said. "So I know you arrived safely."

For a second, watching him close the door, I almost suspected he'd been teasing me—here and in the tunnel. But no. Jeremy was nothing if not responsible. At a time like this, flirting would be the last thing on his mind.

Damn.

He jogged around to give the driver directions and a few bills. As the cab pulled away from the curb, I remembered his coat and rolled down my window.

"Your—" I called, but he had his back to me, hurrying to the shelter of the awnings. A second later, he vanished into the shadows, looping back to Botnick's shop.

I rolled up the window.

"Forgot his jacket," I said to the driver, who was watching me through the rearview mirror.

The young woman gave a slight roll of her eyes, as if to say *she'd* never accept a man's jacket in the first place. Too bad. I'd never been one to refuse an opened door or a pulled-out chair. As long as the man understood I could open my own doors, could pull out my own chairs, then I wasn't adverse to a little chivalry. With Jeremy, it wasn't so much that as old-fashioned good manners.

He may not have grown up with women in his life, but he'd had Elena around for over fifteen years now, and knew better than to underestimate "the fairer sex." Had it been Elena back at that shop, she would have gone down the chute first and taken on those rats herself, protecting *him,* watching *his* back. And he'd have let her. With me, it was a question of limitations and experience. While I wanted, someday, to have the nerve and the know-how to do such things myself, in the meantime, I wasn't going to protest about being carried past a nest of rats. Or taking his coat when I was cold.

I pulled the jacket around me, savoring the warmth for the rest of the cab ride.

PLAYED

WHEN I ARRIVED IN BRENTWOOD, a guard met me at the door. Like being sixteen again, arriving home after curfew. I even got the "what have you been up to?" arched brow from him as he surveyed my ruined outfit.

As I passed Grady's bedroom, I heard my name and stopped.

"You aren't listening to me, woman!" Grady hissed, loud enough for his voice to reverberate down the hall. "I was *possessed.*"

"Yes, yes, I know, but they really want us to stick to these ridiculous celebrity séances, so, perhaps for a while, if you could choose to be possessed only by people fitting their criteria—"

"You think I chose to have this happen? This—this power—this evil thing, it stole my body. I was powerless, unable to see, hear, speak, trapped in some limbo." He took a deep, shuddering breath. "I need to speak to Jaime. While that thing had hold of me yesterday, I had some . . . sense of her. I think she might understand what happened."

The creak of a chair. "So that's what this is about? You don't need to pull this possession nonsense, Bradford. If you want to take the woman out for drinks and a quick shag in some tawdry hotel, be my guest. I've never stopped you before, have I?"

"I'm telling you I was possessed—"

"Oh, I know what you're possessed by. Get it out of your system so we can get back to business."

"This *is* business, woman. Something happened out there and I believe Jaime Vegas holds the key. I've told you she has the gift. Her performance with Tansy Lane—"

"—was a remarkable performance. Props to her for it, and for finding that memo, giving her the advantage of knowing in advance who she was about to contact that night."

"Becky never said Jaime found—"

"The poor girl is terrified of losing her job, so she doesn't dare do more than hint. If Todd Simon found out that she'd left that memo on Tansy Lane in the kitchen—"

"I don't believe it."

"No? Well, I've done my research, because that's what you pay me for, Bradford, and Todd Simon is a cutthroat—"

"I meant about Jaime. She didn't need to warn me about Amityville—Becky certainly wasn't going to. If Jaime Vegas is as conniving as Becky would have us believe, then why not let me fall on my face..."

Footsteps sounded on the stairs. One last glance at Grady's door before I hurried down to my own.

I'd been played by Becky. We'd *all* been played by her, but that was no excuse. I consider myself a good judge of character—showbiz character, at least. But I'd fallen for the nervous young director routine. Conned. But not for long.

I TURNED off the bedside light, laid down and called Jeremy. He answered on the second ring.

"Checking in as requested," I said. "Safe and snug in bed. How's the hunt going?"

"Badly. I followed his trail to his car. Then presumably he drove off."

"Which makes tracking impossible. Was he alone when he left?"

"Yes. He seems to have persuaded the others to go on without him. No sign of the police being called for the break-in."

"Can't take the chance of them finding the blood-flecked dungeon downstairs."

"No doubt. I'm parked behind his house, but he hasn't returned. While I hope he simply stopped to grab a late-night snack, I think he's done exactly what I feared he'd do."

"Run to his contact to try to get in touch with the group."

"Which would be perfect if I were still following him." A soft sigh. "I'll wait another hour or so, in case he returns."

"If he does, will you talk to him?"

"Only if it can be done safely. Otherwise, I'll regroup and try again tomorrow."

I laid my head on the pillow. "Thanks. For looking out for me tonight. I know you're used to having a partner who can take more of the risks."

"*All* of the risks, you mean. If I'd been there with Clay or Elena—or anyone from the Pack—I'd have been the one sitting above the hatch and being escorted past the rats. I'm the Alpha, remember? I'm not allowed to have fun."

"Fun?"

"Fun might be pushing it," he said, echoing my words from earlier. "But it's nice to say, 'I'm going down the hatch first,' and not have four werewolves scrambling over themselves to do it for me, lest I stub my toe."

"Can't lead the Pack with a stubbed toe."

"Evidently. And while I have no objection to devising strategies, giving orders and letting them have their adventures, it can be a bit... much at times. You mentioned those diseased rats in Toronto?"

"Right."

"At least you were allowed to whack one. When we initially discovered the nest, I wanted to determine what disease they might have contracted. I was allowed a split-second glance at the nest, then they let me examine a nearby rat corpse, with Clay hovering over me, twitching as if he expected the thing to jump up and bite me in the nose."

"He can be a tad overprotective, can't he?"

"A tad. But it's his job and it's also his nature, so I can't argue. And, yet, I'll admit it's refreshing to turn the tables now and then."

"And protect instead of being protected?"

"You can take care of yourself. But..."

"I can just tell myself I'm humoring you."

A soft laugh. "Yes, you can."

We kept talking as he watched Botnick's house. At some point, I drifted off. When my alarm rang, I was still clutching the phone to my ear, the call long since disconnected.

MY MORNING began with another call to Jeremy. There'd been no sign of Botnick all night. Jeremy had retreated to his hotel just before dawn. He'd swing by and survey Botnick's house and shop before coming to breakfast.

Since he'd been up all night, I certainly didn't expect him to put on his game face and make nice to strangers. But he was already on his way—or so he said, though I could have sworn I heard the shower running in the background.

As for Hope, she'd left a message on his hotel answering service, saying Bigfoot had kept her up until dawn.

After I hung up, I took last night's clothes from the garbage can and put them in a bag for private disposal later. If Todd Simon had cameras installed in the house, he wasn't above having the cleaning staff root through our trash. Next thing I knew, Hope would be given a new assignment—investigating Jaime Vegas's ripped, sewage-stained, rat-hair-strewn clothes. I'd hate to see the story *True News* would come up with to explain that one.

Then it was time to take care of Becky.

ON THE way to breakfast, I popped my head into the room the guards and staff were using as a base station. With apologies for intruding, I mentioned that I'd spotted a paparazzi lurking about the night before. It was a lie, but within minutes, I was perched on the edge of the desk, surrounded by the trio of guards as I regaled them with tales of life in the limelight.

"Last month I got a letter from this guy who said he'd written a story about me and posted it online," I said. "I thought that was so sweet. Look at me, inspiring fan fiction and I'm not even a fictional character. So I type in the link he sent and I start reading it, and it's really cute, all about him meeting me at a show, then being taken backstage..."

"Uh-huh," one guard chortled.

I nudged him with my foot, letting my black silk skirt ride up my thigh, their gazes riding up with it. "So you think you know what happens next? You don't know the half of it."

He grinned. "Gonna tell us?"

"Let's just say that being able to contact ghosts makes for some very interesting ménages à trois . . . and ménages à quatre, and ménages à . . . whatever five is in French."

They laughed.

"I never knew I had a thing for geishas and Amazons, but there it was, in vivid detail, and even more vivid color illustrations."

"Spirit photography?" one of them said.

I smacked his arm, letting my fingernails graze his biceps. "Drawings, of course. Very imaginative drawings."

The youngest guard swung around the laptop on the desk, fingers poised over the keys, brows raised in a dare.

"You think I memorized the URL?" I said.

All three of them teased me until I sighed and said, "Try these keywords. Jaime—spelled J-A-M-I-E, his attention to detail not extending to my name. Vegas. Geisha. Amazon warrior. And, ahem, Nubian slave master."

A howl of laughter.

"Found it," the guard said. Then, after a moment, "Holy shit."

"Did I mention it was imaginative? I don't know where I got those missiles." I waved at the picture, then at my chest. "But apparently there's more to me than meets the eye. A *lot* more."

As they laughed, Angelique passed the door, heading for the dining room. I jumped off the desk.

"Angelique!"

She stopped, frowning as she saw where I was.

"I need to talk to you. Someplace—" I glanced at the guards, "—private. Sorry, guys. Maybe there's an empty room someplace—"

"Take this one," the head guard said. "We'll clear out."

"Are you sure?"

They were. As they left, I thanked them and agreed to come by later with more stories. They waved Angelique in and closed the door behind them.

"We're supposed to stick to the common rooms," she said.

"Do you know why? I'll show you in a minute." I moved behind the desk and sat. "But first, I bet I know who fed you stories about me. It's either Becky or Will, but my money's on Will. He tried the same shit with me the second day—hinting that you were talking about me behind my back. I wouldn't bite, but if I had, I can guarantee you'd have seen my response on the show."

Confusion, then dawning horror.

I continued. "Whatever you said about me, Angelique, it's now on film. And when it airs, you won't see what led to your comments, just the end results. Just you spouting seemingly ungrounded insults and accusations."

Her face paled. I waved for her to sit down.

"Whatever you said about me, I don't care, but you won't see me saying a word against you because I haven't. I've been around long enough to know better. I also know better than to do anything that will make me seem *too* good, and risk pissing off my costars. For example, sneaking a peek at a file on potential subjects. Did Becky tell you I did that?"

"Will. But he said he wasn't supposed to tell—" Her pretty face hardened. "That was part of the setup, wasn't it? Let on he's sneaking me secrets, and I won't go after you about it. They played us against each other."

"Becky *did* get me to look at a memo," I said. "Accidentally. On Gabrielle Langdon. That's why I tried to pass you the tips. And that's why I wouldn't make contact myself. It wasn't fair."

She flushed. "Guess I haven't been very fair myself. But Todd Simon warned me I had to be on the defensive, especially against you. He said everyone's out for blood in this town, and I'd get eaten alive if I didn't come out swinging."

"Well, you can stop swinging now, because I'm not your enemy. As for why I told you all this in *here,* let me take you for a little stroll. Show you a few features of the house they didn't cover in the tour."

I SHOWED her the hidden cameras in the common areas. She managed to hold it together until we were back in the guard room, then collapsed into a chair.

"I can't believe... my dad said I wasn't ready for Hollywood, but I was so *sick* of the revival circuit. I thought this was going to be my big chance." A strained laugh. "My big chance to make a fool of myself on national television."

I took the chair opposite hers. "Maybe not."

AFTER TALKING to Angelique, I tracked down Becky and apologized for my poor performance the day before. I promised to do better that afternoon.

"I just... I guess I get nervous about contacting famous people who died fairly recently. With a case like Gabrielle Langdon, it was all over the news and so many people know the details. If I get them right, I'll look like I'm just remembering the case. If I screw up, everyone will know it."

She nodded. "I can see that. But you won't need to worry about that this afternoon. This guy hasn't been in the news for..." She calculated. "About thirty years."

"Thank God."

She checked her PalmPilot, then said casually, gaze still down, "You live in Chicago, don't you?"

"I do."

"Then you'll have an edge, because what he was famous for is a lot better known in Chicago than Hollywood, though he himself lived here. And there's no murder involved. Not *his* murder, that is, though he certainly sent a lot of people to their graves." A slow shake of her head. "Live that kind of life and die in your sleep. Proof that life isn't fair."

She studied my face, trying to see whether I needed any more hints. I didn't. I thanked her for her time, then went in search of Claudia and Grady.

JEREMY AND I dined alone. That seemed wisest—letting Becky believe that her stars had passed the stage of feigning civility and now were avoiding one another even for meals.

The next séance segment would be later that morning, so I had to stick around. I tried persuading Jeremy to go—to hook up with

Hope, maybe pay a visit to Botnick at his shop—but he insisted there was no rush. We'd leave together after I was free.

In the meantime, I wanted to go into the garden, to try contacting the ghosts again.

"I know I'm not going to have some sudden breakthrough, but..." I let the sentence trail off.

"At the very least, you're letting them know you're still here. That's hardly a waste of time, if they're comforted."

Before we went outside, I collected my necromancy kit, then picked up a package I'd ordered from town. A little gift for Jeremy. Not much of a gift, I thought, as I looked into the bag. Unoriginal. Probably unwanted, under the circumstances. I wished I'd chosen something better. I wished I knew what better would be.

I took it out to the patio and thrust it at Jeremy with a mumbled "Just a little something."

He opened the bag and smiled. Reaching in, he pulled out a sketch pad and pencils.

"Okay," I said. "Probably the last thing you need on this trip. But I thought, well, maybe if we had some downtime like this, you could use a distraction from the research."

"I could. Thank you. It'll help me clear my mind so I can see fresh angles. It's perfect timing too. I know you prefer to work without an audience breathing down your neck."

"Strange for a stage performer, huh?"

"No, not really." He folded the bag and put it into his pocket. "Let's get out there, then, before they find work for you."

BETTER LATE THAN NEVER

SO WE "WORKED" TOGETHER at the back of the garden, me kneeling on my ritual cloth, Jeremy seated off to the side out of my field of vision. If anything, I was more relaxed than when I'd been alone, maybe because I knew he'd detect—and warn me of—any intruders before I was "caught." Or maybe it was just comforting having him nearby, the steady scratch of his pencil underscoring the children's whispers. Even they seemed more patient with me, their encouraging caresses never turning to jabs and slaps. For all that, though, I made no progress.

Finally, I stopped, stretched and walked over to Jeremy.

"What are you draw—" I caught sight of the page. "Hey, that's me."

I bit my cheek to keep from grinning. I'd never known Jeremy to sketch anyone outside the Pack. While it might have meant that he didn't like flowers, and I was the only living alternative, I knew it meant something. With Jeremy, that's what art was about—a medium to explore an idea . . . or a person.

"It's recognizable, then? Always a good sign." He closed the book. "Are you done?"

"I think so. Can I see?" I hesitated with my fingers outstretched toward his book, then curled them back. "Or maybe I shouldn't ask. Your art and all. Private, I guess."

"No more private than your rituals and you share those with me." He handed me the pad. "Just a series of sketches. I'm thinking of doing a painting."

"Of me?"

His smile grew, touching his eyes. "If that's all right. I'm working on one of the twins right now. For them, when they're older. It's taking awhile. I originally meant it to be just Kate and Logan, but decided to add Clay and Elena. A bigger project, but I thought the children might prefer that when they grow up."

"More meaningful, with their parents in it."

"I thought so."

I opened the book and flipped through the sketches. There were quite a few, all raw, some no more than an outline, maybe with a feature or two. Preparation for a painting—Jeremy preferred to work from sketches and memory rather than from live models. An interpretation rather than a photograph, he said.

His interpretations were often surprising. Like the older portraits of Clay and Elena in his studio. Clay—brash, difficult, violent—depicted as a young man with an almost boyish innocence. Elena—the more sociable, more easygoing of the pair—painted with a dangerous edge, the beast within revealed.

On first glance, you'd say Jeremy got them wrong, misinterpreted. But I'd seen that feral side of Elena, protecting her loved ones, and I'd caught glimpses of Clayton's gentler side, playing with his children or talking to his wife. Not their dominant personalities, but an aspect of the whole—a side you had to dig to find.

So it was with no surprise that when I first looked at the sketches Jeremy had done of me, I thought *No, that's not right.* Not the way I saw myself. Not even the way I saw myself reflected in others. In those sketches, I looked . . . quiet. Intent, almost introspective. My gaze was focused on something to the side, my expression serious, solemn even, rapt in concentration.

Yet the more I stared at them, the more I thought *Yes, I recognize that.* Like seeing a photo of myself shot at an odd angle.

"Oooh, nice," said a voice at my shoulder. "I like the one in the corner there."

I wheeled to see a woman a few years younger than me, with straight black hair almost to her waist. Six feet tall with the remote, slightly exotic look of a fashion model. That illusion of aloofness vanished the moment she glanced up from the page, her eyes dancing in predatory amusement, like a cat always on the lookout for something worth pouncing on.

"Eve!" I spun to Jeremy. "It's Eve."

I knew I looked ridiculous, gesturing at empty air, but he only smiled and said, "Hello, Eve. Glad you could join us."

"Glad to be here." She looked at me. "Am I interrupting? If you guys were just getting to the naked-portrait stage, I can come back."

"Ha-ha. We were just finishing some stuff. I was contacting—" I looked around. "They're gone. Or being quiet."

"Probably trying to figure out what I am."

"Jaime?" Jeremy said, rising. "I'll go inside and get you a cold drink. If anyone's looking for you, I'll stall them."

"Thanks."

"What a sweetie," Eve said as he left. "And visiting you all the way from New York. No family in tow. Sitting in the garden sketching you while you fondle corpse bits. Positively domestic. So does this mean you guys are—"

"No," I cut in, then smiled. "I can't believe you're here. Kristof was certain it was a no-go."

She perched on the edge of a retaining wall. "Well, it wasn't easy getting out of there, let me tell you. First there were the chains, tying me to my rock. And that big vulture that keeps picking at my flesh. Then the fires of hell, and that three-headed demon dog guarding the exit..." She reached out to smack my arm, though her fingers passed through. "You're looking at me like I'm serious. How evil do you think I am? Sheesh."

"Speaking of evil, I met one of your old friends the other day. I just popped by to talk to her and ended up knocked unconscious, thrown in her car and driven to a body-dump site."

"What?"

I left out the part about Savannah coming to my rescue and taking on Molly. Good call, because as soon as I mentioned that Molly had been in contact with Savannah, Eve's face twisted with a cold fury that chilled my blood no matter how many times I saw it.

"That two-faced smarmy bitch. You tell Savannah she is *not* to—"

Eve stopped and turned away, her lips curling in a snarl scarier than any of Jeremy's. She stood with her back to me. I waited. After a moment, she relaxed and turned around, smiling again.

"Okay, let's take that back a step. Ahem. Would you please convey a message to Savannah that Molly Crane is not to be trusted? As a contact, I only used her for what she could do for me because that's exactly how she treats everyone else. With Savannah, she only wants—"

"To see whether Savannah can be useful. Savannah already figured that out."

"She did? That's my girl." She planted herself on the retaining wall. "Back to business, then."

"First, about you being here. It's . . . okay? With everyone?"

"I didn't go AWOL if that's what you mean. The Fates investigated Kristof's story and, well, they're a little freaked."

"Freaked?"

"Yeah. Kind of discomfiting in a higher power. I mean, they're deities, right? They should just calmly survey the problem and say 'Yes, we're aware of that.' But if they *were* aware of it, that would be even scarier. No excuse for letting it continue."

"So they had no idea this had happened?"

"Zip. It's an isolated incident. So seeing that they have a problem involving dark magic, they realized there was only one—" she faded, then came back, "—for the job."

"You were bleeped."

"Damn. I hate it when that happens. What did I say?" She frowned, searching for the word the higher powers had censored—some topic she wasn't allowed to discuss with mortals. "Let me rephrase: they realized there was only one *ghost* for the job. That being me. So I've been reassigned. Now bring me up-to-date."

I did, then said, "Am I on the right track?"

"Yes, the Fates confirm that we have trapped child ghosts. They confirm that the bastards responsible for it have, as Aratron said, done what should be impossible—performed magic without hereditary spellcasting genes. And that's what has them freaked. Who found a loophole? How big is it? What else can they do? How many of them are there?"

"In other words, they're no further along than I am."

She gave me a look as if to say: what did you expect? "Finding them and finding out exactly what's going on is our job now."

"That's what I've been doing."

"I know. But, well, you're moving a little slowly." She raised her hands against my protest. "You're going about it the right way—the safe way. But unless you want to spend months reading reference books and canvassing contacts, I'd suggest it's time to jump-start this baby."

"Jump-start it how?"

"Those kids are here, right? In this garden. And they don't follow you any farther than the house. Why?"

"Well, I guess being fragmented or whatever means they're weakened, restricted in their movements—"

Eve's head shot around, her gaze following something. Then her face lit up, not with her usual cat-with-the-canary grin, but with a gentle smile.

"Hey, there," she said as she leaned down to a child's level. "Coming out of hiding?"

"You can see them?"

She shook her head. "Just glimpses." She looked away sharply from the ghosts, before her gaze chilled. "Dark magic or not, you don't do shit like this. It's just understood. No ritual requires children, so no one uses them."

"Maybe they don't know that," I said slowly, the thought still forming as I spoke it.

"Hmmm?"

"They're humans doing magic, right? They don't know they don't need children. Maybe they assume they do. Maybe whatever faith or magic system they're building on uses children. That's what we always hear about in tabloids and movies. Child sacrifice."

"Could be . . ." she mused, gazing out as if still looking for the spirits. "Use it and it works, so you keep using it." She swung her gaze back to me and stood. "Forget why. We'll get to that later, after we stop them."

"But it's another avenue to look into. For finding them. If we know what faith and magical systems use child—"

She waved me off. "More research. You've got to cut through that, Jaime. Take action. We start by going back to why those spirits are stuck here. Presumably the ghosts are weakened and can't travel far. Far from what?"

"Their bodies, of course—" I stopped and looked out over the gardens. The endless raised beds. A breeze rippled past and I shivered. "They were buried here."

"I'd say that's a fair guess." She walked along the path, her hand passing through the roses as she peered around. "Perfect place. You wouldn't even have to dig down into the earth. Just get through lightly packed soil."

My gaze went to the house. "So you think the people who live here—?"

"Don't count on it. I've buried a few corpses in my time and I wouldn't put one in my own garden. But if I had a neighbor down the road with a yard full of raised beds? Or if I was an employee there? Or on a crew doing their gardening or pool cleaning? Plenty of people could see and get access to these gardens. You can go that route, checking possibilities, but it's just more research. You need to—"

"Take action. I heard. But how—"

"Say one of these poor kids' corpses . . . appears."

"We find a body, you mean? Dig one up and get clues that way?" I shook my head. "There's a house full of people a hundred feet away. People with cameras."

She smiled. "Which makes it perfect."

"Perfect? How would we ever hide—?"

"You don't. That's the point. You're thinking like a supernatural, Jaime. Hide the evidence. Cover the crime."

She crouched and reached out, as if coaxing one of the children, a smile playing on her lips. Only after a moment of this did she look back up at me.

"This time, there's no cover-up. These are humans. You can't just canvass supernaturals in Los Angeles looking for them. You have millions of suspects, not a few hundred. You need to draw them out."

I wasn't sure I agreed. In fact, I was pretty sure I didn't, but rather than argue the concept I honed in on the specifics. "How would I ever find a body? It could take weeks, even with Jeremy and me both out here every night digging."

"You don't need to dig, Jaime. They'll come to you."

"They'll—" My throat went dry. "You can't mean— Raise their

bodies? My God, Eve, I can't believe you'd suggest that. You're a mother."

"Yes, I'm a mother, Jaime, which is exactly why I'd do this instead of pissing around with research. You think I don't know what I'm asking? I do, but if it means stopping these bastards, then I'd let you do it to Savannah herself." She walked past me, silent. "I know it won't be a very pleasant thing to do, Jaime. Not for you or them."

"If it would solve this, I'd do it. But we've got a lead with this Botnick guy and I think we should play that through first."

With her back still to me, she said, "Your call. I can't dig up the corpses myself. If you really want to do more book reading, look into African folk magic."

"Did the Fates suggest that?"

"No, I did. Couple of years before I died, I had some sorcerer kid offer me body parts. From a child. He'd hooked up with these... witch doctors. Fucked-up stuff."

"This kid... Where could I find him?"

"Over on my side somewhere. Not my doing. I tore a strip out of him and scared him off that shit, but he only got into something worse, with worse people than me. Guy was looking for a shortcut to power. Typical kid—didn't want to work for it. Point is, I did some digging into this folk magic after he told me about it. There are some branches that use children, either selling parts of their corpses or stealing their so-called life energy. You mentioned fragmented or weakened child spirits..."

"And something like that might explain it."

"So you go ahead and do your research. It'll give me time to track down Kris, tell him I'm back for a while. If you need me, just shout, but..." A sly smile. "If I'm slow responding, give me a few minutes."

"Gotcha."

JEREMY DROVE me to the séance site.

"All right," Becky said as she ushered us into the backyard. "Our subject for today is Mickey Cohen."

"Is this his house?" I said, surveying the small stuccoed home.

"Um, I can't say," she said. "Liability issues. Him being a mobster and all, we have to be very respectful of the current residents."

"A mobster?" Angelique's eyes went wide as she shivered. "Like the Mafia? I don't think my daddy would want me talking to someone like that. Maybe I shouldn't do this one . . ."

"Cohen . . . Cohen," Grady mused. "The chap who founded Las Vegas, wasn't it?"

He glanced at Claudia, who gave a "don't ask me" shrug.

Becky smiled. "I'm not telling, but I'm sure he will. Now let's set up over there."

WE ACED the séance. All three of us. Becky was fuming, knowing I must have passed on her tip about Cohen to Angelique and Grady, and I realized I'd just made an enemy in the business. It was the first time I'd ever done so intentionally. I'm always careful not to burn bridges—that incompetent junior assistant you tell off today could be a studio executive in ten years. But in ten years, I'd be out of the business, and Becky didn't have the clout to do more than spread "difficult to work with" stories about me.

But if I was wrong? If she turned out to be the mistress of a network exec currently considering my new show? The thought passed with a surprising lack of alarm. Right now, my priority was freeing these kids. Anything else I could deal with later.

After the séance, Jeremy and I headed to Botnick's shop, which had been closed when he checked earlier. On the way, I told him what Eve had said.

"She may have a point."

I looked over at him sharply. "About raising the corpses?"

"No, but I think I know a way we could find a body without raising the dead. For now, though, it's simply something to keep in the back of our minds."

THE SHOP windows were still dark, the sign turned to Closed.

"Lunch break?"

"Perhaps." He found a parking place. "I'm going to walk past. Care to join me?"

"Around here, it's probably safer than staying in the car."

RUNES

ACCORDING TO THE SIGN on Botnick's shop, it opened at eleven and closed at seven. It was now almost one. Jeremy peered through the darkened window as I looked for a Gone for Lunch or Back in Five Minutes notice. Nothing.

"It doesn't look as if he opened this morning," Jeremy said. "The mail is still under the slot."

He glanced at the adjoining stores. An adults-only video shop and a tattoo parlor. Putting his fingers on the back of my arm, he steered me toward the latter.

It was empty except for a woman sitting sideways on an old armchair, her back against one arm, her legs sprawled over the other. She had a sandwich in one hand and a pen in the other as she sketched something on a pad. Late twenties with spiked black hair, she wore torn jeans and a T-shirt with the sleeves ripped off.

Her gaze flitted over me and came to rest on Jeremy.

"Sorry to disturb you," he said. "We're here about the shop next door. Atrum Arcana appears to be closed, and I was hoping you might know whether that's temporary or it's shut down for the day." He gave a wry smile. "I'm sure you don't keep an eye on your neighbor's comings and goings, but we've traveled some distance, so I thought I'd ask."

"Atrum Arcana?"

She looked at Jeremy with renewed interest, her eyes glittering behind her cat's-eye glasses. If she noticed me, she gave no sign of it. It seemed that the further I got from thirty, the more invisible I became to twenty-somethings—the men I was with became fair game.

"I don't know what's up with Eric today," she said. "I haven't seen him. But maybe I could help. I know some people who sell pretty much the same stuff. What exactly did you have in mind?"

"Wiccan amulets. For a niece. I heard his store carries a large selection."

"Oh."

As her interest cooled, Jeremy walked to a display of mystical symbols. "These are very nice. Not for her just yet, though I'm sure she'll be asking for one in a few years. Are you a practitioner?"

"Nah. I just draw what the customers want. Occult stuff is hot."

"This is your work, then?"

She nodded.

He traced his fingertips over an ankh. "Beautiful. Maybe when she's older. Thank you very much for your time."

She stood as he turned to go. "Here's my card. And about Eric? No idea where the guy is, which is weird. He never opens late, never closes early. Takes his business seriously. I was a little worried when he didn't open, so I tried his home number. Left a message. Nothing."

"Something probably came up," Jeremy said. "We're in town for a couple of days. We'll call tomorrow, before we come out."

"And if he doesn't answer, give me a ring. Maybe I'll know something."

As she retrieved a business card, he eyed a smaller display of symbols. Simple ones in black and white. Even as she handed him the card, he pulled his gaze away from the display only for a moment, with a distracted "thank you."

Another lingering look at the symbols, then he put his fingers on my arm and headed for the door. He made it halfway, stopped and slowly turned.

"I noticed you have a number of runes there," he said, nodding at the display.

The young woman beamed. "Yep. A specialty of mine. I love them. Elegant, you know?"

Jeremy nodded, still hesitating, as if contemplating something. After a second, he walked back toward the woman.

"There are a few I've seen, and never been able to place."

"What do they look like?"

He nodded at her sketch pad and murmured, "May I?"

She passed it over. He sketched two symbols. I watched with a vague sense that I'd seen them before, but couldn't remember where.

"You're an artist," the woman said, her appraising smile returning. "I can tell."

A small nod from Jeremy, not quite admitting it. He finished his sketches. The young woman studied them, then shook her head.

"They look kind of like a couple of the Elder Futhak ones, and a bit like Hungarian but not quite either." She picked up the paper, lifting it into a better light. "Very nice, though. Can I keep them?"

I expected Jeremy to say, "Yes, of course"—his usual good manners—but he hesitated, as if he'd like to refuse but wasn't sure how. After a moment he nodded.

"So, what's your medium?" she asked.

His gaze was distant, mind elsewhere. A blink as he reluctantly returned. "Oil, mainly."

"Cool. Mine's ink, as you might have guessed."

She chatted for another few minutes, Jeremy murmuring appropriate responses and complimenting her work. He gave no sign of his preoccupation or his impatience. Only someone who knew him would pick up the subtle hints, that cool veneer to his words, that emptiness in his eyes. I laid my fingers on his arm.

He nodded. "We should be going."

"Here," she said, plucking the business card from his hand. She wrote two numbers on the back, then smiled at him. "My home and cell. In case you ever want to discuss runes or art."

Art, my ass. But I followed Jeremy's cue, smiling and thanking her for her time.

As we stepped onto the sidewalk, I said, "Those are two of the runes on the babies' blankets. The ones Elena said you had quilted for them."

He nodded.

"Like the symbols in Clay's room. On his comforter and his walls. Elena said you found Clayton's comforter years ago and painted the walls with the same symbols, to match. She said you had the babies' blankets done that way as a joke. Only you didn't find that comforter, did you? You had it made. Like the blankets. And they aren't a joke."

He looked over sharply, brows arched.

"Where do they come from?" I asked. "The symbols."

A pause, then he tapped the side of his head. "As for how they got in there?" An odd look crossed his face, frustration with a chaser of something sad. "No idea. I just . . ."

He shrugged and kept walking, as if he wanted to leave it at that. Then, when we were almost at the car, he said, "It's a . . . compulsion, I suppose. With Clay's room when he was younger. With the babies now. Even Elena has some in her bedroom." A twist of a smile. "Hidden, of course. If she found them, she'd think I was mad."

She wouldn't think that. But she'd ask questions, probing and worrying, exactly what he didn't want.

"Do you think they're connected to the other things?" I asked. "Your visions? Your . . . sensing?"

"I've thought about that, but I don't see how. Maybe they're just . . ." he shrugged, "images I saw once that made an impression subconsciously."

"Do you want to go somewhere, maybe get a coffee, talk about it?"

He blinked, as if startled by the very suggestion. Maybe even taken aback. Then he shook his head. "We have to meet Hope."

That was all he said. No "maybe later," not even an "I don't want to talk about it." All day I'd been fighting a mounting frustration, pretending I wasn't just a bit disappointed with the way things were going. Last night had been . . . special. Clichéd, yes, and an odd choice of words to describe a night spent hiding from an S & M cult and running through rat-infested tunnels, but I really felt that shared experience meant something.

I'd been saying that a lot lately. Meant something. Coming to L.A. meant something. Touching me all the time meant something. Talking to me about his duties as Alpha and the dangers of a relationship meant something. Drawing my picture meant something. But I was beginning to wonder whether I was just seeing what I wanted to see.

WE MET Hope. She'd done some research on missing children. The results were not encouraging.

In a city the size of Los Angeles, kids go missing. Most are not the sort whose pictures ever appear on milk cartons and transport trucks. As Jeremy said, these would be the children the group had targeted.

Next, we mulled over Eve's proposal. Was there a way to uncover the bodies without "satanic cult" being splashed across the six o'clock news? Hope would think about it. Jeremy probably could have asked Elena the same thing. But had he called Elena, she or Clay—if not both—would have been on the next plane out. As far as they knew, we were conducting exactly the sort of investigation Eve had groused about—reading books, researching news articles and canvassing safe supernatural contacts.

AT 4 P.M. we found ourselves at Botnick's shop again, preparing for another break-and-enter. Hope had asked to come along, on the chance she'd pick up some chaos vibes and help us unearth any occult evidence we'd missed.

She stood guard at the parking lot entrance and I watched from within the lot, in case anyone stepped outside while Jeremy reopened the window behind the trash bin.

"Done," he said as he walked up beside me.

"More of a challenge for you this time, I hope?"

His brows shot up. "Challenge? Heavens, no. Why would I want that? I'm a responsible Alpha, and as such, I hope all such dangerous endeavors are as straightforward and risk-free as possible."

I smiled, put my hands against his chest and lifted onto my tiptoes. He lowered his head, getting close enough for me to reach.

"Speaking of challenges," I muttered.

"Speaking of risks," he murmured back.

I met his gaze. "I'm willing to take them. Whether you are is, I suspect, another matter."

He hesitated, and I knew I'd guessed right.

"It's not—" he began.

"Okay, it looks like—" Hope's voice, across the lot. "Uh, sorry. I thought I heard voices."

"You did," I said, stepping away from Jeremy. "We should get inside while it's clear."

GETTING INSIDE wasn't the only thing made more difficult by daylight. Although the windows were smoked glass, anyone peering in could see us. But the alternative was to wait five hours.

Hope had contacted Karl earlier and hinted that his skills might be needed, but she'd pretended the occult case was her work assignment, not mentioning Jeremy or me. Jeremy seemed reluctant to get Karl involved. I could chalk this up to Jeremy enjoying the "challenges" of doing it himself, but knowing his feelings about Karl, I suspected there was more to it.

"I'll start in the office," Jeremy whispered as he adjusted his gloves.

"Can—?" Hope began, then pulled a face and reached for her cell phone. "Sorry. I'm supposed to be investigating crop circles. Thankfully, I can write a crop circle story in my sleep." A glance at the phone. "Oh, it's Rona Grant. Should I—?" She glanced at us.

"Go ahead," Jeremy said. "Perhaps she has something."

She didn't. Hope kept the phone a half-inch from her ear, volume jacked, so even without werewolf hearing, I could listen in.

Seemed May had asked Rona to follow up on whether any of those contact names had panned out. Hope strung her a story with the ease of a professional huckster, insinuating that we were indeed making use of those contacts, when we'd dismissed the lot of them yesterday. She probed around the subject of Botnick—nothing overt, just leading questions that might have gotten Rona talking about the cult leader, but obviously the woman had no interest in steering us down that seedy path. So Hope promised to keep her in the loop and hung up.

"As I was going to say, can you spare Jaime to show me those dissected bits?" Hope asked. "Not that I have a prurient interest in seeing dried-up body parts, but you were wondering whether they were taken from someone who was already dead . . . or someone they helped get that way."

"And you'll be able to tell. Jaime? Would you rather take the office?"

"Dried bits don't bother me."

WE CREPT to the storage room. Just inside the door, Hope stumbled. I went to catch her, but she brushed me off, regaining her balance herself. She turned, hands out, fumbling, as if dazed. Her face was white, her eyes wide and unseeing.

Having a vision. I knew better than to interfere—it's like shaking a sleepwalker awake. Instead, I stayed there, ready to grab her if she fell.

Her hands found the curtain and she grabbed it, as if for support. For a moment, she clung to it, head dropped forward, eyes closed, breaths coming deep and fast. Then her head whipped back and she gasped, eyes flying open.

"What's in here?" she asked hoarsely.

Before I could answer, she threw open the curtain. A sharp intake of breath as she stared at the bondage gear. Then a shaky laugh. "Well, that explains it."

A pause, then she glanced at me. "I have to— I can't do this here. Too strong. Can you get the . . . stuff and bring it out to me?"

I nodded.

A COUPLE of minutes later, I slipped into the cleaning closet and found Hope there, rubbing the back of her neck.

"Sorry about that," she said. "It was just—"

"Too much."

A wry smile. "Yeah. Asking me to get a sense of those—" she waved at the bags in my hand, "—while I was in that room, would be like asking a bloodhound to pick out a month-old trail in an airport terminal. Way too much else going on."

"Are you okay?"

Nodding, she took a bag from my hand. She stared at it, but I could tell she was still watching the movie playing in her mind. A sharp shake of her head.

"Maybe you should get some air," I said. "I know whatever you saw couldn't have been very pleasant."

"I'm okay. It's not . . . They don't disturb me." She lifted the bag. "Nothing here. Let's try another."

She went through three of the half-dozen bags, then stopped on the fourth, eyes closing, eyelids flickering, like someone in the throes of a vivid dream. Her breathing accelerated. Sweat beaded on her forehead. Then her eyes flew open and she handed the bag back to me.

"Car accident."

The next two gave her nothing.

"One accidental death, five chaos-free deaths. My sensors aren't perfect, but if all those folks were murdered for their body parts, I should have picked up something from at least one. All I got was a car accident—single-vehicle collision. Not pretty, but normal enough."

"So they're likely morgue or cemetery pickings. Like necromancers use."

"You guys use . . . ?"

I nodded. "Only we don't get the nice protective wrapping. Physical contact is a must."

"Ah."

"We get used to it. Like you and your visions—a nasty part of life."

She glanced at the bags. "So could this guy have been selling to necromancers?"

"Only without knowing it. More likely, he was just selling to humans wanting the stuff for medicine or magic. We use our own black markets, but even those are iffy. If I want quality goods, I have to go to the source."

"You mean . . ."

"Grave digging. Fortunately, it's not something I have to do very often."

Hope found one more violent death in the next batch—electrocution—but again it seemed accidental.

"So this cult draws the line at murder?" she said. "That surprises me. You'd think if you're going to kidnap and torture your victims, you'd kill them, if only to cover your tracks."

"Kidnap and torture?" I shook my head. "It may seem hard to believe, but they don't need unwilling victims. That bondage stuff is for the cult members. Consenting adults."

"Maybe that's what *you* saw. What *I* saw was definitely nonconsensual. And it was recent. I've been working on distinguishing past and current images and I have no doubt about that one."

"What did you see?"

"Not much. I was watching it from the victim's point of view, and his or her head was covered. Not just a blindfold or leather mask either. This thing was heavy."

"Like a metal helmet?"

She nodded. "But it was solid—or almost solid. The person inside could barely breathe."

I hurried back to the storage room and checked the shelf. The helmet was missing.

SUPERNATURAL CSI

HOPE PACED FROM ONE END of the storage room to the other. "No, it's not helping. I just keep seeing the same scene. That's usually how it is. If there's some way to see more, I haven't figured it out yet. I just get a snippet, playing over and over."

"Go through it again," Jeremy said. "In case I'm missing something."

From the frustration in Hope's face, I knew she thought he meant in case *she'd* missed something, but she took a deep breath and closed her eyes.

"Scene starts. Blackness. Can't breathe. Struggling. Restrained. First by hands, then those are gone but he still can't get away. There's a voice, but it echoes inside the helmet. Can't make out the words. Can't even tell whether it's a man or woman. Trying to scream, but can't, as if gagged, but . . ."

Hope opened her eyes. "It's like the person is gagged, but I don't feel one. Same with the restraints."

"A binding spell," Jeremy said.

"No, I've been caught in one of those before. It's not the same. This is . . ." She struggled for a comparison, then said, "Here, I'll try again."

Eyes closed. Back into the vision.

"Not a binding spell. Not restraints. The person wants to fight, but can't. Like his body won't respond. No—" She lifted a finger. "One more time. I'm getting it." Eyes closed. Deep breath. "The person is struggling. Screaming. But he's so weak, it doesn't matter." She opened her eyes. "That's it. Weakened. Like sedated but there's no feeling of being tired or sleepy. Just . . . drained."

"Magically drained," Jeremy said.

"I'd say so."

"If it happened here, let's see whether I can find a trail."

I TOOK Hope to the office, saying we should take a look, see whether fresh eyes found anything new, but really, I was just giving Jeremy privacy. There's something very undignified about getting down on your hands and knees to snuffle the ground.

After about ten minutes, Jeremy called us back. The room was thick with trails. From our excursion the night before, he had a good idea which trails belonged to group members, but picking out "which of these doesn't belong" in the tiny closet was probably close to Hope's analogy of a bloodhound in a busy airport terminal. He'd sorted out three, maybe four scents he didn't recognize. One of them, presumably, was the victim.

"The others are probably cult members who missed last night's meeting. All the trails, though, eventually lead there." He pointed down at the trap door, having rolled back the carpet.

"Not surprising," I said. "If they're going to kill someone, that's where they'd do it."

"I'm not sure we have a murder victim. That was my first thought—that Botnick made contact with the group and they demanded proof of his loyalty."

"Human sacrifice," Hope said.

"But for all of the trails that go down, there's one coming back."

"Maybe Botnick lost his nerve," I said. "Or it was just a test to see whether he'd go through with it. In either case—" I pulled open the hatch, "—that means I'm not going to stumble across a corpse or a ghost screaming for vengeance, so I'm good."

"Hope?" Jeremy said. "A lack of a corpse won't make this any easier for *you*."

"I'll be fine."

HOPE STOPPED at the bottom of the ladder, rigid, as if she'd known this vision was coming, and braced for it. When it finished, she gave a soft sigh of relief.

"Same old, same old," she said. "He or she is in the helmet, can't see, can barely breathe, can't fight or scream. For chaos, it ranks about a four. Terror, but it's just fear of the unknown."

We looked around. The cavernous, crate-lined room looked exactly as we'd left it.

"Flecks of blood," Hope said, walking to the middle.

I followed her. "They're from last night. The meeting."

Her face scrunched in distaste. "In other words, as you said, it was consensual. Which explains why I'm not getting much in the way of chaos vibes."

Jeremy hadn't said a word. Not unusual. But when I looked over, I saw him staring out across the room, nostrils flared. He turned his head slowly, inhaling, as if trying to get a fix on a scent. Then his gaze came to rest on a wall of boxes along the wall—the wall with the embedded hooks.

"Those boxes weren't like that last night," I said, walking toward it.

Jeremy called to me, but I was only a few feet away and by the time I realized he was trying to stop me, I could see a foot protruding from behind the stack. I backpedaled to avoid an attack. Then I saw the hook, and the chain pulled taut and, without thinking, I stepped sideways for a better view.

A man hung suspended from the hook by the chain. His feet touched the ground, knees bent, dangling. My first thought was *How do you hang yourself if you can touch the ground?* Then I saw the choke chain around his neck.

Jeremy put his hand on my shoulder, but didn't pull me away. If I wanted to look, that was my choice. He moved past me to examine the body.

The man's head drooped, but even before I saw his face, I knew it was Botnick. His eyes were bulging. His fingers were wrapped around the chain at his neck, as if he'd tried to pull it free.

"He couldn't get it loose," said a soft voice behind me. Hope's. "They took off the helmet and kicked his legs out from under him, and the chain tightened, but something kept it from loosening, even after he got his footing."

Jeremy moved alongside the body, looking without touching. Watching him, my gaze moved down Botnick for the first time, and noticed something . . . unexpected.

"He's not wearing any pants. Did they . . . rape him?"

"Doesn't appear so," Jeremy said. "There's no sign of struggle. I think that was intentional—using a spell to restrain him—so there wouldn't be any marks. Nothing to indicate he didn't do this to himself. As for the pants, though . . ."

"That's intentional," Hope said. "They've set the scene for autoerotic asphyxiation."

I explained to Jeremy.

"Ah," he said. "And, given the nature of this room and the equipment upstairs, that's exactly the sort of thing the authorities would expect someone like Botnick to do."

SO WE *did* have a murder. Jeremy had found a return trail because Botnick had been in and out of this basement several times in the last twenty-four hours.

Had he made contact with the group? Gotten in touch with his former lover, who'd called her former lover and they'd set up a meeting with Botnick? It wasn't the only possibility. Maybe that cult member he'd whipped last night had her "I'm not going to take it anymore" epiphany, and had come back to kill him. Or maybe it was a customer, furious that his "ground rhino penis" hadn't outperformed Viagra, as advertised. Guys like Botnick had their share of enemies—not all the most stable individuals.

But that would be mighty coincidental and wouldn't explain the magical weakening Hope had picked up. So we set to work playing CSI. The supernatural version. The werewolf untangled and followed scent trails. The half-demon reviewed the death vision. And the necromancer tried to contact the spirit of the deceased.

I summoned Botnick repeatedly, with no luck. Not surprising really. Rigor mortis had set in and the body had cooled, meaning he'd been dead for hours.

Newly dead spirits don't hang around long before someone whisks them off to the afterlife, and once they're gone, necromancers can't make contact until the powers-that-be decide they're ready to receive visitors. Still, I tried, in case Botnick hadn't been scooped up yet. I was about to give up when I spotted a shape slipping through a stack of boxes across the room.

"You!"

I advanced on the ghost. It was the voyeur from the night before. He started to fade.

"Don't you dare," I said. "Unless you want to be reported for loitering at the scene of an unauthorized occult gathering, I'd suggest you tell me what you saw."

"I didn't—"

"Yes, you did. You're the only witness to a murder and you'd better tell me what you saw or you'll add 'failing to remain at the scene' to those charges."

He peered at me, his eyes narrowing. I tried to look severe. Even fierce. I think I blew it when I went for fierce.

"Pfft," he said, and started to fade.

A bolt of energy sliced through the boxes and hit him in the stomach. He yelped and stumbled. Eve strode from the crate pile and kicked the man's legs out from under him. When he fell, she planted her boot on his throat.

"Feel more like talking now?" she asked.

He yowled as she ground her foot into his neck.

"Oh, stuff it. You can't feel pain, remember?" She leaned back and fixed him with a look. "Or, considering your 'proclivities,' I'm guessing that's the tragedy of your afterlife, huh?"

His eyes narrowed to slits. "I deliver pain, bitch. I don't receive."

"Right. So that convention in Hawaii... eighty-nine, wasn't it? So that's not you I see wearing the grass skirt and getting... Eww. Let's stop right there."

His face went slack and his lips parted, as if to ask how she'd known that. Then he settled for spewing invective.

"Oh, quit your bitching," Eve said. "I'm not here to discuss your sex life—much rather not, thank you. You're going to tell the nice lady—"

"I'm not telling either of you anything."

She began again, in the same calm tone. "You're going to tell—"

"You've already admitted you can't hurt me, so how are you going to—"

"Hold that thought." Eve lifted a finger, then looked at me. "Could you . . . ?" She motioned with her still-raised finger, telling me to turn around.

So she didn't want me seeing how she was going to persuade the ghost to speak. I could have protested that I wasn't skittish—I'd just found a dead body and hadn't run screaming from the room. An old argument, and not worth rehashing now. So I settled for a glare, and turned my back, resisting the urge to cross my arms.

Jeremy and Hope had already figured out that I wasn't talking to myself. From behind me came a commotion of muffled cries, most of it "bleeped" out, the rest incoherent babbling.

"—sorry, very sorry—didn't understand the situation—no offense intended—none at all—"

I waited. More babbled apologies.

Then, Eve, impatiently, "Are you done? Because we really need to get on with this, preferably before the cops show up."

"Yes, yes, but I just want you to know, I meant no disrespect. I—"

"—didn't understand the situation. Well, now you do. So shut up and answer our questions. Jaime?"

I started to turn around.

"Uh-uh," Eve said. "Gotta keep looking that way or we aren't going to get the truth out of this bastard."

The ghost yelped in protest. "I will. I assure you, now that I understand—"

"—the situation. Got that part. As for telling the truth, let's just say I like to be thorough. So the—" her next word was bleeped, "—stays. Got it?"

"Whatever you say, ma'am. Or, er, is there a proper form of address? I've never met—"

"Ma'am is fine. Jaime?"

The ghost—Stan, as he finally introduced himself—had been hanging around the basement last night, hoping for further excitement after our hasty exit. The cult members had followed us a little ways into the tunnel, but retreated once they hit the drop-off. Upstairs, Botnick convinced them that nothing had been touched, no doors left unlocked, and, had anyone broken into the basement, it had probably just been some vagrant or addict who came in through the tunnel looking for shelter.

The man had left then, but the woman had hung around, obviously suspecting something was up, and only left when Botnick went with her. Stan stayed. Jeremy returned and wandered around, picking up Botnick's trail, then left. Twenty minutes or so later, Botnick came back alone, probably hoping we'd show up again. He'd stayed for an hour, then made a phone call on his cell. He'd had to go upstairs to get decent reception. Stan hadn't followed, so he hadn't heard the content of that call. Botnick had then done some wandering of his own, nervously pacing as he waited.

A couple of hours passed. Then Stan heard a cry and a thump. He'd gone up to find Botnick facedown on the floor, unconscious, surrounded by three dark-clad figures. They seemed to have come up on Botnick from behind and knocked him out before he could say a word.

Jeremy had me press Stan for details on Botnick's attackers, but he could give little. And whatever Eve was doing to him, it meant he couldn't lie.

All three had worn dark boots, pants, jackets and balaclavas. They'd ranged in height from about five foot six to six feet. Their clothing had been too bulky to determine weight. They spoke in whispers, and little of that, communicating only brusque commands, never using names. From the timbre of the voices, he guessed all had been men.

One of the three had brought a leather mask and the helmet from the storeroom. They'd wordlessly decided on the helmet. Botnick regained consciousness as they were putting the helmet on him, but the biggest of the three had restrained him. One of the others had done some "magical mumbo jumbo" as Stan put it, and Botnick's struggles had turned to twitches, his stifled cries to whimpers.

I questioned Stan further on the "magical mumbo jumbo." Being a nonsupernatural, the finer points of spellcasting eluded him. According to him, the person had "said foreign stuff and blown something on Eric."

Eve recited a few lines in the most common spellcasting languages—Latin, Greek and Hebrew. He thought Greek sounded right . . . but Latin was close too. Jeremy tried French and Spanish, but I doubted Stan would recognize the language even if the exact lines were repeated. He was more a "foreign stuff" kind of guy. Likewise for the "blown stuff." It had been powder, maybe gray, maybe white. In other words, anything from ash to cocaine to dust. Eve knew of no spells requiring such a thing.

Nor had she heard of anything like the "weakening" spell. As she said, there was no point using something like that if you had a binding spell. Meaning whoever used it *didn't* have a binding spell.

Once Botnick was subdued, they'd taken him downstairs. There, the tallest of the three had done all the talking. Interrogating, I should say. Not much different than what we were doing to Stan now. They'd wanted to know all about the "visit" we'd paid him.

Botnick had described us only in the broadest terms—a couple in their late thirties, dark-haired man, red-haired woman. They'd pushed for details, but, like Stan, Botnick wasn't an eagle-eyed observer. He'd gotten the best look at me, but his only description was that I was "a real looker."

Jeremy had been behind him most of the time, and he'd only gotten a glance at Jeremy's back as he'd followed me into the tunnel. Apparently not being one to check out a guy from the rear, Botnick could say only that he "wasn't a huge, brawny guy," thus supporting his belief that Jeremy's strength was preternatural.

They'd questioned him a lot on that—Jeremy's strength. Had I displayed any uncanny abilities? No. Had Jeremy displayed any others? No. What had we asked him? He told them. Where did we go? He told them.

Like Stan now, Botnick had been almost falling over himself to respond, probably thinking he was being tested and working hard to impress.

Once they'd been certain Botnick had nothing more to tell them, they'd killed him. Then they'd staged the scene and left. Stan hadn't bothered to follow them, having no interest in secret societies that didn't involve sex.

IV

She glanced up at the bat. Its desiccated eyes stared back from its perch on the shelf overlooking the tiny concrete room. Beside it was a legless terrier—one of their earlier experiments, along with the other mammals and reptiles on the shelf ringing the room, dating from a time when they'd hoped animal sacrifice would be enough.

The remains now served a dual purpose. When they performed a human sacrifice, they had only to glance up to be reminded of why they'd needed to take this difficult step. The other reason was purely practical. While they'd taken every step to hide and secure this room—by both normal and magical means—if it was ever found, the animal corpses would serve as a valid explanation for its existence, making them seem guilty of nothing more heinous than animal sacrifice and dissection.

She knelt under the watchful eyes of those preserved beasts, waiting as Don explained to the group what she was about to attempt.

"This spell is far more ambitious than any we've tried before, but we've been working on it for months and finally, in this past week, we've seen a glimmer of success."

Her gaze slid around the circle, studying and evaluating each expression. Everyone was here. Under the circumstances—the promise of stronger magic—it should have been no trouble getting full attendance. But Brian had tried to duck out, claiming a pressing work deadline. And, to her surprise, Tina had also wavered, saying her in-laws were in town.

Murray's death three weeks ago had shaken them more than she'd anticipated. She'd given them time to bounce back, and now she needed to follow the slap of his death with a reward. Reassure them that the prize was worth the price.

"We insisted you all be present today," Don continued, "in hopes that this will provide the boost we need to successfully cast this spell. All of us here, our combined life energy in this place, where the power has been harvested many times and where vestiges of that supreme power may still remain."

Don lied with the fervor of a true believer—convinced that what they were doing was right and, more than right, to his benefit. That's what set him apart from the others and what had made her choose him years ago as her confidante. Well, her confidante in most things...

Here, in this room, they'd killed six children, slitting their throats as they slept, drugged, on this floor. Here they'd watched a young man burn to death, the spell making him too weak to do more than mewl and rasp, his screams pouring from his eyes instead. Here they'd stabbed Murray in the back, watched their longtime fellow and, yes, friend slide to the floor, his lifeblood trickling down the drain.

And here, in this same place, they would now be reminded of what they were striving for. Here they would witness a breakthrough into the world of power they dreamed of. Or so Don hoped. She could see the anxiety in his eyes, the sweat beading on his bald pate.

She smiled reassuringly. She didn't tell him *all* her secrets.

"I'll need a volunteer to test this on," she said. "Brian? Would you be so kind?"

"Depends on what you're going to do."

A whoosh of laughter from the group, more tension relief than real amusement.

"It might hurt, but not too much." She smiled. "I hope."

More laughter. Brian took up the position she indicated, in the middle of the floor, standing over the drawn symbols.

"I ask you all to be patient with me," she said. "I'm sure this will take a few casts."

She adjusted the cue card on the floor. She'd memorized the spell, but there was some reassurance in having the words close by. Sometimes even she needed reassurance.

She took a moment to mentally prepare. Getting "into the zone," as her personal trainer would say. Then she reached into the open jar, took out a generous pinch of ash and laid it on her palm. She closed her eyes, sinking deeper into that zone. Around her, no one even shifted position, however uncomfortable the cold concrete beneath them. Silence and concentration were paramount.

When she opened her eyes, she saw only the mound of ash on her palm, all her attention on that focal point. One deep breath in. She let it out slowly, the human remains fluttering from her hand. Still exhaling, she began the incantation.

With the last words, she flung her hand toward Brian. The unexpected movement startled him and his mouth opened to say something. Then he jolted sideways, knocked off balance, almost tumbling to the floor. As he recovered, she cast again, faster now. And this time, the moment she flung out her hand, he jerked, as if struck by something. His eyes went wide, then closed as he slid to the floor.

Around her, everyone had gone as still as Brian. Finally, Don found his voice.

"He—he's just unconscious. It—it worked."

She tried to look surprised, as if it hadn't worked for her when she'd tested it on derelicts, no one the wiser when they slumped to the ground, presumably passing out drunk.

Don remembered his lines. "Our first truly defensive spell. Imagine how it could be used. No more fear of muggings or carjackings or home invasions. One spell, and your attacker falls to the ground, unconscious." He cleared his throat, then gestured at Brian's still form. "This is what we've been working toward. Magic truly worth the price."

She looked around the circle and knew, finally, that they were one again.

DEATH BODIES

ONCE STAN WAS GONE—Eve and I made sure of it—we left too. Interrogating Stan had only confirmed what we'd already suspected, but I suppose that was progress. Botnick had been killed, not by the Disciples of Asmodai or random customers, but by members of the group we were seeking. And they had magic.

While Eve stood guard outside, Hope, Jeremy and I looked around the store and made sure there was no trace of our visit—far more important now that it was the site of a murder, not just a break-and-enter.

"Thanks for coming by," I said to Eve as we headed back to the car. "Your timing was perfect."

"Actually, I arrived a few minutes before that, but thought I'd give you a chance to handle it on your own. I liked 'loitering at the scene of an unauthorized occult gathering.' Had him going for a minute. Trouble is, when you try to bluff, you tip your hand. We'll have to work on that."

EVE ACCOMPANIED us back to Hope's apartment, arguing her case for drawing out our prey instead of tracking it down. After her help, I couldn't refuse to listen and she knew it, making herself almost as much of a nuisance as Stan.

As we walked from the parking lot to Hope's place, the debate slid into a two-way discussion between Eve and Jeremy, with me there to "interpret." Hope stayed out of it from the beginning—being her first prolonged ghost encounter, she probably found it unnerving.

"Fine, you're right," Eve said to Jeremy. "Minimal press exposure, to protect everyone involved and keep things from getting out of hand."

As I relayed her message, I dropped change into a street musician's guitar case.

"I hope you're paying him for music lessons," Eve said. "Or, better yet, to stop playing."

I shook my head and glanced at Jeremy, but he was busy scanning the street. I thought he was thinking until I saw his nostrils flare.

"Jeremy?" I said.

He inhaled again. Then a nod.

"What do you smell?" I asked.

He shook his head.

BY THE time we reached the apartment, we'd made a decision. If we didn't find anything in our search of Botnick's house, we'd take that next step tonight. We'd try to find a body in the garden . . . but not using necromancy.

BOTNICK LIVED in an old two-story working-class house in a working-class neighborhood. His was little more than a cereal box—long, rectangular and very narrow. Hardly the Gothic mansion one expected of a sex cult leader.

The interior was generic. Off-white walls throughout. Interior decoration by IKEA. Functional, contemporary furniture, all matched sets. Even the art on the walls looked like it came from the Scandinavian company. Maybe Botnick had gone through the IKEA catalog, found a sample page for each room and ordered everything off it.

After we knew the layout of the house, we split up. Hope would randomly scout for vibes. Jeremy would take the office. I'd look for secret areas—locked closets, trap doors and the like—the sort of hidey-holes Botnick seemed to like.

The only Gothic thing about the place was the ghosts. Three of them. That was a lot for one place. Botnick seemed to attract them. Not surprising. People pursue magical answers to their problems even after death. While humans try to find a back door into the afterlife—to gain the knowledge of the ages by communicating with the dead—ghosts are busy trying to find a back door out, to leave eternity and exchange the divine for the profane. The "grass is always greener" syndrome.

Now this trio of ghosts, who'd been hoping this cut-rate occultist would show them the path, had hit the jackpot. There was a necromancer in the house.

At first they only whispered among themselves. To nonsupernatural ghosts, necromancers are the stuff of legend. Like spotting Elvis in the afterlife. Everyone says he's there, they know how to recognize him if they see him and some have even met him. Most, though, will go through eternity and never encounter the man. So it was with necromancers. These ghosts recognized my "glow," but wanted to be sure they weren't mistaken. So they followed me.

The apparent leader was a woman in pioneer gear: a shabby dress with a yoke and apron. I guessed she was at least sixty—with iron gray hair and sunken, leathery cheeks—but on second glance, I wondered whether she was really any older than me. The second ghost was a young woman in a high-collared Victorian dress, her hair pulled so tight it acted like a face-lift. The third was a man in modern working clothes. Big and shambling, he lagged behind the women like a faithful dog.

They "tested" me, trying to determine whether I could see or hear them, and I willfully failed every time. Got away with it until I was checking an interior wall that seemed larger than normal—perhaps hiding some secret compartment. I tapped along it, listening for a change in tone, intent on my task—

"Hello!" The pioneer woman's face shot through the wall right in front of me.

I jumped.

"Ah-ha!" she screeched. "You *can* see us."

I tried to cover, looking around as if some noise had startled me. Then, fearing that wasn't enough, I faked a hiccup, as if *that* had made me jump. I overdid it with the hiccup. Tipped my hand, as Eve would have said.

I kept examining the wall while all three ghosts tried their hand at "spooking" me. Finally I gave up. The ghosts hadn't appeared when the others were around, so I found Hope in the master bedroom.

"Hey," I whispered. "Getting any bad vibes?"

"There's something here," she said. "I can't tell whether it's just his S & M stuff. Maybe a less-than-willing partner. Hard to pick up, though."

"Hey, pretty lady," the male ghost whispered in my ear. "Got something I think you'd like to see."

I kept my attention on Hope as she closed her eyes to pick up the vibe or vision. The ghost stepped between us.

"Here," he said, leering. "Take a look at this."

He reached—predictably—for his fly. Not like I hadn't been flashed before.

His zipper whirred. Then he reached inside and . . . his torso fell back, intestines spilling out, the top half of his body nearly severed.

I stumbled backward. The ghosts roared with laughter.

"Gotcha," the man said, his head nearly on the floor, walking toward me, insides quivering, his upper half held on only by his spine.

"Jaime?" I heard Hope say, her voice distant.

I lifted my hands to wave her off and murmured something like "I'm all right"—words that didn't penetrate the pounding of blood in my ears.

The bisected ghost cavorted in front of me, his intestines bobbing. I took a deep breath to steady myself. This was his death body. He'd probably died in some industrial accident and could now revert to that "form" at will. Knowing this, though, didn't make the sight any less gruesome.

"Jaime?" Hope said again.

"Sorry," I said as the ghost pranced between us. I forced my gaze to Hope. "Are you getting anything?"

"I think so. Weak, though. Just random images. Blood, crying . . . It's faint, which could mean it's old—"

The pioneer woman leapt through Hope. Her scalp was ripped off, bloodied skull exposed over empty bird-pecked eye sockets. I slapped my hand over my mouth as I shrieked.

Hope caught my arm to steady me.

"Just ghosts," I said before she could speak. "I shouldn't have interrupted. Go back to what you were doing."

As I hurried away, the ghosts pranced and darted around me in their death bodies, the Victorian woman wasted and naked—a dancing skeleton sheathed in gray skin.

"Not bothering you, are we?" she trilled. "Shall we stop?"

"Yes," lisped the pioneer woman, her tongue half gone, her empty eye sockets turned my way. "Shall we stop?"

She mimicked the younger woman's proper accent. The man joined in and all three circled me, chanting, "Shall we stop? Shall we stop?"

"Jaime?"

I turned to see Jeremy in the office doorway.

He strode over, his hand going to my arm. Then he looked around, his face hardening. "Ghosts?"

I nodded.

The pioneer woman circled Jeremy. "Oooh, look, a proper gentleman. Isn't he a fine one?"

"Very fine," the younger woman said. "Very proper. Too much a gentleman for the likes of this whore."

I wheeled on her, then chomped my lip hard enough to taste blood.

Don't give them the satisfaction, Nan always said. Let them see they're getting to you, and you've lost.

Jeremy said something, his head leaning down to mine, hair in his eyes, lips moving. Asking me what I was seeing, what I was hearing. I knew I should tell him—get that distance by sharing it, laughing it off. But all I could hear were the damned ghosts.

"She does look like a whore, don't she?" the pioneer woman said, coming close, her eyeless sockets studying me. "All fancied up with her colored hair and her painted face, acting like she's quality, but she's wearing pants tighter than riding breeches, her shirt's half undone, giving any man who wants it a good view of her titties. Like the fancy ladies at the mining camp. Act like they're something special, but give 'em a dollar and they'll spread their legs fast as any street whore."

"I got a dollar," the man said. "Think she'll give me a ride?"

"Course she will. And being dead you don't have to worry about catching anything."

They all cackled.

"Did you bring your banishing mixture?" Jeremy asked, his voice finally penetrating.

"Forgot."

"Isn't *he* worried about catching the pox?" the pioneer woman said. "Your fine man?"

"Fine men like that don't think of such things," the Victorian woman said. "They don't know better . . . until it's too late."

The pioneer woman snickered. "And he finds out her cunny's so well used it's like fucking a bucket."

"I'm going outside," I said to Jeremy. "Get some fresh air. See if I can lose them."

"Oh, you won't lose us, pretty lady," the man said.

Jeremy tried to accompany me, but I insisted he stay behind. Bad enough I couldn't help him search the house. He argued, but I stood firm and, after a long look in my eyes, he brushed his lips across my forehead, then whispered a suggestion about a coffee shop a block east.

The ghosts followed me out the rear door into the backyard, cycling through the same insults as if they could think of nothing new. I considered making a run for the road and trying to lose them.

"What the hell?" said a voice behind me. Eve strode around to my front. "Why didn't you call?"

She wheeled on the severed man when he got too close and slammed a kick into the side of his dangling head. His torso flew sideways so fast he toppled.

"Now put yourself together or the next kick is going to knock that half clean off." She turned on the other two. "Clothes on. Scalp on. Eyes back in."

She marched in front of them like a drill sergeant. "Is this how you think you get a necromancer's attention? Well, congratulations. You've just placed yourself on their blacklist. No necro, anywhere, is ever going to speak to you, no matter how nice you are."

The pioneer woman aimed a sulky scowl at Eve. "Who do you think you are, giving us orders?"

"Let's just say you don't want to find out," Eve said, peering down at the woman from her full six feet. "Now—"

"You don't scare me," the Victorian woman said.

She advanced on Eve. The other woman circled around behind her. The man stepped forward, his hands clenching into fists. Eve stood her ground, looking bored.

"You spooks wanna rumble? I've got a better idea. What you need is a break. A vacation. I'm thinking Scotland. Got some great castles there."

She drop-kicked the man, then shot an energy bolt into the Victorian woman's stomach. The pioneer woman ran at Eve, then froze in a binding spell.

"Hey, Kris?" Eve called. "That's your cue."

Kristof appeared, leaning against a tree, as if he'd been there all along, watching from the other side.

"Sorry," he said. "It looked like you were having fun. I hated to interrupt."

"I was, but now it's time for transport and I could use some help. You take the ugly guy. I'll take the ugly women."

The Victorian woman squawked as Eve grabbed her arm and that of the still-frozen pioneer woman.

"Back in a jiffy," she said as she vanished.

UNGRATEFUL

WHEN THEY WERE GONE, I looked at the house. Should I go back inside? No. Not just yet. I crept from the yard and found the coffee shop Jeremy had mentioned. Some Starbucks clone in a strip mall, the kind of place it seemed no neighborhood could be without.

I ordered, calling Jeremy while I waited in line, so he'd know where to pick me up. I told him Eve had shown up and "solved the problem." Another day, another rescue.

I sat in a too-comfortable armchair, the kind these places always seem to have, that look so cozy and inviting until you sink down and realize you can't reach your coffee. So you clutch the mug in your hands and tell yourself the comfy chair makes up for the inconvenience.

Two women about my age plopped onto the sofa next to me, though the coffee shop was three quarters empty. They then proceeded to speak loudly enough to entertain us all.

"And I told her, 'You are *not* quitting ballet, not after I paid for lessons for five years.' All those hours shuttling her to the dance studio, watching her rehearsals . . ."

"Ungrateful kids," her friend said, shaking her head. "You want them to grow up with some culture, some grace, and all of a sudden they have better things to do."

"Well, if that's what she thinks, she can think again. I made an investment. And like all my investments, it damned well better pay off. Ungrateful little . . ."

My jaw clenched so tight my head hurt. I lifted my cup to sip my coffee and watched the surface quiver as my fingers shook.

How many times had I heard some variation on those words from my own mother? My earliest memory was of her dragging me from a preschool pageant, her fingers clamped around my arm, where I'd have welts for weeks, all because I'd been ungrateful enough to cry when the hair stylist's curling iron had burned my scalp. Even the last time I'd spoken to her, I'd heard the speech. My eternal ingratitude for the sacrifices she'd made on my behalf.

As the women continued, my mother's voice rolled over me, taking me back to when I was first coming into my powers.

"Do you have any idea what it's like, Jaime? Getting calls from high school that you're cowering in the bathroom? Having to delay a commercial shoot because some ghost is bothering you? Changing your wet bedsheets? Pissing the bed at your age because you're *scared*? I've worked my ass off to make something of you. Your father saddles me with his screwed-up family problem and his screwed-up kid, then kills himself—takes the easy way out. Your precious Nan is no help, always coddling you, putting me down because I ask a little of you in return. You should be tripping over yourself to help, not complaining because you missed a week of school, failed another test. As if you wouldn't have failed anyway. At least I gave you an excuse. Any other parent wouldn't put up with this, you know. They'd have shipped you off long ago."

I'd grown up believing her—that any other parent would've gotten rid of me. A child has no other point of reference, no wider view of the world.

I'm sure I wasn't easy to raise. I had my problems, supernatural and otherwise. But now I look around and see the way other parents raise supernatural children. Jeremy taking in a feral child werewolf, no relative or responsibility of his. Paige adopting the daughter of a dark witch, a stranger. Even other human parents faced with supernatural children handled it just fine. Talia Vasic raising Adam on her own, helping him deal with his demonic powers before she knew what they were. Hope talking about how close she was to her mother, a woman who probably still didn't know why her daughter was "different." It didn't matter. A parent loves. A parent helps. A parent accepts.

Still, I wasn't the only supernatural raised by an unloving parent. Jeremy talked little of his father, but from what I've gleaned, the man had been a cold killer with nothing but contempt for his quiet, nonaggressive son. Jeremy got over it. Flourished. Grew up to be a leader, a man who accepted his differences and didn't complain about them or feel sorry for himself.

"You should have called."

I looked up. The other women were gone and Eve now sat in their place. She propped her long legs on the table between us.

"Yeah," she said, cutting me off as I started to answer. "You wanted to handle it yourself. I know. But see, that's not how this arrangement works. We're partners. If I need a ghost contacted in another plane or I need something done in the living world, I call you. If you need a pesky spook scared off, you call me."

"I—"

"And you know what? I'd love to be able to find any ghost myself, to surf the Internet when I need information. But I can't. No more than you can deal with jerks like those three."

I looked around, then took out my cell phone, pretending to talk into it. "You took them to Glamis, didn't you? To Dantalian."

"Oh, they'll have fun," she said. "Dantalian's not so bad. Gets lonely, though. Six hundred years is a long time to be cooped up, even for a demon. Like a cat confined to a small apartment. He appreciates new playthings to bat around." She stretched one leg and "nudged" my knee. "And if you think *that* distracted me from my lecture, you're wrong. You need to call me, Jaime. If I'm around, there's no need for you to deal with shit like that."

"I know. I just—"

"—don't want to *need* help. Fine. But everyone has her specialty. Yours is helping ghosts. Mine is kicking their asses. Whole different skill set."

"I didn't help them," I said as I looked out across the shop. "Didn't even try."

"You were breaking and entering, for God's sake. You can't stop to take requests."

She went on, trying to convince me that I hadn't been wrong to ignore the ghosts. But I knew I hadn't handled it well. I should have told them I was busy, but would speak to them later, outside. They still might have turned on me, but at least I could say I'd done my duty.

Duty? I balked at the thought. I wasn't their servant. I didn't owe them anything.

Or did I?

I thought of the analogy I'd made earlier. Necromancers as the Elvises of the ghost world. They all want to catch a glimpse of us, to talk to us. Just a little of our time. And, yes, it can be overwhelming, as I'm sure it was—or is—for Elvis. But if someone walks up to him and just wants to say, "Loved your stuff," does he have the right to ignore them?

I've spent enough time in Hollywood to know this is a contentious issue—the artist's obligation to the public versus his right to privacy. While I don't think you owe it to your fans to provide tabloids with your vacation itinerary or details of your sex life, I don't think an autograph or thirty seconds of your time is too much to ask, not when these are the people who fund your dream—buying your movies, albums, books, whatever.

I told myself the analogy wasn't a fair one. I'm quick with a signature or a smile for my fans. What obligation do I have to ghosts? They don't pay for seats at my shows. Yet, without them, without my ability to speak to them, I'd have no career. Sure, I could fake it—I usually did—but it was my real contacts, like my séance with Tansy Lane, that kept me in business.

But ghosts ask for more than an autograph or a handshake. Am I obligated to provide it more often than I already do? Am I obligated to at least listen more often than I do?

Jeremy arrived and I started to get up, but he waved me down again and told me Hope had taken a cab and I should finish my coffee. He got one for himself, then started to sit on the sofa.

"Uh, not there," I said.

He looked over his shoulder at the seemingly empty seat. "Hello, Eve."

"Tell him I said hi . . . and bye," she said. "I need to check a few things, then I'll come by the gardens."

AFTER WE left the coffee shop, Jeremy told me the results of their break-and-enter. He had hoped to uncover the name of the lover Botnick had shared with a member of the magic group, and he had found a book with dozens of women's names, all classified by codes. Find the key to the code and he might find the right lover—but he suspected that key had existed only in Botnick's head. Eve was trying to gain access to Botnick, but those first few postdeath days were difficult.

Hope hadn't fared any better. As she'd feared, the vibes she'd picked up were old. She'd finally tapped into the chaos enough to see what she'd been sensing—a vision of a man killing his wife with an axe, back in the twenties. A gruesome reward for all her effort, and one with no bearing on our case.

I hesitated for a minute, then told Jeremy about the women in the coffee shop and how they'd reminded me of my mother.

"I guess I was feeling sorry for myself, thinking of how other parents handle supernatural things so much better. But you didn't have it easy yourself."

A half-shrug. Did that mean he didn't want to talk about it? Or just didn't want to complain? After a moment, though, he said, "I just wasn't what Malcolm hoped for in a son." He often referred to his father by his first name, which said a lot about their relationship.

"You weren't a fighter, you mean." I flushed. "Not that you aren't—"

"I'm not. I can be, but it's not who I am. A wolf instinctively wants to pass on what he knows to his son. I just wasn't that son. He tried transferring his attentions to Clay, but—" a shrug, "—that didn't work out so well."

"Your father and Clay?"

"At first, Malcolm wanted nothing to do with Clay. But as he grew, my father interpreted his strong wolf side as . . ." He paused, as if searching for a word.

"A violent streak?"

"Sadistic even, which I'm sure any psychiatrist would say was projection. Malcolm liked to kill. There's no other way to put it. He wanted to train Clay to fight. I knew that as long as I supervised, it was what Clay needed. Clay hated Malcolm, but he was astute enough, even at that age, to take what he could from the lessons. As for a father-son bond, it never happened."

"Is that all your father wanted?"

"I'm sure he hoped to turn Clay against me. Malcolm vacillated between ignoring me and planning petty revenges. He hated being beholden to me."

"Beholden?"

"His father left Stonehaven and all its assets to me. While my grandfather intended to protect me, the result was that I was then responsible for Malcolm. I had to dole out an allowance and hide his killings, because if the Pack found out, he'd be banished, and become an even greater threat."

I was silent for a moment, then said, "That's the real problem, isn't it? You're tired of being responsible for others."

He looked over sharply.

"Your father. Clay. The Pack. Elena after Clay bit her. You've always been responsible for others, and now that you're hoping to retire from Alpha-hood, the last thing you need is a relationship with someone else you might need to protect."

"No. That's not true, Jaime. Clay and the Pack were responsibilities I wanted. Even with Elena and my father, there were other options available. I like being responsible. I like helping. I like protecting. And I'm sure that says something less than admirable about my character, but I can't help it. If anything, with you, I struggle not to overdo it. I want to give you advice, to help you, and I know that's not what you need from me."

"Sometimes it is," I said softly.

A crooked smile. "In small doses, yes. If I gave free rein to my impulses, you'd run screaming the other way." He eased back in his seat, smile fading. "I am a leader, Jaime. I like to be in control and be responsible for others, and I take that responsibility very seriously. That means I don't take chances. Ever."

I met his gaze. "Well, maybe it's time to start."

A long pause. Then he murmured, under his breath, so softly I had to read his lips to hear it, "Maybe it is."

BY THE time we returned to the house, it was past midnight. Jeremy and I snuck around to the garden.

I sat under a gnarled dwarf tree, the long twisted branches tickling my arms, while Jeremy . . . got ready. Overhead the nearly full moon brightened the garden to twilight, casting a yellow glow. Some night bird or owl gave a mournful cry, raising the hairs on my neck. The faint smell of wood smoke drifted past.

"Nice night for grave digging," Eve whispered as she sat beside me on the bench. "Did you know you have a ghostly audience already?"

I glanced around. Tansy and Gabrielle were almost hidden behind a fountain. Tansy lifted her fingers in a sheepish wave. I waved back, but my stomach clenched. Was she still waiting for me to talk to her?

"There are more," Eve said. "Probably a dozen of them. They seem to be trying to stay out of your way. Just curious. But if you want me to shoo them off—"

"No, they're fine."

She tilted her head, hearing the *click-click* of claws on cement. "Here he comes. I'll get out of your way too, so I can guard the guards—warn you if *they* get curious."

"Thanks."

A black wolf stepped from the shadows into the moonlight. He moved slowly, as if wary of startling me. I suppose if there's any sight worth being spooked by, it's a 180-pound wolf in a residential garden at night. But Jeremy in wolf form never frightened me. Not even the first time I'd seen him. A changed werewolf looks like a real wolf, but their overall size stays the same, as do their hair and eye color. I'd taken one look in those dark eyes and I'd known it was Jeremy.

He padded over to me and nudged my hand, his nose as cold and wet as any dog's. I laughed at that and he gave me a look, but I didn't share. Comparing a werewolf to a dog might be considered an insult. But as I stood, I did let my hand brush his fur. It felt like . . . fur. Coarse on top, soft underneath.

I turned to ask where we should start, and was struck by a sudden thought. "You can understand me, can't you? Do you need me to speak slower or louder . . . ?"

A soft snort and shake of his head. The movement was awkward, as if he wasn't accustomed to "human" communication in wolf form. How did they communicate? Did they understand barks? Did some canine language interpreter click on when they changed form?

"So I guess we should do this systematically, one bed at a time, starting—" I looked up to see his tail disappearing into the shadows. "Or I can just follow you."

CADAVER DOG

FOR THE NEXT HOUR, Jeremy sniffed gardens, trying to find the unmistakable scent of a decaying corpse. Harder than it sounds because most of the beds were raised within retaining walls, so he had to hop up or—in a few cases—take a running leap.

He stayed at the edge of the gardens and leaned in to get closer to the center, ducking around bushes, picking his way past plants. I erased paw prints as we went.

We'd made it through about half of the garden when I noticed Tansy and Gabrielle watching.

"Is this about those poor trapped children?" Gabrielle asked as I waved them over.

I nodded. "We're hoping to find a body, so we can . . ." I considered how best to explain it. "Find the people responsible and figure out what they did so I can free the spirits. He—" I waved at Jeremy. "The, uh, dog is specially trained for that sort of thing."

"A cadaver dog."

"Right. But not, you know, officially or anything. Just a friend of a friend knew someone who trained them and let me borrow this one."

"Shouldn't he be on a lead?" Tansy asked.

"This one works better off-leash. He's very well trained."

"Huh. Well, it looks like he may have found something."

I leaned past Tansy to see Jeremy gingerly raking back the dirt with his claws. He took another sniff, caught a noseful of dirt and sneezed. Then he resumed his careful digging.

A smell wafted up, strong enough for me to recognize. The stink of a rotting corpse. Jeremy lowered his muzzle into the hole and flipped something out. Even before I got close, I could see tiny stick-like bones and needlelike teeth. A mole or large mouse.

"Eww," Tansy said. "You'd better grab that, before he eats it."

I swallowed a laugh. "I made sure he was well fed before we started."

Jeremy looked at me, as if figuring out what we were talking about. He rolled the tiny corpse back into the hole, this time with his paw.

When he started covering it, I hurried forward. "I'll get that. You just keep— I mean, go, boy. Work. Sniff."

Jeremy rolled his dark eyes, leapt from the garden and headed toward the next one as I refilled his hole.

"Here comes Pete," Tansy said. "Wonder why he left his post? Uh-oh, he looks worried."

A gray-haired man hurried down the path, his broad face gathered in concern.

"Where is he?" Gabrielle asked.

"Inside the house. Upstairs I think." Tansy looked at me. "Some of us took up posts, keeping an eye out. This looked like something you wouldn't want to be found doing, so we were keeping watch."

"Oh? That's very thoughtful. Thank you."

"Someone's watching from upstairs," the portly man—Pete—said as he drew up beside us. "The English chap. He's been looking out the window."

"Grady? Damn! Jer—uh—boy?" I called softly. "Stay. Okay? Stay."

Jeremy peeked from the garden a few yards down and dipped his muzzle, telling me he understood. I stepped back farther into the shadows and looked up at the house. Grady's curtains were parted, a dim glow silhouetting his figure.

"Thanks for letting me know," I whispered to the ghost.

"I don't think he saw—" He stopped, looking up. "Oh, he's gone. False alarm. I'll head back."

"Wait," I said. "Your name's Pete?"

"Peter Feeney, miss. Used to work a few blocks away. Chauffeur, gardener, butler . . ." He smiled. "Whatever they needed."

"And what do *you* need? From me, I mean," I blurted. Alarm bells sounded in my head. But I steeled myself and pushed on. "I mean, is there anything I can do for you? I'm pretty limited. I can't find your killer or anything like that."

Peter smiled, showing small, even teeth. "My killer was me, miss. Me and my bad habits. Now, I'd love to bring *them* to justice, the folks who told me all those cigarettes weren't bad for my health, but I know you can't do that." He chewed his lip, the urge to be polite warring with the fear that he'd never get another chance to speak to a necromancer. "There is something, but I know you're really busy . . ."

"Go ahead."

"It's not urgent, but maybe when you're all done, if you have the time . . . I'd like to find my son."

"Has he . . . passed over?"

"Oh, no. At least, I hope not. We had a falling out a few years before I died. Silly thing. They always are, aren't they? But then I passed and when I went to his old apartment to check on him, he'd moved out. I don't want to make contact—just to see him. Finding him is probably as simple as looking through an L.A. phone book or dialing 411 but . . ." A wry smile. "I can't do that."

"No, of course not. But I will, as soon as I get a chance—"

The whoosh of the screen door sliding open sounded. I froze. Peter motioned for me to stay still and the ghosts fanned out, heading for the back of the house.

"I saw it," Grady hissed, his voice traveling through the still night air.

"A dog," Claudia said.

"Not a dog!" Grady roared before Claudia shushed him. "A demonic beast. A huge black wolf with glowing eyes and fangs as big as your fingers."

Jeremy peeked from a bush, ears swiveled, head tilted, as if to say, "Who, me?"

"It was a dog," Claudia said, her tone wavering between exasperation and frustration. "A large black dog. Yes, his eyes probably seemed to glow—reflected in the moonlight—but it was a dog. You've been under a lot of strain—"

"Bloody hell, woman. Something is going on here, and if you start nattering at me about jet lag and a change in diet—"

"Where's this wolf, Bradford?"

"I don't know. Out there. Somewhere."

"Are you going to take a look?"

"For a wild beast? I'm not mad, woman."

"Do you want me to take a look?"

"Of course not. Just—" A sigh. "Maybe it *was* a dog."

"Um-hmm."

The scrape of shoes on patio stones. Then the whir of the patio door closing. And all went silent.

GRADY'S LIGHT went off minutes later and stayed off. I spoke to Peter some more, getting his son's name and some other info—birthdate, last known job, schools attended—in case finding him required more than just looking it up in the phone book. Then I hurried to catch up on my paw-print-wiping duties.

Over an hour passed. Jeremy found a dead bird and a dead cat—the former probably a casualty of the latter, which must have been a family pet before death turned it into garden fertilizer.

I reburied the animals and followed Jeremy through the last few beds. No bodies.

While he changed back, I stood watch, more careful now than I'd been the first time, aware of our spectral audience. Seeing my "cadaver dog" change into a man would require a more elaborate explanation than I could dream up.

The ghosts seemed to have left, and I'd asked Eve to circle the perimeter, just to be sure. But I was still on edge, so when I heard a mutter near the neighbor's pool house, I slipped through the hedge to find Jeremy crouched on all fours near the outbuilding.

I stammered an apology and spun around.

He let out a soft laugh. "It's all right, Jaime. I'm human. And decent. Well . . . pretty much." The sound of a zipper. "There."

"Sorry," I said as I turned. "I thought I heard someone talking."

He bent again, as if examining the ground. "That was me. I

picked up my shoe and forgot I'd tucked my watch and pocket change inside." He glanced up from his search. "Still frustrated from my lack of results, it seems."

He brushed his hair from his face, finished gathering his spilled belongings, then stood. He was barefoot, dressed in dark jeans, his dark shirt thrown on, but still untucked and unbuttoned. His hair was tousled from the Change. Sweat-soaked stray strands clung to his face.

I knew from Elena that the Change wasn't some Hollywood-style morphing where not a single hair gets mussed. Jeremy's face was shiny with exertion, spots of color on his cheeks, his eyes gleaming, lips parted as he caught his breath.

My gaze traveled down his open shirt front, along the thin line of dark hair, the lean muscled chest, the flat stomach...

My heart—and other body parts—started doing flip-flops.

He snapped his watch back on and ran his fingers through his hair, trying to brush it into some semblance of order.

"Sorry," he said. "I'm a bit of a mess."

"That's okay." *Really* okay.

He motioned me closer. I tried not to trip over my feet in my rush to get there. He backed farther behind the shelter of the pool house.

"Not much chance of being spotted back here," he said, nodding at the brick wall beside us. "Grady didn't seem like he was going to raise a fuss, did he?"

"No, Claudia convinced him nothing was there."

He started to button his untucked shirt, leaving the top half undone. He plucked at the neck with an apologetic smile. "Hot."

"Uh-huh."

I was two feet away, but I swore I could feel the heat from his body, smell the faint scent of his sweat. And his eyes... They glittered with something that was not quite predatory, but different. Less civilized. Like he'd forgotten to pull that mantle of control completely back into place.

If I didn't know better, I'd say he'd had a few glasses of wine. That's what it looked like—the gleam of slight drunkenness, that lowering of the inhibitions. I looked into his eyes and shivered, body straining against the urge to cover those last two feet—

He did it for me. His arms went around me and he lowered his lips toward mine, but stopped short. I looked into his eyes and saw, not uncertainty, but a teasing smile. I lifted my lips an inch, covering half the distance, then said, "Your move."

His brows arched. He brought his lips so close I could feel his breath, then waited for me to close the gap.

"You like having me give in first, don't you?" I murmured.

A fraction of an inch lower, lips brushing mine as he said, "No, I'm being courteous."

"Bullshit."

A low laugh. I hung there, in his arms, our bodies barely making contact. His hands slid up my back, his touch so light I shivered. A gentle tug as he wrapped his fingers in my hair, then brought them up to the back of my head. His lips moved down, eyes closing, and I shut mine, reaching up for him, waiting for that first contact, expecting a kiss as soft and teasing as his touch.

His mouth crushed against mine so hard my eyes flew open. A low growling chuckle rippled through him. He started pulling back, to soften the kiss, but I wrapped my arms around his neck and returned it hard enough to make him gasp.

He swung me up, lifting me easily, hands going to the back of my thighs. My legs parted to wrap around him, but my skirt caught. His hands slid down my thighs and pushed my skirt up, his touch firm, fingers splayed, gripping me as they traveled up my thighs to my ass. Then he let out a soft breath of surprise.

I pulled back from the kiss enough to say, "I don't like panty lines."

Another delicious growl of a chuckle as his fingers dug in, pulling me against him. I wiggled until I could feel him hard against my crotch, then tightened my legs around his hips, rubbing against him.

My hands dropped to his sides and squeezed between us, finding the button of his pants, then . . .

I broke the kiss. He dove to find it, but I brought my hands to the sides of his face, holding him back. His dark eyes wavered there, his face indistinct, my vision still clouded with lust.

"Just a second," I said as I squirmed from his grip and lowered myself to the ground. "I think I'm making this too easy for you."

"Easy?" The word was almost a growl. "Do you know how many

times I've thought of this in the past year . . . and had to see you at council meetings and pretend the idea never even entered my mind?"

A quiver of excitement raced through me. So he hadn't been as oblivious—or immune—as he'd pretended. It was almost enough to make me throw myself into his arms. Almost . . .

"A year?" I murmured. "That's nothing."

I lowered my lips to the base of his throat and tickled my tongue up to his chin, tasting his sweat.

"If it hasn't been easy, you have only yourself to blame," I said. "I've been here, ready and willing the whole time."

I leaned against him. My fingers skated over his hip, then stroked the back of his thigh, heading between his legs. His growl sent tremors through me and I had to stop for a breath before looking up at him.

"Four years, Jeremy, and I'm thinking . . ." I looked into his eyes. "Maybe you can wait a little longer. Just to be fair."

I inched back, my hands going to his chest, as if to ward him off, but sliding under his shirt, feeling his heart thumping under my fingers, feeling the beat of his quickened breathing, the sheen of sweat over his lean, muscled chest . . . all of which didn't make it any easier for me, but I closed my eyes and savored the tease. Then, his shirt parted, I leaned forward, my nipples pressing hard against the silk, brushing them against his chest as I arched up on tiptoes, kissing the bottom of his throat, tongue sliding out to feel his pulse. He shuddered, but didn't move, and I wondered how long he'd stand there, and what I could do to tease him, to tease both of us, to break that legendary control . . .

I swallowed a moan and stepped back.

"It's late," I murmured. "I should get inside. Are you coming tomorrow?"

A pause. "Well, apparently, that depends on you."

I choked on a laugh and swatted his arm. "I meant to the house. Breakfast is at nine." I looked up at him. "As for the rest . . . we'll see."

I turned and started to walk away.

"Are you sure?" he called after me. "When I've had time to clear my head, I might change my mind."

"Oh, I think I can change it back."

I could feel his gaze glued to me as I sauntered off around to the front of the house.

UP IN my room, I let out a deep, shuddering sigh. Part of me screamed that I'd gone crazy. I could have had Jeremy in my bed—or in the backyard—tonight. Wasn't that what I wanted? What I dreamed of? I should have seized on the chance before the adrenaline rush of his Change passed and he realized he wasn't ready yet.

But that was exactly why I'd walked away. Because if he wasn't ready, I didn't want him. I wasn't taking the chance that he'd wake in the morning, apologizing and backpedaling furiously. Let him sleep on it and make up his mind. Because that's how I had to win Jeremy—body *and* mind—or I'd never keep him.

So I tried not to think about what I'd just walked away from, and was busying myself checking cell phone messages when a patter sounded at the balcony door. I froze. Jeremy? Tossing up pebbles to get my attention? I'd ignore him. I had to ignore him or—

I turned. And there was the man himself, at the glass balcony door, his shirt still undone, shoes off, hair mussed, lips curved in a small smile.

I looked past him. No ladder or other sign of how he'd gotten there. I cracked open the door just enough to be heard.

"How the hell did you get up here?"

"Magic?"

"Well, I haven't changed my mind so—"

"You forgot to say good night."

I struggled not to look at him, at that sexy crooked smile, at his unbuttoned shirt, at his black eyes still glinting with the heady exhilaration of the Change, still hungry—

He moved to the gap and leaned against it, his right hand pressed to the glass, one eye peeking through, a sliver of bare torso close enough to—

Oh, God. I couldn't do this. Screw my resolve.

I reached for the door handle, then stopped. Seduce him? An amazing night of sex and he'd be mine forever? If I honestly believed it would be that easy, I'd have done it four years ago.

"Good night," I said.

"No kiss?"

"Absolutely not."

His lips twitched. His left hand slid through the crack, grabbing the door frame, ready to open it. With one wrench he could be inside, but he just stood there.

"Just one kiss," he said. "Let me in."

"Or you'll huff and you'll puff?"

A throaty laugh that sent a wave of heat through me.

"I could," he said. "If you'd like. Or I can stay right here. Just open the door a little more . . ."

He moved his face against the two-inch crack. His lips parted, the tip of his tongue showing against white teeth. My knees quavered as I imagined cracking that door open, just a couple of inches more, and pressing against the gap, feeling his body, the heat of it, tasting his kiss, his hunger—

"No," I said, so fast it came out as a squeak.

"Then why don't you come out here?"

"Because in two minutes I'd be on that cement floor, getting strips ripped from my ass, and I wouldn't be able to sit for a week."

He laughed—a full deep laugh that made me want to throw open the door. But if he wasn't opening it himself, that meant that despite that adrenaline inebriation, part of him was still thinking clearly enough to hold back. That part that wasn't ready to take a chance.

"Good night, Jeremy," I said, and closed the door.

I stepped away, reached back and started unzipping my dress.

He pressed his hands to the glass. I could read his lips. "That's not fair."

I smiled and finished unzipping. The dress slid off my shoulders, but stayed there. I looked at him, his gaze fixed on me, eyes dark with lust.

"You wouldn't dare," he mouthed.

I turned, then let it fall off the rest of the way. And, once off, there was nothing else to remove.

"Jaime!"

I heard him through the glass, heard him say my name in a deep growl that made me shiver, but I didn't turn around, just lifted my fingers to wave over my shoulder, then strolled into the bathroom for a very long, very cold shower.

RUNAWAY

THE NEXT MORNING, I snuck downstairs, hoping to avoid Becky. One of the guards said she was closeted in a teleconference with Todd Simon and several network execs.

I took my coffee into the garden. My plan was to visit the child ghosts as if to reassure myself—and them—that I was making progress. But something else was gnawing at me. Something I needed to do, however difficult it was. Tansy had helped me last night. Now I needed to return the favor, at least by hearing her out.

It took only a few minutes of summoning before she appeared.

"You wanted to talk to me the other day," I said. "I'm sorry it took so long to get back to you. I've been—"

"—busy with far more important things." She sat beside me on the low wall. "What a mess, huh? Those poor kids. We didn't even notice them until we saw what you were doing. We keep trying to talk to them, but they can't hear us."

"I'm not sure they can hear me either. But I appreciate the help. I really do."

She nodded, then went quiet for a moment. I braced myself, waiting for her to ask for help in return.

"I'm sorry about springing Gabrielle on you like that," she said finally. "I thought maybe you could get inside information, and I feel awful about raising her hopes."

"I'm sure she would have found me anyway. I only wish I could do something. But in some cases, I just can't. Finding a murderer. Bringing him to justice. Beyond my realm of influence, no matter how much I might want to."

I gave the words extra emphasis, trying to prepare her for disappointment. But she only stared at me, uncomprehending. Then her eyes widened.

"Oh, shit! Am I a moron or what? You guys are trying to figure out who killed Marilyn. I was the warm-up, wasn't I? That's what that Angel chick wanted to know. Who killed me."

"But you don't know who did it," I said, tensing.

"You should see your face," she said with a peal of laughter. "You're waiting for me to ask for help. Bring my killer to justice, damn it!" Another laugh and a shake of her head. "I already know who killed me and I have no interest in bringing him to 'justice.' "

"What?"

She pulled her knees up to sit cross-legged. "I couldn't remember for a while, but eventually I did. It was this guy I came to the party with—I'm not naming names 'cause he's still alive. Anyway, I was high on winning the Emmy and too much champagne. I found this gun in the house and I was showing it to him outside. He was playing with it and—" She shrugged. "The end of Tansy Lane."

"I'm sorry."

"We were being stupid. Drunk kids goofing off with a gun."

Turned out, the only thing she wanted from me was conversation. She peppered me with questions about the shoot and my career, topics of interest to someone who'd grown up in the biz. Then she left me to try contacting the children again, and promised she'd be around, should I need help from the other side.

All my worrying about how to get out of the obligation, and I could have avoided it just by hearing her out when she'd first asked to talk to me.

BEFORE I could try to summon the children, a guard called my name. I stashed my kit under a bush, and turned the corner to see Jeremy on the patio with a guard, Grady and Claudia.

"Maybe we should go find her," the guard was saying.

"She's fine," Jeremy said. "She doesn't like to be disturbed when she's meditating. If she doesn't answer, I'll wait—" He saw me. "Ah, here she comes."

He nodded and murmured a good morning. I studied his face. It was as inscrutable as ever. He turned to answer something Grady was asking.

Okay, this wasn't the greeting I'd hoped for. Was he upset about last night? Or hoping I'd forgotten? I brushed off regrets. I'd known that once the thrill of the Change wore off, he might reconsider. But if that adrenaline rush had been the only thing driving him last night, then it was a good thing we'd waited. Or so I told myself.

As I drew closer, Jeremy lifted his hands, a steaming mug in each, the smell of fresh coffee wafting my way.

"Thank you."

Another nod. "I trust you had a good night?"

I bit back a smile, but when I met his gaze, I saw no twinkle, no sign that his words were anything more than a polite inquiry.

He continued, "Were you meditating? I could wait here—"

"Nonsense," Grady said. "If Jaime's busy, join us for breakfast."

Claudia seconded the invitation. Jeremy glanced at me, as if he didn't care one way or the other and I wanted to scream that I'd been up since six-thirty waiting for him. But I certainly wasn't going to give him that satisfaction. So I settled for a shrug and a "Your choice."

"If I won't be in the way, I'll join you."

I had to look up and follow his gaze to see whom he was talking to. His eyes were on me.

"Sure," I said, voice as neutral as I could make it. "Come along."

He stayed at my side as I wended my way back to my summoning spot. When we rounded the third corner, he reached over and, without a word, took my coffee and laid both mugs on the garden retaining wall. Then he swept me up in a kiss that left me gasping.

My relief must have shown, because he smiled and said, "You weren't worried, were you?"

I smacked his arm. "Bastard."

A brow arch. "I don't think anyone's ever called me that before."

"Keep pulling stunts like that and you'd better get used to it."

He moved in for another kiss. I studied his gaze, trying to see whether any hesitation lingered. I couldn't tell, and I wasn't taking chances. Even if he'd made up his mind, there was something to be said for making him wait a little longer . . .

So I kissed him lightly, then headed into the garden to do what I'd come out here for.

I RECOVERED my necromancy bag, then sat beside him on a bench and sipped my coffee as I listened to the bird calls and the whispers of the children, felt the wind ruffle my hair, felt the children's fingertips brushing me.

Once I'd reestablished contact with the children, and reassured them I was back, I spoke to Jeremy.

"I was thinking about the kids. About the families." I put my hand out and felt small fingers tickle mine. I tried to close my hand around them, to hold on, but caught only air. "Whether I do the raising or not, I think we should find a way to alert the authorities, even if it's after this is over, so they can find the bodies and give the parents closure."

He nodded.

"Or maybe just, I don't know, give them graves. Headstones. Something to say they were here. From what you said, the parents probably don't care."

"I didn't say that. The children may have been taken from the street. Or kidnapped from families or neighborhoods where the police would presume they'd gone to the street. That's safest. Minimizes the search. But it doesn't mean no one cared. However bad things are for a child, someone usually cares."

His gaze moved out across the garden.

"You're thinking of Clay. His family."

A small look of surprise. Then he nodded.

"There was nothing to be done, though, right?" I moved closer to him. "You didn't kidnap him. Elena says he'd run away after he was bitten, was on the street for a year, maybe more, before you found him. You couldn't take him back to his family and say, 'Here's your son. By the way, he's a werewolf.' "

"No. I couldn't."

"Did he ever ask about them?"

"Never. That used to worry me. At first, I thought he wasn't asking because he didn't want to upset me. When he was young, I'd find ways to bring up the subject of mothers, fathers, siblings. He never nibbled. Later, he pretended he'd forgotten everything that happened before he was bitten. He tells Elena he can't remember."

"But he does?"

"I think so. Before Elena became pregnant, he asked me if there was a way to check on his medical history."

"Look for any hereditary conditions. Something he might pass on to a baby."

"Yes. I found his family. It was easy enough. There was some media coverage when he disappeared. I'd always assumed there was, but I'd never looked before." He went quiet for a moment, as if thinking about that. "Paige helped me get medical records. She never asked what they were for, but she probably knew. I didn't find anything significant, medically."

"And Clay. Did he ask about them? His family?"

Jeremy shook his head. "All he wanted was the medical information. I always had the feeling his childhood wasn't . . . easy. That running away, even as young as he was, really . . ." He struggled for a word.

"Didn't bother him."

"I don't think it was an unlivable situation. Bad enough, but not the sort of thing that would cause your typical six-year-old to walk away and never return." A tiny smile. "But I suspect Clay wasn't the most typical child even before he was bitten."

"He's happier being a werewolf and sees no reason for regrets. Maybe, if he hadn't been bitten, he would've turned out like these children. A runaway."

I thought about that as I felt the tinkling touch of the children's fingers, listened to their whispers. How old were they? It was impossible to tell. From the touches and pokes, I'd guess some were quite young, though the voices had sounded like preadolescents, which meant they should be able to understand my instructions, supporting the theory that they couldn't hear me any better than I could them.

The older ones could be passed off as runaways. The younger ones? Vanished children, like Clay had been.

I thought of Clay, the life he'd gone from, the life he'd had instead.

I wondered whether any of these children had run away. Just up and left their homes, their families, maybe even only for a day or two, cooling off after a fight. And then . . . gone. Killed. Sacrificed.

What did they make of their situation? Were they frightened? Suffering? Were they *aware* enough to be frightened? To suffer? Were they together? Or separate, unable to contact the others, alone. No way to tell. Not until I set them free.

"Have you heard from Elena and Clay yet?" I asked finally.

"I called them when I woke up, checking in, but no one answered. They're probably outside with the kids. I left a message."

I nodded.

"Sir?" a voice called. "Ms. Vegas?"

I waved the guard over.

"Your cell phone has been ringing, sir," he said to Jeremy. "You left it in your jacket inside. And someone thought they heard Ms. Vegas's phone ringing in her room."

We gathered our things and headed for the house.

IT WAS Elena calling with their "research notes" on folk magic.

"So how does that help us?" I asked when Jeremy finished explaining.

"I don't know if it does. Not at this stage."

"What about those body parts in Botnick's closet? They're used in this kind of magic. Maybe if we knew his supplier . . . No, I guess if he had a direct link to this group, he wouldn't have been trying to find them."

"But it does shed some light on what we're looking for. Like Botnick, this group is likely eclectic in their choices, and their magics."

"Experimenting to find what works. Like that kid who tried selling body parts to Eve."

Jeremy nodded. "If they practiced African folk magic, Botnick would have known that and known how to refine his search."

"And we'd now know how to refine ours, looking for this group. Without that, all we have is a nice theory."

CAUSE AND EFFECT

AFTER LUNCH, WE STOPPED BY HOPE'S PLACE to update her. While she talked with Jeremy, I asked to borrow her phone book. I looked up Peter's son's name and found a handful of direct matches, plus a lengthy list of possibilities. When I explained to Hope and Jeremy what I was doing, Hope offered to help.

"With all that information you've got, I should be able to find him. Just tap into a few databases, unless . . ." She looked at me. "I don't mean to jump in."

"No, I'd appreciate it."

As I said it, I realized I meant it. Like Eve said, we all have our specialties. Finding people wasn't mine.

"I'd love to see how you do it, though," I said. "For next time."

"Sure." A watch check. "I've got twenty minutes before a meeting, so I'll boot up my laptop, try a few things. Might not find him, but we'll try."

She'd just cleared a spot on the table when my cell phone rang. I answered.

"Speaking of meetings," I said after I hung up. "It seems I have one. Becky wants me back at the house and she sounds pretty tense." I glanced at Jeremy. "You stay. I'll grab a taxi."

"No, I'll go with you."

Hope paused with her finger over the power button on her laptop. "Should I wait on this?"

"Not on my account. If you get a chance to look, that'd be great. If not, we'll do it later."

HOPE'S DOOR exited at the rear of the building. As we passed the adjoining alley, Jeremy glanced down it. He tried to be discreet, but the flare of his nostrils told me it was no casual sweep of his surroundings.

I stopped and peered into the alley. "What's down there?"

"Nothing."

I stepped into the shadows. "I could have sworn I saw you looking down here earlier too, when we first arrived."

He hesitated, as if trying to decide whether to brush me off. "I was just . . . checking."

"Someone's following you, aren't they? Is it a werewolf?"

He walked over. "If that happened, I'd tell you, for your own safety. I'm just being cautious."

I wanted to press him, but he'd tell me if he wanted to—and wouldn't if he didn't. Still, I couldn't resist walking another few feet into the alley, testing his reaction. But he didn't grab my arm or call me back. When I glanced over my shoulder, his face was relaxed, meaning there was nothing to worry about.

I took two more steps and glanced back. "Not going to follow?"

He smiled. "Sorry. I was just . . . watching."

"Ah. Enjoying, I hope."

"Very much, though I must admit, it's igniting a question I've been trying not to think about all morning."

"And that would be?"

He tilted his head, gaze traveling over me, still standing at the mouth of the alley, making no move to come closer. "Whether you're as . . . unencumbered by extra articles of clothing as you were last night."

I laughed, then turned to face him. "I'm afraid yesterday's outfit wasn't very undergarment friendly. This one is." I unbuttoned my blouse and spread it apart. "See?"

"I do."

"Sorry to disappoint."

His gaze stayed fixed on my raspberry demi bra, the lace thin enough to leave little to the imagination. "I wouldn't say 'disappointed' is the word. Are there a matching pair of . . ." His gaze dropped below my hips.

"You don't expect me to show you that too. In a public alley? In the middle of the day?"

"Expect, no. Hope . . . ?" He smiled.

"Well, it would be hard to show you that. This skirt isn't easy to lift up. It's too tight."

"So I see."

"I'd have to take it off."

The smile twitched. "Pity."

I looked around. There was no sign of anyone. I reached around for the zipper—

My cell phone rang. Jeremy let out a curse as I answered it.

"Jaime?" Angelique said. "Has Becky called you? There's a meeting."

"Angelique," I said, with a glance at Jeremy. "Yes, she called and we're, ah, on our way."

"Oh, thank God. I think—" A sharp intake of breath. "I think I'm being kicked off the set."

"What?"

"Will came by my room and asked whether I'd made my plane reservations for home yet or would I like him to do it. I said I didn't know what he was talking about and he wouldn't tell me, just apologized and hurried off."

"I'm sure he's mistaken. Or trying to spook you. Don't be surprised if Becky shows up in a few minutes, trying to bully you into agreeing to something—after he's scared you into thinking you're leaving. If she does, stall. I'll be there as soon as I can."

THE SHOOT was over. All of us were leaving.

Grady, Claudia, Angelique, Jeremy and I sat in the living room as Becky explained.

"Mr. Simon thinks we have more than enough footage for the lead-up bits," Becky said. "We'll film the Monroe séance live, as planned, but the preshow work here is done."

We stared at her.

"I had two interviews scheduled for tomorrow," I said. "I don't mind staying to do them—"

"Thanks, Jaime. Really. You're a trouper. But Mr. Simon wants everyone cleared out today."

"Today?"

I glanced at Jeremy, sitting silently beside me.

I turned back to Becky. "Aren't there more séances for us to film? You said there were six—"

"I'm afraid they just aren't going as planned, Jaime. Mr. Simon is pulling the plug."

In other words, we weren't giving the kind of reality TV footage they'd hoped for. I argued—we all argued—but it did no good. We'd had our chance.

"I hope you aren't telling us to pack our bags," I said finally. "I can't catch a flight to Chicago until tonight and I'm not going to sit around a terminal all day waiting."

"We have until the end of the day, I'm sure." Claudia's glare dared Becky to argue.

After a moment, Becky said, "As long as you're cleared out by sundown, because that's when the staff has been told they can leave."

WE WENT back to my room. Jeremy closed the door behind him and watched me getting out my necromancy kit. I double-checked, making sure I wasn't missing or low on anything.

Finally I looked up at Jeremy. "I'm doing the raising now."

"I see that."

I studied his expression. Blanker than usual.

"You're wondering why I practically announced it down there, telling Grady and Angelique I'm going into the garden for a while."

"The question did cross my mind."

"I'm setting the stage," I said as I checked my supply of vervain and hoped it would be enough.

Jeremy frowned. "Setting the stage for the discovery? I'm not sure that's—"

"Wise?" I finished. "Maybe not. But I'm trying to come up with something worthy of a television event. The spiritualist, summoned to the garden by the restless dead, uncovers their bodies. There's no way Todd Simon will shut us down after that. It'll add a whole new dimension to *Death of Innocence*. The show will go on and we won't need to leave before we've solved the mystery and freed the ghosts."

After a moment Jeremy said softly, "It could backfire, Jaime."

"Yep."

Another quiet moment, then, "It could cost you that TV show you want."

"I don't really want it anymore."

The words startled me at first. Then the sensation settled into one of relief, as I realized I'd given voice to a decision I'd been longing to make.

"I hate television," I said. "I don't need the added boost to sell tickets. So the only reason I have for pursuing it is self-satisfaction. To reach a goal I was raised to believe I should want, above all others. Well, I don't want it. These last couple of days I've hated it more than ever, because it was interrupting something I really wanted to do."

I looked up at Jeremy. "You said you like to help. So do I, but I've been fighting it all my life. Maybe I'm not very good at it. And I'm sure I'll never run around chasing down problems like Paige or Hope. But this is what I want to do—now, not five years from now, after I've had a TV show that I'll hate every moment of. Time to do what will make *me* happy: stage work and council work."

"Good." He smiled, then went sober. "But this could still damage your professional reputation."

"Yep. It could." I opened a small tin of grave dirt and sniffed it for freshness. "But what matters right now isn't the show or my reputation, it's the children. What's best for them is to have me here, close by, with all-hours access, working to free them. Whatever the cost."

"But you can do this without the premonition angle. You happened to be in the garden. You saw something sticking from the dirt. You alerted the guards, who called the police. Their interviews alone will delay all plans to pack up today."

"Maybe. Maybe not. But giving this a spiritualist angle guarantees they won't pull the plug on the final show, which I suspect they're considering, despite all the promotion they've done. They'll back out and blame 'problems on the set'—meaning us. But if I find a body and claim it had something to do with spirit communication? The buzz will be too big for them to cancel it. Personally, I don't care anymore, but I feel . . . guilty, I guess. I'm responsible for getting us shut down, and now I may have ruined Angelique's big shot at stardom and Grady's chance to pick up a North American audience."

"We'll have to handle it carefully."

"I plan to."

OUR THEORY about this human magical group was that they were "scientists" of the occult world, trying and discarding various theories and practices, maybe latching onto a ritual or an ingredient that seemed to work, and experimenting until they found just the right combination, the one that did *something*.

As I prepared to raise a body, kneeling at my altar cloth while Jeremy and Eve kept watch, I pondered on how we—true supernaturals—weren't much different. There's no single way to raise a corpse. Every necromancer family has its way—one it swears is better than everyone else's.

Some use poppets—small dolls stuffed with hair or nail clippings from the target. The O'Caseys prefer a more complicated method, but one that doesn't require body bits.

As for the ingredients and invocations, again, they vary. Like spellcasters, we use what's been "proven" to work. As with spellcasters, there are those who say the whole thing is hooey—that we don't need to sprinkle grave dirt over a chalk symbol, we don't need to blow corpse dust to the four winds—that the power to raise the dead, as the power to communicate with them, is within us.

But we keep using what works. That doesn't mean we're too stupid and superstitious to try without the bits and bobs of ritual. This group had probably done the same—tried sacrificing an adult. Maybe it failed, as did our pared-back rituals. That could be psychology at work—at some level we're convinced we need ingredient X and therefore we fail without it. Or maybe I was thinking too much to avoid what I was supposed to be doing.

Paige told me once that her mother always said the main function of ritual was that it provided the spellcaster—or necromancer—with a gradual transition from the everyday world to the magical. That the act of concentrating on placing ingredients just so, on drawing symbols, on laying out tools and lighting censers was for focus, to release the brain from thoughts of shopping lists and luncheon dates. If that was the case, I'd probably never needed that refocusing more than I did this afternoon.

It wasn't thoughts of shopping lists cluttering my mind, but the horror of what I was about to do.

Raising the dead. If you're a religious person, you call it resurrection and it's a miracle. If you're a horror buff, it's Armageddon at the hands of a flesh-munching mob of shambling corpses. In truth, it's some of both.

Like miracle workers, we return the ghost—the soul—to the body, conscious and aware. So unless you raise a Hannibal Lecter, the person's not going to start eating brains. But the body is the dead one, the broken one, the rotting one, just like in a horror flick. So now the ghost is trapped, fully aware, in that broken and rotting corpse. Could anything be more horrific?

Yet every well-trained necromancer is taught to do this. Must practice even. Whether he or she ever chooses to raise a zombie, we know how, should we need that knowledge.

And now I did. To raise a child.

THE DARKEST POWER

I BEGAN THE INVOCATION. Jeremy stood just past the nearest garden bed, watching for anyone coming from the house. Eve patrolled for ghosts, warning them off. I think Kristof was helping too, but I didn't see him; didn't see anyone.

As much as I tried to clear my mind, every sight, every sound seemed to vie for my attention. The poke and scrape of pebbles under my knees. A prop plane buzzing overhead. A fly walking over my chalk symbol. The sickly sweet smell of lilies. To me, they smell of funeral homes and death. Sweet yet off-putting, like the stink of rot.

Rot . . .

How long had these children been in the garden? How much had their bodies decayed? Were they even whole? What if they weren't and I'd return a soul to a partial corpse, one without arms, without legs, unable to fight to the surface, trapped under the earth as I sat, oblivious, listening to airplanes and watching flies—

Enough. Focus.

It took awhile, but I finally found a mental place without sights, without smells, feelings, sounds, even thoughts. Just me, commanding any nearby soul to return to its body.

A soft sound came to my left, so faint that I first mistook it for the rustle of a leaf. Then I heard Jeremy, softly calling my name.

I leapt to my feet and hurried toward the sound. Jeremy was walking toward a garden of rosebushes, moving fast, his gaze on a shifting patch of earth. Something small and gray darted back and forth as if pushing the dirt away.

Jeremy slowed. "Isn't that the spot where—?"

The ground erupted in a flurry of dirt. Even Jeremy reeled back.

"Raw—raw—raw—"

The garbled raucous cry echoed through the garden as the dirt continued to fly, the thing at its center moving so fast it was only a blur under the geyser of dirt. I saw something long and flat and broad, flapping against the ground. A wing.

The dead bird. The one Jeremy had uncovered and I'd reburied.

Once I realized what I was seeing, I could recognize all the parts—the eyeless head lolling, neck broken, one leg grabbing dirt, trying to find its grip, the other leg jabbing at the earth, the claws gone, wing beating frantically, trying to take off. The bird kept screaming in fear and pain, battering itself against the ground as it tried to make its broken body work. The stink of it filled the air, that horrible rotting—

"Jaime!" Eve's voice was harsh at my ear. "Send it back."

All I could do was stare at the bird.

"Goddamn it, Jaime. Send it back!"

I snapped out of it then, my lips flying in the invocation that would free the bird's soul from its body. The garbled screeching stopped and the tiny corpse fell to the earth, dirt raining down on its still form.

For a moment, nobody moved. Even Jeremy seemed shocked into speechlessness.

Life from death. The darkest power. In my hands.

After a moment, Jeremy moved in to clean up. He said something to me and I responded, but I don't know what I said. I walked past him, as stiff and unseeing as a sleepwalker. He caught my arm, tried to get me to stay, but I mumbled something—again, I don't know what—and kept going.

I walked back to my ritual setup and dropped to my knees. A rock jabbed into my shin hard enough to cut me. Warm blood welled up. I couldn't find the energy to wince.

"It's over," Eve said, from somewhere close. "Yeah, it was bad, but it's over and the bird's free and it happened so fast it probably doesn't remember anything."

She kept reassuring me that the bird was okay, but we both knew that when I closed my eyes, I didn't see a broken and rotting bird, screaming and flapping in terror. I saw a child. Until now, I'd only imagined what I intended to do to these children. Now I saw it, heard it, smelled it.

"We'll find another way." Jeremy's voice, somewhere above me, his words drifting past.

Eve said nothing, but I could feel her tension as she held her tongue.

"We'll find another way." His voice was beside me now, as if he'd dropped to his knees.

"He's right," Eve said finally. "This was a bad idea—"

"No. I'm going to do it."

"You don't need—" Jeremy began.

"Yes, I do." I followed the sound of his voice, forced my gaze to focus and saw him crouched beside me. "This time I'll release the soul as soon as we see something. We don't have time to back off now and do more research. Better to—" I swallowed, "—just do it and do it fast."

Jeremy hesitated, then nodded. "Would you like me to go? Leave you be?"

"No." I met his gaze. "Please don't."

So, with him beside me, and Eve scouting, I began again. My heart beat so hard I could scarcely breathe. When I closed my eyes, I saw the bird again. Every time a child's ghost touched me, I jumped, as if in guilt.

"Take some time," Jeremy murmured. "Everyone inside is busy packing. No one's going to bother us."

When I couldn't relax, Jeremy tried distracting me with a story from his youth. Any other time, I'd have hung on his every word, sifting through the tale for insight. But even though his story took place in his late teens, it made me think of childhood. Of the children. And underscoring his words, I heard them whispering.

As I leaned forward, sweat dripped onto the chalk symbol. I picked up the chalk to fix it, but my fingers were trembling so badly I snapped the piece in two. Moving to grab the fallen end, I accidentally erased the chalk edge with my knee.

"Here," Jeremy said, reaching for the larger piece of chalk.

I managed a weak smile as he filled in the missing parts. "Now I'm a true celebrity necromancer. I even get professional artists to draw my symbols."

A joke weaker than my smile, so I didn't blame him for not smiling back. When I looked, though, he seemed not to have heard at all, but had withdrawn into his thoughts. After a moment, he lowered the chalk to the paving stones and drew something to the side of my ritual setup.

"Remember those runes I mentioned? The ones I see?" he said as he drew. "This is one of them. Not for protection, but for calming."

He finished the simple design, then took my hand and laid it on the symbol.

"Now, maybe these are just part of some secret code I found on a cereal box when I was a boy but—" He met my gaze. "I think—I feel—there's more to them than that."

And as I knelt there, his hand light and warm on mine, the rough stone beneath, the edges of the rune running past my fingers, I could feel the anxiety and panic seeping from me, as if drawn into the stone.

I began the incantation, my hands on the rune, his on mine, and the words flowed with a confidence I rarely felt.

The sound came quickly. The same soft noise I'd heard earlier. Coming from the same direction. My gut twisted, half bitter disappointment, half frustration.

"The bird again," I said as I pushed to my feet. "It's that damned bird. I tried focusing on a child, but—"

"Wait," Jeremy said. "Let's be sure before you release it."

We followed the sound to the same garden. I could see where Jeremy had reburied the bird, but the ground there was undisturbed. My gaze shot to a spot a few feet away.

"The cat?" I said.

But that patch of earth was still too. The whole garden was still. And quiet.

I glanced at Jeremy. "The sound. Is it gone?"

He shook his head and leapt into the thirty-inch-high garden as easily as if it had been a mere step up. He cocked his head to listen, then picked his way deeper into the hexagonal rose garden, following the sound straight to the center.

As he bent, I heard it again, faint, coming from the ground. I climbed onto the retaining wall, stepped into the bed and almost fell back as my pointed heels sunk into the soil. My arms windmilled, but I caught my balance before Jeremy scrambled to my rescue.

"Two words," Eve sighed behind me. "Sensible shoes. Preferably sneakers. Not pretty, but I swear, someday they'll save your life."

"I know. I know."

I took off my shoes.

"Can you stand watch?" I asked Eve as I walked up beside Jeremy.

"Kris has it covered."

In other words, she wasn't leaving. Probably expecting me to panic and screw up again. As I crouched, a high patch of earth shifted from a disturbance under the surface.

I raked back the dirt. Jeremy helped. Eve hovered. The garden seemed to go silent, no sound but the sifting and shifting of earth as we dug. The smell of damp earth soon mingled with something danker, mustier—the stink of the grave.

I kept digging. Probably a dog or another cat, an older one, buried deeper, under more seasons of added soil, more layers of rotted vegetation. The family's designated pet cemetery, amid the roses, so their dearly departed wouldn't stink the place up.

I was scooping away a handful of dirt when a dark stone appeared at the bottom of the hole. Then it moved, jabbing upward. A long, dark claw. Another poked through. Then a third, the last only white bone. The long thin bone of a human finger.

"Th-there," I said, lifting my hand to stop Jeremy. "Good enough. I'll send the soul back—"

"No," Eve said. "Dig a little more."

I swung around to look at her. "It's a hand. Even I can tell it's—"

"Yes, it is." Her gaze met mine, eyes cold and unreadable. "Keep going until you have the hand exposed—"

"It *is* exposed," I said, voice going shrill as I watched the fingers—bone and rotted flesh—reaching for the air. "That child is trying to dig his way out and I'm not standing back and letting it happen so we can have a whole body to show the police—"

"Then stop him."

"Stop—?"

Her gaze bore into mine. "Stop the child from digging and keep him calm. This will only take a minute, Jaime."

When I hesitated, she said, "Trust me."

I yanked my gaze away, closed my eyes and commanded the child to stop digging. That impulse to claw his way out was so strong, so deeply rooted, that zombies had been known to batter themselves to pieces trying to get free of a casket. And yet, when I gave the order, the hand stopped moving.

Again, for one moment, there was silence, Eve and Jeremy both staring at that still hand.

Here was the other side of that darkest power. Not only could a necromancer raise corpses, we could control them. Enslave the dead.

Looking at Eve and Jeremy, seeing awe on the faces of two of the most powerful supernaturals I knew, I realized it was more than just the darkest power. It was the most fearsome. The greatest power a supernatural could wield. Jeremy could tear his victims limb from limb. Eve could torture them with magic. But with death came release—unless I stepped in. Then death was only the beginning of the horror.

As I held the child still, murmuring words of comfort—mental and aloud—Eve knelt beside the hole. Then she reached in and took hold of the child's hand, fingers wrapping around the small ones as if she could reach through the dimensional barrier and touch them.

Her eyes had barely closed when her body went rigid. Beneath her eyelids, her eyes moved, twitching like someone dreaming. At a movement to my left, I looked to see that Kristof had joined us, standing back but watching Eve, his face taut with worry.

"Her name's Rachel," Eve said, her voice tight, as if pushing words out. "Rachel Skye. She's eleven. She lives . . . no, I can't get that. An apartment building. A city. A busy street." A noise in her throat. "Not important. She's coming home from school. Taking the bad way. The one she's not supposed to take. But it's shorter and there's a TV show she'll miss if she takes the other way. She cuts through the alley. She hears something behind her. Something flies down over her head. Everything goes dark."

Eve pulled her hand back from the child's and crouched there, head bowed, hair falling forward to hide her face. Kristof moved up beside her, hunkered down and said something, too low for me to hear. A whispered exchange. Then he squeezed her hand and backed off.

Eve looked up at me. "That's all I get. Darkness, then she passed over."

I relayed everything to Jeremy, who'd been waiting patiently throughout, never asking for an explanation. As much as I longed to ask Eve what she'd done, I could tell I wouldn't get an answer. The what and how didn't matter. Only the results.

"So they probably drugged her or knocked her out," Jeremy said. "They kept her unconscious until they killed her. They're uncomfortable with what they're doing. They feel guilty."

"Cowards." Eve's face darkened, but she shook it off. "Hold on. I want to get this done so we can let her go."

She started again. Like Hope, she seemed to be experiencing a vision, getting her information that way rather than through questioning. Unlike Hope, though, this wasn't random flashes. She controlled the vision, as if guiding her way through the girl's memory.

The second foray added little to the first. Rachel had never regained consciousness after her attack. As she'd been losing consciousness, though, she'd heard a voice. A British-accented woman's voice telling someone else to make sure he grabbed Rachel's knapsack. In that command, she'd heard a name. Don. And that was all we had.

BLUFF AND BLUSTER

I RELEASED RACHEL'S SOUL. Then Jeremy covered our tracks as I hurried back to clean up my equipment. Eve didn't stay. She mumbled something about continuing to work on getting access to Botnick, but even if she did, I had a feeling he'd say the same thing Rachel did—that he'd been attacked from behind and immediately hooded, seeing nothing.

I was erasing the rune as Jeremy walked over.

"This," I said, pointing down at the rune. "It's not for calming, is it?"

"What makes you say that?"

"Because, if it was, I'd see it all over Kate's bedroom."

He let out a laugh, but only shook his head and picked up my kit.

"You said earlier that you don't know what they're for," I said as I finished erasing it. "That goes for this one too."

"It *could* be for calming."

"But all that mattered was that I believed it was." I straightened, stood on my tiptoes and brushed my lips across his cheek. "Thank you."

I examined the area, making sure we'd left nothing behind.

"All set, then," I said finally. "If you can run the kit out to your car, I'll—" I took a deep breath. "I'll go find Grady."

MY PLAN was to let Grady discover the body. That would divert most of the media attention away from me and give it to someone who'd love the spotlight, leaving me to step back and concentrate on luring in the group. I'd use my influence with Grady to ensure that all reports said I'd instigated the search and pinpointed the burial site. That would tell the group that *I* was the threat, not Grady.

I found Grady and Claudia in the living room. While Grady thumbed through the daily paper, Claudia was arguing with the caterer, insisting on getting dinner before we had to leave.

Nearly dancing with impatience, I waited until Claudia dismissed the poor woman, who took one look at me and fled before I could add any culinary demands.

I knew the camera was there, probably still on. In fact, I hoped it was. This was one private performance I didn't mind making public.

"Bradford? Can I talk to you?" I glanced at Claudia. "Both of you."

"Certainly. Where's Jeremy?"

"Outside still. Something happ—" I swallowed and sat beside him on the sofa. "I know you have a strong sixth sense for these sorts of things. Have you . . . sensed anything in this house? Or in the garden?"

He aimed a hard look at Claudia, and I knew she'd been holding him back from discussing this with me, not wanting him to make a fool of himself.

"I have," he said. "I picked it up as soon as I arrived and it's become steadily stronger. You remember that séance I did, don't you? That poor young woman, killed in this very yard, brutally slaughtered in the prime of her life? Cut down by nefarious forces. Demonic forces."

Claudia motioned for him to tone it down, but he kept going.

"I believe, Jaime, that in contacting her, I caught the attention of those forces. The other day something possessed me. Something demonic. It was trying to communicate with me. To show me something."

"Yes, that's exactly—"

"Then, the next night, there was a dog. A hound of hell, I'm certain. I saw it prowling the gardens, its red eyes glowing. It was trying to draw me outside, to lead me to whatever that demon had failed to show me."

I nodded vigorously. "I'm sure you're right. I've been feeling the pull too. There's something in that garden."

"I fear so. You know what we must do, then, don't you?"

"Yes. We have to—"

"—avoid that garden at all costs. I wanted to warn you earlier, when I realized you were spending so much time out there."

"But—"

"Claudia, however, felt I was overreacting." Another pointed glare her way, then he reached for my hand. "Fight the urge, Jaime. For the sake of your soul, don't let evil win. We'll be gone from this place soon, but until then, we must all avoid that garden."

"But—"

He stood. "Now, Claudia and I are going into town for tea. Would you and Jeremy care to join us?"

DAMN, DAMN, damn!

I'd been so sure Grady would take the bait. The more I thought of it, though, the more I saw that my plan had one very big hole—it presumed that Grady's "hunt for evil" was pure showmanship. Yet when I'd heard him talking about the possession and seeing the wolf out back, I should have realized that his fervor was fueled by the passion of a true believer. Not unlike May Donovan and the group, he'd searched for some sign of the paranormal, but had always been disappointed. When the real supernatural world reared up in his face, he'd looked it in the eye and realized he wanted nothing to do with it.

Now, once again, I'd tipped my hand. I'd asked him to come outside, and he'd refused, an exchange that had probably been caught on the hidden cameras. So how suspicious would it look now if *I* went outside and found the body?

"Jaime?"

Angelique was coming down the stairs. I darted into the back hall, hoping to avoid her.

"Jaime?" Her voice sounded right behind me.

I turned and flashed a wide smile. "There you are. I thought I heard you. What's up, hon?"

"I wanted to thank you for trying to keep the show going."

"The fight's not over. Now, I have a call to make—"

"One more thing. There's this huge revival meeting in Nebraska next month and I was wondering if you might go with me. I know it's not your thing, but it attracts thousands of people."

"Nebraska? Um, sure, why not? Now, if you'll excuse me."

From her expression, she knew she was being brushed off, and I hated to do that, but told myself I'd make it up to her later.

I LOOKED across the patio for Jeremy. No sign. He'd probably overheard me with Angelique and slipped back to guard the burial site.

I was about to follow, then stopped. If I went back to that site, I had to be prepared to find the body. Was that wise? Or should I call Jeremy first and make sure we didn't have an alternative?

No. The more fussing we did now, the more likely we'd be caught trying to stage the discovery.

I headed into the garden.

"Jaime?"

Grady. I turned as he rounded the corner. I opened my mouth, then took one look at that gliding, almost feline gait and amended the greeting.

"Aratron."

He smiled, brilliant blue eyes twinkling. "I believe you wanted Bradford Grady. For a small matter of corpse discovery?"

I hesitated. "I'm not sure this—"

"—is a wise idea? Not the sort of thing to accuse me of, child. I am nothing if not wise." He motioned for me to continue walking and joined me. "It is clear that these people you chase are patient—this magic is not something they could have mastered overnight. From Eric Botnick you learned how careful they are to avoid the limelight, and how decisive they will be in ridding themselves of a potential threat. If you are surrounded by attention . . ."

"They'll stay clear until it dies down, then strike . . . after I think

I'm no longer in danger. Which is why I wanted Grady to do the discovering."

"That is the obstacle, which I am generously offering to help you overcome."

JEREMY WAS back at the site, standing guard with Eve and Kristof. He heard—or smelled—me coming and rounded the corner.

"Had some trouble with Grady," I began.

"Aratron, I presume," Jeremy said. "Hello."

Aratron smiled. "I'd extend my hand, as I know is the proper greeting among humans, but not one so welcome among your breed, so I'll settle for a respectful 'well met' to the Alpha of the North American Pack."

No surprise that Aratron knew who Jeremy was. As for Jeremy recognizing the demon, I suspected it had to do with those extrasensory abilities he didn't like to discuss.

The demon turned to Eve and Kristof. "Eve. Mr. Nast, sir. Keeping out of trouble, I presume."

"Within reason," Eve replied.

As Aratron passed Eve, he reached out and gave her shoulder a fatherly squeeze, his fingers even seeming to make contact. Then he peered down the path on the far side.

"Speaking of trouble, I was hoping to meet Lucifer's daughter at this gathering. She's not here?"

"Lucifer's . . . ?" I began.

"The half-demon girl," Eve said. "Hope. No, she's not. We didn't see much use for her powers here."

"Then you're underestimating them," Aratron said. "Which is not only shortsighted, but a dangerous thing to do with an Espisco. The most fascinating subtype of the half-breeds. And exceedingly rare. Lucifer is most particular about where he spreads his seed. Her mother must be a remarkable woman." He turned to Eve. "I'd like to meet the girl sometime. You'll arrange it, I presume."

A look crossed Eve's face. If I didn't know her so well, I'd chalk it up to jealousy—having Aratron take an interest in a more interesting half-demon. More likely Eve just didn't like being ordered to do something, no matter who was doing the ordering.

Not waiting for an answer, Aratron stepped up into the garden and stood over the shallow grave.

"So the child lies here. We'd best get on with it, then, before Bradford Grady's woman begins to wonder about his protracted bathroom visit."

He crouched, cleared his throat and affected Grady's tone. "Here, Jaime? Is this where you sense it?"

He switched to an eerily accurate imitation of my voice. "Yes, Bradford. Don't you feel it?"

"Yes, I believe I do. Evil, great evil permeates this place." A dramatic shudder. "We must uncover the source of these demonic emanations. Only then will the tormented spirits be at rest."

"Enjoying yourself, Aratron?" Eve said.

He cast a haughty glower in her direction. "I'm a eudemon. We are incapable of enjoyment." Back to my voice. "It looks as if the dirt has been disturbed here, Grady, but I'm afraid to—"

"Never fear, sweet lady. I will dirty my hands for you."

He sifted his fingers through the dirt. "What's this? It looks like a finger." More digging. "A finger attached to a hand. Mother of God, Jaime, we've found a body. We must alert the authorities at once."

"I think you'd better leave that part to Jaime," Eve said.

"I have a better idea." He glanced at me. "What is his woman's name?"

"Claudia."

He cleared his throat and gave a bellow worthy of Marlon Brando. "Claudia!"

Two more shouts, then from the patio, a guard's voice. "I think it's Mr. Grady. He sounds like he's in trouble."

"I'll get help," someone answered.

Aratron smiled. "Two minutes to a suitably dramatic discovery, one with enough witnesses to ensure it can't be covered up. Now, I'm going to return Bradford Grady to his body, but I will remain close by, should he fail in his duties."

"Thank you."

A gallant nod. Grady's body stumbled back, almost falling in the bushes before Jeremy caught him.

Grady blinked. "Where—? What—?"

"You just found a body," I said.

WHEN GRADY saw what he'd "done," I'm sure his first thought was to get the hell out of Dodge before the cops arrived—or the evil forces sucked him into that grave. But by then, the guards were there, along with Claudia, Becky and Will, and he quickly sized up his options. If he played along, he'd headline the local papers as a hero. If he claimed he'd discovered the body under the thrall of a demonic force, he'd headline the papers as a nut-job. Astute man that he was, he went with number one.

COVER STORY

THE POLICE CAME. They saw. They called for backup.

Excavating the body would have to wait until the scene had been processed. The detectives interviewed me first, with a warning that there would almost certainly be more questions to come.

They weren't happy with my "lured into the garden by psychic vibes" explanation, but I toned down the spiritualism angle, feigning reluctance to put a name to whatever had drawn me there. Still, I think they would have been more comfortable if they could make the most logical deduction—that I'd "found" the body because I put it there. But even a cursory look proved this was no day-old corpse. There was little chance that I'd killed and buried this person months ago, then just happened to be billeted in the same house where, driven by my guilty conscience, I'd coerced Grady into uncovering my victim.

I'm sure they'd still consider that angle; without it, they were left with a possible true case of a spiritualist responding to the calls of the restless dead.

HOPE BROUGHT Zack Flynn over as planned, and ducked past the crowd surrounding Grady to the sunroom, where Jeremy and I were lying low.

She waved Zack into the room. "She's all yours. An exclusive interview for the *L.A. Times*. Be nice to her."

Zack thanked Hope far more fervently than the situation warranted, then stood there, puppy dog eyes following her from the room, turning to me only when she was out of sight.

"Great girl," I said.

"She is, isn't she? She's got what it takes to play with the big boys, but she isn't interested. She's having a blast chasing alien abduction stories and doesn't give a damn what anyone thinks about that."

His gaze slid to the spot where he'd last seen Hope, his expression a mix of envy and infatuation. Aratron's words came back to me. Lucifer's daughter. From what little I knew of demonology, Lucifer was just another lord demon, no more powerful or "evil" than any of the other lord demons. But the name still gave me a chill. I wondered what Zack would think of having Lucifer for a father-in-law. Convenient for any "my soul for a Pulitzer" ambitions, though.

The interview went well. Like the police, he seemed to appreciate that I wasn't going off on an "I hear dead people" rant with this. Unlike them, though, he *did* press that angle, journalistic instinct backed by a personal interest in the paranormal.

I spoke with reluctance, as if I knew more, but wasn't comfortable admitting it. I said I sensed that the victim was young and female and had likely come to a violent end.

"Though," I added with a wry smile, "one could probably guess the violent-end part by where she ended up. Not exactly a psychic feat."

Zack jotted down my words. He had a recorder, but seemed to use it only as backup. As he wrote, I leaned back in the armchair, catching a ray of late-day sun across my face.

"Did you get a sense, as you call it, of anything else? The girl's age? A name, perhaps?"

I shook my head. "Preteens, maybe, though I could be judging that based on the size of the hand. As for female?" Another self-deprecating smile. "Well, I have a fifty-fifty shot there, don't I?"

"Anything more?" He studied me, as if certain I was withholding something.

"I . . . sensed more, but it's out of context and I may embarrass myself if, let's say, I gave you Holly as a name and it turns out to be that of her cat."

"Holly?" he said, pen poised over his paper.

I shook my head. "Just an example. If I had to . . ." I toyed with a strand of hair hanging over my shoulder, then looked up at him. "R. S. That's all I'll say. It could be her initials. It could be the initials of her school or the street where she lived. I don't know."

He nodded and wrote. A few more questions, then Hope rapped at the door.

"Interview's over, Flynn," she said. "My turn now . . . and quite possibly the only chance I'll ever get to show you up, which, by the way, I intend to do."

He grinned. "Think so, do you?"

"Know so."

She sauntered past him. There was no sway in her stride, but his gaze was glued to her every step of the way.

"How about a wager?" he said. "Whoever's story gets more inches gets dinner at Patina."

Hope laughed. "You think I can afford Patina on my salary?"

"Oh, right. Forgot. Hmm. McDonald's, then?"

Another laugh and she shooed him from the room. He was too busy bantering to notice she hadn't agreed to the wager.

"Not your type?" I asked when Zack was gone.

"As a friend, yes. But I don't—" A cloud passed behind her eyes, then she forced a wide smile. "Between playing weird-tales girl for *True News,* girl Friday for the council and chaos demon-in-training, my life is pretty darned full. I'm trying to set Zack up with a preschool teacher at our gym—a nice normal girl who doesn't see death and destruction on every street corner. More his speed, I think."

I glanced around. "Being here . . . is that okay for you?"

"If you mean because of those poor kids, I'm not seeing anything, so I'd presume they weren't killed here. I'm exaggerating with the 'every street corner' thing. On average, I get maybe a couple of visions a day and most aren't so bad. Though I did notice something in the dining room when I passed."

"The hanging guy?"

"You can see him too?"

"Every time I sit down for a meal."

"And you eat in there? Seeing that?" She shook her head. "I've got a lot of work to do before I hit that stage. They still catch me off guard. Sometimes badly off guard. Like when I met Karl. Hugely embarrassing."

She stopped there.

I tapped my watch. "We have about another twenty minutes to make this look like a real interview. Spill."

"It was in a buffet line, which probably isn't the strangest place to meet a werewolf. I'm minding my own business, eyeing this nice roast duck centerpiece. Then everything goes black and I'm running through a dark forest. I snap out of it and there, on the table, is the duck—now freshly killed, blood and entrails everywhere. I freaked."

"Don't blame you."

"I spun around and hit the guy behind me. Knocked the plate from his hands. Snagged my bracelet on his sleeve. Generally made a fool of myself. Being Karl, he was as cool and suave as could be, which only made it worse."

She shook her head, but the smile playing on her lips told me she hadn't taken it as badly as she pretended.

"And the vision was Karl . . . chasing someone?"

"Nah. Just a general 'hi, I'm a werewolf' image tag."

"You can tell what kind of supernaturals we are?"

She waggled her hand. "Iffy. The stronger the power, the more likely I'll get a vision. It's like detecting chaos. If that hanged guy was jumping off the table right now, I'd probably get a flash. If he was just thinking about it, I have about a twenty percent shot."

"You can read thoughts?"

I must have looked worried, because she lifted her hands.

"No, no. Not like that. I pick up chaotic thoughts. For example, if you're sitting there thinking my shirt is god-ugly, I wouldn't know. If you're thinking about wrapping your hands around my neck and strangling the life from me, I may pick it up."

"Handy."

"The key word is 'may,' I'm afraid. Not as useful as it sounds."

We chatted for a while longer, swapping stories.

As for the interview, she might still do a story, but that would come later. *True News* came out weekly, meaning it wasn't a timely way to get the group's attention. But if Zack's interview and the other media bits didn't lure them out, Hope's article would run next week, with more damning details that would definitely spark their interest.

AFTERWARD, I gave some sound bites to the biggest TV news crews—just enough to ensure they knew whose vibes had led to the body—then slipped away in search of peace and Jeremy. As I passed the living room, I heard someone being pelted with questions. Those crews who hadn't been lucky enough to get an interview with Grady or me had tracked down a substitute.

"Um, yes," Angelique was saying. "I have picked up some, uh, feelings in the yard."

"You mean the garden, don't you?" someone said.

"Have you heard voices?" another voice asked. "Or seen anything?"

Angelique stumbled through an answer. The kid was just too young to give a full improv performance. She'd been kept out of the loop on all this, and now microphones were being shoved in her face. As much as I wanted to find Jeremy, I felt guilty.

"Hey, guys," I said as I walked into the living room. "Are you boys pouncing on this poor girl? We just found a body in the garden. She's a wee bit shaken up, aren't you, hon?"

I put my arm around her and squeezed her shoulder. Angelique shot me a grateful look.

"I've never seen a dead body before," she said, her honeyed southern accent pitch-perfect again. She shivered. "I only hope that poor child has gone to a better place. She'll be in my prayers—"

"Jaime," a hook-nosed man cut in, motioning for his cameraman to swing the camera to focus on me. "You led Bradford Grady to that body. What did you sense?"

I tugged Angelique on camera with me. "We've *all* sensed things in this house, for days now—"

"But you helped discover the body. What was *your* experience?"

I kept trying to steer the questions back to include Angelique, but they were having none of it, and it soon became apparent that I was only hogging any camera time she might have received. So I made my excuses and fled.

I found Jeremy in the kitchen, where he'd cornered Becky. Being Jeremy, he didn't make it obvious—none of that werewolf posturing. Instead, he'd taken a spot a few feet away, out of her personal space, as she fixed a coffee. To leave, though, she'd need to shoulder past him.

"I presume you don't expect Jaime out of the house by tonight," he was saying. "Under the circumstances, packing has been the last thing on her mind. And, in speaking to the officers outside, they made it clear they'd prefer everyone to stay where they are."

"We haven't made any decisions yet."

"No? Perhaps the staff is receiving inaccurate information, then. They've apparently been told they're staying on for another day or two."

"They are, but the actors—"

"You told Jaime she had to be out tonight because the staff wouldn't be here. If they're staying on, I see no reason to hurry her departure, particularly under the circumstances. I'll tell her we're here for the night."

He turned to go.

"We?" Becky said.

"Jaime has just discovered a murder victim. I'm concerned for her safety, so I will be spending the night. I believe there's a pullout sofa in the living room. That will suit me fine."

He walked out before she could answer. I followed him.

WE WATCHED the six o'clock news with Grady, Claudia and the guards. Even the cleaning woman joined us after hearing the commotion. It took me awhile to realize Angelique wasn't there but, after seeing her fumbling on screen, I decided maybe it was better if I didn't drag her in to join the party.

And a party it was. A victory celebration. We were splashed all over the news, Grady and I both finding opportunities to plug the *Death of Innocence* special and dropping teasers about the material we'd taped so far.

As for the discovery of the crime, it played out just the way we'd spun it. Yes, Grady had found the body. Yes, he claimed to have sensed the "poor child" calling to him. But in every newscast, it was clear that I'd been the one to lead him there, based on my own experiences in the house—experiences I was less eager to share. When the group heard the story, the person they'd think who was most likely to know more than she was saying—perhaps something that could expose them—would be me.

As I watched myself on television, imagining the group watching too, I had to admit that I hadn't really thought it all through. Finding the corpse would, we hoped, draw out the killers. Being of a scientific bent, they'd leave nothing to chance, so they'd get closer, maybe even try to beat the police to other bodies in the gardens.

I'd already hinted I knew more. Having unlocked magical secrets themselves, they'd know it wasn't impossible that I *did* know more, that my ability to communicate with the dead wasn't a put-on. They'd want to know how much more I knew.

Jeremy would do everything in his power to keep me safe. Hope had promised her help, as had Eve.

But had I really considered the danger I was now in?

No.

Would I have backed out because of it?

No.

RISKS AND REWARDS

AT EIGHT O'CLOCK, AS WE WERE FINISHING DINNER, the door swung open. In strode a man—no more than thirty with blond-streaked hair, a cultivated five-o'clock shadow and a shark's grin. Two assistants flanked him, each a decade or more his senior.

"Todd Simon," he said. "I know you were probably hoping to catch a flight home tomorrow, but in light of recent developments, I see grand new possibilities for this little show of ours, and I'm personally taking the helm to guide us there."

Claudia pushed back her chair. "I presume this new direction means a renegotiated contract? With a renegotiated salary?"

Simon flashed a smile. "Absolutely. My lawyers are on their way here to handle that. This show has just climbed to the top of the network's specials list, and we have you all and your amazing talents to thank for it. I intend to make every member of this team a very happy camper."

BETWEEN THE reporters, cameras, cops and Todd Simon's crew roaming the house and garden, Jeremy and I couldn't steal a moment of privacy. So I'll admit it was with no small disappointment that I realized he had every intention of sleeping on the pullout sofa.

Old-fashioned, yes, but kind of sweet. I returned to the kitchen for an aspirin after the others had retired, giving him a chance to slip upstairs with me. But the living room remained dark and silent.

At some level, this was what I expected from Jeremy. Responsible and controlled to the core. As passionate as he'd been the night before, and despite his teasing today, he'd be wrapped up in the case and presume I'd feel the same.

Damn.

I trudged upstairs. Eve was in my room, keeping watch, slung sideways over a chair by the balcony door, reading a book. A textbook, of course. I couldn't imagine Eve picking up a novel. Reading was for learning, for research, and even then only as a last resort, when there wasn't a more active way of finding out what she wanted.

I glanced at the title. *Abarazzi's Complete Genealogy of Demons, Demi-Demons and Associated Subtypes.*

"A little light reading?" I said.

"Catching up on some family history. Dull enough I won't get caught up in it. Not so dull that I'll fall asleep." She looked over the edge at me. "So..." She glanced behind me. "I see you didn't find the aspirin."

"Ha-ha." I kicked off my shoes and dropped onto the bed. "It's been a long day, and definitely not the time to make any—"

A rap at the balcony door. Jeremy stood there, shielding his eyes to see past the light reflecting off the glass.

"You were saying...?" Eve began.

"Scoot."

"Leave? Weren't you just saying...?"

I mouthed an obscenity. She grinned and closed her book.

"I'll be on patrol. You need me back, just shout. But something tells me you won't."

She left. Jeremy was leaning against the railing now, confident in his welcome. He looked as sexy as he had last night—hair slightly mussed, feet bare, lips curved in a smile, long fingers tapping the railing with just a touch of impatience, eager to get inside.

A spark of heat flickered. I remembered the night before, him leaning into the gap, that hunger, that desire—and the spark exploded into a flame that licked through me, burning all the hotter as I remembered what had brought him here last night. This time, there was no adrenaline intoxication to blame. He'd made his decision. He was ready to take a chance. After four years of waiting and hoping, he was here, at my door. And just seeing him was enough to make me dizzy with lust.

As I walked to the door, I realized my nipples were already hard, pressing against my shirt. I tugged it looser to hide them. I'd waited years for this, and no matter how ready I was, I was going to make this last.

I cracked open the door. "Bastard."

His brows shot up. "What did I do now?"

"Pretending you were staying downstairs. Faking being asleep when I slipped down there."

"I've been outside since you first went upstairs, Jaime. I was talking to the officers on duty, then scouting to ensure I could still get up here without being seen." He paused, lips twitching. "So you came back down? Hoping to do what? Sneak me back up to your room?"

"Of course not. I was getting an aspirin and a glass of water."

"You have a headache?"

"No—yes. A bad headache. So sorry. Better luck tomorrow."

I started to close the door, but he wedged his fingers in the gap. A tug and it opened a little farther. Then, one hand still on the door, he reached the other in, fingers brushing my cheek, hand going behind my head to pull me to him. For a second, I hung there, straining for his touch, aching for his kiss . . . and knowing if I let him get me closer right now, I wasn't going to make it as far as the bed. And as delicious as that thought was, it wasn't quite what I had in mind. So I stepped back and snapped the lock down, stopping it at a six-inch gap.

"Headache, hmm?" His expression went serious. "Do you know what's the best cure for that?"

"What?"

"Orgasm."

He said it so matter-of-factly I had to sputter a laugh.

"Multiple, if possible," he continued. "It's a proven medical fact that one physiologic event, like orgasm, can cancel out the effects of another physiological process, such as a headache."

His expression was perfectly serious, but I said, "You're full of shit."

"Perhaps. If so, you should call my bluff. Just open the door and we'll test it out."

He gave me a look that was almost enough to let me test it without so much as a touch. Which gave me an idea...

"You're right. Maybe I should." I backed up to the bed, then settled onto the edge. "But I think I can manage by myself. I'm a strong believer in self-reliance."

"I see."

I smiled. "Not yet."

As I eased back onto the bed, my skirt hiked up until it was bunched at my hips. I ran my fingers along the hem, then under, to the inside of my thigh.

"You wouldn't dare," he said.

"That's what you said last night and, as you may have noticed, I'm not the sort of woman to let a challenge pass."

I leaned back and brought my feet up to give him a better view. I stroked the inside of my thigh, fingers climbing higher. A surreptitious look his way. He was pressed against the gap, his nostrils flaring, eyes glinting. His lips parted, tongue slipping between his teeth—

I shuddered and pulled my gaze away. I was already so wet I'd need to peel these panties off.

I slipped my fingertip under my panty leg, running it along the edge, tugging it up just enough to give him a peek at what lay beneath. Then, holding the panties aside with one hand, I teased myself with the other, gasping and arching my hips.

Jeremy gripped the edge of the door frame, fingers flexing as if readying for that lock-breaking yank. But he didn't do it, just stood there, watching me, nostrils flaring, holding back—controlling it and drawing it out until the last possible moment—

I stopped before I hit *my* last possible moment. I let go of my panties, but kept my finger under them, where he couldn't watch.

"You could open that door, Jeremy," I said. "But that would break it, and then you'd have to explain things and, well, that just wouldn't be proper, would it?"

I leaned back on the bed, fingers still teasing us both. His hand tightened on the door frame, but he only said, "Open the door, Jaime."

"You'd like that, wouldn't you?" I slid a finger inside myself and gasped. "I'm doing just fine on my own."

"I can do better."

"Think so? I'm pretty sure I have more practice."

A laugh. Then a roll of his shoulders, as if trying to snap out of the mood. He glanced over his shoulder.

"You really should let me in, Jaime. Before a guard walks by and sees me. That's trouble we don't want."

"Oh, so now you're getting all responsible on me. I thought you said it was safe."

"For climbing up, not camping out."

I walked to the door, stopped at the opposite end—out of his reach—and peered into the night.

"All anyone can see from this angle, in the darkness, is a very big tree."

"Are you sure?"

"Yes."

"Absolutely?"

"Yes, so you're not using that as an excuse to come inside."

"I wasn't thinking of excuses. I was thinking of a little show you promised me in the alley this afternoon."

"I never promised—"

"An implied promise, cut short by a phone call, which I never complained about."

"You're such a gentleman."

He stepped back, leaning against the railing.

"Please," I said, rolling my eyes. "You expect me to strip in front of a patio door? What kind of woman do you take me for?"

His lips twitched in that sexy, crooked smile, gaze locking on mine. "I dare you."

"Bastard."

"Keep calling me that and I might get offended and leave."

I mouthed the word, checked the lock on the door, then backed up and started tugging my blouse from my skirt, slow and deliberate. Then the unbuttoning. I shrugged and the blouse slid down my shoulders, but no further. Reaching behind, I unzipped the skirt. A shimmy and it went down to my waist and caught at my hips.

"See, I told you it was too tight."

I gave a halfhearted tug. It fell a half-inch. Another shrug and my blouse slid to my breasts and stopped.

"Hmmm, seems that's a little tight too," I murmured.

Another shimmy. Another half-inch. The lace on my panties showed over the waistline. I plucked at it with one hand and ran the fingers of the other under my bra.

"Seems I could use a hand."

"I believe I already offered that."

I laughed, then tugged off the shirt and let it float to the ground. The skirt followed, pooling at my feet.

"Is this okay?" I asked. "Or do you prefer au naturel?"

"I didn't get much of a look at au naturel last night. You turned away before the dress came off, if you recall."

"Did I? Nasty." I stepped out of the skirt and moved closer to the door. "I suppose you want to do a comparison."

He nodded, but his gaze kept traveling over the sheer lace bra and matching G-string panties. I backed up, then bent, picked up my discarded clothing and headed for the bed. As I turned, he made a low noise deep in his throat.

I leaned over the bed to lay my clothing on the far side. Then, still bent over, I glanced over my shoulder at him. His expression was enough to make me lean over farther, feet spread a little wider.

"Seeing something you like?" I said. "A position maybe? Judging by that look you're giving me, I think you're more of a wolf than you let on."

A low chuckle. "Normally, I wouldn't say it's a preference, but at the moment I believe I could be persuaded."

I stretched farther, arching to enhance his view . . . and the invitation. My hand glided between my legs. I pushed the fabric aside, then slid a fingertip in again.

"Jaime . . ."

I pushed the finger the rest of the way in. Jeremy grabbed the door frame. I smiled.

"One tug, that's all it'll take. I'll be right here. Waiting and . . ." I slid my wet finger out for him to see. "Ready."

His grip tightened on the door and I braced myself. Then he stopped short, nostrils flaring as he glanced over his shoulder. I backed off the bed and hurried over.

"Is someone down—?"

He lifted his finger to his lips and stepped to the edge for a better look. He frowned, then, gaze still riveted to something below, eased back to the door. His lips moved, but I caught only a murmur.

I moved to the gap and whispered, "What's that?"

He pressed against the opening. "I said—"

A sharp tug on my panties. I gasped and pulled back, but he had the front of them wrapped around his hand.

"You—"

A yank on the front of my bra and I smacked into the door frame, the curse cut short as his lips found mine. I gave a token struggle, but hated to ruin a very expensive lingerie set, so I gave up and kissed him back. The door frame pressed against my face and sides, cold and hard, an unwelcome contrast to the heat of his skin, and I wriggled to get away from it, to feel only him.

As his fingers crept into my panties, I tried to arch back, to give him better access, but the door was in the way. His fingers grazed me and my hands clenched, wanting to grab him, to dig my fingers into him, but all I could feel was that damned door.

He teased me, his fingertips slipping inside, but the angle was wrong and awkward and, after a moment, he pulled back.

"Don't stop," I said, voice ragged.

"Sorry, I'm a perfectionist. I'd hate to leave a bad first impression. Perhaps if you opened the door . . ."

"You open it."

"The door lock is on your side. True, I could break it—but that, as you pointed out, would be wrong. Irresponsible. Just reach over, flick the switch—"

"Never."

He yanked on my bra, pulling me into a kiss that sent my brain reeling, nails clawing at the door frame.

Okay, enough was enough. Time to tip the balance.

I reached through the gap and unbuttoned his pants, slid my hand into his shorts and wrapped my fingers—

He groaned and pressed against the gap, as if he could shoulder his way through.

That was more like it.

I stroked him, my grip tight, and his groan turned to growls that made my eyelids flutter and my panties flood. I arched my hips toward the door and pulled him between my legs. A sharper growl, frustrated now as he tried to get closer.

I let go and backed up, then slid my panties down. I looked at him, caught that flare of the nostrils, that dark lust in his eyes as he pressed into the gap, his erection—

I pulled my gaze away before I said "to hell with it" and opened the door.

I undid my bra and let it fall, then stepped from my panties and moved to the door. Fingers wrapped around him, I arched onto my tiptoes, guiding him between my legs.

He chuckled. "I don't think that will work."

"Is that a dare?"

I slid him between my legs and thrust my hips forward. I couldn't get more than a couple of inches, just enough to tease. I slid down, eyes closed, arching back, gasping—

The door slammed open, lock breaking. His arm went around my waist, lifting me up and dropping us both to the floor. His arm broke my fall, but we hit with such force that we slid across the hardwood. His hand flew to the top of my head a split-second before it crashed into the bed leg.

I smiled up at him. "Always a gentleman."

"Not always," he said, and, with one hard thrust, he was inside me.

V

She knelt on the living room floor of her condo. The blinds were drawn, but that wasn't suspicious, given the hour. If anyone *had* seen her, he would have been shocked—this upright professional kneeling before an ancient spellbook, surrounded by candles, arcane symbols chalked on the floor. Unexpected, but hardly criminal, worthy only of whispers and raised brows.

The grayish powder in the bowl could be anything—probably wouldn't even be noticed. That was the beauty of it, unlike the dried body parts her nanny had used—those disgusting relics that had to be kept hidden and, when accidentally found, had cost the old woman her job. All that secrecy, shame and pain for something that hadn't even worked. Oh, her nanny had claimed otherwise—taking responsibility for accidents and strokes of good luck. That was how the ignorant practiced magic, seeing success in every coincidental occurrence.

Unlike the rituals her nanny swore by, this magic worked. As for why it worked, the group was convinced the ashes were the key. She'd believed that too. That was the one thing that made the difference between failure and success, ergo it must be the key.

And yet...

What if the magic worked with the ashes because they thought it would? Because they'd wanted this to be the key? Because they'd *needed* it to be the key, to excuse what they had done—taken the life of a child. Guilt, fear and conviction. All powerful motivators.

Three years ago, she'd started experimenting with using lesser amounts of ash. It had taken months of daily practice to see any results. All that practice meant she needed more than her share. Being the one in charge of the burning and the division of material had let her take that extra unnoticed, but she'd hated it. Like a company CEO who pilfered copy paper and printer ink—disgraceful and undignified.

After that initial breakthrough, though, success had come faster with each reduction. It was as if having proven to herself that she could cast with less, she'd overcome a mental barrier that said otherwise. It didn't work with all the spells. Thus far, the group had mastered just over a dozen, and fewer than half of those worked with significantly reduced amounts of human remains. But it was progress. Moving toward the ultimate goal, the one she was testing tonight.

She cast the spell again. A simple one that created a spark—barely enough to light a cigarette, but a building block to better things. One must master the elementary levels first, in magic as in all things.

After casting, she blew a fingertip of ash. The spark flared. She tried again, and was again successful. Then she reached over, picked up a moist towel and carefully wiped her finger, removing all traces of the ash.

She cast the spell. Nothing happened. Again. Nothing.

She swallowed her disappointment. Must remain calm and focused. She dipped her finger in the ash. Cast. Blew. Spark. Again. Another spark. Wipe the finger off. Cast. Failure. Cast...

The air ignited in a tiny pop of light and heat.

She took a deep breath and leaned forward, palms pressing into her thighs as she exhaled. Then she allowed herself a smile.

Only a small spell, to be sure, but she had proven her theory. She could cast without the ash—without aids of any kind.

She resisted the urge to try again. Take the success and hold the memory, untainted by later failure. That would bolster her determination, knowing that the last time she'd tried, she'd succeeded.

She picked up the bowl of ash and poured it back into the jar, watching it slide down. Here was the cement that bound the group together. Bound them in fear and guilt.

There was more than one kind of power and this one was just as essential to her quest as anything magical. She must keep the group together and striving forward, seeking and searching, working with her to achieve her goals.

To do that, she had to keep them killing.

MORNING AFTER

I WOKE UP TO AN EMPTY BED. For me, that's usually a "morning after" relief—saves those invitations to an unwanted breakfast and the "I'll call you" lies, an awkwardness topped only by "what was your name again?" For the first time in my life, on waking to an empty bed, I rolled over and cursed.

I wasn't surprised that he'd left, but I'd hoped the promise of a passionate wake-up call would override his usual sense of propriety. Apparently not. He must have slipped out in the night so I'd be spared curious stares and knowing grins when we walked downstairs together.

Old-fashioned, but I couldn't complain when it was one of the things that had drawn me to him in the first place. Always a gentleman. Well, not always . . .

I smiled, thinking of some deliciously ungentlemanly behavior from the night before. I stretched and felt a protesting throb between my thighs. Maybe that wake-up call wouldn't have been such a wise idea. One unexpected part of having a werewolf as a lover? All that extra energy.

I grinned and rolled over. More pangs of protest. That dull throb between my legs. Tender breasts. Even my lips hurt.

Damn, that was good.

The patio door opened. Jeremy walked in, pants on, shirt undone, feet bare, cell phone in his hand. Seeing me, he lifted the phone.

"My morning check-in with Elena. I didn't wake you, did I?"

I shook my head and was about to peel the covers back when I noticed that faint wrinkle between his brows had deepened.

"Everything okay with the babies?" I asked, pushing up onto one arm.

"They're fine. But Elena's already read the L.A. news online. She thinks it's just as it appeared in the articles—that you found a body. I confirmed that." A hand raked through his hair as he looked around distractedly for a place to put his cell phone. "I don't like lying to her."

"I know."

"They're going to find out, after this is done. The council has to know and Elena will need to know first. It'll take some careful explaining."

"Do you want to call Clay in? Or Antonio?"

He shook his head. "The more people we have around you, the less likely the group will reveal itself. If I need help, I have a backup plan."

He laid his phone down on the dresser. I glanced up at his hair, glistening and damp.

"You've showered?"

"Yes. I didn't disturb you, did I?"

"No, it's just—" I motioned to the front of his pants. "Forgot to zip up."

He frowned. Before he could look down, I stretched and caught his waistband.

"Come here. I'll get it."

He moved to the side of the bed.

I undid his button, opened it, then looked at the zipped fly and smiled. "Whoops. My mistake."

I undid the zipper, reached inside and lowered my head to give him a proper good morning.

LATER, I was curled up against him. "I was just thinking. This is probably the safest place to be."

"Hmm?"

I propped myself up to look down at him. "If I'm in danger, maybe we should just stay here until it's all over."

He gave a low laugh and rose to kiss my neck.

I sighed. "What you're politely refraining from pointing out is that the problem won't end while I'm in bed with you."

"I'm afraid not."

"So I suppose we should . . ." I eyed the cold room beyond, "get up."

"Probably."

He pulled me down to him in a kiss that said we weren't going anywhere for a while yet.

IT WAS midmorning by the time I finally got into the shower. As I dressed, Jeremy slipped out. I was pretty sure it was too late to pretend he'd spent the night on the sofa, but that wouldn't stop him from trying.

I'd hoped we could get a complete update from the police, but even Jeremy's polite charm could win only a grudging summary from the young woman guarding the scene. Yes, they'd uncovered a second body. Yes, they were looking for more but, no, she wasn't confirming that they *expected* to find more.

I'd also hoped to sit out in the garden, maybe find a quiet corner and let the children know I was still there, but the best I could manage was permission to sit on the balcony off my room, and I only got that because—after a brief conference—they seemed to decide there wasn't much they could do to stop me, as long as I wasn't taking pictures of the scene.

We gathered breakfast and went up, leaving the bedroom door open so no one could accuse me of holing up with my lover while I was supposed to be "on the set." Not that I had anything scheduled yet. I'd passed Todd Simon in the hall and he'd only blathered, "Plans, big plans. Be ready for my call, Jaime." My guess? He had this big opportunity and no idea how to use it.

Grady was doing the morning-show rounds. As for Angelique, I'd looked for her, wanting to make sure she didn't feel left out, but I must admit, with the case and Jeremy on my mind, I hadn't looked very hard. I'd make it up to her at that revival in Nebraska.

As Jeremy ate, sitting on a patio chair, I watched the scene below. There wasn't much to see. Two technicians were working on the spot near where we'd found Rachel Skye. Tools and equipment scattered about indicated there were more people involved, maybe taking a coffee break.

"The children aren't making contact," I said. "I don't know if they can, with me being up here. Maybe they don't know I'm around. Or maybe they're gone. If they move the bodies, the ghosts might go with them. And then—"

"When this is over, Eve will find them. But, as you both said, it's more likely they'll stay here."

I nodded, staring out over the yard. "Do you think they know what's happening? Can they see what's going on?" I nibbled my lip. "I've never been able to tell how well they see or hear things on this side of the veil. Maybe they're watching their bodies being dug up—"

He'd moved up behind me, hands going to my hips, pulling me close. His lips tickled the back of my neck. I leaned into him.

"Stop worrying, right?" I said. "There's nothing I can do about it."

"Yes, there is. We can catch whoever is behind this. Then you'll free those souls—"

"What if I can't?"

His kisses circled to my ear. "You will. Once we know what was done to them, you can free them. Eve said—"

"Maybe she's just saying that to calm me down, so I don't freak out—"

He turned me around to face him. "Does that sound like Eve?"

I shook my head.

"The children are fine," he continued. "It's unlikely they will leave, and if they do, we'll find them. It's also unlikely they understand what's happening, and if they do, they'll get over it once they're freed, which you will do just as soon as you're able to." His lips brushed my forehead. "Now come inside. Hope's probably wondering why we haven't called—"

"Ms. Vegas?" A rap at the open door. It was one of the guards. "Are you in here?"

I called an invitation and we stepped back into the room as he entered.

"Do you know a May Donovan?" he asked. "Lawyer? Works for some paranormal group?"

"Sure. What's up?"

"She was here this morning. Demanded to speak to you. Started off nice enough, but when I said you weren't available, she got pushy. Came right inside looking for you. We stopped her before she got far, but then she went out back and questioned the police . . ."

Jeremy stepped up beside me, frowning. "Did she seem upset?"

"Pissed off. Like we were hiding something. She wants you to call her. That Simon guy doesn't want you to—didn't even want me giving you the message—but that didn't seem right."

THE LESSON OF THE NYMPHS

"DAMN IT," I said as I sat on the bed. "She must think this is some kind of scam. A publicity stunt."

"If she didn't lob accusations, she may only want to speak to you," Jeremy said. "There could even be some benefit in doing so."

I looked up at him. "How?"

"The longer we keep this in the news, the more worried the group will become. Having you claim further 'messages' from the victims may not be wise. But working with May Donovan's group . . . ?" A graceful shrug. "Put the right twist on it, downplaying the spiritualism and playing up the ritualistic aspects of the killings, and she's likely to be quite willing to help."

"To uncover the worst kind of paranormal scam—one with real bodies. Perfect. I'll call now, tell her I want to talk."

I phoned the number May had left. The phone rang four times, then voice mail picked up. As I listened to her inviting me to press one to leave a message, I stopped, finger over the button. Then I hung up.

I laid the cell phone on my lap and thought. Then I thought some more. And while I did, Jeremy didn't question, just waited.

"May Donovan," I said finally. "Her accent. It sounds British, doesn't it?"

"I'm not very good with accents, I'm afraid. My language skills come from books, not conversation."

"But it could be British, right? I was just thinking about what Eve said—that Rachel's killer was a woman with a British accent. And I know that seems like an enormous leap, but . . ." I took a breath, slowing my thoughts and organizing them. "Zack Flynn said May had it in for Botnick. Imagine if she *was* part of this group and knew Botnick was searching for them. What better way to keep tabs on him? Purely professional interest. Even *he* wouldn't be suspicious."

Jeremy looked thoughtful. Dubious? After a moment, though, he said, "I think it's South African."

"Hmmm?"

"The accent. I believe it's South African."

"Like the folk magic we were investigating?"

He nodded. I called Eve.

I'd barely finished saying her name when she appeared.

"I see you haven't left the bedroom yet," she said, plunking onto the bed.

"You got here fast."

"She says, avoiding the subject. I didn't have far to travel. Kris and I have been patrolling. So far, nothing."

"What about this morning. Did you see a woman like this?" I described May. "She talked to the police earlier."

"Yeah, Kris saw her. She said she was a lawyer for the family, freaking out over the damage to the property, wanting to know how much longer they'd be digging up the backyard. Kris listened in, but he knows a lawyer when he hears one."

Jeremy and I exchanged a look.

"Did *you* overhear her?" I asked.

Eve frowned. "No."

I picked up the phone and dialed May's number, then held it out for Eve to listen. At first, she just fixed me with a "what the hell are you on?" look, but after a moment, she said, "That sounds like . . ." She stopped herself. "It *sounds* like the woman Rachel heard when she was kidnapped. But it might just be the accent. Who is she?"

I explained. As I spoke, Eve's frown deepened.

"Okay," she said when I finished. "She *does* sound like the woman Rachel heard. And she might be from South Africa. And, yes, falsely representing herself as the family's lawyer to get a look around is suspicious, but this is exactly the kind of thing a scam-buster *would* take an interest in—a potential child sacrifice, pseudosatanic shit. Someone who's so hell-bent on proving the paranormal doesn't exist certainly isn't going to get involved in it."

"It could make a good cover story," Jeremy said. "But Eve has a point. If she's been actively trying to disprove the paranormal for years, that's a very elaborate cover."

"Is it?" I settled onto the bed. "Do you remember what she said when we first met her? She started off on the opposite end of the spectrum. A seeker. Only after getting burned did she switch sides." I turned to Jeremy. "Eve met this guy in the afterlife who was running a poltergeist school. He had the gift, which is rare, but instead of trying to seriously teach others, he used it to entice nymphs to his school . . . and his bed. Nymphs made an easy target because, in the afterlife, they're always looking for power. They get plopped into a world full of supernatural ghosts, but they themselves have lost their powers."

"Except cheerleading," Eve said. "They make very good cheerleaders."

"When Aratron was here, he talked about the evolution of the supernatural. There are people out there who have supernatural blood, but because their original powers are no longer useful, they don't know it. Isn't it possible that some sense they might be different? I've met people like May Donovan, who seem driven to seek out magic and supernatural answers. Maybe because they have the blood, but not the power."

Eve snapped her fingers. "That could explain why the magic is working. Latent supernatural blood. Like quarter-demon crossbreeds." When I looked at her, she said, "Half-demons don't pass on their powers to the children, right? But they say that the blood still counts, gives any other supernatural powers a boost. So Savannah doesn't have my demon powers, but she probably gets an added bump to her spellcasting."

I passed her words on to Jeremy, who considered them as I went on. "Let's say May Donovan has this drive because of her latent powers. She seeks out knowledge, but gets nowhere. So she flips sides—

works out her frustration by uncovering scams while still secretly searching those scams for truth. Even after she found a backdoor in, she'd keep up the front—both searching for new magics and to protect herself." I paused. "Do you think she knows about Hope's powers? Maybe that's why she made contact in the first place."

"Possible," Jeremy said. "But it's equally likely that she simply makes it her business to be involved in everything paranormal in this city, including offering her assistance to a new tabloid reporter who covers the supernatural. If Hope uncovered something, May would be among the first to know."

"Which is exactly what happened."

WE SET about brainstorming. The most obvious way to test our theory would be to take advantage of May's invitation and trap her. But we had no way of knowing how many people were involved or what magics they had.

Almost an hour passed. Then Jeremy's cell phone rang.

"It's Hope," he said before answering. "I should have called her."

A couple of minutes later, he hung up. "Zack Flynn wants to meet with us. He says he has news."

"The reporter? But he's part of the Ehrich Weiss Society, which means he's probably in this magic group with May too, so why—" I stopped. "Because I wouldn't see May or return her call. Now he's giving it a shot."

"So it would seem. I told Hope to stall him and said we'd meet her in thirty minutes."

"Go out? Is that safe?"

"We'll be careful. But we have to go to her. There's someone I need to talk to."

SINCE IT WAS Saturday, Hope had spent the day at her apartment, waiting for instructions from Jeremy. When we arrived, he walked to the head of the narrow road leading around her building. There he stopped, sniffing the air. When the way was clear, he crouched to pick up a trail.

When he straightened, he led me down an alley. I knew if he didn't explain, it was either because he didn't want to worry me or because he didn't want to speak prematurely.

We looped around another building coming out . . . somewhere. My sense of direction is lousy and here, surrounded by buildings, I didn't even have the sun to check. Another road, another alley.

When the dirt under our feet turned to gravel, Jeremy motioned for me to wait. Then he carried on, slowly and silently, not so much as a rock rolling underfoot. As he approached an alcove, he eased along the wall and stopped at the edge. Though he was too far and too hidden in shadow for me to see clearly, I could picture him sniffing, listening, waiting.

Then he stepped out into the opening.

"Hello, Karl."

His voice echoed down the empty alley and was drowned out by a curse of surprise. Jeremy motioned me toward him.

There, in the shadows, was Karl Marsten.

A recent addition to the Pack, after several years of "fence-sitting," Karl was a jewel thief, and looked like Hollywood's version of one. Dark haired with sharp features and sharper gray-blue eyes. With his pressed pants, linen shirt, Italian loafers, faint tan and manicured fingernails, he looked like an action hero idling on the sidelines while his stunt double worked up a sweat for him. But from what Elena said, he was quite capable of working up that sweat all by himself, and those expensive clothes did little to disguise a powerful build. A dangerous man hiding beneath the veneer of a bored sophisticate.

By the time I arrived, he'd overcome his surprise and was eyeing Jeremy with a half-smile that seemed almost rueful.

"Dare I ask how long you've known I was around?" Karl said. "Or, perhaps not. You'll shatter my delusions of stealth."

I looked at Jeremy. "So that's whose scent you've been picking up these last couple of days. Elena didn't have him standing by in Arizona after all."

Jeremy said, "I'm not the one he's been watching."

He directed my attention across the way, where we now had a perfect view of Hope's backdoor entrance.

"I was . . . concerned," Karl said.

"Because she called and told you she was investigating some occult business, and you thought she was doing it on her own."

"Which isn't to say that she couldn't handle it on her own, but I knew Jeremy was in town and Elena wanted me nearby in case of trouble. Discovering that it involved you meant there was no reason not to stay close, keep my eye on—"

He stopped, gaze fixed on something over my shoulder.

Hope started toward us. "I sensed a werewolf and thought it was Jeremy, so I came down to meet him. I should have known better. Werewolf plus chaos equals only one person I know. Care to finish that sentence, Karl? *Who* were you keeping an eye on?"

Genuine dismay rippled Karl's composure. "I was—"

"Doing his job," Jeremy cut in. "Watching me, at Elena's behest."

"Ah." She gave Karl another hard look, one that said she didn't believe it, but would take it up with him later. "I suppose you might as well join us, then."

"With such a welcome, how can I refuse?"

"With such an entrance, how can you expect a welcome?" Hope turned on her heel and headed for her backdoor. "At least I didn't come home to find you in my living room again."

"I was testing your security."

"You just like pushing your luck. One of these days you're going to spook me on the wrong night and push it right into an early grave."

WHEN WE reached Hope's apartment, Karl looked around.

"I see your mother's been here," he said. "She has impeccable taste."

"She does. And she's single. Close to your age too. Want her number?"

He only strolled into the living room and stretched out on the sofa.

"Make yourself comfortable," Hope said, tossing her keys on the counter.

"I am, thank you. And I'll take a Scotch and soda when you have a moment."

She flipped him the finger. He smiled. As she invited us to sit and offered coffee, his gaze followed her, lips still curved. She tossed him a bottle of Perrier. He caught it easily and we started to plan.

DIVISION OF DUTIES

JEREMY TOLD US HIS THOUGHTS as Karl scavenged through Hope's fridge, pawing past the take-out cartons and pulling out the leftovers.

When Jeremy finished, he looked at me. "I know you should accompany me. After all, this is your investigation—"

"No. Well, yes, I'd love to follow through, but under the circumstances, you don't need to be checking over your shoulder, making sure I'm okay." I glanced at Karl. "I presume you're going with Jeremy? As backup?"

"I am." He turned to Jeremy. "Fried chicken or pork vindaloo?"

Jeremy's gaze slid to Hope.

"Eat up. I have so many leftovers, I can barely squeeze in a carton of milk. The perils of cooking for one. Jaime?"

"Nothing for me, thanks."

"The vindaloo, please," Jeremy said to Karl.

"Good choice," Karl said, scooping out the stew for Jeremy and some of both for himself. Then he opened a container of what looked like potatoes au gratin. "So, if I'm playing bodyguard, someone needs to stay behind with Jaime."

"Not if I'm in Brentwood," I said. "The house is surrounded by cops, so Hope can go with you two—"

"I'd prefer you had backup, Jaime," Jeremy said. "If Hope doesn't mind."

From the disappointment that flickered across Hope's face, she *did* mind. Not much fun babysitting when there was an adventure going on.

She could have played the sexism card, but she didn't, probably realizing gender had nothing to do with it. Out of a necromancer who can talk to the dead, a half-demon who can see visions of chaos and two werewolves with superhuman strength and senses, it was obvious which two should head into battle. They could have used Hope's chaos detector, but someone had to stay behind to guard the main target.

Hope covered her disappointment with a smile. "Sure. That's fine."

Karl paused, spoon in a bowl, his gaze on her, steady and piercing. She glanced at him and they exchanged a look. He nodded, and put one of the plates into the microwave.

AN HOUR later we were all back at the Brentwood house, where Hope and I would wait while Jeremy and Karl met Zack Flynn and, with any luck, used him to infiltrate the group.

With the ongoing confusion at the house, no one questioned me bringing guests in. Didn't seem to notice, even when I took three people up to my room.

Karl and Hope were on the balcony, door closed to give them privacy as they talked. Though I couldn't hear a word, I could tell it wasn't their usual banter. Karl was doing most of the talking, his fingers resting on Hope's arm, leaning down to her, face grave.

Hope's fingers grazed the gun under her jacket. Jeremy had been happy to see that gun . . . and even happier when Karl assured us that Hope could use it.

I pulled my gaze from the balcony as Jeremy returned from scouting.

"All clear?" I asked.

He nodded. "Nothing has changed with the police, and May hasn't returned."

"Before you go, could you draw a couple of your runes for me? The protective ones?"

"You don't need to humor me, Jaime. I know that whatever

irrational urge I have to draw those is just that: irrational. A symbol can't protect someone."

"Please?"

He looked around, fingers drumming against his leg, as if almost hoping he wouldn't see anything to write on. I took a sheet and pen from the tiny writing desk. He sketched a few runes, not even pausing to consider which to do, as if he already knew. Then he quickly folded the sheet in quarters and reached around me to tuck it into my back pocket, using the opportunity to lean close, body pressing against mine.

I whispered, "If we finish this tonight, you won't need to rush back to New York before morning, will you?"

"Make a mess and leave you to clean it up? That wouldn't be right. I'd have to stay an extra day or two, to help."

"Good."

AFTER JEREMY and Karl left, Hope slipped away to get a better picture of the house—entry points, escape routes, "safe" rooms and such. I doubted we'd need any of them. Jeremy had told Zack Flynn that I'd flown back to Chicago to escape the media attention.

But scouting the property probably made Hope feel more useful, so when she suggested it, I said it sounded wise and promised to stay in my room until she returned.

While she was gone, I took a moment to sort out my thoughts. I was worried about Jeremy. Though I didn't doubt he could look after himself, I wasn't comfortable having Karl Marsten as his only source of backup. And I knew Jeremy was equally uncomfortable with it, as much as he'd pretended otherwise.

Six years ago, a group of outside werewolves had banded together to overthrow the Pack. Clay had been kidnapped and tortured. Two of Jeremy's Pack brothers had been killed. Only one member of that rebel group survived: Karl Marsten.

In the final battle, Elena had spared Karl because he'd helped her. Then, with Clay's support, she'd asked Jeremy to pardon him. Before the uprising, Karl had never caused any trouble for the Pack—even been on good terms with them. He hadn't participated in the killings or Clay's torture, and had joined the group for a reason the werewolves could understand—the wolf's instinctive need for territory, which the Pack had denied him.

So Jeremy had granted Karl his reprieve and territory in a distant state on the condition that he at least consider joining the Pack. It was all very fair, very Solomon-like, very Jeremy.

Now Karl had joined the Pack and proven himself a loyal and useful member. And the Pack had accepted him. Including Jeremy . . . or so everyone thought.

Jeremy gave every appearance of supporting and even encouraging Karl's membership. It was what he considered the best way to deal with Karl.

Yet he couldn't forget what Karl had done. Maybe Karl hadn't personally killed Peter or Logan. Maybe he hadn't beaten Clay. Maybe he'd even acted as a buffer, keeping Clay from the worst of his captors' hate. But he'd sanctioned all that by standing aside until he saw the tables turning and only then had he flipped sides.

Jeremy strove to accept Karl as a Pack brother. Clay had been the one tortured, and he'd forgiven Karl, so why shouldn't Jeremy? But, to me, that was the very reason why he couldn't. It was easy to forgive someone for what he did to *you*. Not so easy when he did it to someone you love. Clay looks at Karl now, shrugs and says, "It was just business." Jeremy looks at him and sees the man who stood by and watched his son be beaten within an inch of his life.

Obviously, though, whatever Jeremy's feelings toward Karl, he trusted him enough to track him down this morning and ask him to join us. But I knew he'd rather have any other Pack member at his side. And so would I.

NEXT I contacted Eve, as I'd promised Jeremy. While she couldn't physically protect me, she could keep watch even better than Hope—with no chance of looking suspicious—and could alert me if she found trouble.

When I explained what was happening, Eve sat cross-legged on the bed, considering it in silence for a moment.

"So Jeremy's meeting this kid who says he has info on the group, but really he's a *part* of the group, or so you presume. Meaning he'll likely lead Jeremy into a trap. Being forewarned, though, Jeremy will be springing the trap, not walking into it."

"Right."

Another moment of quiet thought, then she nodded. "Not bad. But I do have a problem with one big part of it."

"Which is?"

"The part that has you sitting here guarded by a chaos demon."

"Hope's not—"

"Oh, I know what she is. A complete stranger, and your life is in her hands."

I shook my head and started emptying the dry-cleaning bag dropped off earlier. Eve strode over and parked herself "on" the bag, her form obscuring it.

"You're ignoring me, Jaime. I'm raising a valid point."

"No, you're being paranoid, which comes from a lifetime of *needing* to be paranoid. Hope isn't some black-market contact like Molly Crane. She helps the council. Jeremy knows her—"

"Elena is her contact, isn't she? And that's mainly professional. They don't hang out together."

"Jeremy knows her and he trusts her."

There was nothing she could—or dared—say to that, so she started pacing as I emptied the bag.

"So while he's gone, you're here, guarded by a chaos demon who's not even around—"

"She's scouting the property. She checked in on me before I called you."

Eve walked to the window and looked out. "Who's backing Jeremy up?"

"A Pack brother. Karl Marsten. He's—"

"Oh, I know who Karl Marsten is. A career criminal and a drifter." She shook her head. "I know guys like Marsten. You and Jeremy don't, so you can be forgiven for not seeing past that suave show of his. How old is he? Your age? Older, probably? He's spent the last forty years not giving a shit about anyone. Guys like that don't wake up one morning and turn team player. He's using the Pack. He doesn't care about anyone in it—"

"Not true. Even before he joined, he got along fine with them, and he was always fond of Elena."

Eve snorted. "The cute blond who's also the only female of his species? Oh, I bet he's fond of her."

"It isn't like that. And he's always been on good terms with Antonio and Nick. Even Clay doesn't mind him."

She met my gaze. "Elena, Clayton, Antonio and Nick. Leaving someone out there, Jaime?"

Hearing my own fears echoed in her words, I busied myself stuffing a blouse into my closet. "You're right. Karl Marsten isn't my first choice to be watching Jeremy's back. And you're right about him being self-centered. But that doesn't mean he isn't capable of loyalty. Look at Hope. He's very protective of her and that's not the behavior of a guy who thinks only of himself."

Eve turned slowly, her eyes narrowing. "Hope? He knows the half-demon?"

"Sure. That's how she hooked up with the council."

"Through Karl Marsten?"

A rap at the door, then Hope's "It's me." She slid in and looked around.

"Oh, sorry, I thought I heard you whispering and wanted to make sure everything was okay."

I waved toward the balcony door. "It's Eve."

"Ah, right, the ghost."

Eve circled Hope, sizing her up. "At least she's tiny." She towered over the girl by almost a foot. "Even you can probably take her."

"Thanks," I muttered.

Hope looked around, obviously uncomfortable. "If you'd rather I stayed away a little longer, so you can talk to, uh, Eve . . ."

"Tell her to go," Eve said.

I glanced at Eve.

"Five minutes," she said.

"Maybe that's a good idea," I said to Hope. "I feel rude talking to ghosts in front of people. How about giving me five minutes?"

"Sure, can I get you a drink while I'm downstairs?"

"Coffee would be great."

"Don't drink it," Eve said as Hope left.

"Wha—?"

"The coffee. Don't drink it."

I rolled my eyes and sat on the edge of the bed.

She flipped her hair back over her shoulder and crossed her arms. "You think I'm being paranoid? Let's see whether I have this straight. You and Jeremy call this Hope girl for information because she just happens to be in L.A. on some work exchange—"

I opened my mouth, but Eve continued. "You go to her for local information and the first people she introduces you to just happen to be the same people you now suspect are responsible. She noses her way into your investigation like an eager puppy, following you two around. Then, just when you and Jeremy figure out who the bad guys are, who shows up to protect Jeremy? This half-demon's boyfriend. He takes Jeremy to 'uncover' the group while she 'guards' you. Damned nice setup."

"Setup for what?"

Eve pretended not to hear, strolling over to the balcony doors, eyes narrowing as if distracted by some sign of danger.

"Setting us up for what, Eve?"

"That half-demon thinks she's got a nose for trouble? It's nothing compared to mine, and this stinks to the heavens."

I shook my head. "Only if you slam the pieces in until they fit your conclusion. *We* went to Hope, on *Elena's* suggestion. Hope didn't even know we were in town. Yes, it may seem coincidental that she just happens to introduce us to the very people we're looking for, but consider what they do. They play paranormal investigators to watch for new magical leads and for any signs that they themselves are in danger of exposure. Who would be one of their main contacts? Tabloid reporters covering occult activity. They worked with Hope's predecessor, then they contacted her. She had no reason to suspect them."

"Really? Seems her nose for trouble doesn't work so well after all."

I hesitated, then shook my head. "She says it's not perfect. She's young and we both know she won't have come into her full demon powers yet, especially when she's untrained."

"Convenient . . ." Eve murmured.

I pushed on. "As for her and Karl, I don't think she's his girlfriend—" I caught Eve's look. "And I know you only meant that they have a relationship, which they do. But he came to L.A. to protect *her*."

"So it can all be explained away. And you aren't the least bit worried that they're somehow involved?"

"The key word is 'somehow.' How? What could they hope to gain? They had nothing to do with me finding these ghosts or starting this investigation."

"Let me think on it."

"You do that."

TRUST ISSUES

HOPE RETURNED WITH MY COFFEE, which I only sipped. I trusted her, but Eve had left me a little unsettled.

Past experience had taught me that Eve was quick to jump to conclusions about people—always conclusions that saw the worst. If you deal with the magic black market and the people in it, you have to expect the worst of everyone.

Even now, whatever she was doing on the other side, it wasn't playing a harp in the choir of angels. Whenever she needed something from me, it was "contact this dead killer" or "research this unsolved murder case." She might be working for the Fates, but she still had every reason to be overcautious, even paranoid. So I took her fears about Hope and Karl with a whole *teaspoon* of salt . . . but didn't dismiss them.

As Hope and I waited for news from Jeremy, we talked, mostly about life in L.A.—sharing anecdotes, favorite restaurants and clubs, that sort of thing. As time ticked past, conversation became more strained, both of us worrying about Jeremy and Karl.

Eventually Hope took up Eve's earlier occupation—pacing. She'd head to the window or balcony door, look out, then return to me, try to resume conversation and falter as she returned for another look outside . . . or at her cell phone.

"Marsten isn't involved," said a voice to my rear.

Eve strode around me.

"New theory. Marsten's not in on it. Unwitting dupe. Werewolves don't need magic, so the group wouldn't interest him. And he knows if he betrayed Jeremy, Clayton would put him through a hell worse than anything the Fates could dream up. Marsten's only crime is middle-aged delusions. Even players aren't immune to pretty young things."

I opened my mouth, then glanced over at Hope.

Eve continued. "Girl like that, with her powers, she'd be easy prey for this group. Thing I can't figure out is why she's holed up here with you."

"Uh-huh," I murmured under my breath.

"It'd be easier if she'd convinced Jeremy to take you along. Did she try?"

I shook my head.

"Huh. Well, she needs to get you out of this house and away from the guards. Has she suggested you two go anywhere? Out for a drink or a walk?"

Another shake.

"If she does, you stay put. In the meantime I'll keep patrolling... and thinking about this."

EVE HAD only been gone a few minutes when Hope's nerves took a sharp turn for the worse.

"Keep up that pacing and you're going to wear a hole in the floor," I said.

She jumped, as if surprised to hear a voice. Her eyes were wide and blank.

I pushed to my feet. "Hope? Are you seeing—?"

A sharp shake of her head and her gaze focused. "N-no. Just..." She seemed to struggle for words, then said abruptly, "They should have called by now."

"Not unless they're in trouble. Whatever Jeremy has in mind, it's going to take awhile. I know waiting is tough..."

I let the sentence trail off as I realized she was no longer listening. She'd resumed her pacing, gaze jumping from the window to the balcony door, then back, searching the gardens. Her face was taut, but instead of looking pale and drawn with worry, her eyes glittered and color splashed her cheeks. A vein in her neck throbbed.

She walked faster, slowing to gaze out the window, then striding to the patio doors, slowing again to look out, veering and striding back to the window. Like a house cat spotting a bird just outside the window, its whole body quivering in anticipation, unable to take its eyes off its prey.

Lucifer's daughter.

"Hope?"

She wheeled, lips curling back at the interruption. Then, in a blink, the look was gone.

"I just . . . I'm sorry," she said, her eyes still darting toward the window, as if she couldn't pull her attention away. "There's something out there."

I walked to the window. She reached out, as if to yank me back, then stopped herself and motioned for me to keep my distance. "J-just to be safe. Something's going on out there."

"Someone's here?"

A long pause, and I thought she was considering it. But her gaze stayed fixed on the window, straining to see. Not thinking of an answer—she probably hadn't even heard the question.

Something in the garden. The empty garden vacated by the cops, but still off-limits to anyone in the house.

Voice neutral, I said, "Do you think we should investigate?"

Another long pause. I was about to repeat myself when she strode to the door.

"I'll go," she said. "You stay here."

"Hold—"

I grabbed the door before she could get it open. Her head swung my way, eyes filled with a fury that made my stomach go cold. I stood my ground, and again she blinked it back.

"Something's happening," she said. "I have to go."

"We aren't supposed to leave the house."

"I have to go." Each word was icy with warning. A shudder, then she looked at me. "You'll be fine. Just stay here. Whatever happens, stay here."

She tried yanking open the door, but my foot acted as a stopper. "What good will that do? You have the gun."

A flare of frustration, jaw setting, then another hard blink. She yanked the gun from her waistband and slapped it into my hands.

"There. Now—" She jerked the door so hard I stumbled back. "*Stay* here."

EVE WAS right. This was a setup. If Hope really was chasing some "chaos event" in the garden, she wouldn't leave her gun behind.

But if it was a setup, why give her weapon to me? Maybe it wasn't loaded. Clever ploy. Let me think I was armed, so I wouldn't try to escape or fight when someone came for me.

I turned the gun over in my hands, trying to figure out whether there was any ammunition. It was an automatic. Marksmanship was one of Jeremy's hobbies, mainly bows and rifles, but he had a pair of revolvers and had shown me how to use them once. Had this been a revolver, I'd have been in luck. As it was, I had no clue. Even if I could tell whether it had ammo, the gun might be buggered up so it wouldn't fire.

But why leave me in a house filled with potential witnesses . . . and security guards? I'd offered to come along. Why not just say "sure"?

Maybe because that wasn't May's plan and Hope didn't dare mess with the plan. But why not try to convince me to go with Jeremy in the first place?

I remembered when Jeremy first asked Hope to stay with me. She'd wanted to argue. I recalled Karl, carefully studying her reaction. Maybe her expression had suggested she was up to something, and when she'd seen his suspicion, she hadn't dared argue. So May had switched to a backup plan—this one.

Did that make sense?

Damn it! In my gut, I didn't believe Hope would turn on me. Even seeing that flare of anger in her eyes hadn't changed that.

But I couldn't ignore the possibility. I needed to get out of this room.

I WENT downstairs with every intention of hanging out with the guards. But then I started to wonder whether that was safe. We knew these people had magic, including something like a binding spell.

Would human security guards, ignorant of the supernatural, be able to protect me? Could they get killed trying?

Even if sticking close to big men with guns convinced the group to keep its distance, it wouldn't resolve the question of Hope's allegiance. If she was on May's side, she'd just try again, another way, and maybe that time I wouldn't see through the ploy.

The only way to know was to follow her.

AS I slipped out the side door, I eased the gun out and wrapped my hand around the grip, finger on the trigger. It would help if I knew how to fire it. I told myself it didn't matter. As Eve would say, bluffing is enough. Act as if you can shoot it—and more important, *will* shoot it—and that should give any would-be attacker pause.

I slid through the shadows along the side of the house, heading for the rear. Ahead, a yellow ribbon of crime-scene tape waved in the breeze, broken from its moorings, as if someone had walked right through it. Hope? Breaking the tape hardly seemed wise, but if not her, then who? Last time I'd looked, the officers guarding the gardens had retreated to their cruiser.

I darted behind a hedge, then stood on tiptoes to see over it. There, about a dozen feet ahead, Hope walked into the garden with the slow, deliberate pace of a sleepwalker.

"What the hell are you doing?"

I almost fell backward. Eve's glare was murderous.

"I don't know what you think you're doing, Jaime, but you get your ass back in—"

I cut her short with a whispered explanation as I snuck around the hedge, following Hope.

"I don't care what your reason is. Get back in that goddamned house right now."

"It's not a setup. Look at her." I waved toward Hope as she banged her shin against a garden wall and kept walking, oblivious. "She's in some kind of trance."

"She's luring you in. Making you curious. Making you think it's safe to follow."

I kept moving. "I've seen her when she gets a vision and that's just what she looks like."

"And she can't fake that? Don't be—" Eve bit off the rest with a click of her teeth. Then she strode in front of me. "Stop and look around, Jaime. Notice anything about where you are? And where you're being led?"

I glanced over my shoulder at the hedge, which wrapped around the garden, cutting me off from the view of anyone stepping out the side or rear doors. Then I turned to see Hope heading toward the most secluded corner of the yard.

"She's not following any 'chaos trail,' " Eve said. "She's leading you to a spot where no one's going to see what happens next."

Damn. She had a point.

I glanced back at the house.

"Finally," Eve breathed.

"Jaime?"

Hope was walking back through the garden.

"What are you doing out here?" she asked, blinking like a wakened sleepwalker.

"Damn it, Jaime, ignore her—"

"I was worried about you." I lifted the gun. "You left this behind."

She frowned and looked down at her waistband, as if trying to figure out how the gun got from there to my hand. Eve shoved me toward the door, but her hands passed through.

"What happened?" I said.

"I'm . . . not sure. Someone . . ." Hope shivered. "I think someone was killed back there. Just now. I can still feel it."

She wrapped her arms around herself, shuddering, but her expression wasn't one of fear or concern. She looked almost . . . rapturous. The hairs on my neck rose.

"Don't listen to her bullshit," Eve said. "She'll say anything to get you—"

I tuned her out. Hope glanced over her shoulder, toward that far corner.

"I think we should check it out." Her voice was high with barely contained excitement.

"Do you?"

Her gaze stayed riveted to that deepest, most remote, shadow-enshrouded corner of the garden. My fingers tightened around the gun. Eve had gone silent now, tense, as if waiting to jump in, as if she *could* jump in.

Hope motioned for me to follow, took a couple of steps, then, seeing I hadn't moved, wheeled back. Her fingers grazed my arm. Eve started a cast. A spell? But it wouldn't work in my dimension.

Hope's fingers wrapped around my arm. I raised the gun. Eve lifted her hands over her head, something materializing between them.

I swung the gun. A crack as it connected with Hope's temple. Her eyes went wide. She stood there, staring at me in disbelief. Then her knees gave way and she crumpled to the flagstone path.

I dropped beside her, my hands going to the side of her neck.

"Forget her," Eve said. "Get your ass back in that house before they realize you didn't fall for the bait."

Hope's pulse was strong. I pushed to my feet.

"Good," Eve said. "Now grab the gun and, next time, try *firing* it, presuming it still works."

"It probably didn't work even before that. Why would Hope hand me a working firearm?"

"Good point. You did the right thing, then, braining her with it."

"Don't sound so shocked."

"And you're even wearing sneakers. I'm doubly impressed."

I grimaced and started for the house.

"Eve?"

Kristof's deep voice sounded behind us. We turned as he strode around a garden bed. A brisk nod to me, then his gaze returned to Eve. "There's something I think you should—"

He stopped as he walked through Hope's still form. He frowned down at her.

"The Espisco half-demon," Eve said. "Bitch tried to lure Jaime out here with some bullshit story about sensing a murder."

"Mur—?" Kristof rubbed his chin. "I, uh, think she might have been right. There's a body in the back corner, and a very confused spirit hovering over it, trying to figure out why she's not *inside* that body."

I turned toward the back corner, but Eve jumped in front of me. "Uh-uh. Even if Hope wasn't lying, that doesn't mean it isn't a setup. You're getting back in that house right now."

I stepped behind Hope and grabbed her under the armpits.

"What part of 'right now' don't you understand? There's a body in the back corner. That means there's a killer in this garden."

"Then I'm not leaving Hope out here, am I?" I glared up at Eve. "Not when she didn't betray me."

"We don't know that. Now put her down."

"She's probably a hundred pounds, if that," I said through gritted teeth as I heaved her up.

"And you're a hundred and twenty, if that. Now put her *down*—"

"Eve's right," Kristof said. "I'll watch over her. You get back in the house—"

"Jaime?"

A small woman with long blond hair staggered from behind the hedge. For a moment, I thought it was Gabrielle Langdon. Then she looked up.

"Angelique?" I said.

"You—you can hear me?"

She lurched toward me, but stumbled. Kristof caught her. As his hand made contact, breaking her fall, my gut sank.

She looked up at him as he righted her. "You can see me. You can touch me."

Kristof's face stayed neutral as he nodded.

"Oh, thank God," she said, the words tumbling out on a deep sigh. "I thought I was—" She shuddered and didn't finish.

I stepped closer to Angelique, careful to keep out of touching range.

"What happened, hon?"

"Jaime?" Eve's voice was brisk but gentle. "Get inside. We'll handle this."

"Angelique?" I said.

"I—I knew you and Grady were up to something finding that body, and you kept me out of it because I'm the new kid."

"We never—"

"Jaime, in the house. Now."

"I understand," Angelique said. "I probably would have done the same thing. But I wanted to know what you were doing. Not to mess things up, but just to prove I could help."

Oh, God.

She went on. "That woman came back. The one who was here

this morning looking for you. From the paranormal society. The guards said you'd left with your boyfriend. So I followed her out and told her to meet me in the garden."

Eve motioned for me to stop listening.

"She was there," Angelique said. "I told her I was working with you. That I knew all about the bodies and the murders. She lifted a gun. I saw it, but I couldn't believe it, so I just stood there and she fired and—" Her fingers flew to her breast, searching for a hole that wasn't there. "It was special effects, wasn't it? The bullet and the blood and my—my body, lying there..."

I stepped toward her to say—

To say what? The same thing I'd been telling her all along? *Don't worry, hon. Leave everything to me. I'll fix it.*

I couldn't fix this.

Angelique reached for me. Her fingers passed through my arm and she gasped. Kristof pulled her back.

"Jaime," Eve said. "In the house *now*!"

Something smacked into the side of my head. As I tottered, I stared at Eve, as if she'd somehow reached through the dimensions and slapped me. I swayed, my legs suddenly too weak to hold me up. Eve's mouth opened, alarm in her eyes. Kristof pointed at something behind a row of bushes. A shout.

The second blow knocked me out.

THE KILLING ROOM

I WOKE LYING ON A COLD, SMOOTH FLOOR. I opened my eyes, but the world stayed dark. To my left, someone was breathing deeply. A voice came from above the breathing. A male voice, young and anxious.

"Come on," he said. "Wake up. You need to wake up."

A second voice, older, weary. "She can't hear you."

"How do you know? People see ghosts all the time. Maybe if you'd help me . . ."

Ghosts . . . ?

I thought of Angelique and my gut twisted. I'd genuinely wanted to help her, but when helping her interfered with my own agenda, I'd brushed her off and promised myself I'd look after her later. Well, there was no later now. Not for Angelique.

"I think she's waking up," the younger voice said.

"It's probably better for her if she doesn't."

I blinked and lifted my head. High above me a tiny greenish light, like a smoke detector, was the only source of illumination. I blinked hard. After a moment, I could make out figures. One on the floor, long dark curls pooling around her. Hope. That was the breathing I heard. I let out a soft sigh. Unconscious, but alive. Thank God.

A young man hovered over her. No more than a teenager, from what little I could see in the darkness. Pale hair. Wiry. Small for his age. He looked more like a hologram than a ghost; I could see Hope through him. Another ghost stood at his side, this one opaque, like most spirits. Middle-aged and stout, his arms crossed, he watched the boy try to wake Hope.

"She can't hear you." My voice was breathy and weak, as if I'd strained my vocal cords.

Both men turned to stare at me.

"She can't hear you," I said. "But I can."

The boy smacked the man on the arm and grinned. "See? Told you." He turned to me, grin fading fast. "You need to get out of here."

"Where am—?" I swallowed the rest. My throat was dry, eyes burning, brain fuzzy, but slowly it came back. Someone had knocked me out with a spell. Kidnapped. Again. If I had the energy, I might have laughed.

I struggled to my feet.

"That's it," the young man said encouragingly. "Now, find a way out—"

"There is no way out," the older man said.

The boy turned on him. "And how do you know? Obviously we didn't find it or we wouldn't be here. But no one was here to warn us." He glanced at me. "Okay, now the door is to your right, about three steps—"

"And you think they left it open for her?"

I let the boy guide me to the door. I found the edge of it and ran my hands down either side, feeling nothing but smooth metal.

"Where's the handle?" I asked.

"Problem number one," the man said.

I turned to the boy. "Is there another door? A window? A vent?"

"It's an eight-by-eight concrete box," the man intoned, like a contractor reciting dimensions. "Soundproofed walls. One way in and out—a six-inch-thick steel door. Oh, and the drain. But unless you can transform yourself into a mouse, you aren't fitting down that."

"And *you* aren't helping," the boy snapped.

"Ignore him," I said.

I peered around, and could now make out the walls. Solid walls.

As much as I'd love to free myself from this mess, there was a point at which I had to call for help—and being locked in a concrete box qualified.

"Maybe I can't get out," I said. "But I know someone who can get in."

Not being able to act in the living world, Eve couldn't get me out of here herself, but she could always be counted on to come up with a plan. And she'd be able to stand guard and scout the house for escape routes. When I'd been kidnapped, she would have tried to follow, so she probably wouldn't be far.

I reached into my pants pocket and breathed in relief as my fingers closed around the silver ring nestled at the bottom. If they'd patted me down for weapons, they'd probably ignored that. Little did they know...

I smiled, clasped the ring and called for Eve.

"It's not going to work," the man said.

"Shut the fuck—" the boy began, then looked sheepishly at me. "Sorry, ma'am."

I motioned for a moment of silence while I summoned Eve again. Then I calmly returned the ring to my pocket.

"It might take her a minute to get here," I said.

"If she can." The man lifted his hands as the boy turned on him. "I'm just saying..." He glanced at me. "What is this friend of yours? A ghost, right?"

"Among other things."

"Well, there's a reason we're hanging out in this box...and it's not for the scenery."

"We're trapped," the boy said. "It's like we aren't—"

He disappeared. A moment later he returned, still talking.

Seeing my expression, he said, "I faded out, didn't I? It happens. It just started happening awhile ago. Just now and then at first, then more and more."

Fading. Like the children.

"Anyway, as I was saying, it's like we aren't really ghosts. I mean, we are because I pass through you." He demonstrated by walking through Hope's still-sleeping form. "But the walls are real, even for us. That doesn't mean a ghost can't get *in,* though."

The man rolled his eyes at this youthful optimism. I took out the ring to summon Eve again. As I pulled it out, my fingers brushed a folded piece of paper. Jeremy's protection ward. I touched it, and let out a deep breath. "Even if my friend can't get here, I know someone who will."

"If he tries to break you out, he'll end up in here with us."

"That's fine. No metal door can hold *him* in a room."

I walked the perimeter, feeling the walls, then searching the center. It was small, as the man said. A concrete box with a drain in the middle of the floor.

"I thought you said help was coming," the man said, voice dripping sarcasm.

I knelt, squeezed my fingers into the drain grid and tugged. Bolted down. Maybe, with enough pulling, I could get it off, but the man was right—unless I could turn into a mouse, it wasn't going to help.

"What's this for anyway?" I said, down on all fours, peering into the dark drain.

Silence.

I glanced back at the ghosts. The boy shifting under my gaze. Even the man looked away.

"There's no tap in here. So what would they need to drain away?"

"Blood," the man said after a minute. "That's what this place is. A killing room."

"HOPE?" I shook her shoulder harder. "Hope? Come on. Wake up!"

I'd been trying to rouse her for at least five minutes. Five long and precious minutes. Twice she'd stirred, only to fall back asleep without opening her eyes. Had they drugged her? Or had I hit her harder than I thought?

There'd been no sign of Eve. Whatever magic these people had used to keep ghosts in here was either keeping her out or preventing her from hearing my call.

As for Jeremy, I couldn't wait for rescue. Not this time.

"Hope. Hope!"

She mumbled something, her eyes still closed. I drew back my hand and slapped her. She started awake, eyes wide and unseeing, kicking and flailing.

"Hope! Stop—"

Her foot connected with my shin.

"Ow. It's me. It's—"

Fingernails raked across my cheek, coming dangerously close to my eye. I grabbed her by the wrists, pinned them at her sides and leaned over her.

"Hope, it's me, Jaime. I know it's dark and you can't see anything, but we're in trouble and I need you to listen."

I TOLD her what had happened. As I spoke, she just lay there, not reacting. I explained why I'd hit her with the gun. I told her about our solid concrete cell. I even pointed out the drain, its purpose and what that probably said about why we were in here. She sat through it all, unflinching.

At first, I chalked it up to steady nerves. Or maybe shock. But then I realized she hardly seemed to be listening. She could hear me—I made sure of that several times. But her gaze kept sliding around the room, as if I were chatting about something as inconsequential as dinner plans.

She seemed dopey too, unable or unwilling to sit up. When I asked how she was, she motioned for me to keep talking.

Her gaze darted about the room, like me in a room of ghosts, my attention pulled every which way. I realized then what was distracting her: visions of murder, of human sacrifice. I had to get her out of here.

Easy to say . . .

"So we're trapped in this room," I said. "Unless you've got some secret power I don't know about, something that will knock down walls . . ."

She blinked, focusing on me, then shook her head.

I turned to the ghosts. The boy had faded again. I waited for him to return.

"You two were killed in here, weren't you? By these people?"

The boy nodded. "They talked about there being others before me. Kids, I think. But they aren't here. It was just me until Murray came along."

So why weren't the children here? There was no sense asking him, so I just said, "And your name is?"

"Brendan."

"Good. Okay, Brendan, tell me everything you know about these people."

———

NORMALLY, A ghost doesn't remember the circumstances surrounding his death unless you intercept him before he gets to the afterlife realms. But these ghosts had never crossed over, so they hadn't been granted postdeath amnesia, and they remembered everything.

I relayed Brendan's experience to Hope, partly in hopes that she'd catch some clue I'd missed, but mostly just to distract her from the visions.

I plucked every potentially useful tidbit from his story. We were in a basement. There was a TV room nearby, plus a small bedroom. The house was in Brentwood, probably close enough to where I'd been staying for the group to transport the bodies.

From Brendan's account, there were at least five members. May was one of the leaders, working closely with a middle-aged man. They'd introduced themselves as a couple, but that was probably a front. None of Brendan's descriptions matched Rona Grant or Zack Flynn, but that didn't mean anything. May had said there were more members of the Ehrich Weiss Society, so we just hadn't seen any overlap except for her.

As for getting some idea of what they were capable of, the only spell Brendan had seen them cast was the weakening one. When he finished, I turned to the older man—Murray.

"So you were killed after Brendan?"

He nodded, his head down. A hell of a thing to put someone through, but I had to do it, so I pushed on.

"How were you approached?"

He hesitated. "I—I don't remember. It's all very foggy. I was at work and then . . . That's all I remember from that day. I woke up here, like Brendan."

He shot a furtive glance at the boy, as if worrying about what effect his death had on him, but Brendan said, "I didn't see it. I was blacked out. It happens a lot when they're doing magic in here."

I relayed that to Hope. During Brendan's account, she'd barely seemed to be listening, but now she went still, as if struggling to pay attention.

"So he was sacrificed?" she said. "Like the boy?"

"Right."

I gave her a quick recap of Brendan's story. She looked confused, but waved for me to continue questioning Murray. She listened as I relayed the story of his death, his tale almost identical to Brendan's, offering no new insight.

As he finished, Hope moaned and began writhing on the floor. I knelt beside her. Her face was ashen, eyes rolling back.

"They—they must have done something to me," she whispered. "I—I feel sick. Something . . ."

Her voice dropped and I had to lean closer.

"He's lying," she whispered.

"Wha—?"

"Shhh. The older one. Murray. He's lying."

Her voice was so low I struggled to make out the words.

"He wasn't burned. They stabbed him in the back. He was one of them. They turned on him." She swallowed. "I'm sorry I'm not much help. I'm . . . having a hard time."

I squeezed her shoulder. "You focus on blocking the visions and I'll get us out of here."

Her gaze dipped, cheeks flushing.

I couldn't imagine what it was like for her. Seeing ghosts in their death bodies was nothing compared to seeing them in their death throes. I'd never complain about seeing a death body again.

Death body . . .

I turned to Murray. "I know something that might tell me more about the magic these people have. As ghosts, you can revert to what we call your death body, how you looked at the moment you passed. If you can do that for me, maybe I can take a closer look for signs of magic."

"I don't know how," Murray said quickly.

"I'll tell you."

"Sure," Brendan said. "Whatever helps."

"I don't see how it will." Murray crossed his arms. "They used gasoline and matches to kill us, not magic."

"Humor me."

He shook his head.

"Why? It's not as if you're lying, right?"

His expression chased away any doubt.

"Wha—?" Brendan began.

I shot him a look and he went silent.

"Are you ever planning to get out of here, Murray?"

"Of course."

"So then what? You waltz up to the higher powers, say 'My name's Murray and I was a human sacrifice' and expect them to take your word for it? You've got some serious bad karma to undo, and not a lot of time left to undo it. I'd suggest you start now."

His eyes said he wasn't convinced.

I imagined Eve at my shoulder. *Bluff, damn it. He's human. What the hell does he know about our world? Bury the bastard in bullshit.*

"Do you know what I am? A necromancer. You can see a glow around me, one you won't see on regular people like her." I waved at Hope. "My job is to act as a mediator between this world and the next, and to do that, I have a partner on the other side. That woman I was summoning? I called her a ghost... among other things. She's not just any ghost. She's a direct link to the higher powers. Every necromancer is assigned one."

"Cool," Brendan said. "Like a guardian angel."

I imagined what Eve would say about being called an angel, but kept a straight face as I nodded. "Something like that. One of a necromancer's jobs is to ease the passing of spirits. When we escape here, I'll turn you over to her and she'll take you to the higher powers who will decide where you belong. When she hands you over, she'll make her report. What you do in the remaining time you have on this side will have a big impact on that report."

Hope's strained voice floated over. "And if Jaime doesn't get out of here alive, then she can't help you cross over, meaning you'll be at the whim of the first necromancer you meet when—if—you escape."

"But I don't know what I can do," Murray said. "I can't get you out of here—"

"You can help by telling me about them. The group you were a part of before they killed you."

Brendan turned on Murray. "What?"

"Yes, he was part of that group, but he changed his mind after hearing what they did to you. He wanted to turn them in. That's why they killed him."

Murray nodded emphatically. I doubted that was how it happened, but Brendan was mollified enough to relax.

"Now," I continued, "tell me everything."

THE GROUP HAD BEEN STARTED almost fifteen years ago by May Donovan and another man, Don Rice. Don was also in the Ehrich Weiss Society, but otherwise the groups were separate, on May's advice. As we'd suspected, she and Don had used the society to research new occult groups and to track rumors of their own.

"And Zack Flynn?" I asked.

"Who?"

"A reporter for the *L.A. Times*. He's part of the Ehrich Weiss Society."

"I think May's mentioned him. Just a kid, right?" A moue of distaste. "We don't allow young people in our group. We're serious practitioners."

Had Jeremy and Karl realized their mistake, left Zack and gone back to Brentwood? Or had they teamed up with Zack and used his connection to May to infiltrate her "real" group?

Hope's face was red and beaded with sweat as she was swept into another vision. That jolted worries of Jeremy aside. He could take care of himself.

I continued grilling Murray.

Three years ago, after over a decade of trying, the group had found the so-called "key" to unlocking the mysteries of the magical world.

Human sacrifice. Or not so much the act itself as the by-products. They cremated the victims' organs and used the ashes in spellcasting.

The ritual they'd used must have bound the spirits to the earth so the magic could draw on their energy, draining them as their ashes were used. That's why Brendan was fading. He was disappearing as his energy was consumed in spellcasting.

Even with that ingredient, their success had been limited to a few spells in a select number of books—simple magic from real *grimoires,* I'd presume. The spell they'd used to knock me out was a fairly recent addition, and the strongest thing they had.

When I asked about the children, he said that over three years, they'd killed six children and buried them in the garden down the road.

"But their spirits aren't here," I said. "Were they killed here? In this room?"

"Some. But that was before May performed the encircling ritual."

"Encircling ritual?"

"To protect this room from . . ." he fluttered his hands, "evil spirits. Nosy neighbors. Who knows? May was getting paranoid. Kept worrying that we'd conjure up some demon or tap into something ugly."

"Did something like that ever happen?"

"Not to us."

"But to May?"

He glanced around, then lowered his voice, as if he could be overheard. "May is different. The magic always works better for her. Comes easier to her. Some of us can barely cast the simplest spells. May's always first and best. It makes some of us wonder . . ." He shrugged. "There'd been grumbling. About what else May might be able to do. What she might be hiding from us."

"Which would explain the 'encircling' ritual. If she did something that spooked her. So presumably, this ritual is what keeps you two in."

I had a good idea why May was the strongest. Tapping into real supernatural blood. As for what kind . . .

"These rumors," I said. "About May Donovan—"

"They're coming."

The raspy voice made the hairs on my neck rise. It came from Hope's direction, but didn't sound like her.

When I looked over, she'd twisted onto her side, her hair tumbling over her face. In the dim lighting, her expression seemed to be fear, but as I bent to reassure her, I saw she was smiling. Her amber eyes glittered. Her lips were drawn back, white teeth glowing in the darkness.

"Hope?"

She blinked and that smile wavered, but returned, less feral, more . . . blissful, eyes rolling back. Her lips parted and she let out a hissing sigh of pleasure.

The sound raked down my spine. I recognized that look, that sigh. When I'd made my deal with a demon, he'd taken human form for the summoning. As I'd squirmed, listening to the killer describe his crimes, I'd seen that same look on the demon's face as he drank in the chaos.

But half-demons weren't demonic. Like every other supernatural, evil was a choice, not a blood destiny. I remembered Hope's words: "Other half-demons get a special power without a demon's attraction to chaos. That attraction is *all* I get," and I understood. All those times she'd looked away, guilty, embarrassed, when I'd offered sympathy for the horrors she had to endure.

Horror, yes. Horrible? Horrifying? Not for her.

Now, hearing our would-be murderers approaching, she felt not fear but—

I turned away from Hope. I had to think . . .

"Jaime?"

I steeled myself not to look at her. I remembered the demon I'd dealt with, how seductive he'd been, how easy to trust . . . and how much I'd paid for it.

"Jaime?" Her voice quavered, but that hoarse bloodlust was gone. "Help me. Please."

Still I resisted. But did enjoying chaos make Hope demonic? She had helped us find this group. Never once had she led us into trouble, double-crossed us or done anything to *cause* chaos. She'd honestly seemed to want to help—to find some balance for the impulses she hid.

I turned. We'd been in this room long enough that my eyes had adjusted to the darkness and I could make out Hope's face, slick with sweat, her eyes still glowing, but filled with fear, even despair.

"They're outside," she said. "Talking. I can hear their thoughts. This place—all the chaos—it must be boosting my power. I'm getting all these thoughts, every bad thing—" She inhaled. "May's the key. Tricking them. Lying to them. You can use that."

"How?"

Frustration flared in her eyes. "Just . . . use it. Somehow. Not much time."

I leaned in to listen. She talked fast, throwing out snippets of information about May and the others. Random thoughts, out of context, left to me to interpret.

Then she gasped. "They're getting ready. Gas. Matches."

Her face contorted, excitement warring with true fear. She grabbed my arm.

"Knock me out again," she rasped.

I took her other arm and drew closer. "They won't hurt you. I'm going to get you out of here."

"You don't—" She bit off a snarl and took a deep breath. "You need to knock me out."

"I really need you awake, Hope. I might need your help—"

"To kill you?" Her gaze met mine, hard and sharp. "If they want to kill you, I might not try to stop them. I might even help them."

I didn't believe that, but I could see that she did.

"Grab my hair and hit my head against the floor."

"What if I accidentally—"

She flew at me. Seeing that snarling face, those glowing demonic eyes, I reacted instinctively and flung my arms out, knocking her back. As I hit her, she veered, as if launching off my hands, twisting to fly, headfirst, into the nearest wall. She hit it and slumped to the floor.

DEMONS AND WEREWOLVES

I RUSHED OVER and dropped to check Hope's pulse. There was a muted jangle at the door, as if someone was turning a lock.

I sprang to my feet.

Light filled the tiny room. I stumbled back, blinking after straining so long in the dark. Then I followed the light up and saw a panel inset in the high ceiling.

Ringed around the room was a high shelf dotted with what looked like stuffed animals. The taxidermy types, not the toys. That caught me off guard and I stared at a crow for a moment before yanking my gaze away.

Another click. The door was opening. I looked around frantically, hoping I'd see some weapon missed in the darkness. There was nothing. Shoes! My heels. I could use them as I'd planned to with Botnick, to stab or—

I stared down at my sneakers. Oh, goddamn it!

"Hello, Jaime."

May Donovan walked in, dressed in a blazer and skirt, as calmly professional as if we were meeting in her office. Even smiled and extended her hand.

"I trust I won't need to use that spell again," she said, stopping before me. "You're a bright woman. You know when you're outnumbered."

Her gaze dropped to Hope. "Still unconscious? I suppose that's just as well."

A click as the door closed. I looked past May and saw four others crowding into the tiny room. Three men, one woman, all on the far side of forty. At a gesture from May, two of the men walked to Hope and carried her into the middle of the room.

Something was etched into the concrete—a symbol they'd found in a book, presumably. As the men laid Hope on it, her hand flopped onto the stainless steel drain, sparkling and spotless, no sign of its purpose evident. Of course there wasn't—the point of having a concrete room with a drain was to wash away all the evidence.

I swallowed.

One of the men retrieved the gas can he'd left by the door and set it down on a lock of Hope's hair. The other woman held the matches, flipping them in her fingers, not nervous, just toying with them. I glanced at their faces, relaxed, unworried and unhurried, as if they were preparing the room for yet another dull but necessary business meeting.

I opened my mouth to stall them, but my mind and gaze stayed caught on Hope, on that gas can carelessly laid on her hair, on her graceful fingers and chewed nails stretched over that immaculate drain.

"You really can talk to the dead, can't you, Jaime?"

I jumped, startled, and looked at May. Her face was impassive, but her eyes were fever-bright. The eyes of a fanatic spotting proof of the divine.

The other woman harrumphed. "She's a good actress, that's all. Just like the rest of them."

"I don't think so. Someone—or something—led her to those bodies."

In her voice was the longing I'd heard so often from the bereaved, those desperate to believe. In May, it was magnified a hundredfold.

"I can," I said. "I see them, hear them, speak to them."

"May, don't let her—"

"You don't believe me? There's a ghost right next to you. A seventeen-year-old named Brendan, though you may not have bothered asking his name before you dowsed him with gas and set him on fire. May, you picked him up at—" I glanced at Brendan, who told me the place and I relayed it. "You tricked him into your car, you and Don—" Another look at Brendan, who pointed to a tall balding man with a cleft chin. I nodded to him. "Over there."

Expressions ranged from May's exultation to incredulity to grudging acceptance.

May smiled. "You and I have a lot to talk about, Jaime."

In other words, I'd just bought myself a temporary pass. I tried not to let my relief show.

"First, though . . ." May continued.

She waved to Don, who held the gas. He uncapped it and stepped over Hope's body.

"No!"

I leapt forward, but May grabbed my arm.

"Please don't make us restrain you, Jaime. You know we can't let her live. She knows—"

"But she's one of us. Magical."

May shook her head. "Don't—"

"She's a half-demon. That's what we call them. Demons take human form and impregnate women. The children look human, but they have special powers. The ability to control an element, or improved senses or—"

"The X-Men." The other woman rolled her eyes. "I may be a bit old for that sort of thing, but I have teenage boys, Miss Vegas. Try something a little more original, please."

"It's not just elements and senses. Like Hope. She can pick up chaos, senses it and sees—"

May cut me off with a look. "So you're telling me that sweet Hope Adams is really . . . a chaos demon?"

"Half-demon."

"And your companion the other day? The one Eric Botnick swore had superhuman strength? I suppose he's one of these half-demons."

"No. Werewolf."

May cast a look at the group. I couldn't see it, but everyone laughed. Then she turned back to me, her hand still on my arm, squeezing gently.

"I understand why you're doing this, Jaime. You want to protect your friends. But—" The squeeze tightened. "Please don't insult our intelligence."

I opened my mouth to protest, but knew I'd overplayed my hand . . . and I hadn't even been bluffing.

A smell filled the air. The slosh of liquid hitting concrete. I turned to see Don trickling gas over Hope.

I wrenched from May's grasp. May lifted a handful of gray powder and started to cast. I stopped.

"I'm sorry. I just— I just want to talk."

"Tell more tales of demons and werewolves?" the other woman scoffed.

"Why not? Couldn't there be—?"

A quick look around told me I was losing my audience. I glanced down at Hope, her small form, her faded jeans freckled with splashed gasoline, more dripping from her fingers, into the drain . . .

"Why kill her like that? It's a horrible way to die."

"The suffering enhances the potency," May said, voice as cool as her eyes.

"No, it doesn't."

Her face hardened, but she hid it behind a condescending smile. "You may be able to talk to ghosts, but that doesn't make you an expert on magic."

"Maybe, but I know people who can cast spells that make yours look like parlor tricks. Even for the rituals that need human sacrifice, it doesn't matter how you kill the person. It's the *fact* of death that counts."

I could see this wasn't getting me anywhere. "Never mind. I know you don't believe me about Hope, but if you gave her time to wake up, she could demonstrate—"

"Not interested," said the other woman—Tina, as Murray called her.

May shot Tina a look. Then she swung that look around the group. Judging their willingness to let Hope live a little longer, just to be sure there wasn't some truth to my preposterous tale. But their faces were hard. If she made the wrong decision, they'd see it as weakness—her hunger for magic overriding common sense. An unacceptable flaw to this bunch.

"No, Jaime," she said finally. "I know she's your friend—"

"She is. And if you kill my friend in front of me, exactly how willing do you think I'll be to teach you what I know? Show you how to contact the dead?"

"Don't threaten—"

"Tie her up and put her outside this room, as a show of faith. Then, in a return show of faith, I'll show you how to communicate with Brendan's ghost. When we're done, Hope will be awake. She'll show you her powers and, if she doesn't, you can . . ." I swallowed for dramatic effect, "finish with her."

Another look around the gathered faces. Tina's expression stayed resolute—gaze fixed on Hope as she toyed with the matches.

"Don?" May said.

"It sounds reasonable."

The other men agreed. At a motion from May, they bound Hope's hands and feet, gagged her and carried her into the room beyond.

MIRACULOUS

WHEN THE MEN RETURNED a few minutes later, they closed the door all but a crack—presumably leaving it open so they could hear if Hope woke up.

Phase one accomplished.

On to phase two.

"What you were saying earlier," I began, "about needing to kill them horribly. That really isn't necessary. But I suppose slipping a lethal drug in someone's drink wouldn't have the same effect for the group, would it?"

"What—?" May began.

"You're all in this together, right? You watch them die. You each play your part. Share the murder, share the horror and the guilt. A bond that's probably very hard to break. Must have made it really tough to convince them that Murray broke it, huh?"

May's gaze swung to mine.

"You remember Murray, don't you?" I continued. "He's right here."

I described Murray. Several of the group members paled, but May's face remained impassive.

"You don't believe me?" I said. "Ask him something. He can hear you."

"Remind her of the time—" Murray began.

"If Murray says I tricked the others into killing him, he's lying." She turned to Don. "You found that—"

"Realtor's card," I cut in.

"Card?" Murray sputtered. "What card?"

"Or so you told the group, Don," I said. "But there wasn't one, was there? It was May's idea. She convinced you that Murray really was planning to leave the group, but that you needed some solid evidence to convict him."

Don's expression answered.

"They lied?" Murray said. "I was killed for a lie?"

He continued raging, but I focused on Don. "May lied to you too. She wasn't convinced Murray was leaving. She thought he might, but it was only that—a possibility. What she saw, though, was the opportunity to cement your allegiance by making you an accomplice in Murray's murder. And, in killing Murray, she'd prove to the group that the pact was more than idle words. If they didn't believe the group would kill them, now they knew better."

"She'll say anything to save her friend," May said.

She lifted her hand to blow the ash at me. Don caught her wrist.

"Don't bother," I said. "You don't need that to cast magic. Or, should I say, *May* doesn't. Not that she was going to tell you that anytime soon. Better to keep you working for her, digging for better magic, killing for the group . . ."

They had all turned toward May. I searched for something else to say, to give that extra shove, then reconsidered before I overplayed my hand again.

So I waited as they moved toward May, blocking her in, questions rising, sharp with accusation. Then I began inching toward the door. Get out and lock it behind me.

One more step—

"Where do you think you're going?"

Tina swung into my path. I threw myself at her, fingers hooked, aiming for her eyes, but she moved at the last second and my nails scratched her cheek instead. She howled and doubled over. My knee flew up, aiming for her stomach—

Hands grabbed me and yanked me back. I twisted and struggled, but Don held me by the shoulders. He kicked my feet out from under me. As I fell, I saw May, pinned by the other men.

"Looks like we'll have a triple dose of new material," Tina said, wiping blood from her face as she bent over me. "Your parlor tricks don't interest me, Jaime Vegas. But if you and that girl are what you claim to be, that will add an extra boost to your remains, won't it? Truly magical ash."

I twisted in Don's grip, but he held me tight. Behind me, the men were taking turns casting the weakening spell on May. After the third, she slumped to the floor. And there, with her, went my chance to escape. I'd turned them against the only person in this room who valued my powers. The only one willing to let me live.

I looked about wildly, searching the room. My gaze went up to the light. If I had a spell, I could break it, plunge us into darkness and escape. If I was a werewolf, I could fight my way out. If I'd worn the damned heels, I could at least stab Don in the knees. If wishes were horses . . .

Damn it, Jaime. Focus on what you do *have, on what you* can *do!*

I looked across the room to see Brendan and Murray frozen in helpless horror, watching as Don pinned me to the floor and gave orders to the others to douse May with gasoline.

"Brendan! Murray!" I shouted. "The door!"

Don frowned at me.

Murray's look said he didn't understand my plea any better than Don. "But the spell. We can't get out."

Brendan was already racing across the room. When he reached the door, he stopped short, as if hitting a physical barrier. Then he poked his fingers into the inch-wide gap. They passed through. He grinned.

"Good," I said. "Get out there and look for a ghost. A woman. My age. Long dark hair. Her name's Eve. Show her where I am."

As I spoke, Brendan shoved his shoulder against the crack, but it stopped, as if the breach in the spell was only as wide as that gap. He kept pushing. Murray strode over to help.

"She's stalling," Tina said. "Cast the spell, Don. At least it'll shut her up."

He reached into his pocket and pulled out a small bag of ash.

Again, my gaze rose to the light. Then it shifted to that high shelf and stopped on a stuffed bat perched beside a legless dog. In my mind, I saw an image of the bird I'd accidentally raised in the garden.

But I couldn't. Not without tools. Not without time to prepare. Not without—

Don lifted his hand to his mouth, ash on his outstretched palm. He inhaled.

"Wait!" I said. "You want magic? I can give you the most powerful magic of all."

"She'll say anything—" Tina began.

"The power to raise the dead. I can do that."

"Really?" Tina's overplucked brows arched. "That'll come in handy in a few minutes... assuming you can do it to yourself."

She motioned for Don to continue with the spell, but he'd lowered his hand. The other men watched me. Seeing their expressions, I bit back a burst of hysterical laughter.

Communicating with the dead wasn't enough to sway their intentions. But to raise the dead? To play God? No matter how strongly logic told them it couldn't be done, they couldn't help hoping.

"It's a trick," Tina snapped. "Can't you see that? Now she'll tell us she needs a body, so we'll need to take her outside—"

"No, you won't." I waved at the ceiling. "Plenty of bodies here."

"And I suppose you want us to take one down, meaning we have to find a ladder, bring it back, give your friend time to recover—"

"I'll raise the bat. It has wings, right?" I flashed my best showbiz smile. "No need to be carried down when you can fly."

Even before the men agreed, I knew they would. Why not? In return for a few minutes' forbearance, I offered the possibility of a miracle. Who could refuse that?

Are you nuts? my brain screamed. *Have you forgotten the minor fact that you can't do this without your equipment?*

But I could try. At the very least, I'd stall them for a while. Maybe Hope would wake. Or Jeremy would find my trail.

And if that's all I hoped to do, that's all I'd accomplish. Forget stalling. My only option—the only one I'd accept—was success.

Just yesterday, raising Rachel Skye, I'd theorized that the power lay not with the instruments, but within me. If I truly believed that, then it was time to put it to the test. Under the worst possible circumstances, but maybe that was just what I needed. Last year, in Toronto with the werewolves, I'd controlled zombies raised by someone else—a feat I'd said was impossible. But when I saw Elena's life at stake, I'd found the will and the power to do it.

Now there was another life at stake. Mine. And, for once, I was going to be the one to save it.

I closed my eyes and recited the incantation to call the dead back to their nearby bodies. In my mind, I pictured the ritual setup, envisioned myself kneeling before the symbols.

When the chant was finished, I didn't open my eyes to see whether it worked. Didn't even take a breath. Just repeated it. Then repeated it. Then—

"Oh, my God."

The reaction I'd been waiting for. I looked up to see the bat still perched there, motionless. But on an adjacent shelf, the crow's wing twitched.

"It's a trick," Tina sneered. "Even I can do that—like making a pencil levitate."

"Rawr!"

The crow had managed to push itself upright. Its head wobbled, as if its neck was broken. It threw back its head and let out another strangled caw.

"Mother of God," one of the men breathed.

Even Tina stared. Then she wheeled on me. "It's a trick. Somehow—"

A dog yipped. The terrier. Its head whipped from side to side, ears flapping, eyes wild as it tried to stand on legs it no longer had. I fought the urge to release it, sent up a silent apology, and started the invocation again.

The dog convulsed and twisted, its cries turned shrill with panic. On the adjoining shelf, the crow flapped its wings, its head still lolling, beak snapping.

A shriek. Four sets of eyes turned to see a raccoon dragging itself toward the edge...

"Oh, God, no," someone said. "Not that. It isn't—"

The raccoon toppled from the shelf as one of the men dove out of the way. It hit with a bone-crunching thud. For a moment, I blinked, certain I'd misidentified the creature. It was too small to be a—

The beast pulled itself onto its front legs, and I realized it was indeed a raccoon. Half of one. The rear quarters had been removed and a plastic shield had been affixed to the severed end, like an anatomy display.

The raccoon gnashed its teeth and rolled back onto its torso, claws waving as it struggled to get up. Above it, the dog twisted, snapping and snarling, frenzied now.

"Oh, God, what have you done?" one of the men breathed.

"Why, I've brought the dead back to life. I've performed a miracle."

The raccoon fell forward and started pulling itself along on its front legs. It snarled at Tina. When she fell back with a scream, it advanced on Don. He backpedaled out of the way.

"M-miracle?" Don said. "Th-this is an abomination. Stop it right now."

"Stop?" I smiled. "I'm just getting started."

I looked across their faces. In their terror, I saw my true power. The darkest power. The greatest power.

I closed my eyes and shouted the invocation, calling the dead back to their bodies. Someone yelled for Don to cast the weakening spell. Fingers wrapped around my arm. As I yanked away, my attacker reeled backward, grip loosening.

A black blur flashed over his head. The crow, swooping. Then another blur and a high-pitched shriek as the bat flew into Tina. She screamed, arms flailing.

"Kill it! Someone kill it! Kill all of them!"

"Oh, you've already done that," I said. "Once they pass over, they're mine, and you can't do a damn thing about it. Go ahead. Swat that bat. Throw it into the wall if you'd like. You can't kill it. It's already dead."

Another scream, this time from one of the men as the raccoon's teeth sank into his leg. As he shook it, the plastic plate flew off and the raccoon's preserved innards slid out. The man screamed louder, gaze riveted on the mangled beast.

"You wanted magic!" I said. "You killed for it. Well, here's magic. The most powerful kind there is."

The crow swooped past me and flew into Don, who let out a shriek.

"Isn't it everything you imagined?" I yelled to be heard over the din. "And just think. When you die, I can do this to you. Bring your mangled, rotting corpse back to life, with you in it, stuck there for eternity."

I shouted the incantation again. A body tumbled from the shelf. Then another, the air rent with yowls and screeches and screams. I ran for the door. It was half-open now, as if someone had tried to make a break for it. A quick head count as I wheeled proved no one had escaped.

I yanked open the door, spun around and slammed it shut. A body hit the other side. I threw myself against the door, fingers flying to the lock. One twist and it was closed.

My gaze snagged on the light switch for the room. I flicked it off.

JUDGMENT

I LOOKED AROUND FOR HOPE, but she was nowhere to be seen. I ran through the TV room. Still no sign of her. How far could they have taken her?

As I raced into the hall, legs appeared on the stairway. I froze, fanatically searching for a weapon or another escape route.

"Jaime?"

A second set of legs passed the first and I recognized Jeremy's shoes, moving swiftly and soundlessly down the stairs. As soon as he was low enough, he ducked, saw me and nodded. There was no expression on his face, but I could see the relief in his eyes.

He swung around the bottom step and caught my arm, ready to whisk me upstairs without a word, but Karl stepped into our path.

"Where's Hope?" he demanded.

I opened my mouth to answer, but wasn't fast enough for him and he took those last few steps in a stride, looming over me, eyes blazing. I instinctively stepped back, but Jeremy's arm around my back stopped me.

"I—I don't know. They took her out of the room and I—"

"And you what?" he snarled, any remaining wisps of the sophisticated mask falling away.

"Karl."

Jeremy's voice was soft, barely above a whisper, but it stopped the other man short.

"I was looking for her," I hurried on. "She's unconscious and tied up, and they brought her in here, out of the way, but I can't find—"

His head whipped up, nostrils flaring. A slow pivot. Then he strode across the room and yanked open a closet. There, on the floor, was Hope. When Karl started to lift her, Jeremy moved up behind him and leaned down to whisper, "We don't have time. Just move her to another room."

Karl hesitated.

Jeremy said, "We can finish this now. She'll be safe then."

Karl lifted Hope, then turned to me. "Describe the room. Exits. Weapons. How many people? What kind of—?"

Jeremy motioned for him to slow down and look after Hope first. He took her into another room. When he returned, I'd already explained everything. Then Jeremy came up with a plan.

JEREMY STUDIED my face, not asking "are you okay with this?" but looking for the answer. I nodded, then turned my attention back to the door. My heart was thumping so loud I was sure Jeremy and Karl could hear it, but they gave no sign, just waited in their places—Karl behind the door, Jeremy on the other side of the opening.

As I turned the lock, Karl slid his foot against the base of the door, then looked at me. When I nodded, he eased his foot back an inch and I cracked open the door. It was like walking into a horror movie—a soundtrack of human screams and babbling mixed with the enraged and garbled cries of the zombie beasts.

Something—or someone—hit the door, the jolt hard enough to make me jump, but the door didn't move, Karl's foot and hand blocking it.

I closed my eyes and cast the incantation to return those poor souls to wherever they'd come from. I kept casting until the screams—human and beast—dropped to sobs and muted cries.

Then I jumped back. Jeremy swung around the doorway, Karl following. I cast the release incantation one last time as they disappeared into the darkness. Then I slammed the door shut and turned the lock.

I WAS supposed to wait outside the door for fifteen minutes, then unlock it. As I stood there, I tried very hard not to picture what was happening inside the killing room. At least it would be easy to clean up the carnage afterward. I rubbed the goose bumps on my arms.

As I moved, I caught the whisper of muffled voices, pleading. I rubbed my arms harder, torn between wanting to retreat to someplace where I couldn't overhear and wanting to put my ear to the door, to reassure myself the screams and pleading weren't coming from Jeremy or Karl. I might not care for Karl Marsten, but I didn't want to see the man killed.

A thump sounded above me. I started, then strained to listen, but heard nothing. Even the killing room had gone quiet. Another thud, definitely overhead.

Jeremy would have cleared the upper levels, but did that mean they were still clear? Two group members had apparently skipped the emergency meeting. Or were they just late?

A board creaked. I glanced at the door, but my watch said I had eight minutes to go, and I wasn't opening it one second sooner. Nor was I going to cower here and wait to be discovered by an intruder.

I was in the small TV room, the door to the killing room normally hidden behind a wall hanging. I looked around for a potential weapon. A book? A lamp? A picture? I was about to laugh at the last, when I stopped. Picture. Picture frame. Glass.

I grabbed an old eight-by-ten sepia photograph from the shelf and smashed it against the television cabinet. As I reached for the biggest shard, I saw my bare hand. I yanked off my shoe, removed my sock, then put my shoe back on . . . and the sock on my hand. It looked ridiculous, but it was better than sliced fingertips. I picked up the shard with my "gloved" hand, then started for the hall.

I was almost at the top of the steps when I heard another soft thump. I pinpointed the direction and followed, creeping through the kitchen toward what looked like a living room. As I edged along the kitchen cabinets, a blur flew across the doorway.

I backpedaled. Another thump. Then something moved by the base of the doorway. A fat calico tabby peered out. The cat looked at me, then at the glass in my hand.

Great. The one time I'm prepared—weapon and all—and my opponent is an overfed house cat.

As I turned to head back, the doorway darkened.

"Hello, Jaime."

May stood at the top of the stairs.

How—? I pictured the half-open door. When I'd counted heads, I hadn't checked for May, presuming she was still unconscious on the floor.

Apparently I hadn't been the only one who'd taken advantage of the cacophony to escape.

She spoke again, but her next words made no sense. I struggled to understand, then realized they weren't in English. A spell. As I tensed, ready to dive out of the spell's path, I felt a sharp edge biting into my fingertips. The glass!

I ran at May, my hand raised. Her brows knitted, the spell dying in her throat as she stared in bewilderment at the sock sailing toward her. Then her eyes went wide, seeing the glass. Too late. I slashed and laid open her cheek. Blood sprayed. She stumbled back. I kicked, hoping to knock her down the stairs, but my aim was off.

May lunged at me. I swung the glass again, but this time only caught the side of her blouse. The glass snagged and flew from my fingers. As May veered toward me, the glass fell onto a throw rug.

I dove for it, but May cast a spell and something hit me, like in the garden, knocking me sideways. As I regained my balance, May caught me by the back of the shirt. I twisted sharply and pulled free.

I scrambled for the glass shard. She hit me with another spell, this one knocking the wind from my lungs. I blacked out for a split second, then came to as May grabbed my shirt again, yanking me off balance.

"I'm not going to hurt you, Jaime," she said.

"Just kidnap me, right?" I wriggled in her grasp, not fighting, just getting my footing. "Well, you know what? I'm a little tired of being kidnapped."

I swung my fist and hit her square in the jaw. As she released me, I dove for the glass. My fingers wrapped around it and I was turning, flying back to my feet, when a shape passed to my left. I wheeled to see Eve holding what looked like . . . a sword. A very big sword.

I shook off my surprise and dove at May, shard raised, aiming for her throat. But Eve's sword was in flight, sailing toward May, whose gaze was fixed on me, lips drawn back, pushing to her feet. Before I could reach her, the sword cleaved through her torso. She reeled, mouth working as she clutched the left side of her chest.

She tottered. Then she collapsed.

There was no blood. No mark on her body. Yet she didn't move.

"Is she . . . ?"

"She better be," Eve said. "Or this baby needs a recharge."

I struggled from the cloud of shock and turned to Eve. "I didn't need to be rescued."

"Sorry, but my sword outranks your . . ." she glanced at my hand, "sock puppet."

"It's a glass shard," I said, lifting it.

Her lips twitched. "Ah." A pause and she sobered. "You're right, Jaime. You had her, and maybe I should have let you take her down, but this?" She lifted the sword. "Less messy. In more ways than one."

She laid down the weapon as May's spirit began to separate from her body.

I stared at the sword. It was at least four feet long and inscribed with symbols. As the metal glowed, I remembered stories my Nan had told me of necromancers at executions or deaths of criminals, seeing spirits bearing glowing swords, come to claim the souls. The Sword of Judgment. Not a weapon wielded by just any ghost.

"You're a—an—" I couldn't get the word out. "The job you do for the Fates. You're an . . . angel?"

"Maybe." She winked. "Or maybe I just swiped the sword."

She grabbed May's silent spirit by the shoulders, yanked her free and disappeared.

I stood there, staring at the spot where they'd vanished. Then I heard a thump. I glanced toward the living room, expecting to see the cat again. The noise came again, from downstairs. I was late for an appointment.

THE KILLING room was remarkably clean. I guess I should have known that. Jeremy and Karl didn't need to Change into wolves. Part of being such efficient killers was knowing how to kill efficiently.

Four bodies lay in the room, all with broken necks. The only blood came from Karl's nose. Elbowed in the melee. He gave Jeremy a few seconds to examine it, then hurried to Hope.

Once Jeremy discovered May was dead, and I was fine, it was time to consider body disposal. He knew more about crime-scene cleanup than anyone should. He'd said before that it was a necessary "skill" for the Alpha—when he sent Clayton and Elena to stop a man-killing mutt, they often had to clean up. As Alpha, though, he would only need to teach the skills. Yet watching him that day, I remembered what he'd said about having to cover his father's kills.

Whatever my mother had done to me, it paled in comparison to that.

BEFORE THEY removed the bodies, Jeremy checked on Hope too. As I waited in the hall, Eve returned with Kristof.

"Got a couple of bodies for us to look after too, I see," she said.

She waved through the doorway into the TV room, where Brendan and Murray waited, quiet, lost in their thoughts. I explained. When I finished, I headed over to Brendan.

"Ready to go?" I asked.

"I—" He blinked, dazed, as if the fact of his death was only hitting him now, after he'd escaped the room where he'd died. "I guess so."

"I'll take him," Kristof said, his voice uncharacteristically soft. He walked to the young man, his hand outstretched. "Brendan, isn't it?"

He shook Kristof's hand. "Y-yes, sir."

"Kristof." He put his arm around the boy's shoulders and led him from the room. "Is there anyplace you'd like to visit before we go, Brendan?"

Their voices faded as they headed up the stairs. Eve walked to Murray, who sprang off the sofa.

"There are some places I'd like to visit," he said. "See my wife one last time and—"

"You should have thought of that before you butchered six kids," Eve said. "Judgment awaits, and it's getting impatient."

"B-but I helped you guys. Ask—"

He tried to turn toward me, but Eve grabbed his arm.

"Take it up with the Fates."

As they disappeared, Jeremy stepped into the room. "Jaime? Time to go."

JEREMY HAD Karl take Hope and me to her apartment, then he returned to help Jeremy finish the cleanup. During those two hours we spent alone, Hope didn't say a word about what had happened. Instead she worked to make a big meal, as if feeding the men when they returned was mission critical.

When the men did arrive, Jeremy ate, but it seemed more out of politeness than hunger. Then we left. On the way to the car, I said, "So you could follow my trail from the house? I wasn't sure you could."

He hesitated, and I knew he was considering whether to lie, then shook his head and said, "There wasn't a trail. They must have driven you over."

"So how did you know . . . ?" I let the sentence trail off and dug the rune sketch from my pocket. "This?"

"A magical homing device?" He smiled. "I wish it were that simple. I sensed you, as I do sometimes with the Pack. I could tell you were in trouble, came back, found that you and Hope were gone. Then I found you. Somehow."

I fingered the rune.

He shook his head. "Clay and Elena don't carry the ones I did for them, and I've never done any for the rest of the Pack. Whatever let me find you, it's not a piece of paper."

"Well, then, you won't mind if I have it made into a necklace, right? Or, all things considered, maybe a tattoo."

He smiled and pulled me into a kiss.

THE ROAD HOME

TWO GROUP MEMBERS REMAINED AT LARGE, but the council would convene to discuss that. What remained now was the resolution of my primary goal: freeing the children's spirits. Eve and the Fates had "interrogated" May Donovan and now understood what had happened. As for whether it was a fluke or the start of some evolutionary change in the supernatural world . . . that remained to be seen.

As for what *had* happened, Eve said only that the children's spirits had been drained by the magic, which was pretty much what we'd already suspected. If there was a more complex explanation, I wasn't getting it. Maybe Eve didn't think I'd understand, not being a spellcaster. Or maybe the Fates didn't dare go into detail, hoping that if no one in our plane understood, then it couldn't be replicated.

The explanation didn't concern me. All I wanted to know was could we undo it? Could we set the children free? The answer was yes.

Returning to the Brentwood garden wasn't easy. While I had a good reason to return—I was still in residence—I'd likely find myself taken aside for questioning the moment I appeared. I hadn't been anywhere near Angelique's body so we weren't too concerned about the police investigation. Was it safer, then, to plod through the interrogation, then slip out and release the spirits? Or should we sneak back and conduct the ritual right away?

Jeremy, Eve and Kristof debated the options. I acted as "translator," but didn't enter into the discussion. My mind was made up. I had to free those children. No one else could do it for me, and I wasn't taking the chance that I would be prevented from doing so, or even delayed.

I readied my arguments, but didn't need them. No one wanted to wait.

EVE AND Kristof scouted the garden, recruiting and organizing Tansy, Gabrielle and the other ghosts to stand guard. We mapped out all police activity and devised a route that would take us into the garden from the neighbor's yard, and keep us away from the crime scene.

Then Jeremy Changed. Even in human form, he'd be quicker to pick up approaching officers than the ghosts, but if seen on a crime scene, he'd be in trouble. A canine, on the other hand, was just a nuisance—warranting a call to the dogcatcher at most. And if I needed a distraction, a huge black dog would be just the thing.

THE SPOT Eve had chosen for the ritual was ringed with ghosts, most of whom I'd never seen before. They said nothing, as if they feared distracting me. A smile here, a nod there, then they returned to their solemn vigil.

I walked along the path, down the gauntlet of guards. My kit was in the house, but I didn't need it. My role here was simple. I was the magnet to draw the children from wherever they were hiding.

"Are you here?" I whispered.

Silence. Something moved to my left and I looked over sharply, but it was only a breeze rippling the rosebushes.

"Hello?" I said, as loud as I dared. "I'm back. Are you still here?"

No one answered.

"I haven't been around much lately. And maybe, what's been happening here, it's scared you. But it's over now and I can help."

A sigh. My skin prickled. The wind rustled through a tree and the sigh came again, a loose branch creaking softly.

I talked some more, aware even as I did that they almost certainly couldn't understand me even if they were close enough to overhear. Yet I kept talking, hoping the sound of my voice would draw them in.

The garden stayed silent and still.

I closed my eyes and thought of Rachel Skye, the girl Eve had contacted. A child I knew only as a body in a garden. A young girl, taking a shortcut home from school to see her favorite show, murdered and dumped in a garden. I thought of the others, all the children whose touches and pokes I'd felt, whose voices I'd heard, those who didn't have names and stories and maybe never would, not for me.

I thought of Brendan, little more than a child himself, stoic in his fate, as if it was the price one paid for following a dream. I thought of the young teens I passed on the street in L.A. and Chicago and every other big city, all the lost children. And, just for a second, I thought of myself, of my own child, lost all those years ago.

Something grazed my arm. I opened my eyes to see Jeremy. Drawn by my thoughts, concerned. He glanced at me. Then his attention was snagged by something to the left and he tilted his head, confusion in his eyes. I followed his gaze, but saw only the ghosts standing guard.

Fingers tickled my cheek. More brushed my hair. The whispering began. I went still, straining to hear, convinced I was imagining it. Then Eve stepped through the rosebushes.

"They're here," she said.

WITH THE arrival of the children, my role ended and Eve and Kristof's began. They knelt on the path and prepared to conduct the ritual the Fates had given them. Kristof set up the materials. Eve recited the incantation. Jeremy stood silently at my side. The children patted me and whispered. I don't think I breathed through the entire thing.

When Eve finished the incantation, the touches and whispers of the children stopped. I swear my heart stopped with them. I looked around frantically, trying to catch a glimpse of them, praying something hadn't gone wrong.

Then I saw a faintly shimmering form. Then another. A third. A fourth. As faint as Brendan had been.

Slowly the tallest form materialized. A boy about thirteen. Dark eyed, probably Latino, with hair that fell into his face, reminding me of Jeremy. I instinctively smiled, and the boy's gaze went to me, head tilted, as if trying to figure out what I was looking at.

"Hello," I said.

He smiled. "Hi."

Another of the forms materialized. A girl about eleven, with lank dark blond hair held back in butterfly clips.

"Rachel?" I said.

My voice caught as I remembered what I'd done to her, seeing those bony fingers frantically clawing the air.

"Rachel, I—"

She ran over and threw her arms around me and I swear, for the briefest second, I felt them. Then her hands passed through me. Eve came up behind her and knelt, putting her hands on the girl's shoulders as if to reassure her that she could still touch someone.

Behind Eve, another girl had appeared. A couple of years younger than Rachel, with cornrows and glittering earrings that caught the light as she looked around, uncertain, as if she didn't quite recognize the world from this side of the veil. I walked over to her and bent down.

"Hello, there. I'm Jaime. And who would you be?"

Maybe not the right question to ask a traumatized child, but she met my gaze and smiled, as if finding something she *did* recognize.

" 'Lizbeth," she lisped.

I looked up at the older boy.

"Manny," he said before I could ask. "Manuel Garcia."

"Todd," said a voice behind me.

"Chloe Margaret Fisher," said another.

I turned to see a boy about eleven, chubby with wild red hair. Behind him stood a pretty brunette around the same age.

"Pleased to meet you, Todd and Chloe. I'm Jaime. This is Eve."

As Eve approached, holding Rachel's hand, I glanced up to introduce Jeremy, but he'd stepped back, out of sight. I nodded. Explaining to the children why he couldn't see them—that they were ghosts—wasn't something they needed yet.

I looked around the group. "Five. I thought—" I glanced at Eve. "There are supposed to be six."

"Number six coming up." Kristof's voice floated from somewhere in the garden. He rounded a bush. In his arms was a small boy, his face buried against Kristof's chest. "This is Charles. He's shy."

I greeted the boy and he nodded, his face still against Kristof.

"We should go," Eve whispered to me. "Before they—"

"What are we doing here?" Chloe asked. "Where's my mom?"

Eve took her hand. "We're going to take you to someone who'll answer all your questions. Then we're going to throw you a big welcome-back party, with all the ice cream you can eat. Vanilla, right? That's your favorite, isn't it?"

The girl nodded, temporarily distracted. Eve started down the path, holding Chloe's and Rachel's hands, so Kristof shifted Charles to one arm and reached down. Elizabeth took his free hand. He waved for the boys to follow Eve, then fell into line behind them.

"Never heard of a girl who likes vanilla best," Eve said as they walked. "You must be pretty special. Do you know what my favorite is?"

"Chocolate?" Rachel said.

Eve grinned. "Smart girl. Double-fudge chocolate with brownies. Does anyone else like chocolate?"

Their figures and their voices started to fade as Eve passed them gradually over to the other side of the veil.

"My favorite flavor?" Kristof was saying. "Bubble gum."

"No way," scoffed one of the boys.

Eve said something I couldn't make out, and they all laughed. And that was the last thing I heard. The children laughing.

THE WRAP-UP

"IN LIGHT OF THE RECENT TRAGIC EVENTS on the *Death of Innocence* set in Brentwood, spiritualist Jaime Vegas has reevaluated her career and decided to end her regular television engagements on *The Keni Bales Show,* as well as her semiregular spots—" I paused and nibbled the end of my pen. "Does 'spots' sound too informal for a media release?"

Eve looked up from the floor, where she was doing sit-ups. I was also lying down . . . in an extravagant king-size bed, room-service champagne in a bucket on the night table, a chocolate in my free hand, a half-empty box propped on a pillow. If I was leaving television, I didn't need to worry about those three extra pounds. And since Jeremy had given me the chocolates, he obviously wasn't worried about them either.

"Don't you have a publicist for this kind of thing?" Eve asked.

"I want to do it myself. What's a synonym for spot?"

"Blot. Stain. Blemish."

I threw a pillow at her. It landed in her stomach, tassels sticking up from her chest. She shot me a glare. I sighed, got up, walked over and moved it for her. As I bent, I admired my new tattoo. Small and tasteful, as the girl at the parlor promised. Jeremy acted embarrassed by it, repeatedly telling me he didn't think the symbol meant anything, but when it was finished I knew he was pleased.

I'm still convinced the rune is supernatural and suspect it has something to do with Jeremy's mother. When I'd shown it to Eve, she'd said it sparked a vague memory, and she'd promised to dig deeper for me from the other side.

As she continued her sit-ups, I returned to my writing.

The *Death of Innocence* special was dead. No pun intended . . . though that wasn't stopping the tabloids and trade papers from making them. They had dead children, ritual sacrifice, restless ghosts and a murdered young spiritualist. Against that, raising Marilyn was almost anticlimactic. Instead, the network was keeping the footage for a new special: *Death of Innocence: Satanism in Brentwood.* Todd Simon hoped to get Geraldo Rivera to host.

The satanism angle was still only a theory. There was no suggestion that the police would ever trace the murders back to May and her group. As for the remaining members of that group, Paige had called a council meeting for this weekend to plan a course of action.

I struck a line from my media release and checked the clock. Jeremy's plane should be landing soon. He'd planned to stay in L.A. longer, but then he got a jubilant call from Elena announcing that Logan had taken his first steps, and Kate seemed determined to follow. Although Jeremy had brushed it off, saying he'd see them walk when he got home, I'd packed his bag. I wasn't going to start this relationship by letting him miss his grandchildren's milestones. I'd see him on the weekend, at the council meeting.

We'd have to get used to these brief and sporadic interludes anyway. We had separate lives, but as long as they collided regularly, I'd be happy. Even if it was only a weekend a month, I suspected those weekends would be intense enough to keep us going the rest of the time.

I wondered whether Hope would be at that council meeting. I hadn't heard from her. Was she holding her breath, waiting for me to spill her secret? I'd have to talk to her about that. I believed her motives were as pure as anyone's on the council. Maybe part of her reason for helping was to have an excuse to find chaos, but there were a lot worse ways she could do that.

Balance. I'd learned a lot about that this past week.

I'd failed with Angelique. I was paying for that with memories and regrets. I'd go to that revival in Nebraska, in her honor, the proceeds going to her family. Someday I'd contact her, try to make amends, but I wasn't ready to face her yet.

I *was* ready to do more for other ghosts. Maybe I couldn't help every one, and maybe I wasn't obliged to help any. But if this case taught me anything it was that I *wanted* to help, that it hurt more to say no than it did to say "I'll try" and to fail. Whether opening myself up to more ghosts would keep me sane or, as I'd always feared, drive me mad was a possibility I had to deal with. Starting now.

"Eve?"

She stopped in mid-sit-up, then fell back to the floor. "Hmm?"

"That thing you did with the girl's ghost. Reading her mind or whatever. That's part of being an angel, isn't it? A new power?"

She grunted and did another sit-up. I took that for a "Yes, but I don't want to talk about it." I let her do a few more.

"Could you use it to, say, tap the memory of a murdered ghost? Find out what she's forgotten about her death?"

"If you want me to bring a killer to justice, I'd love to, but it's not in the job description. You were in immediate danger as the result of an investigation to help the Fates. So I could intervene. Otherwise, we have to leave justice to the humans on this side . . . and mete it out on our side later."

"I don't mean that."

I told her about Gabrielle Langdon. It took some prompting—Eve was never one to pay much attention to current affairs—but eventually she remembered who Gabrielle was.

"Could you tell her who killed her? If she really wants to know?"

Eve paused, then nodded. "If she really wants to know, I think I can."

"I'll see if I can summon her tonight, then."

Another nod, and Eve went back to her workout.

When I was done here, I'd call Hope both to talk to her and to find out whether she'd ever dug up the address for Peter's son. If not, I'd do some research myself.

That made two ghosts helped. Plus the children, and Brendan. Not bad for a few days' work.

As for fears of madness, there was something I could do about that too. Go visit Tee in Toronto. I'd been trying to push Tee's image from my brain, forget that I'd ever seen this old friend of my grandmother's now driven so mad by necromancy that she was barely recognizable as human. I'd call Zoe and ask her to take me back to Tee and see whether there was anything I could do for her. Through her maybe I'd learn to face my fears—to see how bad it could be, and deal with that—not pull the covers over my head and pretend it could never happen to me.

My cell phone rang. I saw the number of Jeremy's prepaid phone and grinned.

"Just get in?" I asked as I answered.

"I did. Is everything all right there?"

I could hear the concern in his voice, probably worrying that the police had descended on my hotel room the moment he left.

I smiled. "Everything's fine. Lying in bed. Writing my good-bye to Hollywood. Eating chocolates. Watching Eve work out. Thankful it's her, not me."

A soft chuckle. "Did you get the champagne too?"

"I did. And it's making the letter writing much easier."

"Good. Did you hear from Hope?" A pause. "Ah, I see Kate over the crowd. She must be up on Clay's shoulders. I'd better hurry before she sees me and jumps—" A quick inhale. "Too late."

"Clay caught her?"

"Fortunately, though she's not too happy about—"

Kate's scream cut across the miles.

I laughed. "I'll let you go, then."

"So you're fine?"

"Never been better."

As I hung up, I smiled to myself. Never been better, indeed.